BULL RUSH

MAGGIE RAWDON

For the ones who thought they could fix him.
This one has a happy ending.

CONTENT NOTE

A list of content information you may want before reading can be found on maggierawdon.com/content-information

PROLOGUE

Hazel

"MA'AM, I'm sorry, but we can't process this request without your husband's signature."

"Oh. I think there's some confusion. I'm engaged, but I'm not married." I smile at the woman as she slides the paper back to me.

"I don't think there's any confusion. It lists his name here. I can bring it up." She types into her computer, and then she frowns and frowns some more. "Yeah, unfortunately, this might be more complicated than I thought, as it's showing your husband is currently serving the rest of his sentence on parole for a felony. The loan won't get approved if he's on it. We'll need to address that before we can process your application."

"A felony?" I laugh nervously. "I assure you my husband—my future husband—doesn't have any felonies. He's never done anything wrong in his life. I'm not sure he even has a parking ticket on his record."

"Well, ma'am, it's not my place to get involved in any kind of domestic disputes, but I assure you that our records don't lie. You may want to have a talk with your husband when you get home."

I'm not sure what I hate more, being in this stale bank office where happiness goes to die, filing a mountain of paperwork just to be told I have to refile it on a clerical error, or having to find a polite way to insist that she's making multiple mistakes without using a tone that belies my underlying irritation and sounds like I'm one more *ma'am* away from asking for a manager. I flash a bright grin, trying my best to look like I'm just asking questions to help me figure out my error.

"Could you tell me when that information was filed into your system? Or how I might correct it? Because I'm not married. Curtis and I are still very much in the midst of wedding planning."

"Curtis? No, ma'am. I have the name listed here as Ramsey Stockton."

My blood runs cold, and I nearly choke on my own breath. *Ramsey.*

"That's a mistake. We've been divorced for years."

"You're Hazel Stockton, though, correct?"

I nod. This is how I know I'm far outside my hometown of Purgatory Falls, parked in an office chair in a high-rise in the city instead. Because no one at home says the name Stockton like it's Jones or Smith.

"Yes, but only because I've been slow to change my name. I hate paperwork, and so I decided I'd wait until I got remarried. But I'm definitely not married to Ramsey anymore. We divorced years ago." I try to look the part of the confident, reassuring client who definitely should get her loan approved today. Who *needs* to get her loan approved today.

"Hmm. Not according to the records that were pulled."

"There must be a mistake."

"You'll want to phone the downtown office then. It's rare that they make errors like this."

"All right. But I assure you this is one. When can I speak to someone down there?"

"Let me see..." She pauses and stares at her computer screen for a few moments and then looks back up at me, a customer service smile plastered on her face. "That person is on vacation right now, but they'll be back next week. They're available on Wednesdays from one to two p.m. at the downtown office in Pueblo, and on Thursdays from nine to ten a.m. at the downtown office in Denver."

"That's it?"

"Those are the only times they have public office hours, yes. But you can also schedule an appointment online. It looks like..." She scrolls through the list. "They have an appointment available in about seven weeks."

I have to choke back the audible sound of disgust.

"Seven weeks? Okay. Well, then I'll go during their office hours, I guess."

"Okay. Well, if that's the case, then once the error is cleared up, we'll be able to finish processing the paperwork for the refinance of the inn."

"Do you know how long it usually takes for it to show on your end once they clear it?"

"It just depends on the office processing times, ma'am. Sometimes they're very quick, and sometimes they're not." A saccharine smile breaks out across her face, and I have to squeeze the pen I've been bouncing on my knee to keep the smile on mine. "But once they've cleared it up, it should only take a few days for our database to be updated, and then we can get you scheduled to come back in."

"Is it still going to be a week's waiting time to get an

appointment here?" I ask nervously. We need the money, badly. I don't have time to wait, but I guess thanks to this paperwork error, I don't have much of a choice.

"Yes. That's likely so. It might clear up a little by then, but I can't make any promises. Unfortunately, we're very busy."

Apparently, everything around here is unfortunate, including me, if I'm truly still married to Ramsey Stockton on paper. Except... I wouldn't have the inn or the ranch without it —without *him*. It was his family's ranch and their inn that he'd inherited. Then he left them with me when he took off for bigger things and brighter lights. My stomach rolls as I think of him. I need this to be a clerical error because I'm not prepared for what it means if it's not.

Ramsey

THE ONLY THING standing between me and freedom right now is the sky-high pile of paperwork sitting on the table in front of me. The five-month-long sentence for my assault charge has been commuted to parole, and as soon as I finish the last of this exit interview, I get to walk out the doors and finally start living again. But the tired-looking processer currently swishing the last of his stale coffee around in a Styrofoam coffee cup is taking his sweet fucking time, going through every single question like I'm an imminent threat to society.

You'd think I killed some—I keep forgetting that I actually did, in fact, kill someone. In part because I'm still missing time from that day, something the in-house therapist has been working through with me, and another item on my long list of things they've suggested I continue through my parole. I suffered my way through a half dozen pre-parole meetings and checklists that made my eyes twitch from the inanity, packed up everything remotely sentimental in my cell, gave away everything extra I had from the commissary, and arranged to have someone pick me up today. If I don't get to take a long breath of fresh air outside these four walls by dinnertime, I might just lose my mind.

"I see your home of record is in Purgatory Falls, Colorado— is that correct?" The man taps the paperwork in front of him with a blue ballpoint pen that's seen better days.

"Correct. Or rather, it was. I live in an RV now."

"An RV? You need a permanent residence for the period of your parole. Your lawyer should have explained that to you." He rears back like I've told him I hate stuffy pencil-pushing bureaucrats. Which I do, but I have the good sense not to say it out loud. A few of the things my mother taught me stuck.

"I'm moving in with some friends. Parking on their property and using their hookups. I can give you the address. I'm sure they'll give me a bed indoors if that makes a difference." I try to stomp out any semblance of irritation from my tone. I'm happy to be headed for parole, but the idea they can control my life this closely when I'm not behind bars chafes.

"So you're estranged from your wife at the residence of record then?"

I have to pause to process his question. It's been a long time since someone has mentioned my wife to me. Anyone who knows that history knows better than to bring it up.

"My ex-wife lives there." I keep my answer terse.

"Ex-wife?" He flips the page up and then pages through several more. The resulting flutter nearly blows a few of the pages we've already completed onto the ground. I press my palm to them, pinning them to the beige linoleum surface. The last thing I need is to spend thirty minutes watching him pick them up and sort them back into order, checking and rechecking while I wait.

"Ex," I confirm.

A flash of her comes to mind like she's standing here in the room with me. I can't imagine what she's thought about all this. That I'm a murderer now—justified or not. That I'm a felon, and my career playing ball is likely over, at least barring the Chaos is willing to take me back on a discount. Which seems unlikely, even if my last season was my best yet.

I can see her standing in front of me, arms crossed over her chest. Long, soft deep-brunette hair flowing over one shoulder, the rest tucked behind and cascading down her back. Her pale-blue eyes look me over and find nothing but disappointment in their wake. Her lips purse when they fall on the out-of-control five-o'clock shadow I have—the kind she loved and hated in equal measure. A lot like she felt about the rest of me. Until the hate overtook everything else.

"No. It says here she's your current wife. Still married." The processor taps his pen on the desk.

"We've been divorced for five years. Give or take. I don't know the exact date."

"Because there isn't one," he says sharply.

He turns the paper around, taps the blunt end of his pen to the marriage certificate, and then flips to where it shows a bold "M" next to my name. "You're still married. You know lying in this interview could get your parole rescinded." It's half-threat, half-empty irritation on his part. I think he wants me out of here, he just seems to want to take all day doing it. Nevertheless, the threat has me sitting up straighter, and my lawyer puts his phone aside when he senses the tension and turns his attention back to us.

"My client is divorced to his knowledge. If you have documents that say otherwise, I'd like to see them," my lawyer says before I can speak.

My heart skips a beat. A mistake in paperwork sounds a lot like I go back into a cell, and we start over on another day to be determined. Everything about this place is bureaucracy and piles of paperwork. I'm fairly certain there's an employee just printing duplicates and crossing t's and dotting i's. That might be the first rung on the corporate prison ladder before you get to whatever this guy's title is—somewhere in the inner circle of hell.

I've already been imagining the freedom of driving on the open road again, tasting the chili dog and steak I'm going to eat, the cold beer I'll drink at Cooper's, and the feeling of sunshine on my face when I walk out of here later today. Now they're all fading away into the distance like the dreams I have of her when I first wake up. All because of a little black M where there should be a D.

Fuck.

"I'm not concerned about a mistake like that. I'd just like to get out of here today." I look between the two men who seem more concerned about record-keeping than my freedom.

"You'll have to look into that on your own time. All I can tell you is our documentation is never wrong. We don't make mistakes. If it says he's married, it's because there's still an active marriage license registered in the state of Colorado." He flicks his eyes in my direction before he jots something else down in a highlighted box in front of him.

My lawyer turns to me, a question lingering in his eyes, and I shrug. I don't have any answers. I didn't want to air my dirty laundry in front of prison officials. All I know is she asked for a divorce and rode my ass for months to get my signature. Eventually I caved. I signed the papers and gave them to her. Hazel's always been the responsible one of the two of us. I assumed she took care of it, and we never spoke about it or anything else again.

"She filed the paperwork, but I signed it. There's no way she didn't submit it."

"Well, we need to know the exact date so we can get them the updated paperwork, and we'll have to look into the records department for the county in Colorado." My lawyer looks at me thoughtfully, always calm and calculated. I suppose that's why I pay him so much.

I nod.

"I'll make a call. Maybe we can settle this right now. Do you mind?" My lawyer nods to the door and waits for the processor's response.

"Sure." His eyes practically roll, and the sarcasm licks over the word. A few moments later, he excuses himself, and I'm left sitting and staring at the peeling paint on the cinder block walls. My mind's obsessing over the possibility of being put back in my cell. Every hope and excitement I have for leaving this place is wavering in the balance as I imagine they'll use any excuse they've got to make this difficult. It might be one of the nicer prisons, lax security and lots of perks you wouldn't get if you didn't have six figures behind the first number in your bank account, but still a miserable cage I'm desperate to escape.

MY HEART IS POUNDING in my chest when my lawyer walks back into the room, shaking his head.

"County confirmed it. No divorce on record. Just the marriage license."

"As I said..." The processor smirks, satisfied that his paperwork is all in order and I'm the problem. Never mind that it's just shattered everything I thought I knew about my life. But I've got to deal with one problem at a time.

"What does that mean for today?" I ask, looking between my lawyer and the processor.

"I checked with my superior while your lawyer was making calls. We're still good to release you, but your parole officer will want to review the discrepancy. You said you've lost your job. Is that correct?" He asks the question like that's not obvious. I can't imagine many jobs willing to hold over for a five-month vacation, let alone one at this brand of resort.

"I can't play this season. I'm hoping for next if I'm able." Football season's fast approaching, and the guys are already in the middle of camp. A couple more weeks and it'll be preseason, and opening game will be here before they know it. Even if I wanted to play and the Chaos wanted me back, I wouldn't be able to get back in shape that quickly. I'd need a couple months at least, and by that time, the new guy would be in his groove along with whatever rookie they drafted to replace me.

"They usually prefer you reside at the home of record unless you have an outstanding reason, like a job, to remain out of your home state." The processor doesn't bother glancing up from his box checking.

"This is my home state now. I've lived here for five years. Wouldn't they prefer I be here?"

"Usually, yes, but you've never had a permanent address here. Part of your parole is that your home life remains consistent and predictable. Drifting from one RV lot to another won't meet the terms."

"They approved my plans to stay with friends until I can find employment and a permanent residence."

"But you own a family home in Colorado and have a wife who lives at said property. I assume it's where you're from originally?"

"Yes."

"So I'm just the messenger telling you not to be surprised if they press on that issue once they're alerted to the discrepancy." Just as he reaches the end of the paperwork, he flips back two pages and starts reading through something again.

My eyes dart to my lawyer, and he shakes his head, indicating I need to keep my mouth shut. So I do, politely nodding my understanding and forcing a half-smile instead of arguing the point further.

"All right. Let's finish moving through the rest of this so we can get you out of here, sound good?"

I nod again. That promise lifts the iron weight from my chest. I'll do whatever I have to do to get out of here today. The rest is tomorrow's challenge.

Because the idea that Hazel's still my wife? Well, that has possibilities—ones I can only explore once I have my freedom again.

ONE

Hazel

I'M BLEARY-EYED, pressing my hand to my mouth to try to cover the gaping yawn that comes as I grab the iced latte that Kit left out for me on the counter in the inn's kitchen. I take a sip and savor it. It's just the right combination of espresso, milk, and caramel to wake my brain and my taste buds up after one of the longest nights in recent memory. I spent the first half of the night running numbers, and I spent the second half wide awake, stressing over them.

We'll be deep in the red by the end of the year if business keeps up its current trajectory. Anything that might bring in new customers—a renovation, a big holiday event, or pouring some effort into marketing would all require money I don't have. My stomach turns just thinking about the sales projections for next year, and I have to take another sip of coffee to quell it. I have to pull myself together because I have guests to entertain this morning, including a large group of older women who are making the most of the local antique shops and wineries.

When I walk into the dining room, though, four of them are plastered to the corner window that overlooks the expansive yard between the inn and the ranch house. A round of titters echoes against the glass and across the room, and one of the four clasps her hand to her mouth, turning to hurry back to her table. Her cheeks are a bright shade of cherry red that matches her shirt. There's another round of cackling and then a gasp. One of the women grabs the other by the arm, her fingers white-knuckling and glittering as her glacier-size ring catches the light and her eyes go wide.

I feel a sudden sense of dread when I watch the woman with the red shirt, Edna, I think her name was, lean over to whisper something to her friend, and she audibly gasps and clutches her chest at the information.

"Well, I wouldn't kick him out of bed." One of the women at the window snickers.

"Neither would I," another echoes the sentiment.

"Not with those thighs and that butt. Good lord! I need to take a picture and send it to Jane," the third joins in.

"You cannot take a picture. It's rude, and you three are being ridiculous!" the cherry-cheeked woman calls out in a scolding tone.

"It's the shoulders for me. If I didn't have a slipped disc, I'd climb him like a tree." Another round of praising mm-hmms echoes across the room.

I'm trying to think of who the *him* could possibly be. Sam, the groundskeeper, also known as the kid who mows our lawns and keeps the trails, is barely eighteen and as gangly as they come. My maintenance guy is sporting a beer gut and a bald spot, and while I'm positive he still makes his wife's blood pressure rise, I wouldn't exactly describe his flat plumber's butt as something worth writing home about, let alone photographing for posterity.

As I get close, the scolding woman looks at me and shakes her head. "You'd think they've never seen a naked man before."

"What?" I manage to croak before I hurry over to the window.

"You mean it's not part of the day's entertainment? I thought things were finally getting interesting around here," one of the women at the window teases.

A comment that might hurt if I weren't too busy racing to figure out how there's a naked man on my lawn. When I reach the glass and manage to elbow my way into a spot on the side, I lift the sheers to witness a sight that nearly makes me swallow my tongue.

They weren't lying about any of it. The ass, the thighs, the shoulders, every single bit is sculpted perfection. He's rivaling the tree next to him for height too, easily six foot five or taller, and the water that's pouring out of the spigot mounted on the back of his RV is running over every single inch of his naked, glistening skin.

I'm distracted until he turns around, and then I have to close my eyes.

"Oh, wow..." One of the women mumbles in the kind of hushed tone of reverence people use for truly great works of art.

"Good lord in heaven. Can you imagine being on the receiving end of that?"

"Martha!" A gasp echoes against the walls.

"I feel like we should be paying extra for this."

I feel like I haven't had enough caffeine yet for this. I reach around for the edge of the drapes and pull it forward, covering the bay window until I run into a speed bump in the form of two gaping women refusing to budge.

"Excuse me." I start to march forward with the drape,

drawing it across the window to the sounds of disappointment. "I'm so sorry about this. I'll get it taken care of right away."

"Taken care of? Honey, ask him to come in and have some breakfast with us."

I smile at her and shake my head. The last thing we need is him in here having breakfast. He might be pretty to look at from a distance, but up close? With that mouth? He'll ruin any good reviews I might still be hoping to get.

"He's not... He shouldn't be here. Doing that. I apologize, and I promise it won't happen again." I use my best professional voice, but I can feel the burning gaze of several diners who aren't loving the morning's live entertainment.

"Well, tell him I'll pay extra if it does." One of the women at the window nudges her friend in the shoulder and laughs as she finally steps back.

"Betty!" another woman admonishes.

"We're supposed to be having a girls' weekend, Edna! Loosen up and have some fun," Betty sasses back. At least I'm learning their names.

I'm satisfied that the blinds are thoroughly drawn, and a glimpse at the breakfast bar tells me Kit has everything under control this morning. The juice dispensers are all full, the breadbasket is overflowing, and the trays are filled with eggs, bacon, and blueberry pancakes. I look longingly at the pancakes as I make my way across the dining room. We'd just received a shipment of maple syrup from Canada and fresh butter from the Johnson's farm down the street. I'd been looking forward to having a big stack of them with another massive mug of coffee to prepare me for the day.

Instead, I have to march outside and confront my impending nightmare. I didn't think he was due out here for at least two more days, but here we are on what should have been a quiet Tuesday filled with morning bird-watching and a lunchtime talk with the local historian about quilting.

I'd carefully plotted the afternoon too, from the wine tasting in the afternoon, followed by a five-course dinner, pie and fresh whipped cream for dessert, and some time to read in the library. It *was* going to be the perfect day. One they'd write to friends about on the postcards they were going to get in the goodbye gift baskets in their rooms. Instead, it's being interrupted by a giant dick out on the freshly mown lawn.

I excuse myself from the breakfast and politely let them know we'll be heading out to meet the naturalist at 9 a.m. Not that anyone's listening to me because every table in the inn is tittering and fluttering with news of the morning's entertainment—the size, the shape, the general attitude of said diversion are all being discussed—*at length.*

One of the guests, a mother with two children who's already complained about the lack of children's videos in the library flashes me a look of disappointment as I pass her table and shakes her head. I could already see the review from her now; the lack of quality entertainment in the library and the pornographic one-man ensemble would be bolded highlights. I sigh. Another unforced error in the *Hazel gets this ship back on track tour.*

I pause when I reach the side door, my hand already on the ornate, old-fashioned handle. I have to pull myself together, dig deep, and find a professional way to talk to the naked man because, in addition to being a paroled felon who only nearly missed murder charges, he's also my husband. The one I haven't seen outside a football field and TV screen for five years.

TWO

Ramsey

NOTHING FEELS BETTER than a shower after too many days on the road headed west with only truck-stop bathrooms, gas-station food, and a playlist on loop to keep me company. I'm exhausted, parts of my body hurt worse than they do post-game, and I feel like I'm covered in a thick layer of road dust and chip crumbs. A long outdoor shower under the wide-open Colorado sky, a decent home-cooked meal by one of my favorite cooks of all-time, and an even longer sleep under the stars without worrying about getting robbed by whatever's rolled in off the highway for the night is going to do wonders for the state of my fucking mental health. A thing I'm going to need when *she* finds out I'm here early.

I turn the water off and grab the towel hanging off the ladder, wrapping it around my waist. I forgot how much I love it out here—how good it is to be out in the wild again, far away from the roar of crowds and the congestion of the city, where

I'm free as fuck to do whatever I want—within the bounds of my parole, anyway.

It's not the first time I've set foot back in Colorado since I left, but it is the first time I've been in Purgatory Falls. Playing games against the Denver Rampage weren't nearly the same as being up here in the mountains, and it's been way too damn long since I've been home.

"I really need to ask you not to shower in the middle of the lawn where the guests can see." The words cut through my thoughts, and I freeze. There's a razor-sharp edge to her voice, and it's unfortunate since it's the first time I've heard it in years. The brief messages we exchanged about our situation are no substitute for the real thing. I turn around, looking past her to the inn.

I'm not ready to see her yet, not really, and this wasn't exactly how I planned it going down. Not that I thought through this beyond wanting a shower as fast as possible. But I was hoping I could ease her into things slowly after a halfway decent first impression. Guess we're doing it the hard way instead.

I make out the line of sight between me and the Purgatory Falls Inn, the place my great-great-grandmother started over a hundred years ago. The trees obscure most of this area except for one small bay window on the side of the house where a curtain is drawn.

"They can see through blackout curtains now?" I ask, perplexed by where the concern is coming from since I can't even tell if there's a light on inside or not.

"No, but they could see *before* I drew the curtain back into place." If her tone could kill, I'd be lying face down in the dirt right now.

"Well, tell them they're welcome for the free show." I

smirk, trying to make a joke and finally forcing myself to meet her eyes.

They nearly take my breath away. I'd forgotten how perfect the pale shade of blue really is, and how her thick black lashes and high-arched brows perfectly frame them—or at least, they would if they weren't currently being employed at a steep angle to show me just how little patience she has for my bullshit this morning. Unfortunately, this particular brand of fury makes her look even more gorgeous.

"There are children in the dining room, and a mother who I can tell is about to write the nastiest review this year." Her voice raises slightly as her eyes narrow.

"Let her. If she gives enough detail it might bring you a few more paying customers. Ones who aren't knocking on death's door." I don't know a lot of details about what's been going on in my extended absence, but I do know she's having financial problems, and most of her customers are on weekend passes from the retirement homes they live in along the Front Range.

There's a raspy intake of breath, and her hand drops. Steely blue eyes meet mine and pin me in place. Her jaw is hard set as her eyes sweep over me—the offending parts now covered with a towel—and find me wanting.

"You're not in prison anymore, Ramsey. There aren't any rewards for being the biggest prick on the block. If you absolutely must be here, I hope it's to help and not to make things worse."

"You're right. I'm not in prison anymore. I'm standing in my own yard." I nod back to the ranch house. "Fairly certain I can do what I want here."

"This isn't your personal playground. This is a business. People depend on it for their livelihood."

"Well, I can tell why it's failing if this is how you greet them in the morning."

There's another sharp inhale, and her hands go to her hips. Wide ones that have a perfect curve from her waist down to her thighs, ones accentuated by the pants she has on. Ones that look fucking stunning when she's sitting in a saddle or better yet—riding *me*. I smirk again at the thought of it, and she does *not* like that.

"I will have you arrested for public indecency if you do it again," she threatens, her eyes narrow and her lips press together. It's an idle threat because we've both had enough near misses with the law over the years not to invite them over for breakfast.

"You do that. Is there breakfast inside?" I smother my amusement for her benefit.

Her eyes widen, and she's processing the fact that I'm about to invade her little inn. Our little inn, if we're being accurate, because I'm still part owner whether she likes it or not.

"You're not—you can't! I mean, yes, there's breakfast, but they've just seen you all..." Her hands wave over me, and she gives me a distressed look.

"Darlin', like you said, I'm just out of prison. Before that, hundreds of locker rooms. I really don't give a fuck who's seen me naked. It's not like I have to be worried about it being a disappointment." This time, the smirk's return really is her fault because, with the way her lashes flutter, I can tell she must have caught a glimpse that jogged her memory. The way her eyes dart down to my towel and then quickly back up to my face again tells me it might be the one thing about me she still misses.

We stare at each other for a long moment, my smirk widening and her nostrils flaring as she grows more irritated with me by the minute.

"You don't have something to eat out here?"

"Yeah. A granola bar I bought at a gas station somewhere

outside of Oakley. I'd prefer something hot if it's all the same to you."

"The breakfast is for the paying guests."

"Then I'll make use of the kitchen. I assume you've got a couple of eggs and some bacon I can borrow off the kitchen. I'll cook it up myself."

"Kit would kill you if you touched her kitchen." She's not wrong there. That's sacred space as far as Kit's concerned. I'm just hungry enough to risk it.

"Then I'll only use the fifty percent of it that's mine, but I'm fairly certain Kit'll just volunteer to make it. Happily, I might add." Kit's the head of the inn's café and the best cook I've ever known in my life. I'm one of her favorites, and it's a hard-earned position. One I'm not even sure the passage of time could erode, and Hazel knows it.

A silent glare follows, and I just smile and raise my brows in anticipation. The quiet stretches on; the birds in the trees above us chirping their little hearts out like they're rooting for a fight. I can wait all day, but I'm sure she has somewhere she needs to be.

"*Fine.* Get something from the breakfast bar. But you have to put clothes on."

"I'd planned on it as soon as I got some privacy. Unless you want another look for old times' sake?"

"Don't start with the cute shit. It won't work." I get one last look of dismissal, and she turns on her heel and heads back inside.

THREE

Hazel

AFTER I GET the ladies to their bird-watching appointment and arrange to have Grace take them to lunch and the local winery after, I make my way into town. Purgatory Falls, Colorado, is one of the most gorgeous places in the state, maybe even the country. It was founded in the 1860s but grew during Colorado's silver boom over a decade later. Ramsey's family had been one of the first to set a stake on the edge of town, but they hadn't been the only homesteaders out here. The Briggs—my family, the Silvertons, and the McDaniels also made their homes here in the late nineteenth century, and the town still embraces its historical roots—one of the things that continues to draw tourists in by the busload. The other being the massive glittery casino on the edge of town.

Main Street is lined with historic storefronts, quaint cafes, and old-school saloons that have been converted in more recent years to appease visitors who want to feel like they're stepping back in time. Flower boxes line the sidewalks and cloth banners dangle from the lampposts with advertisements for the upcoming fall Harvest Fest. It looks like something from a storybook, and thanks to the local bakery, Hotcakes, it smells like one too when I step out of my car.

One of my best friends, Marlowe, is the owner, and she grins when she sees me enter, nodding at me as she runs back and forth along the cases, gathering an order of breads and Danishes for Mrs. McDaniel. I nod back and make my way to the corner booth. There's a little nook back there with a table and a perfect view of the town square, perfect for quiet people watching or gossiping with Marlowe in between customers. Late mornings are usually her quiet time before she gets a noon rush of people grabbing sandwiches and midday caffeine fixes, and I come here semi-regularly for a chat and early lunch whenever I can get away from the inn. I definitely need the escape today given the dark hulking piece of metal on my lawn. Marlowe raises a brow in question when she sees my face, and I must be doing a poor job of covering my resting *I wish my husband was still in prison face.* I throw my purse over the back of the wooden chair and pull my phone out, flipping through some emails while I wait for her to finish ringing Mrs. McDaniel up.

"I didn't expect you today," Marlowe says as her attention turns to me, and she takes the seat across from me.

"Well, it's already been a dumpster fire of a morning, so I figured I deserved a break."

"Uh-oh. Is Albert giving you grief about not updating the electrical again?" She looks at me thoughtfully. Albert, my maintenance guy, had his own list of necessary upgrades, above and beyond my cosmetic ones, that needed to happen if we want to keep the inn in running order, and somehow, his managed to be much more expensive than the new duvets and bathroom tile I've been coveting.

"It's been okay this week. No major issues, but it's on the list. As soon as I get the refinance to go through."

"How's that going? Have you talked to *him* yet?" Her lips press together warily.

It's impossible for the Stockton brothers not to come up in conversation. They run the casino on land that backs up to the ranch, and it employs half the newcomers in town. They also own half the buildings on Main Street, the one car dealership on the edge of town, and they might as well have their names tattooed on half of the city council members' asses for how much they do their bidding. Soon enough, they'll be renaming the city after them.

But most of my friends are kind enough not to mention the youngest brother's name, the one who ran off to the Midwest to make his millions far away from this little town he grew up in—and me. The only thing he owns in this town is my ranch and inn, but it's enough to make my life hell.

"Funny you should ask." Sarcasm leeches through my tone as I look out the window.

"It didn't go well?"

"That's an understatement. I came downstairs this morning to my Grannies with Gumption group peering out the window, tittering about some guy's ass and thighs. This had me wildly confused because Albert and Sam aren't exactly famous for either... and lo and behold, it's Ramsey, fully nude and showering at the back of his RV on the lawn next to the ranch house."

"Outside?" Marlowe's face contorts with horror.

"Outside in full view of the dining room." I sigh as I watch a group of tourists make their way down the street.

"So he did it on purpose."

"He claims he didn't think any of the windows faced that direction."

"Does he have eyes?"

"Who knows what he has anymore? But he's here. And I can only imagine what that means."

"Is he moving back?"

"Hell no!" I answer her sharply. The thought hadn't occurred to me, and now my nerves can't handle the idea. "He couldn't."

"Couldn't he?" she asks reluctantly, drawing her lips to one side in contemplation. "I mean, if you're still married and all the settlement paperwork didn't go through..." The implication is there. Everything was his to start with, and Colorado law seemed pretty clear about the dispersal of assets in a contested divorce.

"I don't know. I have my meeting with my lawyer this week. Yet another thing I can't afford." I sigh. "I can't imagine him wanting it back. He couldn't run away from there fast enough." I feel sick at the thought of losing everything because he's changed his mind.

"Yeah, but now after everything... He might have changed his mind. Prison can change people. Let alone the kind of things he went through..." Marlowe looks at me thoughtfully.

She's the romantic of our friend group, so she's always had a soft spot for Ramsey's tortured soul. The fact that he went to prison because he murdered the guy who was trying to kill his teammate and friend had her all atwitter when it happened. Frankly, it had the whole town lauding him as a hero and happy to answer media calls about Stockton's humble beginnings in Purgatory Falls. Not that they were very humble. Unless you consider organized crime, theft, racketeering, and three thousand acres humble.

"Well, he can't come back. It's mine now, and I've moved

on. I'm getting married in six months, and the last thing I need is him around fucking everything up." It's that simple. It has to be.

"Did he look as good as he does on TV?" Marlowe can't seem to control the small smirk that spreads as she asks the question. For being the sweet one, she still loves to stir things up. I give her a sour look in return, and she holds up her hands. "I'm just asking, objectively. Inquiring minds and all that."

"The grannies certainly thought so. I thought he was going to give them a heart attack with the way they were clutching their pearls over him."

"And you?"

"He was covered up by the time I got outside." It's not a lie. The fact that I noticed that he's in the best shape of his life and has a couple dozen more tattoos than I remember doesn't need to be mentioned.

"You know I'm not gonna tell anyone, right? Won't even whisper a word to Dakota or Bristol." She raises a brow at me skeptically. Our two best friends would run wild with the truth I'm about to admit.

I sigh and she just watches and waits patiently for me to say the thing she already knows is true.

"He looked good—*really* good," I admit bitterly. "It's not fair."

"I mean... he was in the pros and then in prison. Lots of time and incentive to be in the gym."

"He has more tattoos too. And the scruff." I huff and shake my head. "Too bad it's all wrapped up in that package."

"I thought we liked that package enough to marry it," she muses.

"And then we hated it enough to divorce it," I counter. "I feel sorry for the next woman who falls for it."

"Touché. When is the new divorce happening then?"

"Not quick enough. I'll probably have to play nice to get him to hurry up and re-sign everything. But then, hopefully, he'll be on his way." That was the only upside to him being in town. He's here, and I can sit down with him, redo all the paperwork, and get it turned in without any of the cross-country back-and-forth that we had the last time.

Marlowe's mouth twitches, and then she turns and looks out the window, leaning on her hand and trying to cover the way her lips betray her otherwise serene face.

"What?" I ask flatly.

"Nothing..."

"Just say it."

"I just think you're being a little naïve if you think he drove a thousand miles just to fill out divorce paperwork."

"What? You really think he's going to stick around He hates it here.?"

"I think he's not playing football anymore, and this is his hometown. His family's here. His ranch."

"*My* ranch."

"Technically his." She tilts her head.

"He doesn't want it. And his family? The brothers haven't even spoken in years to my knowledge."

"To be fair, your knowledge of what he's been up to isn't very extensive. Maybe the whole prison and near-death experience changed things for him. Even if the relationships *are* all strained, maybe he's got a mind to mend them."

"Like it changed him the last time?" I ask because it was violence and death that had driven us down the road to divorce in the first place.

"I mean, last time it sent him running away. This time it might have sent him running home." Marlowe gives me a look that tells me I should reconsider my preconceived notions. "I'm just saying... consider the possibility and prepare yourself. He might stick around for a bit."

"Not if I can help it." I'd make the man's life a living hell if he tried. No way does he get to disappear for five years, move on with his life, and then come back home and take it all away again because of a clerical error.

"You do know how to push his buttons," Marlowe notes, and I offer a wry grin in return that makes her shake her head. "All right. Then we'll have to keep you fueled for the rebellion. What'll it be—turkey or ham?"

"Turkey, please. And cold brew? I need something to wake me up before I go back. I barely slept last night, and thanks to him, I didn't get my second cup."

"One turkey on farmer's bread coming up. You can grab the cold brew for yourself if you want." She nods to the small fridge.

We spend the rest of my late morning break chatting about our new business ideas and making plans for the weekend. It's a much-needed break from my current reality. But when the line at the door starts to get longer, she has to say goodbye, and I have to face reality.

"Go find out what he wants. Better to rip the Band-Aid off than be stuck wondering." She raises her brow, and I sigh but reluctantly nod my head. I might as well learn what my fate's going to be and how long it's going to involve Ramsey Stockton.

WHEN I GET BACK to the ranch, I pull down the long dirt and gravel drive, parking in the lot in front of the barn. I want to check to make sure the trail ride the guests took this afternoon was a good one and check in on one of the rescue horses that just got here earlier this week. But when I walk across the lot and into the stables, Kellan, the trainer, and Eli, his assistant and the barn manager, are missing. Instead, I see Ramsey, dressed in all black, with a baseball hat on backward, leaning into one of the stalls, smiling and talking like he's catching up with an old friend. When Wolfsbane lifts his head over the gate and lets Ramsey run his hand over his nose, I realize that's exactly what he's doing.

Wolfsbane is still his after all these years. His parents bought the horse for him for his seventeenth birthday, not long after Ramsey found out he was getting a football scholarship. They'd offered to upgrade his truck and buy him a sports car, but he'd asked for the massive Friesian instead.

I'd been tempted to sell him more than once. The price he'd fetch on the market would keep the rescue horses fed and watered for at least a couple of years, and he'd never been happy after Ramsey left. Giving every other rider but me trouble, and even with me, he'd pout about the fact that I wasn't bringing Ramsey home to him. We couldn't use him for lessons or trail rides, and I didn't get to ride him nearly as much as I would like.

But I felt like I needed Ramsey's permission to sell him, and I wasn't about to be the one who broke the silence between us after we signed the papers five years ago. So Wolfsbane had stayed, first to listen to me cry and scream and commiserate about what an ass his owner was and then to remind me never to put either of us in the position of being left again.

"You miss me? I missed you, buddy. We'll have to go for a ride later. If your mom lets me. She's pretty pissed at me after this morning. But you're not, are you, bud? You're happy to see me." Ramsey leans his head forward, bringing him forehead-to-nose with Wolfsbane, talking to him in a sweet voice. One I've only ever heard him use on Wolfsbane and the dog he had as a kid. It makes me smile despite myself as I try to keep my approach slow. I can tell Wolfsbane is eating up every moment of the attention from him, and I hate to interrupt. I can feel sorry for the horse even if I don't feel an ounce of it for the man.

"I see you two are getting reacquainted," I say as I get closer. Ramsey doesn't even startle; he just glances back over his shoulder.

"Yeah. The big guy and I have some catching up to do."

"Is he in a forgiving mood?" I ask, running my hand down Wolfsbane's nose as he extends his head and neck in Ramsey's direction for more attention.

"Seems like he might be." Ramsey looks over him thoughtfully as he nudges his shoulder again.

"You can ride him later if you want. Kell can help you get him saddled."

"I can still saddle my own horse, Haze." There's a scoffing click in his throat as he shakes his head. "It hasn't been that long."

"Well, it's been a bit. I have no idea what you get up to in the city." I shrug, and Ramsey looks back over his shoulder again to study me.

"Or around here." He smirks as his eyes travel over me. "Finally got the blue hair I see."

His eyes run over my long hair. I'm naturally a brunette, but when Bristol dyed hers, she convinced me to do the same. We spent her birthday down in the city last month getting it done. While Marlowe and Dakota got theirs highlighted, I opted for a dark brown at the roots that fades to a cerulean blue at the tips. I've been threatening to do it since I was a teenager and figured it was now or never.

"Yeah. Bristol and I got it done for her birthday." I shrug.

"Hers blue too?"

"No. She got a rose-gold color. It looks pretty on her with her green eyes."

"You've got lots of new tattoos," I note as I look at his arms, where a geometric pattern swirls around his elbow and meets a bee with a crown. I guess this is our version of small talk.

He shrugs. "The guys and I sometimes go get 'em done for fun. Win a game. Get a bonus. Gotta spend it somehow."

"I think those guys normally buy houses and cars, don't they?"

"Some. A surprising number of us are smart enough to save it. You never know how many good years you'll have in the league."

"Fair enough." I don't want to touch that subject with a ten-foot pole yet. I only know what I heard on the news, but it's obvious he isn't playing this year. Though I imagine that's not the whole story.

As much as I want to avoid the next discussion, I do need to start getting to the point. Ripping the Band-Aid off like Marlowe suggested.

"I assume you're not here just for fun. It's too long of a drive for that. So what is it you want, Ramsey?"

He turns to me, his eyes running up my legs and over my body until they meet mine, and the smile on his face turns ominously dark. I don't even need him to say a word to know—Marlowe was right.

FOUR

Ramsey

"GIVE ME NINETY DAYS HERE. Then I'll give you the divorce uncontested. You can keep the ranch and the inn."

Her brow climbs, and her eyes drift over my face, but she doesn't say a word for long moments, and then her eyes narrow.

"What's the catch?" Her arms cross over her chest.

She knows me too well.

"For those ninety days, you're my wife."

"Obviously." She rolls her eyes.

"No. I mean, *my wife*." I give her a pointed look.

Her brow furrows for a moment and then releases in surprise before she shakes her head.

"You're crazy. Certifiable, honestly. I'm engaged. Remember?" Her eyes slide over me like I've said the most offensive thing she's ever heard.

"You're married."

She levels me with a look of contempt.

"I'm engaged. To a man I love. I'm happy—the happiest I've been in a long time. I don't want you or any of the things that come with you, Ramsey. Not near me or this ranch. I have good things here, and I don't want them fucked up."

I roll my lower lip and dip my head to the side in contemplation, glancing up at her and then shaking my head like I'm unbothered, even though it feels like she just slid a knife through my ribs and into my lung.

"That's too bad. You should have made sure you were in a position to get engaged first."

I see the way her jaw tightens and the furrow in her brow deepens, but a moment later, it fades.

"Just sign the divorce papers, please. This can be civil. You can move on with your life, and I can move on with mine. If we do it now, I'll still have plenty of time to get my paperwork filed for the inn. You can have your life back in time for the end of your parole. We both get what we want." Her eyes go soft with the plea, but her shoulders stay rigid, and I know she's just trying to manage me.

She's bargaining and hoping she can dangle something in front of me that I want more. Unfortunately for her, I've had far too many months alone, staring at a cinder block wall and thinking about exactly what I would do differently if I had a second chance. And fate's dealt me the opportunity for just that.

"Nah. I don't think so. I think I want my family's ranch back. My house. My inn. My horse... I think I want all of it back the more I look around."

"That's not how life works." The brief glimpse of her softer side is disappearing as quickly as it appeared. "Everything here has moved on without you. I suggest you do the same."

I knew she wouldn't come around to the idea easily. I knew

she'd hate it at first, but I didn't plan for exactly how much the unequivocal, unyielding rejection would sting.

"Maybe." I run my hand along the edge of the stall. "But it's how the court system works. I imagine they won't feel sympathetic to my wife getting engaged and nearly committing bigamy, trying to refinance my property behind my back, letting her boyfriend take over my ranch, and then trying to take my ancestral family home all in one go. Yeah. Haze, I gotta say, darlin', you're not lookin' too good in that scenario. But I'm sure you've got plenty of money to fight it with the lawyers, right?" I raise my eyes to meet hers. "I don't imagine you were refinancing because you're hurting for money or anything?"

"You're an asshole." I'm pretty sure she'd throttle me right now if she thought it would do any good at all.

"I just want you to be sure you're making an informed decision before you give me your final answer." I shrug one shoulder, glancing back at Wolfsbane who seems as eager to hear her acceptance as I am.

"Even if I was insane enough to agree to this, and I'm not, to be clear. But even if I was, do you think Curtis would just agree to it?"

"I assume he has a pragmatic side." I take a step closer to her and reach out for a lock of her hair that's fallen over her shoulder, sweeping it back. "Tell you what, darlin'. I'll give you a million to ease his conscience and yours. Instead of refinancing—you can just use that. Think of it like an early wedding gift."

Her jaw drops, and she leans forward to match me, needling her finger into my chest. One manicured nail, her attempt to cover up all the hard labor she does around here from her guests, is threatening to pierce through my shirt and into my skin. Her eyes blaze with fury, and if one of the horses wasn't rattling around in his stall, I'm sure I could hear the grinding of her teeth.

"I don't even know where to start with how fucked up that is," she spits.

"You don't even want to mention the idea to Curtis?" I do my best to stay rational. I can't imagine he'll agree, but it's worth a shot.

She starts to draw up again, like she's going to argue about how ridiculous the notion is that her fiancé would accept my conditions, but there's the slightest flicker of something over her face. A hint of doubt, and that tells me everything I need to know about Curtis.

I wouldn't let a man touch her for a hundred times that. If I could help it, no other man will ever touch her again. But it's obvious—from the flutter of her lashes to the way she nibbles her lower lip—she thinks he might go for it. She shakes her head, takes a step back, crosses her arms, and stares off into the distance; a long sigh escapes her lips before she looks back at me with disappointment.

"Be reasonable and just sign the papers." It's one last plea, but she's caving. I can feel it. Hope floods my chest.

"Sorry, darlin'. Can't do it."

"Don't call me darlin'." She flashes a look of warning at me.

"Sure thing, sugar." I wink at her as her chin dips back and her lips part. I haven't called her either in a long time. Not since we were kids who fell in love and got married because we thought it would always be that simple for us—that we were built differently than everyone who came before.

We stand in an uneasy silence while Wolfsbane rattles the door of his stall, asking to be let out, and a truck rolls up the driveway in the distance. Her eyes follow the sound, and she stares out the door of the stables for a long minute.

"Why would you even want to do this?" she asks without looking at me.

"Nostalgia." I'd rehearsed this answer, knowing she was bound to ask.

She lets out a huff, and her eyes flick over me, then dart back to the door.

"You've never been nostalgic in your life. It was always forward movement with you. Always what was next week, next year, next century. Now, suddenly, you like long walks down memory lane?"

"Yes, but it's also my home of record for the authorities, and I don't feel like refiling paperwork right now. Fuckin' hate bureaucracy." It's not a lie, just not the whole truth. She tilts her head as if acknowledging that much is easy for her.

"I can give you a room in the inn," she bargains, turning back to me with a optimistic look.

"Nah. I don't want to be up at the crack of dawn because your ladies are headed out on one of their daily adventures. I want my house. My bed."

"Fine. Then I'll move into the inn while you play house. It'll keep me closer to everything."

"It's all or nothing." I press my luck, and now I have her attention. Her eyes search my face, and they harden.

"You'd do that? Try to take the ranch and inn away from me? When you never wanted them in the first place?"

"I told you. I've had a lot of time to think over the last few months. Reflecting on what I might have done differently if I'd been in a different place." I offer her a crumb of honesty, but somehow that uneasy admission makes her angrier.

"You get nostalgic and want a do-over, so you just get to crash in here and take everything I've spent years working on? All because things got a little rough out there, and now you think you can come home to hide. Pretend you can put it all back like nothing happened. Fuck the rest of us, right?"

I bite my tongue to keep from responding. It took two of us to get where we did when things fell apart. She was every bit as stubborn as I was when it came down to it. But I'm making a big ask right now, and I know it. I deserve some part of this lashing, even if she doesn't need to be quite so heavy-handed.

"I want a place to stay out of public view, serve out the rest of this parole, and have some sense of stability while I figure out what's next. I'm offering you all of it and a million dollars for the inconvenience. Ninety days and you get it all for the rest of your life. That's like winning the lotto compared to what I could do."

"And you fuck off forever after? I don't ever have to hear from you or see you again? Your lawyer isn't going to show up someday pointing to some loophole where you take it all back?" Her arms tighten around her middle.

"If that's what you want."

"It is what I want. I don't even want to be standing here having this conversation with you now. If it were up to me, you'd fuck off immediately and stay fucked off."

I bite my tongue to keep myself from pouring gasoline on this fire.

"Yes. I fuck off forever after. No loopholes."

"I want it in writing. Tell your fancy fucking lawyer I want everything in black and white. And I want you to sign it in blood. Anything less and I won't do it."

The average person would probably be terrified of her temper, but I love seeing it flare again. Anger means she's still invested enough to feel something for me. Apathy is the real danger. Right now, I still have a shot to fix this. It might be one deep down in the bowels of hell, with rapidly dropping temperatures and the smell of snow, but I'll take it.

"Is that a yes, then?" I have to bite the inside of my cheek to keep the smirk off my face.

"No." She practically hisses the word. "I have to think. Talk to Curtis. Make sure my lawyer can't get me out of this first."

"Your lawyer?"

"I have one." Her eyes narrow and sweep over me before she looks away again. "Not to mention, I'm still hoping this is a nightmare I'm going to wake up from any minute now."

"Afraid not, sugar."

She flicks me another look before she turns to leave the stables.

"One last thing..." I call after her, and she pauses but doesn't turn around to look at me. "I just want to be clear. When I say I want my bed back, I mean with you in it."

I see her bristle, and she flips me the bird over her shoulder before storming out. I turn back to Wolfsbane and run my hand over his mane.

"You notice she didn't say no," I mutter under my breath, smiling as I hear the door to the stables slams shut in her wake.

FIVE

Hazel

"THIS IS INSANE. I can't believe he'd fucking come out here and suggest it. I should kick his ass for even mentioning it to you." Curtis looks like a vein might pop in his forehead as he rants from the bathroom doorway before bed, and I just nod my agreement. I glance out the window where the RV is parked in the distance. What else can I say? If his ex-wife appeared and offered the same deal, I'd probably burn something down.

"It *is* insane," I say softly. There's just one problem. "But the alternative could be worse. If he draws out the divorce... It'll cost me money I don't have, and I could very well lose the inn and the ranch to him. We'd be out a home. I'd be out a business..."

"You never told me it was still his." Curtis looks at me like I've betrayed him.

"I didn't know. As part of the divorce settlement, he agreed to pay all the property taxes for five years, so I wasn't due to take them over until next year. His family accountant was handling it like always." I'm trying to explain, but I'm embarrassed that I could have missed such a glaring mistake.

My ex-husband occasionally bubbled up as a sore subject whenever we got into a tiff over the way I liked something done around the house, or the occasional comment when he thought I spent too long watching the Queen City Chaos on TV. He definitely wasn't a fan of the Rampage-Chaos game I attended last year in person—but in my defense, it's not like Ramsey knew I was there. Besides those little squabbles, we're pretty good together, and I have no idea how much of a mess this news is going to make of us.

"It seems like a thing that should have come up before now. Our wedding date is only a few months away. Were you going to tell me about him paying the taxes before that?" I've never seen Curtis this riled before.

"I don't know. I suppose if it came up, I would have. I honestly didn't think you would care. It's not like it changes anything." I give him a sheepish shrug. I've been so focused on the inn and the improvements we need to make that I'd barely considered the issue myself.

"Well... it does now, doesn't it?" he mutters.

"Unfortunately," I mumble in return.

"It's a nightmare." He stares into the distance.

"It is," I agree. I'm not usually in the position of being this wrong about something, and I can confidently say I hate it.

"How is it even possible that you didn't know you were still married?" His tone belies his otherwise calm demeanor.

I'm desperate to make it clear that I know I fucked up—that I'm trying to fix it. The whole thing makes me sick to my stomach with anxiety. Ramsey could destroy everything important to me with very little effort, and I can't believe I allowed myself to end up in this position. I'm used to being the one in charge, giving the lectures, and making sure everyone else has things in order. Being on the receiving end of this makes me feel like the walls of this ranch house are closing in on me, stealing my breath and suffocating me. I'm half tempted to make a run for the stables to take a late-night ride.

"I thought I filed the paperwork. After the divorce, everything was such a mess. I was just trying to tread water and keep things going around here. It never came up as a question. But I remember the day I sent it. I *know* I sent it," I insist.

I'd been terrified to file the paperwork. I talked myself into and out of getting in the car and taking it to the post office half a dozen times, but then, on the seventh try, I grabbed my keys and charged ahead. Drove the whole way with my hands shaking. Opened the creaky, blue metal door to the mailbox with the rust patch on the upper left corner that I stared at for long minutes before I slipped the manila envelope inside. Even when my heart still hurt. When my lungs burned from the crying. Even though it felt like I was going to die without him.

So I *know* I sent it.

"So you sent it and what, they just never filed it?" His question snaps me out of the memory.

"I guess? Or they never received it. That's what they're claiming."

"You never checked to make sure?" His questions feel like accusations.

"No. I sent it. That was the big thing. We signed on the dotted line. The divorce was uncontested. We didn't even involve lawyers. Just us agreeing, signing, and me sending it in. I didn't think to check. I assumed as long as we did our part, they'd do theirs."

Curtis shakes his head and glances at me, his face twisted with scorn. I'm not sure whether it's for me, Ramsey, or both of us.

"If you'd changed your name or done anything else at all, it would have come up."

"I know. I should have." I have a feeling that's going to be an even bigger regret once Ramsey realizes I never went back to Briggs.

"You should have," he repeats.

"It seemed like more work than it was worth. I just wanted to forget everything, not spend more time on it."

"Well... I'm sure you feel differently now." He says it without malice, but it still cuts. "Fighting this will cost a fortune."

"I have no idea where we'll get the money." I shake my head, trying not to cry. I don't want to give any more tears to Ramsey Stockton.

"My parents won't be able to loan us anything else. They've put in all they can for the wedding, so we'll just have to cancel it. Or push it out. I don't even know how I'll tell them. It's a disaster." Curtis's forehead furrows with the thought.

I haven't even met his parents yet. They're always on one trip or another on the other side of the world, but they're supposed to spend the holidays with us this year to finalize wedding plans. Kit and I had already started planning for their visit. It's just mortifying to know they'll have this kind of impression of me before I even get to know them.

"I know. I'm still hoping I can come up with a plan. Sometimes sleeping on it means having a better idea in the morning." I try to reach out for his hand but he turns his back to me, tucking the sheet tight around his shoulders.

"Yeah. Maybe," he mutters.

My heart sinks. I'll be lucky to keep any of our plans. A divorce could take months, over a year if he makes it particularly messy—and he already promised he would. I know the man well enough to know he's just stubborn enough to hold to his conditions.

———

THE NEXT MORNING we're finishing breakfast when Curtis sets his phone aside and looks up at me. His eyes wander over me thoughtfully before he speaks.

"I think you should do it," he says flatly, like it's a business decision.

"What?" I'm caught off guard.

I expected the anger from last night to boil over to today. I figured we'd have to spend a few more hours hashing out the pros and cons of the options in front of us. I spent the night wide awake working my way up to the idea of being Ramsey's wife again, at least temporarily, but I thought I'd have to convince Curtis it's our best option. The outright refusal and the misplaced rage yesterday all made sense, but this quiet resignation knocks me off-kilter.

"I've thought about it, and I just think we don't have another choice. We need the ranch free and clear of him, and we need the refinancing to go through to keep it going."

"About that..." I say softly.

He looks up at me, confusion marring his face, and his brow lifts in question.

"He'd give us the money." I didn't tell him that part last night. The entire proposal felt dirty enough without adding the money to the mix.

"The money for the refinance?"

"And then some. A million." I practically whisper the words.

"Why?" His brow furrows like he can't make sense of it, and the reaction pricks.

"You don't think I'm worth it?" It's a stupid thing to say. I'm starting another argument when we haven't finished this one. We already have enough problems to fuel them for the next two months straight. I see the flicker of irritation over his face.

"I'm just asking why he'd do it." Curtis's tone turns irritated.

"I don't know why he's doing any of this." Other than the possibility of the obvious, but I can't believe it.

"Don't be naïve. He's an egotistical prick used to always getting his way. He wants you back, and this place too, or to at least prove he can have it if he wants it." His temper flares, but he tamps it down almost as quickly, reaching out and cupping my cheek. "But I know you're smarter than that, and I know what we have is better than anything you had with him, so I'm not worried. If you doing this gets you everything debt free with a bonus..." He shrugs and presses his lips together like it's a painful reality we need to confront. "I feel like we have to seriously consider it."

"I'm surprised that's your reaction. I really thought you'd be dead set against this."

"You know how I feel about things like this. The wedding. The inn business. Your ex. It doesn't make sense to be anything other than pragmatic. Besides, he gets you and this place for ninety days. I get you and all of this for the rest of my life. Ten years from now, three months won't matter." He takes a long sip of his coffee.

He's right about that. He's pragmatic about everything. The opposite of my ambitious daydreams and wild ideas. Always keeping me grounded in reality and making sure I'm thinking about the bigger picture and things like finances and budgets and reality. Something Ramsey never even tried to do. He was as much a dreamer as me. We just were in the unfortunate position of having dreams that ran in different directions—his to Ohio and mine here.

"I guess that's true. In ten years, none of this will matter. But it's... You realize that he wants me in his bed, doing a lot more than just sleeping in it. You don't feel like it's cheating?" We've danced around the heart of this conversation since last night. We've discussed the inn, the ranch, him staying in the house and how much easier it'll make the divorce go if we just play along. But we haven't discussed the fact that Ramsey was very specific in his request.

"It can't be cheating if you're telling me about it and I'm agreeing to it. More like a hall pass. One that gets us a three-thousand-acre ranch, your inn, and apparently an extra million for you to renovate it like you want."

"But it's a hall pass I don't want," I add, because I feel like I have to. For myself as much as him. Especially after the preview I got already. I can't deny the fact that my ex-husband is attractive, but I could remind myself that it came with so many downsides, it ruined everything beautiful about him.

Curtis looks up at me thoughtfully, studying my face.

"If you feel like he's forcing you or he's unsafe and you don't want to do this, tell me. I don't want to be party to anything that makes you uncomfortable." His brows slant down in a deep frown.

"He won't force himself on me." I shake my head. That much I know about Ramsey.

Well, he won't use force *without permission* is probably the more accurate way of putting it. Not that I'm about to share that tidbit with Curtis. Ramsey knows some of my darkest fantasies, ones I've never shared with Curtis, and I don't feel like now is a great time to illuminate that particular discrepancy.

"You trust him?" Curtis asks, noticing the way I'm lost in thought again.

"He respects me. He still loves my family even if we don't love each other. I'm not worried about him hurting me or forcing me or anything like that." I hurry to recover.

Ramsey broke my heart, but he'd never risk breaking my spirit. I'd still trust the man with my life, even if I do hate him with every bone in my body.

"But you're worried?"

"He's a force of nature. He comes in like a hurricane and leaves everything in his wake a path of destruction. I don't want him to make a mess of this place or a mess of us," I explain as Curtis takes my hands in his own.

"He won't make a mess of us. If anything, he's helping us— right? You'll have this place to yourself, finally. Plus, you'll have the money to upgrade the rooms and fix up the stables like you wanted."

I raise my brow at him as I lean back and sip my tea. It's my turn to study him because I can't help the little bubble of apprehension in my gut. The little voice telling me no man is this accommodating, even with these kinds of stakes. Especially not any man who's seen my ex.

"What?" he asks after a long minute.

"I just can't believe you're so unbothered by this. If this was reversed and your ex wanted you to go back to acting like you're still together, I'd be furious. I'd never be okay with it." I'd consider stabbing her for even suggesting it.

"I don't love the idea, Hazel. Obviously, I don't like the idea of someone else touching you. But I can only imagine what a prolonged, messy divorce will do to your mental health and our finances. Not to mention our chances of getting married sooner rather than later. Plus, like I said... he's a fucking loser. No job. No home. Fresh out of prison. It's not like I have to worry about you falling for someone like that." Curtis laughs; it's haughty and dismissive. He gives a sharp shake of his head like Ramsey's the most ridiculous thing he's ever taken the time to consider.

I feel the zip of it in my veins—a rumble of anger and defensiveness. One's I shouldn't feel, given the position Ramsey has me in. But then he was part of me whether I liked it or not. Long before Ramsey was mine, he was part of my family. My brother's best friend. Always at our house to escape the complications at home—ironic since his family had money and mine had none. But my family loved him. Hard. Even after our divorce when my brother and Ramsey grew distant, they were still the first people to cheer for him on the screen against the home team. We all still watched the verdict of his trial on TV with our breath held tight in our chests, hoping for the best. Like any good family, it's one of those things where if I want to talk shit about him—that's one thing, but I'll go down swinging against anyone else who has a bad word to say.

But right now, I have to hold it in. I don't want Curtis to think there's anything more than a business decision being made here—one I'm making under duress.

"And you're okay not being here with me during that time?" I ask because I'm not sure he's thought through all the implications of this arrangement.

"Sure. I'm going to be in Vegas for that training for most of the time anyway. When I come back those couple of weekends, I can rent a hotel." His eyes light up and turn back on me. "Maybe you can sneak away and come meet me there. We can pretend like *we're* having an affair." He grins playfully, and I can tell he's trying to make the best of this. I smile despite the literal truth of his statement reverberating in my head, but something about his casualness has me feeling uneasy.

"You're really not worried about me sleeping with him?"

His grin turns into a smirk. "Not after what you told me about him not being able to get you off."

My eyes dart to my phone and I clear my throat.

"Be serious though. It won't bother you that I'm kissing him? Sleeping with him?" I press. I don't want to do this to save the inn and lose Curtis in the process.

"We saw other people when we were first dating. How's this any different?"

"Because we're about to be married." I try not to let the irritation through in my tone. I don't want to start any more fights with him.

"And we still will be."

"Are you going to sleep with other people then?" The thought hits me like bricks—after all, he'll be in Vegas. What better place to be on a break from your fiancée.

"I don't know. It seems like the hall pass should work both ways." He shrugs like it's nothing but it feels like a brick slamming into my chest.

"But I don't want a hall pass, and if I had one, I wouldn't use it on Ramsey Stockton." I protest. I can think of three movie stars and one singer who would all be in line ahead of him. But knowing he'd still be on the list—even if it would be a hate fuck—is a little unsettling to realize. I'd have to confront that ugly little truth later.

"If you tell me you're not comfortable with it, I can respect that. Although it does seem a little unfair." His mouth sets in a grim line and he tilts his head to the side like he's considering which apple to pick at the grocery store rather than the boundaries of our engagement.

"I'm not comfortable with it," I answer firmly, and his eyes meet mine.

"Okay." There's a resignation in the way he looks at me, but it's an uneasy one.

"Does that change how you feel?" I ask. I want more from him, more fight, more thoughts—more anything really, but he seems at peace with this.

"I trust you, baby. You tell me you're okay with this, that it's what you want to do to make this easier and get his help fixing up the inn, then I'm good. I know who you're walking down the aisle to." He rubs his hand over the back of mine. "Not to mention, I know it's me you'll be imagining and missing anyway."

Apparently, I've underestimated Curtis's ego, and he's underestimated Ramsey.

SIX

Ramsey

HAZEL and I are locked in uneasy silence standing at the kitchen table in the ranch house. It's still my mother's massive old oak table, and it warms my heart a little to know she didn't replace it. Looking around, there's still a lot of my family in the house, even all these years later. Some memories I want and others I wish I could forget.

"Do you want something to drink?" She hovers near a chair.

"I'm good." I shake my head and pull out the one that was always mine to sit.

"Okay..." She shifts on her feet for a moment before finally following my lead. "I've thought about your offer and talked it over with Curtis. We decided that we'll do it but only under a few conditions." She emphasizes the *we* in the sentence like her life depends on it, and I resist the urge to correct her.

"Which are?" I don't like conditions. I don't like that he has any say in something that should be between me and my wife, but then I guess after five years I have to earn that understanding back. Something I have every intention of doing.

"I'm still talking to Curtis throughout the ninety days. He'll be out of town most of the time anyway. But I'm not cutting him off."

"I didn't imagine you would." I'm not worried. I've seen Curtis. He's a fucking speed bump I'll run over in due time.

"I want all the paperwork presigned. We can put it in a lock box at the bank and give the key to Bo."

Bo is her oldest brother and my best friend, Boden Briggs, although my hurting her put some long hard miles on that friendship.

"We can do that," I agree.

"You sleep in the guest room." She looks down at the table when she says that one because she knows what my reaction will be. I was clear about what I want, and I'm tempted to argue the point. I want to insist I'm in her bed—our bed—from the start. But I'm holding back. I don't want to cause friction with her already—not when it seems like she's about to agree to this fucked-up plan of mine.

"I'll start in the guest room. Give you time to adjust." I study her face as her eyes slowly lift to mine. "But once you get used to me around here again, I want my room and my bed back." I see her start to speak, and I cut her off before she can make a comment about her going to the guest room. "With *you* in it."

"I'm not promising anything on that front." There's a steely defiance in her eyes.

"You don't have to promise." I fight the smile that tries to form, but she registers it anyway, and her eyes narrow in response.

"I'm not the girl you remember."

"I'm counting on that."

"Then count on being disappointed. I don't give a flying fuck about men like you anymore. The tattoos and muscles and that little lopsided grin you do when you think you're being clever have lost their luster. They're all just warning signs for me now."

"Well, that explains your choice of boyfriend." That part I can't resist.

"Fiancé," she corrects.

"Use whatever fancy French names you want for him, sugar. It's still Hazel *Stockton*, the last I checked." I see her nose twitch ever so slightly when I say her last name.

"Don't read anything into that. I was too lazy to change it— nothing more."

I'm definitely reading into it. If she hated me as much as I thought she did when she asked for the divorce, she would have changed it. She wouldn't have been able to stand all the times she had to say it over and over again just in the daily course of her life. It meant something that she didn't go back to Briggs— whether she can admit it yet or not.

"Any other rules?"

"We don't tell my family the dirty details of this. Or anyone in town. We make up a lie about your needing to be here for parole and with the glitch in the system that we're still married, it looks better to the justice system if we're a happy family. We'll tell them Curtis and I are on break for the meantime while we work through the mess this still married thing has made."

"I don't like lying to them." I might be an asshole, but honesty is high up there on the short list of morals I do have.

"Bo would kill you if he found out you were treating me like this, and I'm not going to do all this just to lose out on the money when he puts you six feet under."

"You wouldn't lose out. If anything, that's the fastest way to it. Assuming you can stomach being a murderer." She's still the beneficiary of my will. My parents are long gone, and my siblings have their own money. If anyone deserves a payout for all the hell I caused this world, it's her. Her eyes are wide with that information, and then she shakes her head like she's off somewhere distant, trying to process that information.

"I'll leave the murder to you." She realizes she's said it out loud and her hand covers her mouth. "I'm sorry, that was... unkind."

I shrug. "It's true."

A beat passes, and then a curious look crosses her face. "Did you really snap his neck?"

I nod and there's a sharp intake of breath before she considers it further.

"I couldn't believe it when they showed you handcuffed on the TV. I mean, we didn't exactly play by the rules around here. Your family less than the rest, but..."

Murder in the middle of the day with people watching is a bridge too far. That's what she means.

"He tried to kill Bea. Shot Cooper. I just saw red, and it was what it was after." I look out the window. I don't remember snapping his neck, but I'd seen the video in court enough times to know it happened.

"Is Bea... someone to you?"

"Coop's girl. Not mine. But she's some of the best people I've ever known. Coop doesn't love anyone easy. I couldn't stand there and watch him lose her like that." They're one of the biggest parts of my life back in Cincinnati that I miss. They'd gotten me through the trial and the prison sentence.

"I see. I'm sorry that all of that happened. To your friends and you."

"I did what had to be done. It ended well. That's all that

matters." I hate talking about this, but I didn't imagine I was going to get out of the conversation. Might as well have it now.

"Do you have someone back in Cincinnati?" She asks the question quietly, like she doesn't really want the answer.

"You think I'd be here if I did?"

There's a wince on her face, and she pulls back. I realize how she's taken it, and I shake my head.

"I don't mean it like that. Just... you know me. I'm a lot of fucking things, Haze, but I'm not a cheater."

"But you're asking me to be one."

"Nah. I'm asking you *not* to cheat. I'm the one you're married to, remember? Besides, I thought you just said old boy agreed to it."

Her eyes narrow again, but she doesn't disagree with me on the merits of my argument. The uncomfortable silence returns and when her knee starts to jiggle, I know it's my turn to fill it.

"So we're pretending to be a happy family for my parole officer? Is that what we're telling them then?" I ask.

"Yes. It seems the easiest explanation. It's not entirely untrue. I assume that's part of your motivation." Her eyes search my face.

"Are you asking my motivation?"

"I don't think I want to know." She looks out the window, staring into the distance where a couple of her rescue horses are grazing.

"Well, if you ever do, all you have to do is ask."

She glances down at the table, her fingers running over a small dent in the surface that my brother made when he used it as a racetrack for his toy car when we were kids.

"What are we telling the rest of the town?" I ask when I think about my brothers and the gossip mill beyond our friend circle.

"Curtis is leaving. I'll just... let everyone think we broke up when we found out we were married again. He won't care. He doesn't put much stock in what the people here think about him anyway. Beyond that, let them think what they want. I don't care either."

"So the rest of the town thinks we're making things work, and your family is in on half our secret? Sounds like quite the web you're weaving."

"You want me to tell them the truth and let Bo and Anson beat you to a bloody pulp?"

"Unless Anson's right hook has improved, I think I might have a fighting chance," I joke, but she just presses her lips together until they flatten.

"You can move your things into the guest room this afternoon. I'll get it ready and make some space in the fridge if you have any food you want to bring in."

"He already gone?" I'm surprised he left so quickly. I thought he'd draw this out a bit.

"He will be tonight. He leaves tomorrow, and he stays at a hotel down in Denver the night before so he doesn't have to make the airport drive in the morning."

"Where's he headed anyway?"

"Vegas."

"Thinking he can gamble his way out of this?" I smirk.

"Actually, he works at the casino, and he's being promoted. They've got some training and networking he has to do down there ahead of it." The smug look on her face tells me she's proud of him, and it sends a flood of newfound jealousy through my veins. It makes me wonder if she ever looked like that when she talked about me. 'Cause my football career had been a huge part of the reason we fell apart in the first place. But I'm not about to let any of it show.

"Good. How long's he gone for?" I ask.

"Ten weeks."

It's like it was meant to be. I'm grinning before I realize what I'm doing.

"He doesn't have to be here for me to be thinking about him every day." She's dead set on reminding me that I mean nothing to her.

"And yet you both agreed." I shrug.

"Because the inn is having a rough patch and your timing happens to coincide with it. It's nothing more than that."

"Well, given you've been leaning more grandma's getaway and less wide-open skies and Wild West, I can guess why. I doubt those ladies are riding horses or paying to go on hunting or fishing excursions."

"We do bird watching and wine tasting," she answers defensively.

"People come out here to feel alive again. They want to feel whiskey burn down the back of their throat and get lost in the woods, hike two miles to stand on top of a mountain and see how big the sky is up there. Bring home something they put on the table for dinner. Ride into the sunset or ride a cowboy after. You're offering them things they can do in their backyard back East." My mom had kept the inn going after my dad's mom gave it up. She'd been good at keeping a mix of activities to entertain everyone. I didn't hate the way Hazel ran the place or the dreams she had for it, but I worry that she leaves too much money on the table.

"We do just fine." Her arms cross over her chest. Stubborn Hazel is practically an immovable force. She'd run the inn into the ground before admitting she's wrong if she doesn't like the person telling her. So I'll be better off keeping my mouth shut on the subject and changing it to another one that'll piss her off.

"If your boy toy is okay with me even breathing in your direction, things can't be fine."

"I told you. The inn is having a rough patch. He knows it as well as I do, and he wants to do his part. It's not like you gave him much of a choice." She glares at me for even implying there's trouble. "And don't make assumptions about our relationship. You don't know the first thing about what a good one looks like."

I'm tempted to take the bait, but I refuse it. Reminding myself that if I play the long game, I'll get something a lot sweeter than just winning an argument. It's the war and not the battle I need.

"Which room are you using as the guest room these days?" I ask, glancing over my shoulder to the stairs.

"Your old bedroom."

"Fine, and don't worry about the fridge. I'll eat at the inn or go to the cafe in town. I've been missing Kit's cooking so might as well take full advantage."

Hazel always hated cooking, and the few attempts she made after we married were disasters that make me smile just thinking about. I can't imagine she wants to revisit the attempt, and I won't force her to do anything she hates.

I EAT my words and the plate of food she serves her boy toy and me later that night. It's not half bad, and far better than anything I could make. I just hate that it's another thing that's changed about her. One I didn't know about and wasn't part of.

There's a lot about her and this town I could do without, mainly the misery they've both caused. But my heart still aches at all the small moments I've missed. The ones everyone takes for granted when they're happening, but when you're the one who's been absent, they seem monumental in retrospect.

She kisses his cheek as she clears the plates, returning everything to the kitchen and putting them in the dishwasher.

The small gesture nearly tears a hole in my chest, but I smile and stand, taking my own plates in behind her.

"I have to run back to the inn. There's a speaker tonight, and I need to welcome them and get them set up for the guests. Do you think you can be civil with each other while I'm gone for a bit?" She eyes us warily as she pulls off the apron she has on and hangs it next to the fridge.

"No problem on my account," Curtis answers her, but her gaze is locked on mine as I walk back through the kitchen. Obviously, I'm the problem.

"I'll behave." I return to the table to finish my beer and kick back in my chair.

"Don't let him say anything stupid. Just walk away if he tries." Hazel looks at Curtis, and then her eyes fall back on me. "And he *will* try."

"No faith," I muse, threading my fingers together and putting them behind my head as I lean the chair onto its back legs.

"Absolutely none," she confirms, shaking her head and then heading for the door. "I mean it. No bullshit, Ramsey." They're the last words before I hear the door slam shut behind her.

"She's awfully worried I'm going to hurt your feelings." I take a draw off the bottle as he finishes his.

"She's got no reason to be. We've always been honest with each other, and she's told me enough about you to know I don't need to be worried."

"Huh." I grin at him. "Well, that's good. I can't say I'd feel the same if I was on your side of the table and knew how easily she agreed to it."

"I wouldn't say all this..." He waves his empty bottle around. "And a million is easy. I'd say that's a pretty steep bribe."

"If you knew Haze as well as you think you do, you'd know

she can't be bought. She doesn't do a damn thing she doesn't want to."

He gives me a tight saccharine smile and sets his bottle down hard on the table. His eyes lift to mine, and I can tell I've hit a nerve. Whatever she said about him being fine with this, he's not.

"Maybe she just thinks you're an easy way to make a lot of money to start her life with me."

"Does that sit right with you? You knowing you've been living in my house on my ranch with my wife?"

"It certainly seemed like she knew whose bed she was in when she was saying my name last night." The little smirk on his face makes me want to take him outside and wrap his jaw around one of the fence posts, but I keep the smile plastered in place.

"*Last* night. But tomorrow night, and the night after that, and the night after that... she'll forget you even had a name when that engagement ring you got her is sitting on the edge of the sink, and her legs are wrapped around me."

"She might, if you'd ever been able to make her come."

My smile falters at that. I have no idea what he's talking about. I was the first guy who was patient enough and willing enough to try whatever she needed to make sure she could come. It was half the reason she kept coming back to me in college even though she knew then I was a bad bet. His face screws up, and he laughs at my reaction.

"Yeah, Hazel and I... we share everything. Even the painful details of how woefully bad you were in bed. That's gotta suck for someone like you. All that fame and money. But you can't manage the simplest thing a woman needs."

If Hazel told him that—I have to guess she had her reasons. And any protest I make is just going to make it seem like I'm desperate to undermine the narrative. So I keep my mouth shut. Long enough that it makes him uncomfortable, and he stands abruptly.

"I need to head out and say my goodbyes."

"Ah, yeah. It's convenient that you're on the road. Makes this whole thing a little easier for all of us."

"Fairly certain it'll be over before we know it." He gives me another simpering grin and then heads out of the room. I don't see him again for the rest of the night, and I'm thankful for it.

SEVEN

Ramsey

MY WARM WELCOME home the next morning is climbing out of a creaky old bed that's two sizes too small in my childhood bedroom and a cup of cold coffee and a half-stale bagel that my wife has left out alongside a box of bran flakes. Kit's signature farmer's plate with eggs over easy, crisp bacon, and perfectly buttered toast is calling my name right now, but going there would mean seeing Hazel first thing, and I'm trying to give her space. She was prickly as fuck last night when she set me up in the guest room and shoved a few towels in my hands before disappearing into the master. Apparently, returning to marital bliss is going to take us a minute or two.

After I help Elliot, the ranch hand who's been around since my days here, feed some of the horses, I wander into the old pole barn. I'm hoping that my bike has had the same sort of luck as Wolfsbane, and I'll find her right where I left her—pushed in a back corner covered up, figuring I'd be back at some point to get her. I figure the chances Hazel's been back here clearing things out isn't high when she's always stuck in the inn.

I find it tucked behind a new pile of things she must have moved out of the house. They're tarped but covered in a fine layer of dust; among them is my old den couch and a poker table she hated from the day I got it. I smirk at the fact they're still here, too, taking up space. Maybe it's desperate that I'm seeing all this as hope—the fact that she's pushed me off to the edges of her life but hasn't dumped me completely.

Unfortunately, but not surprisingly, the bike doesn't roar to life when I try. So I push it out to the far side of the gravel lot and get some help from Elliot loading it into one of the ranch trucks before he tosses me the keys.

"Just don't tell her I helped you. Lie and say you stole it." Elliot gives me a mock threatening look because he's not trying to get on Hazel's shit list, and I don't blame him. I'd probably be better off buying a new truck, but I have to get to a dealership first. Without heading all the way back into the city, that would mean stepping foot on my brothers' territory—not a move I'm ready for yet.

"No problem."

"Where are you taking it?"

"Down to Briggs's, I guess." Hazel's brother, and my former best friend, owns a shop. From what I've heard, he's more absent owner than worker bee these days, so there's a chance I'll miss him. If I don't, I imagine I'm not in for a warm welcome there either. He never did forgive me for how things went down with her, even if he didn't blame me.

"Oof. I guess they're the best option if you don't want to go to Springs or Pueblo, but good luck to you on that." Elliot's face scrunches with the same realization I'm having.

"Gotta rip the Band-Aid off if I'm gonna be staying here." I answer as I climb in the driver's seat.

"Guess that's fair." He waves me off a moment later, and I crank up the music, trying to drown out all the second thoughts I'm having on every decision I've made lately.

———

I GET the bike into the shop and the paperwork filled out within the hour. I forgot how quick small-town service can be when you're not standing in a ticketed line waiting on the twenty people in front of you. I'm headed back to the ranch truck, contemplating lunch at the café, when I see Bo leaning on the door, his feet crossed at his ankles. His brows raise as he sizes me up, no doubt surprised to see me instead of Elliot or Kell—one of the people he thought would be coming back to the Bull Rush Ranch branded truck.

"Well, well, well. Look what the fuckin' goddamn wind blew in. Haze said you were back with your little bitch-boy tail between your legs, but I told her I wouldn't believe it until I saw it with my own eyes." The smile on his face betrays the words he uses.

"Well, I would have called, but then there was that little thing where you threatened to stuff my balls down my throat if you saw me again. It's rough on a friendship."

"What's rough on a friendship is when you make my baby sister cry for a week straight." His brow raises along with the accusation.

"She seems to have recovered."

"She's done a lot more than that. You seen what she's done with the place? Those ladies love it."

"She's made some choices, that's for sure."

"'Bout to make one of them permanent, and you show up

just in time to try to stop it. I'd say it's fate the way you keep doing that, but I'm starting to wonder if you've got a sixth sense." Bo muses, and though I'm momentarily distracted by the thought of Hazel in college, I frown at my friend's implication.

"You think she's making a mistake?" I ask.

"I think I don't like the fucker she's marrying," he answers flatly.

"She seems to think he shits rainbows. Made it seem like you all were on board."

"I don't argue with her about her choices. You know that best of all. I'd have fuckin' stopped it if I thought she'd listen and saved her a whole lot of heartache in the process." Like I said, Bo won't let me off easy.

"Yeah, well... that's a two-way street with her. She doesn't make anyone's life easy."

"I thought that's what you liked best about her." Bo draws up off the truck and smirks. He's not wrong. A good part of our relationship was built on being fascinated with trying to wrangle each other into submission.

"Well, I'm sure I'm headed for a hell of a lot more of it, so I guess I'll find out." I nod to the door he's blocking. "I should probably get on my way."

"No time for a beer then?" Bo nods across the street to Morton's Bar, and I raise a brow.

"Are we on good enough terms for that, or is this a trick where I walk in the door and you and your brothers beat the fucking shit out of me? 'Cause I gotta say, I'm not in the mood to beat all your asses today."

"I'd guess not after a prison sentence." His smirk draws wider.

"Make a joke about the soap, and I'll fuck you up right here."

"Was it like that?" His smirk drops like lead, and concern clouds his face.

"Nah. Low security. A lot of lawyers and white-collar types. They were more scared of me than anything else." Prison had been fucking awful, but it certainly could have been a lot worse.

"Well... I'm glad you're in one piece after all that. I figure if Haze can look past all of it, I can try." There's a moment of quiet, the death of our grudge passing in between us, transforming into something more akin to a mutual understanding that hard decisions sometimes have to be made.

"It's not like I've got anywhere to be right now." I return his gesture. I could use my friend right now, if he's willing to mend fences, I'm more than happy to help.

"Good." He slaps me on the back, and we head across the street.

WE'RE a couple of beers in and nearly caught up on the state of his life. He's still single, running the garage and a couple of side businesses, still playing enforcer—including moonlighting for my brothers' casino on occasion, and still every bit the lovable asshole he's always been. But then he glances out the window and turns back to me with the kind of look that could send a chill down your spine.

"I'm trusting you with this next part. I'm saying this to you as family—since you still are—and someone who loves Haze. If you use this against her or tell her—especially that I told you—I *will* put you six feet under this time," he threatens. I roll my shoulders back instinctively as a wave of apprehension courses through me, but I nod my understanding. I have no doubt Bo would follow through; we're more alike than either of us want to admit.

"Hit me."

"I'm actually glad you're back. I don't trust that slimy little fuck living with her. I think he's hiding something. Anson and Cade and me... we've been keeping an eye on him. We don't have enough to say anything to her yet. If she has any doubts, she'll dig her heels in and tell me to fuck off. So I don't want her getting a single fucking idea that we think anything's up until I know for sure."

"What has you thinking he's a problem? Seems like a prick, sure. Not good enough for her. But I didn't get an immediate piece of shit vibe from him."

"Not good enough for her." Bo laughs as he shakes his head. "Brother, you got some fuckin' nerve sayin' that."

"I might not be good enough, but you know a grave couldn't hold me down from keeping her safe. So tell me what's going on."

"Just little things." He leans back in his seat, glancing around the room to make sure no one's in earshot. "One day I caught him up in the loft of the pole barn poking around. Another time, he was out in one of the fields with a metal detector. Claimed he fucking lost a watch out there riding, but I never saw him wear one. Then Cade's on his way back one night from Springs, and he sees him arguing with a woman in the parking lot of a motel off 50."

"Did he see Cade?"

"No. Cade didn't get out of the car and was just hitting the drive-thru there."

"I mean, weird, but all of that could have an explanation."

"You have a lot of late-night arguments with women in motel parking lots while your girlfriend waits at home that turn out innocent?" Bo's sarcasm leaks through his words.

"No, but he could have hit her bumper pulling out, or she could be family that we don't know about. I'm just saying there are explanations that aren't sinister." I don't really believe them, but I'm trying to explore all the possibilities first. Hazel really did seem to have her shit together these days, and despite the fact I have my reasons to hate him—I can't deny that they looked like a picture-perfect couple at dinner.

"Occam's razor, brother. If it looks like it... in my experience, it usually is."

"Fair enough. I'm not trying to defend the prick. I'd just as well see him gone."

"Would you?" Bo levels me with a hard look. "What's your plan anyway?"

"Staying out of trouble until this divorce goes through and I figure out what I'm doing next. Just trying to keep my parole officers happy." It's not a total lie. I do want them off my back, and I need to figure out what's next now that the Chaos isn't exactly banging down my door to get me back.

"I don't buy that for one fucking minute." Bo looks at me like I'm a fucking idiot for even attempting to bullshit him.

"Yeah, well, you always were cheap as fuck then, weren't you?" I dodge the accusation.

He ignores my attempt at humor and leans back in, lowering his voice. "You break her heart again, I'll break every bone in your body. I don't give a fuck what you two get up to. You need to let her settle old scores or get some closure—you're both adults. But don't you dare fucking make her cry again, you hear me?"

"Understood," I grit out the word.

"I'm glad." He finishes his beer, and his phone buzzes. Something about the message distracts him, and he stands suddenly.

"I should get back. We'll talk more about everything, but it was good catching up with you." He drops a few bills on the table and stands to leave.

"Later."

He nods as he heads out, disappearing out the back door and leaving me to make small talk with the server while she runs our bill.

I wouldn't exactly call us friends again, but at least I'm off the worst of his shit list. Now I've just gotta worry about what the fuck Curtis has been up to.

EIGHT

Hazel

"SO, THE HUSBAND IS BACK..." Bristol, one of my best friends and the owner of the local antique shop, sips her drink.

"Yes, how is that going?" Dakota sits back against the booth.

We're gathered at Dakota's bar. It's the only place in town with decent vibes. Cowboy's down the street mostly plays to the tourists, and Morton's up the street is just where a lot of the locals go to watch ball and talk politics. Seven Sins, Dakota's place, has the best drinks and a dance floor that's nearly as busy as the bar—especially on weekend nights like tonight.

"I just have to survive a few months while he works through his parole." I've already given them the basics of the arrangement Ramsey and I have agreed to tell friends and family about in the group chat. Leaving out the part about the million and the notion that I might sleep with him seemed like a mistake in retrospect though. I could really use their advice, and none of us are in the habit of keeping secrets from each other.

"I think we should torture him while we can. Revenge for everything he put you through." Dakota's lips form into a devious smirk as she plays with the cherry in her glass.

"I think she should use it as an extended bachelorette-party hall pass. He was an asshole, but he's as hot as he ever was." Bristol's the practical one.

"Given that she's still married, wouldn't it be a second honeymoon?" Marlowe muses, smiling a little when Dakota nudges her with her elbow in appreciation.

"It can be both." Bristol grins and takes another slow sip of the Long Island iced tea she's been hitting hard since we got here.

"I'd get him in bed, get naked, ride that cowboy right to the edge, and then walk out and leave his ass with the worst blue balls of his life. Remind him of exactly what he fucked up." Dakota's the kind of person you never want to cross.

"Is there a version where I don't get naked with him? I think that's probably not in my best interest." Namely, because Ramsey is a lot of things I'd rather forget, but some parts of him are more memorable than others.

"You miss him?" Marlowe looks at me thoughtfully.

"She misses his dick." Bristol laughs.

"It was the one thing he was really good for." It's not a fair thing for me to say. Ramsey had plenty of other virtues; I've just worked hard to forget all of them and focus on the things I hate.

"Be fair. He plays decent ball too." Dakota grins.

I shrug before I take a sip of my drink. I'm nursing it even though I'd rather be having more than my fair share. Drunk me is less ethical than sober me, and with temptation sleeping in my guest room, I need to keep my wits about me.

"Okay, enough talk about him. I need an escape from Ramsey, not a rehash of his greatest hits. He's barely been here a couple of days and already taken over everything. He's driving me crazy." I try to steer the conversation away from Ramsey Stockton, but it's like trying to tame a tornado. He's the whirlwind of destruction that has everyone in town's interest.

"You know we'll help with the body if necessary," Bristol chimes in.

"I might need it. He's literally everywhere. The kitchen. The living room. The stables. Chatting with Kit in the inn. I can't escape him, and now he's started doing little things to help. Feeding the horses and hauling hay with Kell and Elliot. Running around seeing what he can fix at the inn."

"Disgusting." Dakota shakes her head, but a smile cracks despite her attempts to look disapproving.

"Not that!" Marlowe gives me a mock horrified look as she presses her palm to her chest.

"I still think you should torture him. Give him something to do that isn't bothering you. Or better yet, put him to work doing all the shit jobs around the ranch and inn. Make him muck stalls. Send him out to the far pastures to check the fences. Make him do the laundry. Wash the dishes." Bristol's daydreaming about getting that kind of help herself around the house. Bristol's single, but between helping her family out and keeping her business open, she's juggling hard to keep everyone floating.

"That's not torture for him. Torture is reminding him he's about to lose his gorgeous wife in a few short months to another man. Start doing your wedding planning in front of him," Marlowe offers, and I raise my brow at her sudden switch to the dark side. "What? I'm just trying to help," she replies defensively.

"Not the wedding planning. The honeymoon planning." Dakota's eyes glitter with the idea.

"That seems cruel." I press my lips together, letting another sip of the whiskey-laden drink burn my throat. "Then again, I do like to watch the man suffer."

"That Rampage game we went to where the Chaos lost to them? Brutal." Bristol smirks. I'd picked up tickets for my birthday, claiming I won them, and was reluctantly going to go if my friends could go with me. It was a bittersweet sort of regret the minute I watched him step onto the field and heard the home state chant his name right alongside the handful of Chaos fans in the stadium.

"Do you have lingerie you can parade around in? Ask him what he thinks would work best for the honeymoon." Dakota's still planning Ramsey's torture.

"No. I've been meaning to get some. But all the good places are up in Denver." I love living out in the middle of nowhere, but the one downside is needing to travel into the city for any semblance of choice. At least, unless I got wild at midnight clicking the buy button online. A thing I might treat myself to this weekend given the circumstances.

"What do you have going on tomorrow?" Dakota looks like she's plotting something.

"Not much... a few guests are leaving, but Grace could get them checked out." I give her a skeptical look in return, nervous about what her creative mind could come up with.

"So let's go." Dakota's eyes glimmer with mischief.

"Do it!" Bristol adds.

"And then you can ask him for honeymoon spot suggestions. Those athletes are always traveling to the most gorgeous places. I bet he has some recommendations." Marlowe grins when I look to her for a sane opinion.

"You guys are evil."

"Supportive. Evil. It's all the same." Dakota takes another sip of her drink and grins at me. "Pick me up tomorrow at nine."

"Are you going to be ready that early?" I ask, noting that she's already a couple of drinks deep and not an early riser on a good morning.

"I will be for this. Don't worry about me. Just make sure you are, 'cause you're driving. But I'll buy lunch."

"All right. Are any of you coming?" I look around the rest of the table. I might need support fending off Dakota's more devious plans.

"I have to open Hotcakes in the morning and take deliveries in the afternoon. I really need to find someone who can help me with the deliveries at least." Marlowe sighs and gives me a sad look.

"Since Delia quit, it's just me. So I'm working tomorrow too. But send me pictures and updates!" Bristol looks at Dakota.

"Will do." Dakota nods.

A moment later, a couple of guys who look like they might be tourists approach our table, their eyes on Bristol and Dakota.

"Dance?" The younger one holds out his hand for Dakota.

"Can you city boys dance?" Dakota raises her brow in return, clearly unimpressed.

"I imagine you can teach me if I can't." He flashes bright white teeth that nearly blind in the low light of the bar.

"She's not much for teaching. She prefers them experienced." Bristol smirks at Dakota, and they exchange glances.

"What about you then? Do you mind teaching?" His eyes fall on Bristol.

"I'm not much for dancing with guys who had their eye on my friend," Bristol answers and then leans against Dakota's shoulder in amusement. The city boy's grin fades fast, clearly not used to losing out this hard at home.

"Dance with me then. He can watch and learn," the older one interjects.

"How about you both watch?" Anson, my older brother, steps between them and reaches his hand out for Bristol's. He nods a brief hello to the rest of us. "I'll have her right back. Any refills?" Anson nods to our drinks.

"Another whiskey sour?" I ask.

"Another whiskey. Neat." Dakota pushes her empty glass to the side.

"I'm good." Marlowe nods to the drink she's been nursing all night. Bakeries and their crack of dawn opening times don't usually go well with nights out.

"Coming right up." He slips his fingers through Bristol's, pulling her down off the high bench we're on and spinning her once before he crosses the floor with her to a two-step until they reach the bar.

"Should we be asking questions about that?" Marlowe asks as the city slickers disappear to another table, and we watch Bristol and Anson having an animated discussion about something.

"Definitely not." I shake my head. "They bicker like an old married couple without any of the cute moments."

"And they're related." Dakota frowns at the idea.

Bristol and Anson are technically brother and sister-in-law, although his wife—Bristol's stepsister, Fannie—died a few years ago in an accident. Bristol and her mom still help Anson out with their son whenever he needs a babysitter or just a weekend off from being a busy single dad. But Fannie and Bristol were nothing alike, like oil and water, and Anson's complained more than once that my best friend drives him up the wall.

"Hmm. Just asking." Marlowe flashes another look in their direction.

"Anson's just protective because she watches Ford. Doesn't want any bad influences around and all that. You know how he is." Anson's so quiet and so business focused; I can't imagine any woman besides Fannie wanting to deal with him.

"You're just projecting your Briggs brother crush on the rest of us," Dakota teases, and Marlowe's cheeks pink at the implication.

"I still have no idea how you thought Bo was hot." I have to shake the thought off. Growing up with three brothers has left me with all kinds of trauma—dead animals, dirty laundry, and mystery odors of all kinds. The idea that any of the boys I lived with end up with women at all is a puzzle wrapped inside an enigma, only opened with a riddle that probably involves a "that's what she said" joke.

"It was high school. I was young and impressionable." Marlowe attempts to defend herself.

"I mean... he was kind of hot when he played football. I'll give you that." Dakota's always had a thing for athletes. I ended up with one on accident.

"I know a football player who's about to be single if you want him," I offer up, knowing full well that Dakota has zero interest.

"No, thank you. That one is permanently damaged by a previous owner and is currently being returned to sender," Dakota pipes back.

A moment later, Anson's returning with our drinks, and Bristol's hopping back into the booth.

"Miss anything?" she asks, sliding the drink she got for Dakota across the table.

"Nothing worth noting," Marlowe answers, keen to change the subject.

"Thanks." I smile at my brother as he hands me my drink. He nods and then turns to head back to where he came from.

"Who's watching Ford?" I ask Bristol. He's getting older, but not quite old enough to stay on his own. Especially since he's always been a wild child—much to Anson's dismay.

"He's staying the night at Mom's with a friend of his. They're doing some board game thing, so he shouldn't give her too much trouble. He knows she can't handle a lot of noise, but I should probably head out early."

"Okay, but first, dancing!" Dakota downs her whiskey. "With you girls because I have zero tolerance for men and their bullshit tonight."

"Sounds good to me." Marlowe grins.

AS THE CLOCK turns back over to the single digits, and I've had more than my fair share of dancing and drinks, I stand and immediately realize I'm not driving home. And it's way too far to walk. I plop back down in the seat, and Dakota giggles at the flop I make.

"I can get Jasper to drive us home." Marlowe volunteers her brother. For the three of them who live in town, it's a quick trip, but I hate to ask Jasper to come all the way here and then drive me all the way out to my ranch. I could ask one of my brothers. Anson's already here after all, but he also gets up early in the morning. Which leads me to the one person who has nothing better to do.

> Your wife is drunk and needs a ride home.

It takes him a minute to respond, but I see the dots slowly come to life on the screen.

RAMSEY:

Claiming that title now?

At this hour, yes.

You and the girls didn't plan for this?

I could walk or I can ask one of these nice gentlemen at the bar.

One of these cowboys has been lookin' at me all night like he might let me have a ride anyway.

I grin at my phone watching as the dots appear immediately.

RAMSEY:

Fuck no.

You stay right there with Dakota. I'm coming.

Yes, sir.

WHEN HE PULLS UP to the curb in his truck and opens the door, I climb in. He looks over my appearance and smirks. I have a short skirt on, and I don't miss the way his eyes linger on my legs.

"What?" I ask defensively, but he just shakes his head dismissively and looks back to the road.

"Out dancing?"

"Yes. I needed some fun after this week."

There's a mumbled mhmm on his part but nothing more. Suspicious given how much he likes to take shots. I risk a glance over at him. He has on a worn old white T-shirt that's two sizes too small from the number of times it's been washed, and it's currently hugging every curve of his chest and biceps. It's like arm porn with the tattoos, and the tight way the cuff hugs his muscles, and the veins and tendons rise and fall as he moves his arm. When his hand wraps around the gear shift, I start to lick my lips before I realize what's happening.

Get it together, Hazel. He's an asshole. Don't touch.

I manage to tear my eyes away, and I lean my head on the window. I should keep my eyes on the road too. It's the only safe place to look in this truck.

I'M ONLY half awake by the time we pull up into the lot by the barn. He has to park here because some of the guests' cars are blocking the main drive up to the house, but I'm not looking forward to the walk over the gravel in the heels I have on.

I've got my feet braced up against the door to take them off as he opens it, and I nearly tumble out. His brow raises at me, and then he realizes what I'm doing, his eyes falling to where I'm slipping the second heel off. He reaches out a hand as I step down from the truck, and I take it reluctantly.

"This seems wise to you?" He looks down at my bare feet on the gravel.

"Wiser than trying to walk on it in these." I hold up my heels in front of his face, and he takes them before I can snatch them back. "Hey!" I lunge toward him, and it takes exactly one step for me to find fault with my idea. "Ouch!" I pull up and run my fingers over my pinkie toe that I've already managed to smash against a particularly sharp rock.

"That's what I thought." He shakes his head, and then, without asking permission, he hauls me up into his arms.

"What are you doing? Put me down," I gripe, smacking my

purse against his shoulder with less force than a fly smashing into a skyscraper. But I don't need to be touching the man. It's too risky.

"Putting you to bed, grouchy," he grumbles, kicking the truck door shut behind us and starting to make his way across the lot.

"I don't need to be carried!" Given the way he winces, I'm guessing I said that a lot louder than I needed to.

"I don't want to listen to you moan and cry your way across the lot at two a.m., and I doubt your guests do either." He explains his motivations like I'm a child.

"Shit. The guests."

"The guests." He nods.

He has one small point, but I need to make my own—something that ensures he doesn't end up lingering too close once we get in the house. One more stretch of cotton across his chest and I might be a goner.

"Just to be clear." I use my best drunk-girl whisper. "This isn't winning you any points, Mr. Hero. The whole world might love you, but I don't."

NINE

Ramsey

WHETHER SHE INTENDS them to or not, the words cut, but I do my best not to falter. Forcing a smile as I shift her weight in my arms. A whiff of her apple perfume drifts over me, and my stomach clenches. That fragrance elicits an instant response from my whole body, because as much as I try to force myself to forget, it remembers exactly what it's like to have it all over my sheets and skin.

"Are you wincing? I'm not that heavy. Don't act like I'm heavy. You lift weights three times my weight," she complains, snapping me out of my daydream.

"I'm not wincing, just trying to keep you steady on my good arm. You don't want to get dropped, do you?" I cover for myself.

"No. Shit. I'm sorry. I forgot about your bad arm. You shouldn't have picked me up, you know."

"You asked me to pick you up."

"I mean physically pick me up." She huffs and rolls her

eyes. "You know what I mean. You always know what I mean and pretend like you don't. I think you do it just to fuck with me."

"Sometimes." I smile. "How do you know about my arm? It happened two years ago."

"I've seen you play."

"You watched?" I'm surprised. She told me during our divorce if she ever saw another football in her life it'd be too soon.

"Sometimes. Hard to miss when my whole family lives and breathes Rampage football. You play them occasionally, right?"

"Right." I study her face as her nose scrunches up like she's thinking about something else she hates. "I could have gotten you all tickets, you know. Just had to ask."

"I can imagine how that conversation would have gone. Also, apparently, I could have been sitting up in the wives' box the whole time," she snarks as I set her down to unlock the back door.

"You would have asked, and I would have looked into it and sent you the tickets and some field passes. Simple."

"And what would field passes have cost me? A blowjob? Maybe a quickie in the locker room?" More snark piles on as I get the door open, and she stumbles through it. I follow after her silently because I'm fairly certain anything I say in response can and will be held against me, but I'm half afraid she's going to faceplant on the floor if she's not careful. "Why are you following me?" She stops short when she gets to the door of her room. "You think you're coming in? You have a hell of a lot more groveling to do. You can't just fix a few things around the place and think I'm going to get on my back for you."

"I prefer you riding me anyway." I can't help the slow grin when her eyes light at the response.

She lets out a low grumble but turns and doesn't slam the

door in my face. Surprising us both, I think, considering the way her lashes flutter as she notices my proximity to the bed.

"You're still not getting in this bed. So what are you doing?" She tosses her purse onto her dresser and crosses her arms over her chest.

"Putting these in here with you." I hold her shoes up for her to see and then set them gently on the floor inside her door before turning to leave.

"Now you're just gonna walk out?"

I stop short and turn around to look at her. I know this is drunk Haze I'm dealing with, and drunk Haze is the least rational version of her. The one who's either sweet as peach pie or sharp as a razor at your throat, depending on what mood drove her to drink.

"What would you like me to do?" I ask bluntly, because I'm not in the mood for playing games. She looks fucking breathtaking despite the angry furrow in her brow, and having had my hands all over her just now, and that fucking apple perfume, I'm finding it hard to not want more.

"I just think it's something that you're always walking out. You're real good at that." There's the ice water I needed.

"I don't think now is a good time to discuss that."

"It's as good a time as any."

"So we can repeat it tomorrow when you don't remember because you had one too many whiskey sours?" I lean against the doorframe. I don't want to fight with her, not really, but getting her a little more riled than she already is is probably the perfect way to ensure we don't do anything stupid. Because when she finally asks for me again, I want her to be begging for it.

"Oh fuuuuck you. Like you're all high and mighty. Like I never had to scrape you off the floor."

"I never said you didn't."

"You're the one driving me to drink anyway. You just fuckin' show up here one day, naked as a jaybird, telling me I need to pretend to be your wife again. Turning this whole place upside down. Everyone's just so fascinated that you're back. Thinking you're the hero because your face is plastered all over TV. 'Wronged football hero must serve sentence.' Please! Wronged?" She scoffs. "More like attention-loving football jerk. It's like you don't think. But who cares? No matter what you do, people love you anyway. Purgatory Fall's hero!" She's ranting blindly and following rabbit holes left and right while she does it.

"I don't think I'm a hero."

"Good. I don't think so either. I think it was stupid. You could have gotten yourself killed like that. And what did you do it for anyway? Some woman? Who got engaged to the other guy anyway from what I heard." She laughs and shakes her head. "Didn't want to wait for you to get out of prison, I guess. Is that why you're here? She didn't want you even after you nearly killed yourself for her, so now you come crawling back home?"

I'd swear her blue eyes were almost turning green in this light, but I don't dare mention it.

"I did it because they were my friends. I wasn't thinking it through. I thought they were gonna die, and I had to do something. I was never involved with her. She was always with him, for the record."

"And you what? You've just been single this whole time?" Now we're getting to the real questions.

"I haven't been getting engaged, if that's what you're asking."

"I'm asking if you have a girlfriend or someone back in Cincinnati."

"I told you, Haze. I don't fucking cheat. There's no one back there."

"There's been no one this whole time?" Her fingers dig into her forearm, and the motion causes the engagement ring on her finger to glint when it catches the dull light from the hallway.

"I've had a couple of friends who I had a mutual understanding with."

She presses her lips together, and there's a subtle shake of her head. "Of course you have."

"I'm not sure what that's supposed to mean. We both thought we were divorced, and if you remember, you're about to get married to someone else. Got a ring on your finger and everything."

"Yeah, well. He left me with you, didn't he?" There's a quick inhale of breath like she might be holding back tears.

"Haze..." I say softly, taking a step forward. "I think we should get you into bed. It's late, and you've had a lot to drink. I can get you some water."

"No!" She holds out her hand and takes a step back. The motion makes her catch her leg on the bed, and she trips back onto it, falling into a seated position. She recovers quickly, though, and slides back against the pillows, drawing her legs up underneath her. "Don't touch me, and don't do that whole patronizing 'Oh, Haze' bullshit with me. I'm fine. I can take care of myself. It's what I've been doing."

"Suit yourself." I turn to head for the door. I want to help but I'm not looking to get torn open in the process.

"Just don't think you're going to wear me down. You left. And you'll leave again. I know you. I learned my lesson, and I know better this time," she mumbles, her head already on the pillow, her eyes heavy.

I pause at the doorway, holding there for a long moment and bracing myself against it for what I'm gonna say next.

"Haze... I didn't mean to hurt you. I was... finding my parents like that..." I'm searching for the right words and failing. "It tore a hole in me. I was terrified it was going to happen again, and I wouldn't be able to stop it. That it would be you next time."

I turn back when she doesn't answer, and her eyes are already closed. There's a soft little snort, and I can't help but smile at it. I hit the lights, drenching the room in darkness and walk back to pull the blanket off the foot of the bed, draping it over her. She frowns when she feels it fall over her but pulls it tighter around her shoulders.

"Always leaving. Him leaving. You leaving. Why does everyone always leave me..." she mumbles, and I can tell she's half-asleep from the way her words fade.

"I'm not leaving anymore, sugar. Not unless you make me." I kiss her forehead and make sure she's well tucked in, looking back at her one last time before I close the door. She deserves so much better than anyone's ever given her, and I'll do whatever it takes to make it up to her.

TEN

Hazel

"YOU'RE sure you're up for this?" I ask as I pick Dakota up and she climbs into the car with a massive jug of iced coffee and her sunglasses on. Her hair's braided, and she's got no makeup and a baseball cap on. It's not an unusual fit for her, but it's odd that she wouldn't be more dressed up to go into the city. She's always joking that she never knows when she'll find her own millionaire to sweep her off her feet and out of this town.

"I'm good. Just you know, last night was a late one..." She shrugs as she eases into the passenger seat of my old pickup truck.

"And you stayed up *after*?" I eye my friend suspiciously. Ramsey carted me off before anyone else left, but I highly suspect Dakota didn't go home alone.

"Might have." She tosses her purse on the floorboards and starts looking out the window like there's a fascinating sight to behold, that she hasn't seen twenty thousand times before, as she puts her seat belt on.

"All right. Well, if we need to pull over or anything." I'm wary of her being queasy.

"I had toast," she grumbles defensively. "I just need some caffeine to wake my ass up now." She takes a sip and then stuffs the cup into the cupholder on her side. "Do we really have to go all the way up to Denver though? There's a VS in Springs." She looks at me over the top of her sunglasses, and her blue-green eyes glitter in the late morning sunlight.

"Yes, I'm sure. I want the good stuff." I hold up Ramsey's credit card, tapping my nail against his name. "All of it."

"Oh, woman, you are *evil*."

"I made orders at a couple of the bakeries up there too. Dozens of cake samples, and I'm making him try them all with me."

"Death by chocolate?" She laughs.

"Chocolate and expensive lingerie." I smirk, and Dakota mirrors it.

"Well, let's do it then."

"WHAT DO you think of this one?" I ask as I step out of the changing room again, covering my nipples, thankful that it's private back here and we're the only customers in the lingerie store.

Dakota looks up from her phone and blinks rapidly.

"I think he's going to choke when he sees you in that."

"Are you sure?" I turn to the side and look at my profile again. Curtis and I had gotten to a comfortable point in our relationship where lingerie wasn't really happening anymore, and I had never gotten to the point of buying lingerie with

Ramsey. We were college kids, and he thought a crop top and some cut-off shorts were sexy enough.

"Honey, I'm sure. I don't even think you need all this. You look the best you've looked in years. He's come crawling back from the other side of the country to spend time with you. The lingerie is just icing on the cake."

"But I want it to be pretty icing."

"It's gorgeous. I'd bang you." Dakota grins at me.

"All right. Just two more. I want to have a variety to torture him with."

"To torture him with or to seduce him with?" Dakota asks as I walk back into the dressing room, and I whirl around to glare at her. She tilts her head to the side, holding up a hand. "I'm just asking. You can be honest with me."

"To torture him. You were right. He was good... in a lot of ways that I wouldn't exactly mind revisiting. But I love Curtis, and that's what I'm focused on. Where my heart is."

"Your heart, sure. I'm talking about the rest of you." There's a devious upturn of her lips, and I give her a mock gasp.

"What would you do in my shoes then?" I'm curious if I'm the only one who would consider doing something stupid. If Dakota knew there was a bonus million involved, she'd be shoving me into bed with Ramsey herself.

"Hot rich guy wants to spend his parole with me, and oops, we're still married? My fiancé knows and is begrudgingly going along with it? I'm taking advantage of that. No question. I have to sleep with Curtis for the rest of my life, I'm having a little fun with my husband first before I give him up," she says it so matter-of-factly that it sounds practical even to me.

"I don't know why I asked."

"You knew the answer and wanted the encouragement, I'm guessing." She sets her phone aside to give me her full attention. "Like I said. I'm not judging. None of us would. I think even Marlowe would sign on to support it. But..."

"But?"

"Be careful with your heart you're so sure of."

"Says the woman who refuses to ever give hers away." I pin her with a look of skepticism. She rolls her eyes and presses on.

"I've never seen anyone love each other the way you and Ramsey did. The way that boy loved you enough to tell Bo and the rest of your brothers to go to hell. The way you took care of him through everything..." Dakota looks me over thoughtfully as I hover in the doorway. "I'm just saying, I know how much it hurt you when he left."

"I hurt him when I didn't go with him," I admit, because our marriage falling apart had been a mutual sort of thing. No one cheated. No one lied. The tragedies just mounted up so high we were hurting too much to see past them, and when push came to shove, he wanted to run, and I wanted to stay. He needed to start over fresh, and I couldn't imagine leaving the only thing I ever knew.

"Well. I'm not blaming you for that. It meant I got to keep you." Dakota gives me a small smile, and then it spreads. "All right. No more of this sad stuff. Back to plotting torture."

ELEVEN

Ramsey

I RESIGN myself to doing the one thing I've been avoiding since I got here—seeing my family. My brothers, Grant and Levi, run the local casino hotel, The Avarice. It's on family land that abuts the ranch. It was my grandfather's, and then my uncle's originally, then my dad's when he died with no children, and finally, a shared venture between the eldest Stockton brothers. They'd taken a lot of liberties with it from what I'd seen on the website when curiosity got the best of me—modernizing the hotel rooms, adding a huge restaurant and rooftop pool, and even having entertainment in on the weekends.

Kit and the other staff at the inn told me it was becoming a bit of a thorn in the side of the town. Drawing business away from the inn and the other shops on main street during the day and dragging drunken hordes of tourists up into the bars for late night barhops—creating the perfect storm of misery for Purgatory Falls business owners and its small emergency services department. The inn was suffering the worst of it. Many of the visitors who had once come up to stay were now more excited about the all-in-one resort options The Avarice offered. It had made my brothers less than popular with my wife and her friends, but I doubt they care when they count their millions at night.

The woman at the front desk is perplexed when I ask for their offices, insisting that they're not available at first until I tell her I'm their younger brother. She then calls another assistant of theirs who gives me permission to take the elevators up to the top floor where their operations are. I'm given a code to punch in to allow me access to the upper floors, trying not to roll my eyes when I do it. Our family has always had money, but my father had been strict about keeping us tied firmly to the ground with our lifestyle and our expectations. I can't imagine what he'd think of his sons living in a penthouse.

When I get out, it's another maze of a hallway. One direction seemingly leading to residential quarters, and the other ushering me on to corporate offices. I follow the signs and pass through a couple of heavy mahogany doors into an office lobby. This one's much smaller than the first but still grand. The woman offers up a bright white smile, letting me know she'll take me to Mr. Stockton's office in just a few moments. I don't bother asking which one because, for my purposes, I'm not sure it matters.

TWENTY MINUTES LATER, I'm finally in my brother Grant's, office. The dramatic floor-to-ceiling window vista of the surrounding mountainside and valley is extra stunning today with the sun out, and the absence of clouds makes it look like the sky stretches to infinity. I almost forget to greet my brother until he leans back in his chair and makes a clicking sound in his throat.

"Well, if it isn't the prodigal son..." He makes quick work of surveying me and raises a brow as if to ask what I'm here for.

"I won't keep you long. Just thought I should come talk to you given I'll be here for a while."

"I'm not in a hurry. Work will still be here later. You should at least wait for Levi to get here. We can get some lunch down in the restaurant, or we can have it bought up here to the conference room if it's a private conversation you need."

"I don't need both of you down my throat. One of you is plenty."

"Sorry. Two for one deal when our baby brother finally decides to show his face."

"Especially since he's fresh out of prison." Levi appears behind me and pulls me in to slap me on the back before he leans back again to give me the same surly once-over that Grant did. "Gonna have to tell us how that went."

"It went as well as prison can go," I answer tersely. I'm not sure what they're hoping for, a rundown of the meal plan and laundry days, or just the opportunity to rub it in that they've done far more illegal shit than I could ever dream up, and I'm the one who ended up serving time. Which reminds me... "Just being here is a risk for me, so I'd like to keep this chat short."

"You're just visiting family."

"From what I hear you haven't been making a lot of friends here locally, and old habits die hard. I'm imagining those two things are going to converge eventually."

"I don't plan to do anything I'm not forced to do." Lev leans back on a low bookcase pushed up against the windows and crosses his arms.

"Is that what you're doing? Moving back to the ranch?"

Grant's looking at me like he might give me an award for being a clever bastard for moving in on my wife.

"I'm not moving back in. Just staying while I get through parole. It's quiet. Safe. I'm hoping it keeps me out of trouble. Gives me a chance to get some closure on shit, grab my things... Just makes it easy all around, and I finally have time to get it done now that I'm not playing," I lie, using the half-truths that Haze gave me to run with.

"You could have come here." Grant almost looks hurt.

"You miss the part about staying out of trouble?"

"Now, it's been what... five years? We've grown," Lev says defensively.

"I can see that." I look around the office. "I'm sure all of this was built ethically."

"Beautiful, isn't she?" Grant surveys his surroundings because he gives me a smug look of interest. "You should come to work with us. We have a third office up here we kept open for you. Figured you'd be back someday. We could find you space for an apartment up here. Get you out of that dusty old ranch and into something more your speed."

"I can't imagine you were living that rough in Cincinnati." Lev gives me a questioning look.

"I was living in an RV."

"Oof." Grant shakes his head. "I don't know why you insist on that kind of poverty when you have the money to do better."

"I'm happy keeping life simple. I don't need all this fancy shit you all do, or the trouble that comes with it." We'd taken different things away from our parents' death. I'd seen two people who were dead as a result of my father's greed and my mother's complicity in his crimes. My brothers had seen an opportunity for revenge and newfound wealth. I suppose there's something poignant to say about how we all grieve in different ways, but I prefer not to think too long on it.

"Simple isn't always good." Grant shakes his head.

"Simple's boring as fuck," Lev adds.

"You're entitled to your opinions," I counter.

"And the millions our opinions make us." Lev smirks.

"Well I should be going." I give him a flat look and then turn to leave.

"Just have lunch. I'll have it brought up here." Grant's tone softens, and it's rare enough that it compels me to pause.

"We missed our little brother. You can spare an hour, can't you?" Levi spoons on a little more guilt.

"Fine. Just lunch though, and then I've got to get back. I was going to help Elliot repair one of the fences," I reluctantly agree, although I'm sure I'll regret it.

AN HOUR LATER, we've discussed how our sister Aspen and her daughter Fallon are doing, sharing updates we get from her as she's on the road with her job. We cover all the new additions to the hotel and casino, and Grant fills me in on their ambitious expansion plans, and follow it up with a debate on how the town of Purgatory Falls is going to feel about it. Levi presses the same issue Grant did about me moving to the tower, and I shake my head as I put my fork and knife down for the waitstaff to take away.

"I've got business at the ranch. It's easier to just be there."

"Fixing fences? Chasing horses? Be serious. You've got people that can handle that for you." Levi looks at me thoughtfully.

"It's not the fences he's chasing, it's the girl." Grant drops his napkin on his plate and sits back to study me.

"I told you—" I start, but Grant cuts me off at the pass.

"Don't lie. This is the Stockton family vault. You can tell the truth here."

I give him a skeptical look, and he sits a little straighter.

"Can I?" It's an open question. There's a giant chasm between us and where we left things when I went off to play ball. Hazel wasn't the only person I left behind. I divorced myself from every part of this town, including my family.

"The past is water under the bridge. I wish you'd stayed, but I understand now why you didn't. Levi and I make a better team anyway, so no hard feelings." Grant shrugs.

"Gee, thanks."

"Of course." Grant flashes an amused look in my direction.

"You want her back?" Levi asks, circling us back to the conversation at hand.

"Wouldn't you?" I put the question back to him. "If you could have Cora back?" She'd been his near obsession for a while before she left. He doesn't answer. He doesn't have to. We all already know what he'd say. "Then you know."

"But I don't." Grant raises a brow. "So tell me."

"She's my wife. I want it to stay that way. That's all there is to tell." I'm willing to admit the truth, but I'm not ready to have a session where we all discuss our feelings about it.

"Well..." Grant looks out the window, staring out over the expanse beyond as he contemplates it. "Then just let us know what we can do to help."

TWELVE

Ramsey

THAT NIGHT, when I get back to the house, the dining room table and floor are piled with shopping bags and packages that I have to climb over. The kitchen counter isn't in much better shape. It's covered in bakery boxes stacked two and three deep. I'm barely able to get the pizza out of the freezer to make my dinner. I eye one of the dainty pastel cake boxes skeptically.

I have no idea what Hazel got up to today, but apparently, it involved a massive spending spree and a sweet tooth that needed to be cured. I pull the frozen meal out of its box, tossing it in the air fryer after I've cleared enough room on the counter in front of it to do so, and sit at one of the barstools, scrolling my phone while I wait.

There's already a group chat and several messages from Grant and Lev, inviting me to events at the casino and a snapshot his assistant has sent over of an apartment they could turn over for me. I sigh. It's not technically a violation of my parole to be around them, but it's walking a fine line when I'm trying to stay well clear of it.

WHEN HAZEL RETURNS from her dinner at the inn, I point to the piles of bags she's left that are gonna force me to eat dinner on the couch.

"What's all this?"

She grins and walks over to her purse, pulling her wallet out and then a credit card that she slides across the counter. My name is emblazoned on the front. One she must have snatched from my wallet this morning, and I lift my brow.

"Just had a little shopping to do. Figured you wouldn't mind."

"I hope you bought some things I'll enjoy," I answer as I process the small fortune that's been charged to my account.

"Well, I thought you could help me with cake tasting. I need to pick one for the wedding. Curtis is letting me decide, but I could use an opinion. I figured since I was already up in Denver, I'd pop in to get a few things for the honeymoon. You don't mind, do you?" She walks over to one of the bags and extracts a garment from the tissue paper.

It's a sheer lace teddy in pale champagne with delicate white and coral flowers strategically stitched over the surface. She adds a matching set of panties to her hand, ones that lace up the back, and I'm hard just thinking about her in them.

"I'm not sure if I should wear this one for the first night of the honeymoon or this one..." This time, she pulls out a sheer black lace crop top and a matching set of black lace panties, ones that are a barely-there scrap of fabric held together with black ribbon. "So I thought I'd model them and have you help me pick. I mean... who better to give advice, right? I can fix all the things that went wrong the first time."

I crumple the pizza box in my hand and nearly bite my tongue off, trying to calm myself before I respond. It's bait. It's a blatant fucking attempt to try to get me riled, and I'm not taking it. I stand slowly, crossing the room while she watches me.

"He needs all this to get it up then?" I ask, tossing the box in the trash. "I'm probably not the best judge for you in that case. I was happy to fuck you in a torn, old T-shirt."

"Yes well, you were a college boy. He's a man. More sophisticated tastes and all that." She smirks.

"Go put it on then." I grab a potholder and pull the pizza out of the oven. "You can give me a show with dinner. I can try to imagine what the fuck having sophisticated taste feels like while I down this beer."

She rolls her eyes but grabs a few of the bags. I can see the frustration in the sway of her hips that I'm not reacting the way she wants as she disappears to her room. I get to enjoy the satisfaction of that for all of about five minutes when she reappears in one of them, and I try not to choke on my last bite of pizza.

It's the pale champagne one she showed me first. On her fair skin, it makes it look like it's barely there. The only sign that she's wearing anything at all is the boning in the top portion and the lace flowers that make their way up the garment and end where the delicate coral and white flowers make little frames around her breasts.

"Do you like it?" She turns around. The back is cut low, and the lace frames her ass cheeks in a way that's going to live rent-free in my mind for weeks.

"It's... nice," I mumble before I sip my beer.

"The flowers kind of remind me of the ones out in that meadow off the river trail. You know the one I'm talking about?" She looks up at me and smiles. She knows I know. It was one of our favorite places. Two can play this game.

"Yeah." I set my beer down and hold my hands up like a frame, closing one eye and moving them back and forth.

"What are you doing?" She frowns at me, one hand on her hip.

"Trying to decide how close it looks to the real thing. The flowers were a little bigger and covered more of your skin. Did you get some lipstick? Some of that stuff that stains them that pretty color... And your lips were puffier too from all the—"

"Ramsey!" She cuts me off, and her eyes dance with irritation.

"What?" I grin, taking another draw off the longneck bottle. "I thought you wanted my opinion."

"A helpful opinion. On whether it fits well and whether it's pretty enough."

"It fits." Perfectly, if we're being honest. It highlights every feature of her body I love. "I already told you, you're pretty with or without it."

She rolls her eyes and stomps back to her room. "I'm getting a different one."

A few moments later, she reappears in a tight-fitting body-suit. It's not bad, but it's not as nice as the last one.

"It's a bit boring compared to the last one. You'd better save that one for the grand finale. Assuming you get one." I smirk to myself.

"You haven't seen the back yet," she scolds as she turns around and shows off the fact that the whole back is laced with ribbon, and there's a heart-shaped cutout around her ass. She's wearing a floss-thin G-string on underneath. "Does it look cute from the back?" She bends over, and I have to close my eyes.

"Fuuccck" I mutter to myself. Thankfully it's quiet enough that she can't hear.

"What?" She pops again, her brow furrowed like I've insulted her.

"Yeah. It's cute. I don't think you need the G-string though. It just makes for more work." I lift one shoulder as she turns back to me.

"Some people like the work," she sneers and then takes off again for her room without letting me defend my point.

I'm unsure if that's the end of the show or if I'm getting more since she's unhappy with my responses. But I still use the moment to readjust because even if I can keep my face from showing it, my dick's eager to betray me.

It takes her long enough that I assume she might be done for the night, and I pull out my phone to scroll as I finish my beer. I almost don't hear her when she comes back in, and when I look up, it takes effort not to make a sound. This might be the one that kills me.

She has on a sheer lace bra with a cupless corset under it that pushes her breasts so high they almost spill out. The pattern's the reverse of the one she'd had on first: black with blue and black flowers where there had been white and coral. There's a matching set of panties as well, but these ones have little ties on either side of her hips, ones that are begging for me to pull at the ribbon. She's added a set of fuck-me heels this time, too; stilettos that look like they were made to kill with delicate little straps around the ankles.

"And?" She turns around.

"That's the one." I manage to sound like I'm not choking on my own tongue.

"Really? I thought you'd say the slutty-looking one with the heart on the butt."

"Nah. They're all good. But if he's sophisticated and likes taking his time, this one's the one."

"And if he's not? Then the heart one?" she asks.

THIRTEEN

Hazel

"IF HE'S NOT, then it doesn't matter. He'll want you any way he can have you." His eyes drift up my body and land on my face; something flashes across his that I can't read before he presses his lips together like he's getting ready to say something else. My heart thuds faster in my chest with anticipation. I'm ready for him to tell me to go put on one of my old T-shirts, my fingers twitching with eagerness to pull this outfit off and put it on, but he just downs the last swig of his beer and takes the bottle to the kitchen.

"I think I'm gonna head up for the night," he announces before he rinses the bottle out and sets it on the counter.

I blink at his abrupt exit. I trail after him a moment later, trying to come up with an excuse for him not to vanish to the guest room. Then I see the cake boxes.

"Wait!" I call when he heads for the steps. He pauses and looks back at me over his shoulder. "The cake tasting."

"You know I'm not much on sweets." That much was true. He didn't care for them much and was picky about the ones he liked. "I'll leave that to you."

"I need an outside opinion. Curtis already left it to me, and I want help with it." I'm grasping at straws here, but I'm not done torturing him yet—not if he could walk away so easily.

I see a muscle in his jaw move, and his shoulders sag slightly in resignation. My heart takes off again with the hope that I'll wear him down yet. He looks back at the mountain of boxes from the bakeries.

"Why isn't Marlowe doing your cake? Seems like that would make it simple."

"She's a bridesmaid. I'm already asking too much of her."

"Did she say that?" he asks doubtfully.

"No, but you know how she is. She'd do anything for me, and I don't want her stressed out over my wedding. Even if she says she's happy to do it," I counter with the inevitable points he's going to have upfront.

"Fine. But pick two or three. I'm not doing them all."

"Four."

"Three."

My face falls with disappointment, but I nod my agreement. He makes his way back to the living room, sitting back on the couch while I work to fill a plate with samples of cake. One hummingbird cake, one chocolate with ganache, one lemon, and one classic vanilla with a white chocolate raspberry swirl icing on top. Each is split into two bites for us. I grab a fork out of the drawer and follow him into the living room.

I sit down next to him, careful because I'm teetering on heels that are more than precarious on carpet, and then I stab a bite of cake and hold it up for him. His eyes meet mine, skepticism and a hint of confusion in them that I'm asking to feed him.

"Just take the bite," I whisper, pushing the hummingbird cake to his lips.

He takes it gingerly, wiping a crumb from the corner of his mouth as he chews.

"That's good. What is it?" he asks after he swallows.

"Hummingbird cake," I explain. "Now the lemon."

I hold it up for him, and he takes it, tilting his head back and forth like he's considering it.

"Not bad. Lemon's not my favorite though." That much I knew. His favorite was apple. If I'd have been smart I would have asked for something with it. Then I could have brought him to his knees easily. I stab the chocolate piece as I live with that regret.

"Chocolate." I hold it up for him, and he takes it, licking his lips as a bit of the frosting catches there.

"Fuck." He closes his eyes for that one. "I don't hate it."

"I noticed." I laugh at the way he reacts, and his eyes snap open, darkening when he realizes I'm amused at his expense. He reaches for the spare bite I'd cut for myself and holds it up to my lips.

"Try it. You'll see," he insists. So I take it, slowly, from his thumb and forefinger. The taste of rich chocolate floods my senses, and I nearly moan from how good it is. He's slow to pull his hand away, and I grab his wrist and dart my tongue out to lick away the last of the chocolate ganache on the pads of his finger and thumb.

"Mmm." I moan softly. "I think I get it." I lift my lashes to look at him, and his eyes are burning into mine. They shutter a second later like he knows what I'm doing, and he's not buying it.

"Good. It sounds like you have a winner then." He leans forward to stand, and I put my hand to his chest.

"Wait! There's one more." I stab the white chocolate piece with my fork and hold it up.

"I said three. We did three." His tone is short.

"I know, but I like this one. Please?" I plead with him.

He eyes me warily. I see his hand curl around the edge of the couch like he's about to use the leverage to stand, and my heart skips. So I do what any normal ex-wife would do and climb into his lap.

"Please?" I ask again as I straddle him.

His eyes drift over me, and I can see the whirring thoughts written on his face, the war of emotions he's having with himself over how best to control the situation. I bite the inside of my cheek, and I can see when he finally settles on something.

He slides down on the seat, and his hand digs into the flesh of my ass cheek, pulling me forward into his lap. His point is immediately taken when I feel how hard he is, and as he leans back on the couch, I have to squash the little noise that nearly escapes my lips.

"Off the fork." He nods down at the cake, and I pull it off, putting the bite between my fingers and holding it out for him.

He takes the bite and chews slowly while I watch. My hand's frozen in the air while I watch his jaw and his throat move around it. Every little motion holds my attention until I feel his tongue slide over the small web of skin between my thumb and forefinger. It drifts lower, dancing over the pulse point of my wrist, and I close my eyes, biting my lower lip and trying to remember why the hell I put myself in this position in the first place.

"Ask me to fuck you." His voice has a graveled quality that makes it hard to say the next word. But I have to. I've pushed this way too far and let this get away from me, torturing myself as well as him.

"No." I manage to say it clearly and firmly despite how

weak I'm feeling. I'm honestly proud of myself. I open my eyes again, realizing there's a small smile on my lips when I see the scowl reflected on his. Mine fades as his deepens.

His hands go to the ends of the ribbon on either side of my panties, and he twists them around his fingers, looking up at me, his lashes low as he speaks.

"You keep telling me you're not the girl I remember, and I believe you. I think you're smarter, cleverer than you've ever been. So when you climb up here, pleading with me, and spreading these gorgeous thighs over my lap, I want you to remember that I've only just got out of prison after months of nothing but my hand and memories of how perfect my wife felt with her tight cunt gripping my cock and pleading for more of me. Ask yourself if that's wise." His tone is low and lethal, and he starts to pull on one of the ribbons.

"You wouldn't dare," I hiss.

"You're right. I wouldn't. I suppose I could just go down to the Libertine. You think Vic still works there?" There's a conniving upturn of his lips. The Libertine is the local strip club, and Victoria was always obsessed with him. We went to school together, and it was like she'd made it her life's mission in college to try to steal him away from me. Not that it ever worked.

"You're married, remember?" I echo his earlier statement to me.

It's an idle threat on his part anyway. He doesn't like strip clubs, and he'd never touch Vic, not knowing how she treated me. But the thought of it still makes the jealousy curl around my spine, and he knows it. This is tit for tat for all my honeymoon talk.

"Am I?" he taunts, leaning in until I can feel his breath on my neck. "Because if I was, I'm pretty sure she'd remember how good I can be to her. How well I take care of her. All the ways I could put us both out of our misery." His lips are against my throat by the time he's done, whispering the last of his words against my skin, and it's working. Flashes of the two of us are all I can see, like I'm on my deathbed, and I'm granted one last chance to remember all the best things I ever felt and tasted and saw... and they were all *him*.

"Ramsey..." I say softly.

"Just ask."

I don't answer him. I can't. I'm trapped between wanting him and wanting to believe I'm over him. I can feel his hands ball into fists around the ribbons, and he buries his face in the crook of my neck as my silence stretches on.

He takes a deep breath a few moments later, and then he digs his fingers into my ass and hauls us both up to our feet, setting me down on my heels. His hand wraps around my jaw and tightens, and his lips press against my ear.

"Then don't do this to us again until you can." He releases his grip on me and disappears upstairs to his room, leaving me feeling like *I've* somehow fucked up instead of him.

FOURTEEN

Ramsey

> **BO:**
> You coming out tonight for guys' night?
>
> We're celebrating Anson's birthday.

> Am I invited?

FRANKLY, I'm not sure whether or not I'm back in the Briggs family's good graces. I could use a night out, though, some time and distance away from Hazel. She's been invading every thought I've had since I got here, and since she's dead set on tormenting the hell out of me before she'll even consider giving in, I could use a night off from it.

> **BO:**
> You're still our brother for the time being.

> Where are we headed?

Downtown. Grabbing dinner at Brady's at
seven and then to Seven Sins for some
drinks. Try to see if we can play wingman for
the confirmed bachelor and get him laid for
his birthday.

See you at Brady's.

When I get done with helping Kell and Elliot for the day, I take a quick shower back at the ranch house and get cleaned up for dinner. Hazel left a note that she's staying for the dinner talk she's arranged for the guests tonight, so I won't be missed by going out with the rest of the guys.

By nine, we're winding down dinner and having a whiskey and laughing our asses off as they sing "Happy Birthday" to Anson while he scowls at us.

"That was fucking uncalled for," he mutters as he pulls the candle out of the cake and tosses it to the side. One of the wait-staff, a cute blonde who clearly was trying to flirt with him, had made him blow it out.

"You make it too easy." Cade's chest rumbles with laughter as Anson flips his brother the bird. Hazel's youngest brother is night and day from her oldest, wild and free where Anson's quiet and calculated.

"Fuck off. I was promised steak and drinks. Not a fucking musical." Anson's the conservative one of our little friend group, and he'd rather spend his nights at home with his son, watching ball, camping, or hitting his bed early to try to catch the fish in the morning, than be out with us.

"Gotta let us have a little fun." Bo pushes the fresh glass of whiskey the waiter's brought to the table toward his brother. "Drink up, and maybe you'll enjoy it more."

"Doubtful." Anson flashes me a pointed look. "And I expected more from you."

"I'm just along for the ride. Don't blame me!" My laughter dies, but the smile doesn't.

"Some balm for your grumpy ass." Kingston, one of Anson's partners at his construction company and a good friend of his, pushes some cigars wrapped in a black ribbon his way. "You can enjoy an intermission before our next stop."

"Thanks." Anson holds up the cigars and nods to his friend. "Maybe. Or I might just head home to smoke one."

"You're not going home yet," Jasper, a manager from the construction company and Marlowe's brother, argues. "We don't get you out often enough."

"Ready to head to Seven?" Bo looks around at the table as he signs the ticket.

"I'm your captive, apparently," Anson grumps, but I can tell he's having fun despite himself.

Anson out with us like this is a rare occurrence, and we're all trying to make the most of it. His circumstances don't allow for a lot of free time, but he's never been the same since he lost his wife. They'd settled down shortly after high school, bought a small house, had a kid, and started his business all pretty quickly. He never had a wild bachelor streak like the rest of us. He'd still been the grumpy, quiet type back then too, but he smiled a fuckton more then than he does now. I suppose losing your wife so young sucks a lot of the joy out of your life. I know losing mine had been hard enough, and I had the benefit of knowing she was alive and happy somewhere else.

WE'RE NOT at Seven Sins long before we're set up at a corner booth, watching the crowd on the dance floor and nursing beers. Bo's been out a few times, along with Cade and Kingston, and Jasper's already taken off for the night so he can get up early for work, but Anson's remained my stalwart companion for the evening despite his misgivings about staying out.

"That terrible?" I ask when Anson starts to peel the label off his bottle. He looks up like he's forgotten I'm sitting here and gives me an apologetic smile.

"Just not much for dancing or any of this. I'd rather be back at home."

"You don't meet many people that way, I imagine."

"You assume I want to meet someone."

I press my lips together and raise my brows, figuring he has a fair point. I let things fall silent again, watching as one of the two women Bo's been dancing with runs her hands over the front of his pants and kisses him hard.

"You don't have someone back in Cincinnati pissed that you're still married?" Anson's been watching the same dance floor drama as me and seems to be bored of it if he's asking these kinds of questions.

"Nah. Same as you. I'd rather be out in nature or working out. The rest is just too much work for anything less than someone like Haze."

"She's still got you by the balls all these years later, then?" Anson studies me.

I shrug. "If you want to be a dick about it, yeah, I guess you could put it that way."

He lets out a muted laugh and wipes the condensation off the bottom of his bottle.

"You got a plan if she won't bite?"

That's the million-dollar question, and the answer is, I don't. At least not yet. I probably made my stupidest bet yet, and I have no backup if it goes south. I'm about to ask Anson about his own circumstances when Bo comes back to the table, the two women who we were with him trailing behind, and a third friend of theirs has appeared out of nowhere.

Bo helps one of them into the booth between him and Anson, and the other slides in after him. The third woman, much quieter than the other two, eyes the seat next to me but doesn't take it.

"Do you mind?" She nods to it.

"No, go ahead." I scoot over and make sure there's plenty of daylight between us. I don't need rumors swirling that I'm barely back and already cheating on my wife—the small-town gossip mill always needs something to keep it fueled. But she seems about as interested in me as I am in her, so I'm not too bothered.

"Ramsey Stockton. It has been a long time." The woman sitting on the edge of the booth across from me flashes me a grin and her cleavage as she leans over to pat my hand. "I watched all that coverage of you on TV. I'm so glad you're finally out. You didn't deserve to serve any of that time." A breath mint rattles around in her mouth as she speaks, and something about her appearance is familiar, but I can't place it.

"You remember Faith and Holly from school?" Bo points to the women on either side of him. Faith is the one with the breath mint, and Holly's the one wedged between Anson and Bo, her hand currently pressed to Anson's shoulder as she talks to him, and he backs further and further into the corner like a caged animal.

"It's definitely been a while," I answer vaguely on purpose because I have no recollection of either woman.

"You're so funny." Faith smacks the back of my hand, and I pull back.

"I think you need a water." The quieter one at my side is eying her friend like she's a bit embarrassed of her.

"Could you get me one? You know Dakota hates me." Faith

rolls her lip at her friend, and when she notices that I'm listening, she turns to me to air her complaints. "She always wants to charge me two dollars for some cold tap water. It's ridiculous." She rolls her eyes.

Dakota and I were in the same grade growing up, so knowing that those two don't like each other fills in at least some of the pieces of the social politics for me. Dakota was particular about who she was friends with, but if she didn't like you, there was usually a pretty damn good reason for it. Like breaking her best friend's heart.

"I'll get it." The woman next to me hops down and heads back across the bar.

"Sorry about her. That's Avery. She's new in town. Just started working at the casino, and we've adopted her into our little group, but being from the city... well, you know how they are since you've just escaped." Faith is loquacious as hell when she's drunk, apparently.

"Ah. Well, they've got their reasons, I've found."

"You're so kind. You always think the best of everyone." Faith smiles at me, and Bo flashes a look between us. One I answer with a wide-eyed *I'm not encouraging her* look in return.

"I heard it's your birthday." Holly looks Anson over, and when I tell you the man is practically crawling up the wall to put distance between them, I'm not lying. I can't tell whether he hates her or if he just doesn't know what to do with this kind of attention.

"Something like that," he mumbles.

"Mine was last week...." She keeps chattering on about her life, and he just keeps nodding along with her. He gives short answers when she asks him questions about himself, and I can tell she's trying her best to keep the conversation going.

"My birthday's coming up next week too. What a coincidence." Faith interjects herself into the conversation.

"Yeah?" Bo asks her, his eyes drifting over her neck and following the deep vee of her shirt. He pulls her into his lap a moment later, and she leans back against his chest. "You doing anything fun for it?"

"I have some ideas." Her lashes drop as she looks back up at him, and I'm starting to feel like the odd man out, hoping Avery comes back soon, and we can discuss her new job at my brothers' place.

"You should tell me what some of them are." Bo grins at her, taking a sip of his drink and wrapping his arm around her waist. I don't begrudge my friend a one-night stand, but I'm having a hard time seeing what's keeping his interest besides the fact that she's pretty.

"I don't know... Some of them are pretty scandalous. It might be too much for you."

"Haven't found my limits yet."

I'm not a stranger to these situations. It'd been the same with my teammates back East, but it was around this time I usually found myself ducking out for the evening. But it feels rude, given it's Anson's birthday, to be doing it quite this early.

"Have you heard of an Eiffel Tower?" Her gaze snaps to mine from Bo's. "Because I'm really into the idea of that tonight."

I nearly choke on my beer, and I jump up out of the booth as I start to sputter and cough.

"Be right back. I think there's something wrong with this beer." I manage to say before I hustle my way across the floor to the bar, where I see Dakota raise an eyebrow at me as I approach.

"Well, if it isn't the gridiron pimp." She shakes her head and glances back over my shoulder.

"I'm just playing wingman tonight. Trying to help some friends out."

"Is that what you'd call it?" A skeptical brow arches.

"Can I get an ice water?"

"Not if you're taking it back to her." She levels me with a flat tone.

"It's for me. I'll drink it right here if you'd like."

"I would." She reaches under the counter and starts preparing it for me as she glances back in the direction of Hazel's brothers. "She's trouble. Just so you know."

"I think Bo's just trying to give Anson a shot with her friend. She already mentioned you hate her."

"I don't hate her."

"You could've fooled me." I down half the ice water in one gulp when she hands it to me.

"I don't *like* her, but I don't hate her. Hate requires a lot of time and effort. Someone has to be worth it for me to devote those kinds of precious resources, and she's most certainly not."

"I see." I swirl the ice around in what's left and then down it before I put the cup back on the counter and ask for another. She serves it, and I down it again. I'm ready to head home, and I don't want a headache waiting for me in the morning.

"Thanks for that," Bo grouches as he comes up alongside me and orders a water for himself. I look back over my shoulder to see that Faith, Holly, and Avery have all moved on to greener pastures.

"I'm sorry... were you wanting to take a trip to Paris tonight?" I can't suppress my amusement, and he answers it with a heavy frown.

"I'm not excited about going home alone."

"There's a bar full of women and more down the road."

"I had one in my lap already. If you hadn't acted like she disgusted you, it would have been fine."

"I don't want a rumor going around that I'm cheating on my wife, and I definitely don't want a rumor that I'm tag-teaming with her brother," I argue. "And since when do you have a hard time getting women?"

"I'm not having a hard time finding them in general, just a harder time finding ones who don't want to 'take the next step' after a couple of nights together. I want my life simple. I already have Cade taking up space since he's back from college. I'm not about to start watching my bathroom drawers fill with curling irons and tampons."

"You've got a few more years of that before it starts looking sad, just so you know," I warn my old friend. He's a couple of years older than me, and I can't imagine still trolling bars. Even back home, it'd been friends of mine who were up for a friends-with-benefits situation. I didn't trust anyone else.

"You've got a few more weeks of following my sister around like a lost dog before women are going to start seeing you as a pity fuck instead of bragging rights."

"I think I'm at peace with that. Especially if it means I don't fuck it up with your sister."

"You already fucked it up. She's got you on your knees. You're playing defense, and not well, I might add."

"Well fuck you very much."

"I'm trying to help."

"How do you figure?"

"Pretend you know how to run offense. Make a few calls. See if you can get back in the game, or you're gonna lose to that prick." My old quarterback comes out in full force with just enough alcohol in him that he thinks he's clever.

But he's not wrong. Hazel has me right where she wants me, even when I should have the upper hand. Which gives me the perfect idea.

FIFTEEN

Hazel

IT'S BEEN A NEVER-ENDING DAY, and I'm exhausted. I'm in need of a long soak in the bath and a few orgasms. Given that I'm short one fiancé and plus one husband, who I'm desperately trying not to get entangled with all over again, I'm on my own on that front. Especially since I'd barely escaped with the remnants of my dignity the last time I got too close to him. Which means it's battery-operated boyfriends only right now.

Except, I open my nightstand drawer and nothing. Well, not nothing; there's some hand lotion, cough drops, lip balm, and tissues. Plus half a bag of chocolate for a rainy day. But not the thing I need right now. Its case and the contents are missing. I turn on my heel and move to my bathroom. I always keep a charged spare in there. For emergencies and for those days when I need one convenient for water use. I open the drawer, and it's empty too. I glare at the blank space and slam it shut.

There's only one answer—only one explanation for this kind of coincidence, and he's currently sleeping in my guest room. Given that I heard via my bestie group chat that he also spent the night chatting up every local in the bar and flirting with half the single women in town, I'm ready to strangle him. Maybe I can claim justified murder the same way he did.

I move quickly down the hall and through the door. He's fast asleep, sprawled out on his back with the window open and the sounds of the night floating in through the window. He looks so peaceful like this, and somehow that makes me angrier.

I'm on top of him a second later, my hands on his throat, my nails digging into the tattoos there and squeezing. The satisfaction it brings lasts only for the briefest of moments because before I know what's happening, I'm on my back. My hands are pinned above my head, and he's looming over me. His face is a collage of sleepiness, surprise, and irritation as he takes the sight of me in.

I hadn't thought about what I was wearing when I came in here. Too mad to think straight, and he's staring at the thin tank top I have on and the way my breasts are threatening to spill out of it. Given the way we left things the other night, this is probably going to be seen as another attempt to seduce him, and it's absolutely not.

"What the fuck are you doing, Haze?"

"Choking you."

"I caught that part." His brow furrows deeper than before. "For what?"

"Mental distress." I glare at him. "At least that's what I'm going to tell the cops."

"You kill me; you better call Bo to come clean it up so there aren't any cops."

"That's your response?" I huff.

"You wouldn't last in prison. Your smart mouth would get you killed."

"You lasted."

"I was in a Club Fed. You won't be."

"Fine. I'll call Bo. Now let me finish the job."

"What are you so fucking riled about?"

"My toys. What did you do with them?"

He has the audacity to smirk.

"Borrowed them."

"You know I need them." Ramsey knows I have trouble getting off without them. It's one of the few things he knows that Curtis doesn't.

"Which is why I knew you'd come find me when you needed them."

"So give them back."

"I want to know why you lied first. Then I'll consider it."

I frown at the accusation, racking my brain for any kind of lie I might have told him. Don't get me wrong. I love pissing the man off, but we've always had an unspoken rule about not lying to each other—not even the little white ones that you think don't matter. One we never wavered on, even when things got bad.

"What did I lie about?" I shake my head and study his face.

"Telling Curtis you had to fake it with me." He frowns.

I sigh. I wish Curtis could have kept his mouth shut, but apparently, his ego couldn't handle it. He just had to get a dig in on Ramsey, and unfortunately for him, he tried to weaponize the one thing Ramsey would see straight through. I contemplate whether or not to tell Ramsey the truth. The things it'll do for his ego, and the way it'll give him an even bigger upper hand in this make me want to scream.

"I had to tell him that."

"Why?"

"Because of reasons. It's none of your business."

"I don't love you spreading rumors that I can't get a woman off."

"Why? Do you think it'll ruin your chances with Vic? Don't worry. The fame and the money will distract her."

"Not very charitable of you."

"It's not a good idea to be flirting with half the town if you want her, by the way. She's the jealous type."

"Is she? Then I guess she should stop listening to rumors. Because I definitely wasn't flirting." His eyes drift over my face and down my neck.

"Not what I heard. But then I'm just trying to help. The two of you would be perfect together. She'd love living in your RV and being outdoors all the time. Sweating all day in the sun and then fucking her in the dirt somewhere." I make a little gasping sound like I've just realized something amazing. "Then you can come home and shower outside your RV in front of everyone together."

"Is that what *you* want? That why you're being so fucking difficult about everything? You need a rough fuck in the dirt?"

"What?" I let out a weak huff of a laugh. Is he offering? Because... *Shit.* My brain is short-circuiting again.

He leans down, his lips a hairsbreadth away from the shell of my ear before he speaks again.

"You sound jealous. Do you want me to chase you through a meadow again? You liked it so much the last time that we spent the whole night there. We can do that. Then I can spend the morning washing all the grass and mud off you. Let all your guests see you for who you really are." A flash of the last time plays out in my head. I haven't learned my lesson from the other night because now it's not just my brain short-circuiting. It's my whole body.

I force a laugh instead. This one sounds almost as weak as

the one before. Like I might be crying instead. I try to cover it up and laugh a little harder. I need to distract him. Wound his ego a bit so he doesn't clock my reaction to him. I can't be letting him win like this.

"That's hilarious. So funny I could cry." I shake my head.

"Yeah. Weeping your heart out. I can tell. You want me to lick those tears up for you, or just let them keep soaking into my thigh?"

It's that moment I realize his thigh is wedged between my legs, and I'm spread over him like a wanton little whore again. Each fake laugh makes me rock against him, and that little bit of friction sends up a spark that wraps around my clit and tempts me more. I try to think of words to explain how I'm here again, but they all fall short on my lips.

"I... It's just..." I mutter the words, but then I just look to the ceiling and accept my own humiliating defeat.

"I didn't say you had to stop, sugar." His grin is devilish, but his words are soft. "You need it. Use me to finish yourself off."

I take a breath and roll my hips again, teasing my clit with the friction at first and then leaning into it more. Riding his thigh until my breathing gets heavier and my hands are wrapped up in the quilt on his bed. But I can only seem to brush the edges of my release before it drifts away again, and I quickly start to feel the heat of embarrassment rise to my cheeks.

I shake my head in frustration. Ramsey's the one man who's been patient enough to help me get off without toys. But it's been years since we had that kind of connection, since I could enjoy things with him. Even right before our should-have-been divorce, we'd grown too distant for him to be able to help me through it.

"Get out of your head."

"I can't."

"You can. You're thinking too much. Worrying too much. Just grind that sweet little cunt on me."

I return to my former position, and I can feel my clit pulse with anticipation as I start to grind against his thigh. He changes his position, leaning forward a little to give me more friction. It feels good. So fucking good. I bite back a moan as I take another pass.

"There you go. Just like that. Keep going."

I take a deep breath and close my eyes. His breath is warm against my neck and my cheek, and the weight of his thigh between my legs and the possessive way he holds my wrists has me losing myself. I grind away on him like this is a dream where there aren't any real consequences, and I can just enjoy how good this all is—the scent of his cologne, the warmth of his body, the sound of his voice. I take it all in, and before I know what's happening, I'm edging closer to the cliff I desperately need.

"Fuck... You should see yourself. So pretty when you let go like this. What fuckin' dreams are made of."

I switch my position slightly, chasing the edge of the pleasure I feel start to spark. But it's still elusive, and I frown as I lose it, changing my rhythm again to try to get it back and sighing when I can't.

"What do you need? Use your words."

"I need my fucking toys." My eyes snap open, and I glare at him, angry all over again that I had to come in here to hunt them down.

"Ask *nicely*."

"Please give me back my fucking toys." I narrow my eyes. This is where most guys fail the test, and I have to decide whether I play along with the charade for their ego or whether I'm honest and throw them and their egos to the curb.

Ramsey reaches over me into the guest room nightstand,

pulling one of my favorite vibrators out and turns it on. It buzzes to life, and he presses it between my legs. It's like magic, bringing the edge I was chasing back immediately. I close my eyes and start to rock against his thigh again, solid and roped with muscle, just like the rest of him.

"That's it. Soak me while you ride it." He changes the angle of the vibrator, pressing it closer to my clit, and gives me enough to make me desperate to chase the end. I ride his thigh harder; every counterstroke gives another heavy buzz, and before I know it, I'm cursing and practically panting for him. All he'd have to do is ask if I wanted his cock, and I'd probably beg for it. But he doesn't. He gives me mercy instead, pressing the vibrator all the way down on my clit and bringing his mouth down on my nipple, nipping and sucking it through my tank top as I cry out.

"Oh fuck. Ramsey. Fuck... Please. Bite harder," I beg him, and he does as I ask.

I scream out because it's half-decadent pleasure and half-delirious pain. The orgasm chases through my nerve endings, lighting every single one and making me moan as I ride out the last waves of it. My whole body goes limp as it recedes, and the heaviness of the aftershock advances in its stead. He lets my hands go free as he sits back, and I feel the cool air from the AC whip over my body in the gap he's created between us. It feels like heaven on my heated skin.

I enjoy the bliss for whole moments before I hear the buzz of the vibrator go silent, and then I can hear him—in stereo. His breathing is heavy, and I can almost hear his heart pounding through his chest and feel the weight of his gaze. My eyes open and his glimmer with want. His cock is thick and heavy, jutting against his boxers.

"How long has it been?" I ask as I slip my panties off, and he watches the movement like a feral predator about to strike.

"Too long, and prison made it longer." Something about that turns me on. The idea of him, a man who always takes what he wants, having to wait for once in his life. Being starved of his favorite things and driven to the edge like this. I sit up and shift onto my shins until our knees are touching.

I slip my fingers up his thigh and curl them over the inside. "That must have been hard for you. Lots of nights with just your hand. Did you really think of me?"

"I did." The way he looks at me makes me weak. Makes my heart flutter in a way I don't like. The kind that needs to be snuffed out. Crushed. Then set on fire all over again.

"Well..." I force a grin. "Then you'll be well practiced for your time here. But at least now you can use these." I toss my panties into his lap and stand, smirking as his face clouds with confusion. "Enjoy your night, Lone Ranger," I call back over my shoulder before I shut the door. I can hear the loud growl of frustration behind me, and I hurry down the hall, dodging into the master bedroom and locking the door behind me.

I'm winded, still trying to catch my breath, but I hold it for a moment to see if I can hear him follow. It's silent, and I grab my stomach, half a sigh and half a laugh coming out at the same time. I can't help the smile that breaks either as I close my eyes and lean back against the wall while my breathing slows. It's the most fun I've had in a while, which means I'm in trouble if I don't find a way to stop it.

SIXTEEN

Ramsey

I'M in the middle of cleaning my saddle and the rest of my tack in the barn when Hazel bursts in, a bright red backpack flung over one of her shoulders as she roots through a cabinet and searches the wall where the keys are. She brushes a lock of hair back from her face as her eyes frantically scan it a second time.

"Looking for something?" I ask, pausing and adding more leather cleaner the rag as I watch her look through a basket on the counter.

She startles at the sound of my voice but barely spares me a glance. I start toward her just in case I might be able to help with the search.

"Do you know where the ATV keys are? It's an emergency." The anxiety seeps through her tone as she shifts the backpack on her shoulder again.

"I've got them in my pocket." I reach back and hold them

out for her. She whips around, a glare on her face as her eyes flash to the ceiling.

"You've got to put these back where you found them!" She snatches them unceremoniously from where they dangle at my fingertips.

"I'm sorry. I just finished up a few minutes ago. What's wrong?" My brow furrows. I'd like to help if I can, but Hazel has always wanted to do everything herself, and I choose when and where to force the issue with her carefully.

"One of the guests fell off their horse. A rabbit ran out in front of them and startled the horse. It sounds like they broke an ankle. The ambulance is coming, but they're delayed. I want to meet them, just in case, with the trailer and the first aid kit." She talks just as quickly as she walks, and I trail behind her, following to the ATV.

"I took the trailer off this morning to get back into the wooded area. I can put it back on."

"Fuck!" she curses, clearly frustrated that I've made this all harder than it needed to be.

"Just give me a minute, and I'll get it together. I'll drive us out there. Just take a breath." I try to reassure her, but it's a losing battle.

"Don't tell me to take a breath." She gives me a sidelong glare, but she tosses the keys back to me.

"You won't be any help if you're stressed too."

"Kell called five minutes ago. I wanted to be on my way by now."

"I've got you, Haze. Two minutes. Tell Kell we're on our way."

I hurry as fast as I can to get the trailer reattached to the ATV and bring it back around to where Haze is finishing her chat with Kell. Her face clouds with concern as he talks, and she shakes her head, her hand wiping at her brow as she stares up at the sky like something helpful might be there for her.

"Right. Right. We'll be right there. I've got the first aid kit and water. The ambulance is on the way if we need it. Just let them know help's coming and not to worry." She waits for Kell's response, and then she ditches her walkie on her hip.

"More than the ankle?" I try to figure out what has her looking so despondent.

"It doesn't sound like it, but her friend is having a bit of an anxiety attack too. Doesn't want to ride back. I just can't believe this happened with new riders." Hazel sounds defeated, and I'd give her a hug if I didn't think she'd take one of my arms off in the process.

"It happens. There's nothing you can do about it right now but get out there to help. Hop on, and I'll drive us."

"I can do it."

"I know you can, but an extra set of hands won't hurt either."

She sees the wisdom in my plan and reluctantly climbs on the ATV behind me. She slides her other arm through the first aid pack and then wraps both around my waist before I gun it down the trail as fast as the trailer allows.

I'm not quite as worried as she is about the guest. I trust Kell in an emergency. He's seen more than his fair share, and he has one of the coolest heads on the ranch. I'm fairly certain we'll have this sorted quickly and be back to life as usual, but I don't hate the idea of being able to help Haze out with something. Especially after she trusted me to help her last night.

WHEN WE GET to the site of the accident, Kell has everyone comfortable in a nearby break in the woods, including the horses. They're all having the snack he brought along for later in the ride, and he's splinted the woman's broken ankle. Her friend is currently sitting next to him, looking less frazzled and more captivated by whatever story Kell is currently telling her.

"I'm so sorry it took us a bit to get out here," Haze apologizes to Kell and the guests.

"It looks like you've got everything under control though?" I look to Kell for the report.

"Yeah. We just need to get Samantha and Courtney back to the inn and see about Courtney getting some medical attention." Kell stands and meets us to help assess the situation. Haze heads over to the guests and starts apologizing and asking what she can do.

"Do you want to finish out the tour with the other guests, and we can get Samantha and Courtney and their horses back?"

"Sounds like a plan. I can get Lady Luck to ride with me, but if you or Haze wanna ride Teddy back, that'd make it easier." Kell pulls his cowboy hat off to smooth his hair back underneath it, and then places it back on his head.

"We can do that." I nod, watching with concern as Haze tries to help Courtney stand, and she falters, unable to balance well.

"I'm sorry," she apologizes to Haze. "I kinda twisted this one in the stirrup wrong when I slid off and then landed hard the other. I don't think this one is broken, but it doesn't feel good either."

"Oh god. Don't apologize. You're hurt! We'll figure it out. We've got the trailer, so we can get you back to meet the ambulance, and they can take you into town," Haze explains.

"Can I ride with her? I don't want to get back on a horse." Samantha looks skeptically back at Lady Luck. She'd honestly be a better ride back than the ATV, less bumpy and more careful about dips in the road, but I'm not about to argue.

"Of course." Haze gives her a reassuring smile and then turns to Courtney. "Do you think you can make it that way if you lean hard on me?" I'm already seeing visions of them both going down and Haze feeling guilty or getting hurt herself.

"I can carry you." I look to Courtney, and her eyes are glued on her ankle.

"Oh, I don't think that you should—I mean, I'm not light and—" She finally looks up at me, and her lashes flutter, sudden recognition in them. "I guess that could work if you don't mind."

"Not a problem. It's just a few feet, and I'd rather you not do more damage to that ankle." I walk over and pick her up; her hands wrap around my neck, and I can feel her eyes studying every angle of my face.

"I appreciate it." She smiles. "You're good at this whole hero thing."

"Just trying to help."

"Do you work at the ranch? Is that what you're doing now?" She's inquisitive as I carry her back to the trailer.

"It's my family's ranch. I grew up here."

"Oh wow. How did I not know that? That should be part of your marketing. I think more people would visit if they got to see you in a cowboy hat like this." Her tone is decidedly flirty, and I'm just glad it's keeping her mind off her ankle. It's already swollen and looks painful as hell.

"I'll have to take that into consideration." I smile at her as I get her into the trailer, hoping it doesn't cause her too much discomfort on the ride back. She settles in and leans back against the short wall. I'm just grateful this hadn't happened on one of the steeper inclines on the trail or we'd have been at a loss to get her out easily.

"Thank you. I appreciate this so much. When we get back from the doctor's, you'll have to let me buy you dinner or a drink or something for the rescue. I'd love to hear all about the ranch and your family." She beams at me.

"Well, let's get you fixed up first." I flash a polite smile back at her and turn to Hazel to see her talking to the woman's friend.

Hazel looks back at me, a blankness in her expression that seems practiced, before she starts working to calm Samantha and give her reassurance.

"I promise that sort of thing with horses is rare. Especially trail horses. Teddy is an angel; he just got a little startled and didn't want to make a misstep. Lady Luck will get you back safe and sound if you want to go back with the group."

"I don't think so. I just... I wouldn't feel safe. No offense to you or your horses, of course."

"No offense taken. I know it's scary to see someone take a tumble." Hazel gives her a soft smile, but I can tell it's killing Hazel that someone got frightened by horses on her watch. She turns to me, though, all business. "Can she ride back with you? I'll take Teddy back."

"Of course." I nod and turn to Samantha. "Have you ever been on an ATV before?"

"No. But I hope it's safer than a horse." She laughs nervously.

"Just as safe. Hazel's right. The horses are very safe, but I can understand not being sure around them if you're not used to them."

They're safe as hell, especially Haze's trail horses. They're just like people, though, bound to get startled once in a while if something happens they weren't expecting—like a scared rabbit hopping out underfoot.

"It's just, it was our first time. Not my idea. I know I'm a city girl, but I didn't want to be a killjoy. Just watching her fall like that... I have visions of breaking my neck on the ride back." Samantha lets out another self-deprecating laugh.

"Nah. The horses follow each other, and they're so used to different riders and this trail that not much shakes them. The rabbit running out like that and him jagging off to the side was more about keeping your friend and Teddy safe. He doesn't want to step on something, and you both go down hard, you know?" I try to give her my calmest tone like I'm talking to one of the rookies on the field who's just been laid into by the coach.

"That makes sense. They're just big, and I didn't expect how it would feel to be riding downhill. It already felt like I'd fall off."

"That's what the saddle and the stirrups are for. To keep you fully seated in the saddle. I promise as long as you hang on, these trail horses have your back," I explain, and Samantha seems to be taking it in earnestly.

"That makes sense, but honestly, I'm still nervous about heading back on one. Maybe I can hike? Would that be all right?"

"That's a long hike, darlin'. It'll take you two or three times as long as it will them to make that climb back up."

"What about the ATV?" She nods at my ride.

"ATV's just as safe as the driver, and I promise I'll keep it slow and steady. I don't want to jostle your friend and her ankle." I look behind me at Courtney who flashes another flirty smile, and I avert my gaze back to Samantha.

"All right. What do I do?" Samantha looks skeptically at the ATV.

"Just hop on behind me and hold on to me. Like I said. I'll keep it pretty slow, but it'll be a little bumpy through some of these parts," I explain, hoping that warning her will keep her calm rather than scare her off.

"Okay." There's still a wary tone to her voice, but she climbs on behind me.

"See you back at the ranch?" I glance at Haze, and she nods before she heads off toward Kell and the horses.

WHEN I GET BACK to the ranch, it's a whirlwind of activity. Grace is waiting with the paramedics, and they help get Courtney loaded onto the ambulance and on her way to get evaluated. They let Samantha ride with her, and Grace promises to arrange a ride back for them whenever they need it.

I've parked the ATV and am back in the barn, puttering around, hoping to run into Hazel when she brings Teddy back. It doesn't take long, and she's working on putting Teddy back in his stall when I find her.

"You doing okay?" I ask, leaning against the post and keeping a safe distance in case she isn't.

"I'm fine. It's just another thing we didn't need. You know?" She shrugs.

"I know." I nod solemnly.

"We made a pretty good team taking care of it though. I appreciate your help. You and Kell were great with the guests today." Half a smile appears and fades just as quickly. I have to tamp down the urge to preen a little over her praise, just thankful for once I've managed to line up a few things in a row that are putting me in her good graces.

"I was thinking maybe when things have died down tomorrow, maybe I'd take them out to feed the horses a snack or something. Show them that there's nothing to be afraid of."

"Sure. That sounds good." She nods. "Just not Wolfsbane, maybe? They'll never get on a horse again if they have to see him on a bad day."

"Nah. I was thinking Lady Luck and Admiral. But Wolfsbane can make friends when he wants to. He just needs a little extra encouragement." I feel defensive of my old guy. He's temperamental sometimes, sure, but he has a good heart.

"Yeah. I've noticed. A lot like his rider. He eats up the extra encouragement like it's candy." Hazel flashes me a look.

"What's that supposed to mean?"

Her brow arches up. "'Oh, darlin', I'll take it niiiiice and slow. Wrap your arms around me.'" She rolls her eyes and loses the tone that mocks me for one higher pitch. "'Oh, Mr. Stockton, I'd just love to hear all about your ranch.'"

"I was just being friendly." Seems Wolfsbane isn't the only one who can't catch a break around here.

"Uh huh..." She shakes her head, but a smile teases at her lips, and it's hard to tell if she's actually jealous or just teasing me.

"If you don't want me to take them out to feed the horses, just say so."

"Feed all the horses you like." She dusts off her hands on her jeans as she finishes up. I close the distance between us, and her eyes fall to where my boots nearly touch hers.

"I got other cures for that brand of jealousy, Mrs. Stockton." I tease her, and I watch as her shoulders roll back.

"Jealous?" She tilts her head, and then her eyes lift to meet mine in defiance. "Nah. Those kinds of women fawn too much. They don't recognize when he's the kind of horse that likes to be rode hard and put away wet."

She flashes a bright smirk in my direction and then turns to saunter back out of the barn. And fuck, if she doesn't have a point.

SEVENTEEN

Hazel

CURTIS:

You, me, and your toy tonight. It's been too
long. 8 p.m.

I STARE DOWN at the message and glance at the clock. It's
only a few minutes 'til and I'm anxious. I'm not really excited
for phone sex tonight, but I feel guilty that we haven't had
anything resembling intimacy since he left. I've been blowing
Curtis off way too much lately. This last week, I barely
answered his texts, and when I did, they were only one or two
words at a time. Between the inn and Ramsey, almost all of my
time has been monopolized.

If the situation was reversed, and I was in Curtis's shoes, I'd
be panicking. I'd be sure that I lost him to his ex-wife, and I'd be
wanting reassurances. My stomach turns just thinking about

how sick with anxiety I'd be. So I feel like I owe him this much, at least.

But it feels like I'm somehow betraying Ramsey by spending this kind of time with my fiancé. All the torturing each other back and forth, the bickering, and him helping today. The pretending we've been doing is starting to go too far, and all the reminiscing is getting to my head.

I don't know how much longer I can hold Ramsey at bay either if I want to complete the deal. He was clear on his terms. I caved at dinner and told him he could sleep here tonight to buy myself some more time to think it through. But it's only a matter of time until he'll want me to make a decision, one way or the other.

Somehow, someway, I have to find a way to keep my heart safe, even if I do let Ramsey have other parts of me. Curtis has been far too understanding and supportive for me to do anything but the bare minimum to make good on my contractual obligations to Ramsey. Meanwhile, I need to do more for Curtis to show him I'm not forgetting about him.

WHEN RAMSEY COMES through the bedroom door a few minutes after Curtis gets on the phone with me, my heart seizes up in my chest. There's a boyish grin on his face, and his eyes sweep the room for me like he has something funny he wants to tell me. They fall on me a moment later in my bed just as Curtis's voice comes through the phone.

"You got my cock, baby? I don't want you using any other toys while I'm gone. Just mine." Curtis groans, and then the sound of his grunt comes through the phone as he jerks his hand over his dick.

"Yes," I say softly in return, letting the tip of the toy brush over my clit as I tease myself with it under the covers. A torture I deserve.

Regret fills me as Ramsey's eyes darken and his jaw goes tight. I should have locked the door and made sure he wasn't coming back home until later. I'd still tell him I had phone sex with Curtis, because we don't keep secrets. But seeing it on his face—watching that playful grin of his fade to something more haunting—makes me feel awful.

"Good girl. Fuck yourself with my cock. Fill that pussy. I'm already close, baby. I've been missing you. We have to do this more often. I need to hear you," Curtis continues, wholly unaware that my husband is looming over the bed listening to the whole thing.

"So full of you. I wish you were here. I need fucked," I bluster on, my hand shaking under the covers, even though there's no vibration from the toy.

Ramsey's eyes widen and fall over me. I can see the irritated tick of his jaw, and his eyes float back to the phone as Curtis moans through it. Ramsey loses his patience a moment later, ripping back the quilt that's covering me, and the cool air lashes over my skin. I'm bare from the waist down, my panties discarded to the side. I've got the DIY clone-a-dick Curtis made for our anniversary just slipping inside me again as Ramsey fully realizes what's happening. I watch him process it, his face a swift wave of emotion before it goes blank again.

He kneels on the edge of the bed—his eyes locked on me and mine on him. I'm waiting for him to react, expecting he'll say something—do something to mock me or piss Curtis off—but he stays quiet. Just watching and waiting while I keep fucking myself with the toy.

"Oh fuck. I'm close. Are you close, baby? Let me hear you if you are."

I'm not. I'm too distracted by Ramsey. I've lost all ability to focus on my already unlikely orgasm because he's there, glow-ering at me like I'm some kind of harlot who's betraying him.

"Yes," I lie, and Ramsey can tell. A self-satisfied smirk forms in the wake of his realization. He looks like a villain with the way his lips curl into it.

"Tell daddy how much you love it," Curtis half speaks, half squeaks the words as he gets closer to coming.

"I love it, Daddy. I love your cock so much," I answer. And if I didn't regret doing this to Ramsey before, I regret it now when he watches me say those words while I half-heartedly slide the toy in and out. Ramsey stifles a laugh, and I glare at him, pulling the toy away and starting to sit up.

But Ramsey grabs my thighs and pins me in place. My eyes snap to his, and we're locked in a battle of silent wills for full seconds before he grabs the hand I still have wrapped around the toy and guides it back between my legs. He helps me push it inside, his eyes never leaving mine. His thumb brushes over me, and he massages small circles over my clit until I start to raise my hips to meet it with counter friction.

I can hear Curtis coming in the background over the phone. Gasping and stuttering as he fucks his hand somewhere in Vegas. But all I can think about—all I can feel—is Ramsey's hands on me again. Then he does the unthinkable; he leans down and wraps his lips around my tender, swollen clit. The sensation is almost too much, and I buck up under it like I might jump from the bed entirely. His strong arms wrap around my thighs tighter and pin me back down, and he starts to suck on my clit in earnest until I cry out from how good it feels.

"Oh god. I haven't heard you sound this good in forever, baby. You must miss my cock that much, huh?" Curtis laughs through the phone.

I'm too busy coming hard against Ramsey's mouth to

respond, muttering curses and running my fingers through his hair as I fuck his face and Curtis's toy at the same time. When I stop gasping, and my breathing starts to slow to a more normal pace, I brave a glance down between my thighs. Ramsey looks like a fucking devil, his lashes are low, and his eyes are shadowed by them.

He raises back onto his knees and pulls himself out of the sweats he has on. I gasp when I see it—a metal bar pierced straight through from top to bottom. One that wasn't there before.

"You still going, baby?" Curtis asks.

"Yes," I answer absently. "Going again." Because fuck do I want to, but with the real thing this time. The version I've missed in the middle of the night more times than I can count.

"Oh fuck. That fucking horny tonight? You must really miss my cock." I can hear Curtis's smile through the phone, but it's a backdrop to what happens next.

Ramsey's hand slips between my legs and wets his fingers with my come before he wraps his hand around his cock and starts to fuck himself. The sound of it is intoxicating and watching my come make the metal bar on his cock glisten has me in stunned silence.

"Baby?" Curtis asks.

"Hmm?" I respond, my eyes locked on the way Ramsey starts to pick up his pace. Precum starts to leak from the tip of his cock, and I'm so tempted to sit up and lick it off that it startles me when Curtis speaks again.

"Do you miss my cock?" Curtis asks the question like he's already repeated it several times. My eyes lift to meet Ramsey's, and his brow is raised in amusement, his teeth dig into his lower lip as he tries to mute the groans coming from his chest as he fucks himself harder.

"I miss it so much. I want to hear you come again," I answer

Curtis, but my eyes are still locked on Ramsey, and he knows the words are meant for him.

"I can try, baby. Let me see if I can stroke it back to life. I need you to talk me through it though." Curtis sounds doubtful.

I hit the mute button as Ramsey starts to come. He's loud, moaning and gasping as he fucks his hand; his come spills out over me. It paints my chest and abdomen, leaving hot streaks of it dripping down my skin. He jerks out a few more strokes and lets it pool on my lower belly as I watch.

I feel the kind of used and dirty only he can give me as he bends over me, draining the last of himself over my ribs and stomach. He stares down at his work, highly amused at the mess he's made of me. He grabs my panties to wipe himself off and his self-satisfied grin grows wider as he tosses them to the floor.

He looks back down at my stomach and slips the tip of his finger through the mess, drawing letters on my skin with his come. An "M" first, and then an "I." He pauses to admire them before he continues with an "N," and then finishes with a flourished "E." He stares at it for a long moment while Curtis grunts through the phone, clearly frustrated at a lack of progress.

"Baby? I think I need to hear you say it again. You know how much it helps." Curtis breaks the silence that's starting to grow.

I blink, remembering that I started this and asked him for more. But Ramsey's eyes lift from admiring his work, and his eyebrow arches in a threat as I unmute the phone again.

"Yes, Daddy. I'm here. I need more," I say, softly defiant even as he looms over me. Ramsey's expression darkens, and his jaw goes tight. "I need you inside me," I add for good measure. I might be weak for him, but it doesn't mean he owns me.

Ramsey's teeth clench, and a muted growl rumbles from his

chest. He reaches over me and hits the button to kill the call before his eyes return to mine.

"Enough," he roars.

"He'll just call back," I say, whisper-quiet in my response.

Ramsey's fingertips trace up my arm, over my shoulder, and slide between my neck and the pillow I'm resting against. His fingers thread through my hair, and he tightens his grip until my jaw tilts back, and my neck is exposed. His teeth scrape against my skin, and then he sinks them in, biting me hard in a way that's going to leave a mark. Only letting up when I finally yield and cry out his name. Then his head draws up again, his lips against my ear.

"Mine," he growls. "Every single inch for the next two months. You fuck with me like this again, I'll make you pay for it. When he calls back, you can tell *Daddy* you have a husband you're busy worshiping now."

He releases me, and he's off the bed and out the doorway in record time. The door slams shut in his wake, and he storms down the hall while his come is still warm on my stomach. My jaw is still on the floor as I try to process what he's just said, what he's just done.

The sound of my phone ringing echoes on the walls, jolting me out of my daze, and I hit the answer button. It's Curtis again, as predicted, asking me what happened and if I want to keep trying for a second round.

"I have to go. Ramsey's home and I don't want him to hear us."

"Oh. Okay," Curtis whispers in return. "Have a good night then. Love you, baby."

"Night," I mumble and hang up, only realizing when I put my phone on my nightstand that I didn't tell him I love him back.

I grab some tissues from my drawer and wipe the scrawled

word from my abdomen, slowly and deliberately so that I'm not getting it on the comforter when I stand. He'd already made of mess of me, but I didn't have to let him make a mess of everything.

I knew Ramsey had this side in him, but I'd never seen it in quite this way before. The brilliant sort of rage that leaves him completely unchecked. I have concerns about my sanity—because I think I like it, enough that I want more.

EIGHTEEN

Ramsey

I STOP short when the smell from the kitchen hits me. It's my mom's casserole. My favorite thing she used to make, and I haven't had it in years. No one makes it the way she did. I tried once or twice. But I swear I'm about to round the corner and see her standing there in her apron. She always did her best for us, trying to make it feel like we grew up in a normal home with a normal life and had a Susie homemaker for a mom.

I kick off my boots, careful not to get the mud on her floors, and set them in the tray. Another scent wafts around the edge. Apples and cinnamon. I get my answer a second later when I see my favorite apple pie cookies cooling on the counter, caramel dripping over the edge and steam still rising from the top. My girl has a lot of good qualities, but baking and cooking has never been a thing she's eagerly embraced. The last thing I thought she'd do is break into my mom's old cookbooks. So I'm curious if she made the food or if she's just brought it over from Kit's kitchen to ours.

But a couple more steps, and I see Haze standing in front of an open oven, pulling a casserole out with oven mitts and an apron on. She's concentrating so hard on not dropping it or burning herself, I don't want to say a thing to distract her. The look of relief on her face when she sets it on the stove and checks it, finding it unburnt, makes me grin.

Not that I should smile at her. She's done everything she can in the last few days to drive me off, and it was damn close to working last night. Except for the fact that I'm every fucking bit as stubborn as she is when I want to be. I watch her exhale as she takes off her oven mitts one by one and stacks them on top of each other next to the stove. She glances over at the pile of dirty dishes in the sink and sighs, looking exhausted.

"What's all this?" I ask, startling her in the process. She presses her hand to her chest and turns around.

"I thought..." She takes in my sweat-soaked, dirty appearance for a moment, and then her eyes snap back up to mine. "I thought you'd be hungry after all the work you did today. So I cooked dinner."

"I could've just had Kit make something."

"I know, but I..." she trails off, looking into the distance, then shaking her head and looking at the floor. "I'm sorry about the last few days. I wanted to make a point, but I took it too far last night."

"Since when can you cook?" I change the subject. I'm not in the mood for discussing last night. Not until I'm showered and fed. Until then, I'm gonna be too fucking cranky not to say shit I don't mean. Like telling her what a little bitch her boyfriend is for needing her toys to be shaped like his shriveled dick when he isn't around.

"I've been learning. Kit has been teaching me a few things."

"She into my mom's recipe book now?" I nod at the casserole.

"No. I am," she answers softly.

Which means she's been cooking him meals out of it. Serving him my mother's recipes at her table. I see red all over again, even if it's irrational.

"I want the cookbook when we're done here. It should be in the family." I move toward the hallway to take my shower.

"Ramsey!" she calls after me, and I pause, looking back over my shoulder. "Please eat dinner." She gives me doe eyes. The kind that always used to work on me whenever we fought, and my heart twists just that little bit. Enough that my arm twists with it, and I agree.

"Fine. Let me get a quick shower." I need space for a few moments, time to wash the day off and remind myself that if I want to win her over, I'm going to have to swallow my pride more than once. This whole arrangement is going to drive me to the brink of what's left of my sanity.

I FINISH two helpings of the casserole because it tastes that fucking good, and the nostalgia bleeds into my heart with each bite. She serves me my favorite beer with it, like she remembers everything and knows exactly how to weaponize it all against me. It's a war I started; I should have been prepared for her to fight it. But she's winning battle after battle, even when I think I'm on offense.

When she sees my empty plate, she stands abruptly, wiping the corner of her mouth and setting her napkin aside as she eyes it.

"Do you want more?"

"No. I'm good." I set the fork and knife on the edge of the

plate. "It was good though." I'm trying to offer some semblance of a peace offering to her.

"Do you want some of the apple pie cookies? Kit helped me make them so they shouldn't be too awful." She offers up a smile, and that has me wondering what trap she's laying for me now. I lose my ability to keep up the pretense even as she continues. "I have vanilla ice cream too if you want that or whipped—"

"What's all this about?" I ask, interrupting her, and her brow furrows in response. She blinks a few times and then shrugs, looking down at the table.

"I'm sorry. For before. All the tormenting... and Curtis. I think I took things too far with you, and I didn't mean to hurt you, if that's what I did." She hedges her apology, and I want to deny it. I want to tell her my ego is bulletproof, and she didn't touch my feelings. But it'd be a lie. Hearing her talk that way to him had felt like being stabbed after the progress I thought we were making.

"You could have just said that this morning."

"I wanted to make up for it somehow. This was the best I could come up with."

"Why?"

"I told you... I felt bad after last night. I shouldn't have pushed you like that."

"That's what we do best, isn't it? Push each other's buttons." I stand and grab my plate, headed for the kitchen sink.

I want air. Time away from her. Because sitting here eating dinner together. Coming home to her after a long day. It was the kind of thing I dreamed of when I was younger, and I feel like a fucking fool for tormenting myself with it now when I know I can't have it. She might want me in her bed, but she wants him in this seat—and that's going to eat at my heart until it fucking withers.

"Ramsey, please..." She reaches out, and her hand slips around my wrist, dropping when I don't stop. "Ramsey!" she pleads as she hops up from her seat and follows me into the kitchen.

I whirl around on her and study her as she stops short of me.

"What do you want?" I snap, harsher than I even intend.

"I want to..." Her eyes lift to the ceiling and then back down to her hands, where her thumb rubs over the surface of one of her dark red nails. "Live up to the bargain we made. You said you'd give me a couple of weeks, and you did. So I want to make good on it. If you really want to sleep in my—our—bed tonight. You can."

"I think I sleep better without having to listen to your guy moan like a stuck pig."

Her lips quirk up in a smile for half a moment before she smothers it and tries to look remorseful.

"I won't do that again."

"And you know what I want doesn't involve sleep," I press, because if I can't have what I want, I'll take what I can get.

She nods, and she looks at the floor. "I know."

"What's the catch? How are you tricking me tonight?" I slip my hand under her chin, and her eyes lift to meet mine.

"No catch. No trick," she insists.

I study her, her pale-blue eyes taking me in at the same time. They drift down to my lips, and I can tell she's thinking about last night. I lean in, closing the distance between us to kiss her, imagining what it's going to be like to finally feel her warm, plush lips against mine again. I'm drunk on it before I even touch her. And just as I'm about to finally have it—have her—again, she takes a step back and puts a canyon's worth of space in between us.

"But I do have one rule," she says softly. I close my eyes and bite my tongue for a full ten seconds before I speak. I'm doing my best, but even I have my fucking limits. I force a smile when I reopen my eyes.

"You have a lot more than one rule, sugar." I raise my brow to find her matching my expression in defiance.

"No kissing."

"You didn't mind me kissing you last night." I do my best to mask the way the request tears into me.

"I mean on the lips."

"Again…" I smirk.

"Don't be a smartass."

I reach out and run my thumb over her lower lip, trying to make peace with the fact I won't get what I want—yet. But I will. Eventually, she's going to cave, and I can wait as long as it takes.

"Fair enough. This set only spits poison, and the other tastes like sugar, so it's not much of a loss."

She lets out a little sigh and shakes her head at my comment. Her eyes are still on me, though, studying my face and lost in thought. All I can think about is how much I want inside her. How none of the rest of it will matter when I'm buried in her and she's saying my name.

"Any more rules? I want to know them now." I run my fingers down her jaw, and she leans into my touch.

NINETEEN

Hazel

"NO OTHER RULES." I shake my head. I probably need some. A lot of them where he's concerned, if we're being honest. Anytime I'm around Ramsey Stockton I'm in danger of losing everything—my mind, my dignity, *my heart*. I straighten and pull myself out of his grip, leaning back from him. I have to remember that part of me needs distance.

"You sure about that?" He takes one step forward, and I take one step back. I know what he's asking. It's not like I could forget the kind of games we used to play—the ones I asked him for. I nod my yes as I watch him close the distance between us, and my ass bumps the counter behind me.

"There's no other part of yourself you want to save for him?" His lashes lower as his eyes leave my mouth and run over my body. He rolls his lower lip between his teeth as he surveys me, and the sheen it leaves behind has me wanting to lick him already. Not kissing him has nothing to do with Curtis and everything to do with saving myself.

I shake my head.

"Use your words, sugar." He snaps my attention back to the present.

"No," I confirm with a subtle shake of my head.

"You should set limits now if you have them," he warns.

"They're the same as they've always been." With him at least.

Another thing he doesn't need to know is that I've never let anyone else explore them. I might hate him, but there's no one in the world I trust like him. There's not a misleading bone in Ramsey's body, and that kind of blunt honesty makes me feel safe in a way no one else ever has.

"Well then, it's not like he thought he was getting a virgin on his wedding night, right? All the things I taught you. I get why you lied to him. It'd crush his ego to know how thoroughly I fucked you. All the ways you let me have you. How much better I can fill up this perfect body. How loud you get when I make you come..." His hands coast their way down my sides, and everything is already pooling low and warm.

I'm a very weak woman when he's in this sort of mood. Especially because he's also painfully aware of the truth without being told, and I have no intention of confirming that secret for his ego.

"Sometimes, bigger isn't always better. With some men it doesn't matter what size they are, just that they know how to use it to their advantage."

"Some of us are lucky enough to have it all." His lips are on the side of my throat.

"Is that what all your girls told you?" I regret the question as soon as I ask it. I don't really want to know. I'm as bitter as I am curious, even if it's not fair. "I bet they say anything when they see those tight little pants you wear on the field and all those zeroes in your bank account."

He pulls back like I've slapped him, but then a slow light of recognition forms as his eyes search mine.

"You sure did." He smirks, and I shove back at his chest, trying to create space between us, but he doesn't move.

"Fuck you," I grit out.

"That's what this is about, right? The dinner and the sudden willingness to have me in your bed. The apology. You're worried if you don't hold up the bargain, I won't pay out."

I'm in deep now, between a rock and a hard place. If I tell him the truth—that I actually want him, desperately, he'll run with it and use it against me. He already has enough aces up his sleeve for a lifetime. If I agree with him, I'm going to undo everything I've been trying to do today—and despite the fact I still hate him, some part of me is going soft on him too. Like my heart knows its missing piece is back on this ranch, no matter how many times I've tried to snuff it out.

"Maybe you're just so used to it, you're projecting. Maybe you didn't even have to dangle the million in front of me to get me into bed. But now you'll never know, will you?" I taunt him.

His smirk deepens and turns devilish. He leans forward, one hand on the counter, bracketing me in as he tilts his head down to whisper in my ear.

"The bigger question is will I care when this spiteful little mouth is too busy gagging on my cock—and I already know the answer to that."

I reach down and run my fingers over his belt, undoing the leather from the buckle.

"Can't blame you there. Those fancy ones never do learn how to get their knees dirty and swallow gracefully, do they?" I pull his belt loose and let it drop to the floor, my fingers making quick work of the buttons and zipper next. His hands still mine.

"You don't have to rush, sugar. I'm gonna use you all night long."

"All night?" I taunt him, my lashes lifting. "Let's be honest. You're probably gonna come the second your dick hits my tongue."

His eyes darken at the implication, and he grabs me, pulling me close and then turning me around until my back faces his front, pinning me against the counter. He sweeps my hair off my neck and nips his way down my spine.

"I was gonna go easy on you. Break you back in slowly," he rasps against my skin as his hands work on my button and zipper, wrenching my jeans and panties down to my knees. "But we can do it your way."

He wraps his hand around the back of my neck and forces me down against the counter. A moment later, I feel his cock slam inside of me. There's a guttural sound from his chest and a low moan as he eases out and back in again. He takes what he wants from me, and I let him have it.

"Fuck me. Tight as you ever were." He grunts.

He feels so fucking good. Like mine. Like *home*.

"And so fucking wet. Goddamn. You were soaking those panties all through dinner just hoping I'd fuck you, weren't you, sugar?"

He starts fucking me harder, and I can't stop the soft moans that come out of me. Ones he's eating up with every single thrust, gloating and murmuring about how much I've needed him. He grabs my ass cheek and digs his fingers into the flesh, squeezing so hard it hurts, and I hiss out a muted "fuck."

"Use your fingers on that swollen clit. I want you coming with me," he grits out the instruction, and I follow it, slipping my fingers through my own wetness and working slowly around the tender spot.

"You're gonna have to get used to being fucked by someone who knows how to handle you."

I'm counting on it. Curtis treats me like I'm glass. Like the wrong move could be a mistake and send me crashing to the floor in pieces. Ramsey got over that fear years ago.

I hear him spit a second later, the warmth of it slipping down between my cheeks. His fingers slip through it, and then I feel him circle around the second, tighter entrance, one that yields to the tip of his finger a moment later. I gasp at the sensation, and I hear him grunt his approval.

"You let him fuck you here yet, or are you saving that for the wedding night like you did for me?"

"I haven't—" I barely get the words out because I'm already close, muttering another curse before I can finish the sentence. His cock is deep inside me, his finger teasing my ass, and my fingers circling my clit, all of it working in perfect rhythm and giving me more of what I need in a few short minutes than I've had in years.

"That's good, sugar. I'm glad you know what belongs to me."

"I don't belong to you." I manage to get the words out in between moans, and it's less than convincing. So pathetic that he lets out a low, rumbling laugh.

"You might not, but this body remembers exactly who owns it."

"Fuck you, Ramsey."

"I intend to. Over and over again until I break you back in, and you remember who holds the fucking reins."

"I won't. You don't fucking own anything about me." I fight him. I don't know why. Somewhere deep inside I know the odds aren't in my favor—but I still have hope this is nothing but closure for us.

"I own you. Your house. Your name. Your body." Each word is a punctuated thrust. "And every single time, you've come wishing it was me when you fucked him."

I feel him coming inside me, and I tighten the circle around my clit with my fingers. A moment later, the pleasure blooms through me, lightning hot, and I'm nearly screaming from how good it feels. At least until I feel his come, hot and heavy inside me, and the alarm spreads. He didn't have a condom on, and he knows I take medications that make my birth control unreliable. We were always careful when we were married.

"No condom," I hiss.

"I asked if there was something you wanted to save for him." I hear him let out a dark chuckle.

But he pulls out of me and grabs his cock, pressing it against my cheeks as he uses his hand to finish himself, and the last few surges of his warmth seep down between them.

"Fuck me. Look at you covered in me. Just like you should be." He uses his come like lube and his finger presses into my ass one last time. His free hand grabbing a fistful of my hair and pulling me straight again.

"I'm gonna get my money's worth and fill every single fucking part of this gorgeous body. Every fucking day. Until you're so fucking broken for me, you can't even fathom coming without me." His lips make their way down the side of my neck, punctuating the descent with kisses. He bites my shoulder as he pulls away from me. "Now, go get cleaned up so you can put on your dress. You can go back to your guests at the inn and pretend like you didn't just enjoy your husband fucking you like an obedient little wife."

I pull my jeans up while he watches, tucking himself back in and buttoning his pants once more. His eyes follow me as I leave, and I take my time doing it, half wishing he'd come with me and take me again on the bed.

I need to get a grip.

When I get back to the master bathroom, I collapse against the sink, taking in a deep breath and my freshly fucked appearance in the mirror. I'm fucked—in every possible way—because I hate my husband to my core, but I'm also addicted to everything he gives me. One little taste won't be enough to last me as long as I'll need it to in a life without him.

TWENTY

Ramsey

AFTER I HELP with chores in the stables, I take a break, sitting on one of the fences. The sun's setting, and the ranch has that perfect golden-hour glow. It's one of the most beautiful places on earth when it looks like this. I can understand exactly why my family settled here decades ago, and why my parents held on so tight even as their interests drew them away from it. If I have to leave here, walk away from it, and give it to her, I will. I'll know it's in good hands but...

I want to stay. Every moment I've been back on this ranch has made me sorry I ever left. I just don't know how I could have done things differently. Football was the only thing I was ever good at, and staying here, reliving finding my parents in a pool of their own blood on the front porch every day I walked past it, would have driven me mad. It reopened the wound every time I saw the stains in the boards. The ones no amount of scrubbing could ever get out.

Now, at least, they've been replaced. The old wooden porch swapped with a modern one, the door that had been splattered with blood tossed for a gorgeous hand-carved piece one of the woodworkers in town created, and the rare flowers that my mother had always grown along the front, the ones that wilted so quickly in her absence, replaced by wildflowers—Hazel's favorite. But I could still see the good moments—my dad, sitting at the dining table Hazel kept, smiling as my mother made her casserole in the kitchen. Hazel updated the counters to quartz and replaced the backsplash with a color she loves, but the mosaics my mom and she picked out together still sit over the kitchen sink.

This whole place is a patchwork of the people I love, their mark on everything from the house to the stables to the inn, and I'm not about to let it go without a fight. One I imagine is going to be hard fought when I see Hazel leave the inn and cross the lawn to the house in a huff. She's going to make me crawl on my hands and knees over broken glass for any glimmer of a chance at making things right. A chance I feel like is fading faster than I can fight for it.

But for her and this place, I'd do just about anything.

I pull my cowboy hat off the post and put it back on my head before I hop off the fence. I drop the last of the gear back in the stables, take off my gloves, and bid Wolfsbane and the rest of the horses a goodnight before I wave off Kell and Elliot for the evening too. Then I sneak back into the house quietly, hoping I can get a shower in, then find her to spend a couple of hours with my face between her thighs, apologizing for how rough I was with her.

But I only get as far as the door of the master bath when I find her. The massive copper tub that sits in front of the even larger picture window is drawn with hot water. She's spread out in it, looking like a goddess, her blue hair draped over the back, and her hands gripping the sides. Her eyes are closed, and steam rolls off the surface of the water as she takes it all in. Her chest rises and falls, her breasts cresting over the water, and her nipples bob in and out of it with each breath.

"Long day?" I ask. She barely startles, like she knew I was there and didn't care but just didn't expect me to speak.

"Incredibly long. That woman with the kid is leaving tomorrow, but she wanted to air all her grievances first. My asshole ex-husband didn't appreciate the dinner I cooked him that took two hours to make. There's a leak in one of the radiators in the drawing room, and Albert's off for the week."

I cross the room to the tub, kneeling down at the side of it and taking my hat off, placing it at my knees. One of her eyes pops open as she presses the other tighter shut to study my behavior, but she stays quiet like she's waiting for my thoughts on her situation.

"The good news is she'll be gone soon. I can look at the radiator tomorrow and at least patch it until Al can take care of it. I don't know about your ex-husband, but your current husband loved the dinner."

"The dinner or what came after it?" Her eyes close again.

"Both." I clear my throat. "I said some things in the heat of the moment, Haze, that I—"

Her hand, perfumed and damp from the bath, covers my mouth, and she shakes her head.

"Don't ruin it by apologizing."

I can't see the emotion in her eyes, but her lips curl at the edge, and my heart rate thrums in response.

"I hadn't planned on apologizing, just keeping the promise I made earlier." I kiss her fingertips, and her hand slips off my mouth and down my chest.

"Hmm," she hums in response. "I was just thinking that I wish I had my toys, since *someone* still hasn't given them back."

"Let me back in my bed, and they all go back where I found them."

Her eyes open ever so slightly and drift over my form.

"Deal."

I smile at her easy agreement.

"Don't get excited. You smell like sweat and hay."

"That used to turn you on."

"Still does, but you're not getting in the bed like that."

"No?"

"No."

"What am I doing?" I slip my hand down into the warm water, following the curve of her body underneath the bubbles until my fingers slip between her legs. I use my index and middle finger to tease the sides of her clit. Her head tilts back, more of her hair slipping over the edge, and she rolls her lower lip between her teeth as a soft moan escapes.

"More of this. Giving me the orgasm I deserve, and then taking a long shower before you come to bed."

I lean over the edge of the tub, kissing the side of her neck and making my way down to her breast.

"I can do that," I agree, because I might not have my girl back, but she's willing to play, and that's the first step.

TWENTY-ONE

Hazel

I'M BOUNCING around the inn this morning, trying to make sure all the activities are set up for the weekend, confirm the performer for our late-night local history and cupcakes event, figure out what's wrong with one of our dryers, and confirm the menu Kit's put together for the fall menu changeover that's coming in a few weeks. Then, hopefully, we can start putting in produce and grocery orders and be that much closer to set for our next big round of guests. Grace comes back to my office, though, to tell me we have some special visitors. I raise my brow in question.

"Amelia's here, and a couple who say they're friends of Ramsey's?"

I'd forgotten what day it was and missed that it was Amelia's arrival, and that was on me, but I had no idea Ramsey had invited friends out.

"They all have reservations?" I ask, wondering if he comped them on my behalf.

"Yes." Grace looks thoughtfully between me and my book-keeping.

"Okay. Start checking them in, and I'll be right up there." I rack my brain to see if Ramsey mentioned anything, but I don't remember it.

Amelia, on the other hand, has come back year after year to visit the inn. She's a sweet older woman, and she always reserves the same room with a view of the ranch and the mountains beyond it. She's obsessed with Kit's cooking, and I always manage to spend some time with her each visit, listening to stories about her childhood and the exotic trips she and her husband used to take when he was alive. I smile just thinking about her because she's one of my favorite guests.

When I reach the lobby, Grace has already checked the couple in, and they're gathering their bags.

"Can I help you with anything?" I ask. Several of our employees went back to college earlier than anticipated this season, so Grace and I have been doing the check-ins, the request runs, and the baggage until I hire someone new. Which needs to be sooner rather than later and a thing I need to get on the to-do list.

"Nah. I think we've got it." The guy smiles at me, and I immediately recognize him when he does. He'd been on the TV over and over again speaking out in Ramsey's defense and giving testimony about his character to the court. Cooper Rawlings. The former star wide receiver for the Queen City Chaos, Ramsey's teammate, and the guy whose life he saved. The woman next to him also looks familiar. She did a lot of the press work for Ramsey in the wake of his arrest, and she was also related to a football player for the Seattle Phantom, if I remember correctly. I'm racking my brain for her name when she steps forward and introduces herself.

"I'm Beatrix Xavier, and this is Cooper Rawlings. We're friends of Ramsey's. You must be Hazel?"

"That's me." I smile softly.

"This place is gorgeous. I can't believe how beautiful it is out here. And so cozy inside. I can't wait to see the rooms. I hope you don't mind that we just popped in. I saw you had a room available, and I knew if we called ahead, Ramsey would tell us not to bother." Beatrix is all warmth and smiles. The kind of person who's hard not to like from the moment you meet them.

"We just want to check up on him. Make sure he's doing all right after everything," Cooper adds.

"Of course. We're so happy to have you. If you want to go up and get settled in your room, I can go find Ramsey out on the ranch and send him back here."

"Are you sure you don't mind? We don't want to impose."

"No. No problem at all. I think I know where he is anyway." I turn back and wave at Amelia who I can tell is waiting to talk to me. "I'll be right back in a bit! Grace can get you checked in."

"Of course, dear. No problem." She grins, and I nod my goodbyes before hurrying off.

I RUN AROUND HALF the ranch and find Ramsey where I should have looked in the first place—in the stables with Wolfsbane on their way back from a ride. When I let him know his friends have come for a surprise visit, he looks wildly confused, worried, and then happy—his face running the gamut of emotions at the news in rapid order. He hands Wolfsbane off to

Elliot with some protest, and we both go back inside together, breaking for him to follow his friends upstairs and me to find Amelia.

"Hazel!" she gushes when she opens her door. "You didn't have to come all the way back here, sweetheart. I can get myself settled."

"No! Let me help you with your bags, at least. I'll get some tea going and help you get settled in."

"It's so good to see you." She smiles at me, letting me take her larger bag and tuck it in the closet now that she has it unpacked.

"It's good to see you. I'm sorry about that. I was all prepared for your visit when Grace told me you were coming this month after all. But I didn't know about my husband's friends coming. Had to rush around to get things done for them."

"Your husband's friends? I thought the wedding wasn't for a bit yet. I set my save the date out on the mantel!" She looks at me with worry.

"Oh, yes. About that..." I blush because I'm not sure how to explain all of this to my sweet older friend. "Well. It's a bit complicated in that I'm still married from my first marriage. We thought the divorce had gone through years ago, but it turns out, it hadn't. So we're working our way through that mess now."

"Oh no. Don't tell me you've lost the fiancé?"

I hate lying to Amelia, but the truth would make this even more complicated. "We're on a bit of a break while my previous husband and I figure the divorce out."

"Oh, honey! I'm so sorry. I was so looking forward to the wedding. Curtis is such a sweetheart, and I loved how well you two got along when I saw you last summer."

"Me too. I'm sorry it's such a mess for everyone involved,

but I'm still hopeful it'll all get worked out." If I didn't get worked out in the process anyway. Not that I'm about to share that with Amelia.

"Well... we have to catch up. You'll have to tell me all the details."

"Definitely. I'm not sure what the plans are going to be now that his friends are here, but it sounded like they had a short reservation. If I can't catch up with you in the next day or two, we'll definitely do dinner or lunch one day this week."

"I'll hold you to that!" She grins at me as I start up the tea kettle for her and put out a box of teas and a few of the cookies Kit baked this morning.

When I finish getting Amelia settled in, I go in search of Ramsey and his friends. I find them in the stables, surrounding Wolfsbane while they chat. I'm apprehensive as I approach because it's obvious the three of them are close and clearly locked in a deep conversation about something—Ramsey's parole, if I had to guess.

Sure enough. It's the topic of discussion. They move from that one to a discussion of Cooper's proposal a few moments later when Ramsey notices a flash of light on Bea's hand as she pets Wolfsbane. It's enough to make me want to melt into the floor or at least disappear to a dark part of the stables because the next question is about us.

"You must be so excited to have Ramsey back." Bea grins at me. "We're all quite sad we've lost him to Colorado for the time being."

"He's been a lot of help around here for sure." I force my face into the appropriate order.

"She's being kind. I've mostly been a pain in her ass, but she's tolerating me pretty well." Ramsey smiles at me and turns to his friends. "Trying to earn her goodwill back, mucking one horse stall at a time. Ain't that right, darlin'?" He glances back at me.

"I am trying to put him through his paces." I return the beaming smile he has plastered on. I feel simultaneously happy for him and envious that there's this version of him I haven't known before. It's clear he has an easy friendship with them, inside jokes and a softer demeanor than I've seen him have in this town. A whole life outside the one he had here it seems. One I know absolutely nothing about and one that appears so different from my Ramsey.

"Well, someone has to keep an eye on him, or he gets into trouble," Cooper muses, looking back at his friend. I nod, and we stand in silence for a few moments before Bea finally turns it around.

"We need to go riding!" Bea turns to Cooper with a hopeful look.

"I haven't been on a horse since I was a kid. This close to the season, they'll kick my ass if I fall off a horse and hurt myself trying to impress you."

Ramsey laughs. "Yeah, I'm not gonna be held responsible for that. Enough people on the Chaos coaching team are still mad at me."

"I can take you out for a ride if you want," I offer to Bea, and her brown eyes light up as she turns to look at me.

"You wouldn't mind? It's been so long, and I used to love it so much." Bea smiles.

"Of course not. We can ride out to the falls and back. It'll take us a couple of hours, but we can take some food and drinks with us, if you're up for it." She's so kind it's hard not to want to indulge her. I wouldn't mind learning a little about Ramsey's other life in the process.

"Sounds perfect."

"You'll have to pick a different horse though. Wolf's picky about his riders." I flash a look at Ramsey, and he grins.

"Moody like his owner, is he?" Cooper laughs.

"Something like that." I shrug. "But Teddy and Lady Luck over here are both very patient with everyone."

"Ooh, Lady Luck. I like the sound of that." Bea pets Wolfsbane one last time.

"We're gonna head into town. I need to run an errand, and I figure I'll show Coop around town and grab some food." Ramsey looks at me.

"Meet back here for dinner?" I ask, and he nods.

"Perfect." Coop leans over and kisses his fiancée. "Have fun. Be careful, Trix."

"I will. See you later."

I hurry toward Lady Luck, hoping it looks like I'm too focused on getting Bea set up to remember to exchange the same pleasantries with my own husband. I have no idea what he's told them, or how I should behave around them—so for now, I'll just assume it's the same story we've given everyone else.

TWENTY-TWO

Hazel

AFTER KELL GETS the horses saddled for us and Bea puts on a pair of jeans, we head out on the trail. We chat for a bit about her lessons as a kid, how we both fell in love with horses, and we each share our favorite stories about trainers before we go quiet, just enjoying the view. When the trail along the river opens up to a better view of the falls, we slow down, and I direct us to a spot where we can stop and have lunch.

We get the horses set up first and then find a small spot nearby to set up our picnic. It feels good to stretch out, and there's a nice breeze blowing through that takes the heat of the day off my skin. The lunch Kit packed us is amazing, and she even managed to put a small bottle of wine and collapsable wine glasses in here.

"Your chef is amazing. I feel like I don't deserve this kind of lunch out on a trail." Bea beams as she pulls out her sandwich.

"She *is* amazing. Always coming up with fun new things.

She's been trying to convince me to do trail ride picnics for a while. I'm guessing this is her latest lobbying." I smile at how pretty the basket is packed, with matching napkins and containers. Each part of the meal neatly tucked into its own spot.

"I mean, this would be so romantic. With the weather like this and the view? Could you camp out here?" Bea asks as she takes in the expanse of it all.

"It's all still part of the ranch, so we could. If we offered it to guests, it'd be a little more complicated. We'd have to set up some facilities, make it more of a glamping situation."

"I wish Cooper and I could stay longer. He'd love this, and we could probably hike it."

"We have ATVs too for people who aren't big horse fans," I mention, although I doubt the ATVs would be on his allowed list of activities near his season starter either.

"Oh, that's perfect. Do you and Ramsey come out here much?" Bea tries to sneak a glance at me before she picks some grapes from the basket.

"Not recently. When we were younger, we used to ride out here sometimes."

"Please tell me he did something horribly romantic like proposed out here?"

I laugh. "It depends on how you define romantic. He's not much for the traditional sort."

"I get it. He can be so hard on the outside, but when I found out he was married, I was so curious about you."

A zip of apprehension climbs up my spine at that.

"Why?"

"I just imagine that with the right person, he is a complete sap. Or at least I want to imagine him that way. The hard ones falling hard. My brother was that way. But with Ramsey... I had to spend a lot of time with him, doing PR during the trial. We had to have him walk us through anything that could harm his image further."

"I'm sure I was on that list." I press my lips together as I pull one of the small turkey sandwiches Kit made out of its container.

"No. I mean... he thought you were his ex-wife at the time, but I asked if you'd be trouble. If you'd speak to the media or anything. I wanted to reach out proactively and offer any help we could on the media front, but he was adamant that we not 'drag her into anything' and said you wouldn't do anything to hurt him, even if they offered you money for it."

"I wouldn't have."

"The loyalty that the two of you have to each other... that's *something*. I know people who are together who don't have that kind of bond."

I shrug. "He was part of my family before I ever fell for him. He was my brother Bo's best friend for years, and he was always good to me. Even when I was just the annoying younger sister."

Bea smiles as she studies my face. "When did you fall for him?"

I shake my head. "I don't know exactly. I can't really remember a time when I didn't think he was amazing. I guess at some point when I was in my teens, I realized it was more than just friendship."

"Did he start things? Tell me he did. I want to believe he was this cute, sweet kid with a secret crush on his friend's sister. Dying to tell her but too scared to do it at first and then just blurting it out at the worst time."

I grin at her ability to paint a picture. It's sweet to see how in love she is—so much so that she's painting everyone around her with the same rose-colored shade.

"Not quite. My boyfriend at the time canceled plans to go

to junior prom with me at the last moment. I already had the dress, the tickets, and the plans with my friends. Everyone else had dates already. So I wasn't just getting dumped for the dance, but I was going to have to play wallflower too. Miss all the things I was looking forward too. I was crying about it at my locker, trying not to let anyone see. My friends' boyfriends had all these amazing plans—flowers, limos, corsages—and I was going to be the lone single girl with no one to even dance with. I was thinking about not going, but then it was junior prom. It only happens once in your life, you know? At the time, it seemed so important. You know how teens can be dramatic over those things."

"Yeah. I was the same way though, so I get it. Ramsey to the rescue, I'm guessing?" She gives me a hopeful look, and I nod.

"So I'm bawling my eyes out at my locker, and Ramsey walks by, the senior football player and all that infamy it comes with, with his entourage of friends and admirers. He sees me wiping my tears away, and he stops and asks me what's wrong, whose ass he 'needs to beat.' I was so grouchy with him because everyone was looking at me, and I was already humiliated, you know?"

"Oof. Yeah. High school wasn't easy for me either." I raise a brow because I can't imagine someone as prim and perfect as she seems didn't have it easy. I would have picked her for prom queen, if I had to guess.

"Ramsey eventually pried it out of me, and he wrapped his arm around my shoulder and took me with him down the hall-way. All the girls were jealous as hell. And my boyfriend saw me and lost it. He started talking shit to Ramsey, and the two of them ended up outside. They both threw a few punches, and Ramsey came back in, his knuckles all bloody, and he told me he was my ex-boyfriend now, and he'd pick me up for prom at five on Saturday." I laugh when I picture the audacity of teenage Ramsey. I suppose I should have known then how he'd turn out.

"Oh my god. I would have died for that kind of scene in high school. Straight out of a movie."

"Right? But I tried to protest because my brother Bo was his best friend. He was the quarterback, and he wasn't gonna be okay with Ramsey taking me out—even just for show."

"The plot thickens." Bea sits up a little straighter and pops a grape in her mouth.

"But Ramsey was like... 'I don't care what Bo says. You want to go to prom, I'm taking you.'" I deepen my voice as I pretend to be him.

"Oh god. I love it." Bea titters as she waits for more.

"So I went home and then just completely panicked. Ramsey was always just this... untouchable older guy, you know? And now I was going to have his undivided attention, and we were gonna have to talk about things. I was going to have to wear something amazing too because he never went to things like prom. He didn't dance, and he didn't do school-sponsored events. Too cool for all of that. So I knew everyone was going to be watching him—watching us. Some of those girls rooting for me to fuck it up and embarrass myself. I was terrified. I stressed about my dress, my makeup, my shoes... every little thing had to be reconsidered."

"So much pressure." Bea nods. "I can't imagine if Cooper had gone to my school and asked me to prom. I would have melted into a puddle."

"Right? I wanted to feign being sick to get out of it, but then Bo came home pissed off about it, ranting about breaking Ramsey's nose for going near his only sister. I didn't want Ramsey to have gone through all that trouble for nothing."

"Did you pull it off?"

"Yes. Thankfully. I called Bristol, my best friend, and she

came over and saved me. I loved makeup and all that, but she was always better at it than me. She had me all fixed up by that Saturday night and managed to look gorgeous herself too. She really is magic, honestly. When Ramsey picked me up, I think he just stared for thirty seconds first." I laugh as I think about the look on his face. "It was like he didn't recognize me."

Bea grins. "I would pay money to have seen that."

"It was awkward at first, but then the more we talked at dinner and in the car... the more relaxed he was. The more we realized how much we actually had in common. And I realized how hot he was."

"You didn't notice that right away?" Bea looks at me skeptically. "With the dark hair and the green eyes and that jawline? The broody sort of attitude he has. That would have killed in my high school."

"I mean, I knew he was attractive, objectively. But... you know... it was one of those things where he was Bo's friend, and I had never really looked at him like that. He ran around with my brothers, and that was that."

"But then you went to prom and he kissed you and happily ever after?"

I laugh, and she looks disappointed.

"No. More like we went to prom.... He danced exactly once to half a slow song because my friends antagonized him. Immediately after, he dropped me off under the watchful eye of my brothers, and then things went back to the way they were, for the most part."

"But you ended up married?" Bea gives me a confused look as she pours another glass of wine for both of us.

"We ended up at the same college."

"Ended up at?" Bea looks at me skeptically again, like she doesn't quite believe that was entirely a coincidence.

"Well, it was Highland State, so not far away or anything.

A good football school for him. It had a good hospitality management program for me." Even in college, I knew I wanted to run my own inn someday.

"Uh-huh." Bea's brow hikes up higher. "And then what?"

"That's a whole other story we don't have time for." I smirk.

"So you guys are on your third try then?"

I frown. "I don't know about that. I'm just trying to be there for him during his parole. What he did for you and Cooper, that's the kind of guy he is. I hate that they tried to smear him in the media. That that dead piece of shit's sister tried to come for him and his family. It was disgusting, after everything he did stalking you, that she'd even have the boldness to insinuate anything about Ramsey."

"Piece of shit or not, it was her brother. We all defend our family, don't we?" Bea asks thoughtfully.

I nod my agreement on that note. I didn't always agree with my brother's decisions, but I usually defend them regardless. Then again, they're not stalkers and attempted murderers.

"I'm just glad the two of you made it through all that."

"Me too." She gives me a soft smile, and we stare out at the view for a bit before she breaks the silence again.

"I know it's not my place, but the way he talks about you..."

"I was wondering when you were going to start lobbying for him." My smile fades a bit, but I try to maintain it.

"I won't say much. I just want you to know he obviously feels differently about you. You're something special to him, and from what I know, that's rare for him. Everything he's been through; I think you're one of the few people he still trusts."

"Yeah, well, the problem is... that only goes one way these days. There's a lot of water under the bridge. A lot of years and experiences that have changed people. You know?"

"Could you trust him again?"

I shrug. I want to trust him again, even if we can't make

things work. I do trust him with certain things. And given I'm living on his family's property in our hometown, I want us to at least part as friends when this is over. But it feels hopeless.

"There's about a mile's worth of flaming hoops he'd have to get through first."

"I think if you told him what he needed to do, or even just gave him a hint... he'd do it. He came back here for you."

I don't want to argue with her. I already like her after such a short time, and even if I don't agree with her feelings on Ramsey, I'm happy she's in his corner rooting for him. He deserves people like that in his life.

"You're a good friend. I'm glad he has you and Cooper out there."

I can't begin to explain how much pain and irreparable damage lies between us. How much of our past has seeped deep into our bones and become part of the fabric of who we are—for better or worse.

It's not something that can be fixed with one easy conversation, or we would have tried. But I also don't want to upset her, not when she's so adamant about him being here to make things right.

TWENTY-THREE

Ramsey

I TAKE Cooper around town until we end up at Morton's for lunch. He settles in across from me after taking in the bar and studying me for a moment.

"You really fit in here. You know that?"

"I'm from here, so I'd hope so."

"I know, but seeing this place, I get why you came back. I might have to see how Bea feels about it. Maybe we can find a cabin or something for sale up here. I'd love to have a vacation home in a place like this."

"You might be better off closer to one of the ski towns, at least finding something. A lot of the folks here are generational. They're never-sell-their-home types."

"But you're thinking about letting it go?" He looks at me thoughtfully as he takes a sip of his drink.

"I'm thinking about what my next move is in general."

"Well, I think if you want to come back to the Chaos,

there'll be room for you next year. If you stay in shape, keep training, all that... They only signed the guy to a one-year deal. I know everyone fucking misses you, and Quentin, Easton, and I would all kill to have you back. Most of the guys really. The only holdouts would be the ones who went to college with the new guy. You know how that is."

I laugh. "Yeah, I know how that is."

"But the coaches I know have already grumbled about missing you in camps."

"Well, I appreciate being missed."

"Would you come back?" Cooper's question is pointed.

"I mean. I miss playing a fuckton. Being on that field. Playing with you guys. There's nothing like it in the world. I just don't want to set my hopes too high." The idea of never setting foot on a gametime field again haunts me, but I know the reality of my situation.

"I swear, I honestly think there's a ninety-percent chance of you coming back. Barring the new guy being Superman and shooting to the top of the league in sacks or something this year... They'd rather have you out there." Cooper tries to comfort my ego.

"I guess it's wait and see then. I'd like to be back out there. It also just depends on how all this goes." I glance back over my shoulder in the direction of the ranch—not that my chances there are any better.

"All this being your wife?"

"Yeah. Her. The ranch. Being home. I forgot how much I loved everything here." I wince as I admit it.

"Are you guys really giving it a try? I know you mentioned she was engaged, but they broke up? Bea said something about your parole officer wanting you here, and I didn't press her for more information." Cooper's brow furrows.

"They're on a break while we work things out and I get

through this parole. They'll revisit their situation when that's over." I shrug.

"Oh." Cooper looks down at his drink and swirls the ice around once before he looks back up at me. "You gonna be all right if that doesn't end the way you want?"

"Were you gonna be all right if Bea went back to your brother?"

He gives me a flat look and shakes his head. "It's none of my business. It's just that you've been through a lot in the last year. I hate to see anything more for you like that."

"I know. You and Bea are good people. But I have to see some of these through for better or worse. Prison gave me more time to think than I'd had in a long time. I'd been in such a routine with practice and games and off-season training and just all of it... Having to just sit with my thoughts. Fuck. I don't wish that shit on anyone."

"Yeah. I can only imagine." Cooper gives me a sympathetic look.

"I fucked up a lot of things. Ran instead of standing my ground and seeing it through. I don't know if I chose the wrong path or not, but I have to see what it could have been like."

"And she's fine with that?"

"I told her if it doesn't work out, I'd give her the ranch and the inn—all of it and a nice settlement too."

"That's a pretty big bribe to leave your ass."

"Maybe. But it's what she wants, and I'd rather see her have it, whatever way it goes. I just wanted a shot at making it work first." Cooper's the only one I could really admit this too. My brothers wouldn't understand, and her brothers would gut me for trying.

"And how's that going?" Cooper looks at me thoughtfully.

"Ha. Well... she hates me. That's for sure. For everything I did and didn't do." It hurts to say it out loud, but it's the truth.

"But?" He looks at me hopefully. "There's a but, right?"

I shrug. "She likes fucking me. So I've got that in my corner. Having someone to take her rage out on when she's having a bad day doesn't seem to be hurting my cause either."

Cooper laughs and shakes his head. "I guess that's all you can ask for."

"I want a lot more than that, but I'm willing to wait her out. Fuck knows, I deserve a lot of her anger, and then some. I wasn't the best husband after things went down with my parents."

"Understandably." Cooper gives me a look of sympathy. "She knows you're sorry for it though?"

"I think so. I apologized a lot."

"Back then or now?"

I sigh and tilt my head to the side before I take a sip of beer. That was the question, wasn't it? If I could only figure out how to apologize to her now, in a way that meant something to her.

"Right." Cooper nods, understanding me without having to explain more.

WHEN WE RETURN from our trip to town, Bea and Hazel are just getting back from their ride and want showers before they change for dinner. So I take Cooper around the property in the truck, showing him the ranch and some of the trails. We're finishing up in the old pole barn that's full of my family's stuff while we wait.

"So what happens if she takes the ranch and runs? Are you leaving all this stuff here?"

"No. I'll have to move it to wherever I end up. But I need to go through it first, and a lot of it are things that belonged to my parents."

"She kept it all here for you?" Cooper looks at me surprised.

"Yeah. Why?"

"Nothing. I'm just pretty sure Bea wouldn't have done that for Rob."

"What wouldn't I have done?" Bea pipes up, and we turn around to see the two of them have returned, showered and dressed.

"You look gorgeous," Cooper responds, instead of answering her question. He takes her hand and spins her around. She's wearing a sundress and a pair of boots.

"Had to dress the part if I was going to be on a ranch. Hazel let me use them for riding, but I might have to get a pair." Bea grins.

"They look good on you." He returns her smile with the kind of ease that makes me grin like an idiot just watching them.

"Ooh. We should go dancing somewhere." Bea spins again, and Cooper dips her over.

"You think?" Cooper asks.

I turn my attention to Hazel, and she's smiling at them so hard I think she might be falling for them herself. My eyes travel over her; she's wearing a black dress that hugs her curves and flares at her waist with her own pair of black cowboy boots. I couldn't dream up someone more beautiful than her, and I'm racking my brain for something to say that won't make her glare at me, but she speaks before I can.

"Wait... what's on your wrists?" Hazel asks, noting the spot where black ink marks the inside of each of their wrists as Cooper spins her around one last time. "Do you have matching tattoos? That's adorable."

"They don't quite match." Cooper smirks.

"Close enough. I was just a little later." Bea gives him a

look but kisses him softly and then returns her attention to Hazel, holding out her wrist for her to inspect. "They were Cooper's idea because neither of us had one."

"It was really your idea. Your bucket list and all." Cooper smiles at her the way only someone completely lost in another person can.

"Well, true. But the tattoo idea was his. They're the coordinates of where each of us was when we realized we were falling for the other one."

"Oh my god. That's so..." Hazel's eyes go wide, and she looks between them. "That's just... wow." Hazel's lost for words, and that's a rarity.

"Oh, I'm sure whatever Ramsey's done for you is just as romantic."

My mind flashes through all the things I've done since I got here, and I feel guilt swirl in my gut. But Hazel smiles at me like I'm the sweetest man she's ever met.

"He can be very romantic when he wants to be." She covers for me, and that makes the guilt turn into knots. *Fuck.*

"Speaking of romantic... dancing?" Bea suggests again. "Is there somewhere we can go? I've always wanted to learn line dancing."

"My friend has a place in town. Seven Sins. She teaches too. We can get dinner and head over there. Ramsey doesn't dance though." Hazel flashes a grin in my direction, like she's curious to see if I'll try again for my friends' sake.

"I don't mind watching." I shake my head, not wanting to let anyone down. "You and Dakota can teach them, and I can keep the drinks coming."

"Sounds like a plan to me." Cooper looks at me thoughtfully.

"All right. Dinner and dancing lessons it is." Hazel and Bea take off for the car while we trail behind.

"They've become easy friends." Cooper looks at them amused at how they're walking arm in arm.

"Yeah. Bea reminded me of Hazel a little bit. If Hazel was missing the mean streak a mile wide."

"But that's what you like about her, isn't it?"

"I couldn't live without it." Then I look at him. "And when did you become such a fucking goddamn romantic?"

"When I realized I was going to do whatever it took to win her over, despite the odds." Cooper grins like a fool and then looks at me, raising a brow. "I highly recommend it if you're fixed on coming out of this with everything you want to keep."

I LEAN BACK on the porch swing and stare out into the evening after Cooper and Bea have gone off to bed for the night. Even though it's still technically late summer, the temperature has dropped with the sun, and a cool chill drifts over me. A moment later, I hear the creak of the screen door, and Hazel's standing there.

"Mind if I join? I brought beer."

"No, I don't mind." I scoot over to make room for her, and she hands me the extra bottle.

"Your friends are really nice. I see why you did what you did for them."

"They're good people. I'd do it again if I had to."

She stares at me in quiet contemplation for a moment before she takes a draw off her bottle and kicks her feet to make the swing rock.

"They're so in love too. That fresh kind where everything seems possible. I didn't ask how they met. Did they meet at your work?"

I smirk. "Nah. She was his brother's girl."

Her heel catches on the deck, and the swing stops again.

"What? No way!" She looks back at me, mouth agape.

I nod. "Don't say that to him though. In his mind, she's always been his."

"Wow. I would have never guessed someone as sweet as her for something like that."

"Love's love, I guess."

"I guess," she says in a tone that sounds doubtful, starting the swing moving again as she contemplates it.

"Never been in love like that?" I ask. Stupidly, I might add.

"To go after one of your brothers? No, can't say I have. Although Grant does look really good in a suit."

"You wouldn't fuckin' dare." I point the end of my bottle at her.

"If Curtis wasn't around, maybe. Just to piss you off. It might be worth it." She grins at me and takes another sip.

"Don't take this the wrong way, but I don't know if you could lure Grant to his death like that. He's got a strong self-preservation streak." I have a hard time believing any woman could lock Grant down for more than a night.

"He does, doesn't he? Still not married. Living alone in his tower. Has he ever been in love?" Hazel muses.

"Couldn't tell you. If he has, he's never said." I shrug.

"Lev?" she asks.

"Lev's had someone I think he loved once. He might have forgotten her now that he's moved on with life."

"Lev pining after someone is a real vision to wrap my head around." Hazel laughs. Levi is hard as nails, tougher than the rest of us by a long shot. But he has a soft core—one that the right people could reach when they needed to.

"He's not that different from me."

"I have a hard time imagining you pining too."

I give her a flat look, and she smiles, but it fades quickly.

"I know you loved me. I don't doubt that. But I mean... the kind of pining love where you write poems and love letters and can't stop thinking about a woman." Her eyes soften as she looks me over.

"Is that what it takes to win you these days? Love letters and poems?" More stupid questions on my part.

"Maybe," she says quietly. "Would that be so bad?"

"I don't remember you ever being that romantic. Is that how he won you over?" My heart strains in my chest at the idea, and my mind drifts through all the ways I fucked this up. I'm fucking terrible at feelings—processing them, expressing them. After my parents' deaths, I tried therapy. The local therapist struggled to make any sort of progress with me, and he sent me to the city for someone more specialized. I'd gone for a few more weeks after that and then given up. Football was better therapy for me than any talking I'd ever done. I worked my shit out on the field until I had to see someone again in prison.

She looks at me warily. "You don't want to talk about him. Not really."

"Not really," I admit. "I'd rather beat his ass for putting his hands on my wife."

"Bea said she didn't even know you had a wife before the trial. Did Cooper know about me?" She deftly changes the subject.

"I mentioned it once when he asked about my life back here."

"What'd you tell him?"

"That I was married once, but I had a fucked-up life here. A family involved in things that cost them their lives, and the aftermath of that cost me my wife."

We sit in silence after that summary of our end. It was true enough. The black and white bare bones of it, but it lacked all the color that had made it so painful.

"I packed a bag that night after you left." She breaks the silence between us.

"A bag?" I turn to look at her, but her eyes are on her bottle, peeling the label off the front.

"I changed my mind, or I thought I did. It hurt so fucking bad without you in the house. Seeing your stuff still in the closet, your bike still in the barn... It was like you were going to come back any day, when I knew you weren't."

"Haze..." I say softly.

"I'd never felt pain like that... not really. Grieving someone that way. Someone who was still alive. I thought I could just pretend you were dead. Make peace with you being gone like I did my mom and your parents. Then I didn't have to imagine you happy somewhere without me or with someone else. But all the things that people say when they're gone—that they're in a better place, that you'll see them again someday. None of that's comforting when they're still alive." She sighs. "Not that I wanted you to be hurting, but..."

"I did hurt. Like hell. For weeks at night, I'd just stare at that spot in the bed where you were supposed to be. Questioning if I did the right thing. I went to pick up the phone so many times, but I was worried I'd only make it worse." I confess things I never told her.

"How many weeks until you put someone else in that spot in the bed?" she asks, raising her lashes to look at me.

"Haze..." I beg her not to go down this road as her eyes search my face.

"You're right. I don't want to know. Not any more than you want to know about him."

We sit in silence for a moment. I'm desperately trying to think of the right words to say. Something that will salvage what was an otherwise good day.

"I'm sorry," she says at last, breaking the silence. "I fucked it up. Maybe we just need to... make an agreement about that. I don't ask about the in-between, and you don't either. We just live in the bubble we're in for the next few weeks, and we make the best of it."

"If that's what you want."

She downs the rest of her beer and sets the bottle on the windowsill.

"What I want is sleep after this long day." She gives me a soft smile and stands. "You coming in soon?"

"You go on ahead. I'll be in in a while. I just want to sit out here and watch the stars for a bit while I still got 'em at night."

"No stars in Cincinnati?"

"Not like this."

"Well... soak it in while you can, cowboy." She leans down and kisses my forehead before heading back inside.

"I intend to," I whisper after her.

TWENTY-FOUR

Hazel

THAT MORNING, we have breakfast with Cooper and Bea at the inn. Bea makes me promise to come visit her sometime in Cincinnati, and I tell her she needs to come back for a proper vacation. Cooper and Ramsey talk football and his daughter. Then we see them both off to the airport. I go back to the inn, and he goes back to ranch life. Even if he is a little pouty at the loss of his friends.

When I get home that night from the inn, Ramsey's still uncharacteristically quiet. I thought we might have made some progress, especially since Cooper and Bea were here, but he barely greets me when I put my things away in the breezeway. He looks like he's on a mission and doesn't have time to chat.

"Kit put some dinner together for us." I hold up the aluminum foil tray she handed me on my way out the door. "I need a shower after the hike we did this afternoon, but after that, if you want, I can heat this up, and we can eat together?" I try to offer an olive branch.

"Sure." It's a terse reply, and then he heads out the back screen door. It slams in his wake, and I storm up the steps. This is exactly why this would never work. There's no changing the man. I'm busy counting down the list of reasons why I should still hate him when I get in the shower, and I've only managed to work myself back down slightly from my temper by the time I'm done thirty minutes later. Because I'm not about to rush to have dinner with an asshole.

I wrap a towel around myself and walk out into the bedroom to find where I put my body lotion. But there in the middle of the bed is a set of lingerie. One of the new ones I just purchased on Ramsey's credit card. Next to it is an embossed card that's been written over.

I look more closely, picking it up, and my heart sinks. It's the wedding invitations for Curtis and me. They must have come in the mail, and Ramsey found them. No wonder he's pissed. I read the note in Ramsey's writing.

PUT THIS ON AND COME DOWNSTAIRS TO THE DEN.
-R

The den had always been Ramsey's favorite room in the house, the place where he took all his important meetings, so I assume I'm headed there for some sort of dressing down. I stare at the white lace. I should tell him where he can shove it. But something about the demand makes me curious.

I take my time putting the lingerie and my robe on. I'm in no hurry to fight with him, and I'm hoping his temper cools by the time I get downstairs. When I walk through the den door, Ramsey's set up in the big leather armchair near the fireplace. He's got a glass of whiskey in one hand and a white piece of paper in the other. A piece that he stares at for a long moment before he chucks into the fire. He watches it burn to ashes before he finally looks up at me.

"What are you doing?" Dread runs through me.

"Using this invitation as kindling," he answers bluntly.

"You're not!" I gasp as I round the old brown leather couch in the room and see the stack of them he has on the table next to him. The box is half empty, and the fire is roaring at its side. "Did you burn the rest?"

"Yep."

"Are you fucking insane? Do you know how much those cost and how long it took to get them? They were custom. I drove to Denver three times just to get the design right." I feel like I'm going to be sick.

"A waste of time if you ask me."

I lunge at him to take back the invitation he currently has in his hand. He whisks it out of my reach and flings it into the fire, standing as I screech at the way the paper catches fire.

"Give it to me," I demand when he picks up another one but ignores me, holding it up too high for me to reach. "*Now.*" I glare at him, and his expression sours in return.

"He might like being bossed around all the time, darlin'. But I like saving that for special occasions."

"So help me, God, Ramsey. If you toss another one in the fire..." My hands are on my hips as I threaten him, and he looks down at me and smirks.

"Then what?" His eyes glint in the reflection of the fire, amusement dancing over his face.

"I haven't figured it out yet, but it'll be bad for you. I promise that much."

He drops his hand and holds the invitation out for me. I eye him warily before I take it, worried this is all a trap. I snatch it from his grasp and my fears are confirmed a moment later.

"Read it to me." He nods to the paper.

"No." I pull it behind my back and glare at him.

"Suit yourself." He grabs another handful off the pile and chucks them headlong into the fire.

"Stop doing that!" I yell, falling to my knees and covering the rest of the invitations with my arms.

"Read the invitation to me," he repeats, his voice cool and even.

"Fine. You're a fucking psycho, though, you know that? I thought we'd made some progress. But no."

"Read—" he starts, but I interrupt him by doing what he asks.

"You are cordially invited to the wedding of Hazel Briggs Stockton and Curtis Martin Flanagan at Bull Rush Ranch on March 15 at one p.m. Reception will follow at the Purgatory Falls Inn, with a post-reception party at the Seven Sins Bar in town." I look up, and he's furious.

"So you're going to marry him with my name, on my ranch, and celebrate it at the inn my great grandparents built? Do I have that right?"

"Where did you think we were going to get married, Ramsey? There're only a couple of places in town that can accommodate a wedding, and I'm not made of money."

"Somewhere, *anywhere* fucking else," he roars. "Are you going to wear the same dress too? Let him fuck you in it? Make sure he spends a couple of hours on his knees for you first first though. Repeat the whole experience. Then again, I doubt he has the same kind of stamina I do."

"I have a new dress. And I tried to have the wedding at the casino hotel, in the ballroom, but your brothers refused to allow the booking."

There's a flash of surprise on his face before he grins.

"Good for them. At least someone with the Stockton name knows what loyalty means."

I slap him without thinking. The crack of my palm on his cheek is deafening, and my breath catches in my throat when I realize what I've done. His eyes blaze with fury, and I've stoked the fire even hotter.

Might as well lean into it.

"You want to talk about loyalty? I don't think you're ready for that conversation." I steel my spine, holding back the thing I really want to say since it'll only make this fight worse—because loyalty would have meant he stayed on his family land with his family.

We stand in silence for what seems like an eternity, staring each other down and daring the other one to make the next move.

"You're right. We can save the small talk for another day," he answers at last, his calm tone returning.

I turn to leave the room. I've had enough of him, and I'm so pissed I could kill him myself.

"Where's the dress?" he asks. "I want to see it."

I stop in my tracks and turn to look at him.

"So you can burn it too?"

"I hadn't thought that far ahead." A wicked little smile grows on his lips. "Maybe that too."

I turn around and poke him in the chest. "Absolutely not."

"Was I going to get one?"

"Get what?" I frown; momentarily imagining Ramsey in a wedding dress brings an unwanted smile to my lips.

"An invitation."

"No." I look at him like he's lost what's left of his mind.

"Why not?"

"You know why not."

"Because you didn't want me to see you reliving ours or

because you thought seeing me would make it too hard to marry him?"

"Because I hate you with the fire of a thousand fucking suns! I hate how you sweep in and turn everything upside down. How you make me rethink every choice I ever made. How you just walk in and take whatever you want whenever you want and damn the consequences. You're trying to ruin *everything*."

"Not everything. Just you." His hands go to my robe and untie it; it falls to the side, and he sees the lingerie I'm wearing in place of my usual post-shower tee and shorts. I'm mad that I even put it on now.

"I had a misplaced addiction. I'm cured now." I inform him. It's a lie. I'm every bit as addicted as I ever was, or I wouldn't be doing any of this.

"Well, I'm not."

"Clearly." I stare at the pile of ashes in the fireplace.

"I'll buy you new ones in a couple of months. Those needed corrections anyway." He kisses his way down my neck.

"Don't try to kiss up now, Stockton," I warn.

"No? You'd rather have it be rough instead? You can hit me a few more times and tell me how much you hate me if you want. I know how wet that gets you these days." I slide him a sideways look of disapproval, but he just eats it up.

"I'd rather have peace and quiet."

"That's a lie, or you wouldn't have worn this down here." He runs his fingers under one of the shoulder straps and pulls it down.

"I saw the invitation and was trying to placate you," I grumble.

"Is that what you were trying to do just now?" He mocks me as his fingers twist in my hair, and he pushes it off my shoulder.

"It went awry, but yes." I close my eyes as he starts to kiss his way over my shoulder in short, deliberate brushes of his lips on my skin.

"So finish showing me how it was going to go," he says softly.

TWENTY-FIVE

Hazel

"I SAID PLACATE. As in what I planned to do before you burned half of them," I grumble, but I still can't help the sigh when he gently kisses and sucks on the sensitive part of my neck where it meets my shoulder. I arch into him, my ass brushing over his cock, and I can feel him going hard. His hand wraps around the side of my throat, and his mouth continues to tease me for a moment before he speaks again.

"There's another half I could burn. Might still be worth the effort," he threatens, and the defiance floods my chest again.

"Might..." I pull away from him, grabbing his black cowboy hat off the table. I momentarily contemplate tossing it into the fire and watching it burn the way he did my invitations. He pulled it out of his storage closet shortly after he got here and seeing him in it brings back too many memories. But even as I think it, I know I can't do it. So I put it on my head instead and take a step back toward him. I smile as I press my palms to his chest and run them up toward his shoulders.

"Or..." I whisper softly, leaning up on my tiptoes to bring my lips closer to his ear. "You could kiss my ass, cowboy." I shove him hard then, and it knocks him off-balance. He falls back into the chair he was sitting in, and I take off running through the house.

I'm out through the den, down a hall, across the kitchen, and through the back hallway again, racing for the back door. I can hear him on the other side of the house yelling my name in a thundering tone, but I grab the door handle, and my feet hit the deck before I can make out the rest of what he says.

My feet pound against the wood and down the stairs. My heart's racing in my chest, and a nervous giggle pops out as I scan the back to make sure I don't see Elliot or Kellan out at the stables. It's late enough that the sun's setting, and they should be tucked away at home, but I'd rather them not see me running half naked through the yard. This lingerie wasn't exactly made like a sports bra either.

My next regret is when I hit the gravel part of the drive without shoes on. I yelp, and it slows me down, but when I hear the screen door slam behind me, it sends me cutting across the short side and racing across all the tiny stones in record time.

"Haze!" Ramsey bellows from the back deck. "Be fucking reasonable and come back here."

I just flip him the bird over my shoulder, though, grabbing his hat to keep it on my head as I take off in a full-on sprint when I hit the grass. I can move quicker here now that my feet don't feel like they're being impaled by tiny spikes. I'll need it because I can hear his boots on the gravel already.

I take a quick dodge to the right, heading for the outcropping of cottonwood around the stream that runs through this side of the ranch and hope I can lose him in the cover of the turning leaves. By the time I get there, though, he's already gained a lot of ground on me. He's only a few steps behind as I weave through the trees.

I look up, and in the distance, I can see the fence to one of the pastures. If I can hop it fast, it might be enough to slow him down. I can get back to the barn on the other side and shut the door before he can reach me and, hopefully, lose him that way.

"Haze. If I catch you..." Ramsey's on the ridge overlooking the stream as I step into it with something dangling from his hand that I can't quite make out. I glance down at the water and the banks, hoping I'm not surprising any animals here for a late evening drink.

"You can try!" I call back to him as I wade through the water, the mud seeping between my toes and the water splashing my legs as I hurry through the ankle-high section of the current. I lift my robe, careful not to let it get wet, and then I hurry to climb the bank on the other side. I'm half praying he falls into the water. I need the extra time, but the short set of splashes at my heels tells me he's crossed it faster than me.

I'm out across the field, racing like my life depends on it, and it might. The last time I did this to him, he'd been furious with me, yelling about all the ways I could have hurt myself. Between this and the invitations...

I reach the fence, and I don't hesitate. I just pull myself up on the first rung and go to throw my other leg over the wooden rail. But that's when I hear it. The sharp rip and my motion's stopped in an instant. I look down, and my robe is caught on one of the nails, restricting my movement. I try to slip it off my shoulder, but it's twisted, pinning me in place and making it nearly impossible to escape.

I can hear his footsteps, the swish of the grass as it parts for him, and then his heavy breathing as he closes in on me. I yank one last time for good measure, trying to tear myself free where

I'm unable to do anything else. But it fails, and the momentum whips me back, making me tumble off the fence and onto the ground at his feet. I scramble to try to get to my knees and push myself back up, but his knee is at my back, driving me back down.

"No. You're fucking done." He grinds out the words through heavy breaths, pinning me into place. He's able to pull my robe off and untangle me from the nail with ease, making me look like an incapable fawn in comparison. He grabs both of my hands and pins them together with one of his—relentless and thorough in the way he manages me. I can't even think quickly enough to get out of his grip, and I'm realizing at this moment how much power he's let me have up until now. How many times he could have just picked me up one-handed and tossed me over his shoulder like I weighed nothing. How easily he could have put me in my place, but he held back. I forgot about this, what it feels like to be with him and let him have control.

I quickly discover what was dangling from his hand at the ridge line. *Rope.* I feel it, tight and scratchy on my skin as he winds it around my wrists, binding them together.

"Ramsey," I plead, trying to think of something I can say to mollify him.

"Don't talk. I don't want to fucking hear a single word."

"I'm so—" His hand goes over my mouth, and his lips press to my ear as he pulls the rope tight around my wrists until I hiss out a protest through his fingers.

"Don't even try to say that word. We both know you're not." He nips the shell of my ear, and then he stands, pulling me to my knees by holding onto the rope around my wrists. He takes in my appearance, his eyes grazing over every inch of me. I glance down, seeing that I've ripped the lingerie in my struggle with the fence, and one of my breasts is now spilling out over the cup. All of me is covered in dirt and bits of grass, and there are scrapes across my thighs from where I slipped off the fence, little beads of blood pooling where it sliced through my flesh.

He squats down to take a closer look and wipes over it with his thumb. It smears over my skin, and he shakes his head. His green eyes lift to meet mine, ire in them. I can hear his thoughts. The way he's telling me he told me I'd get hurt doing this, how silly I am, along with more patronizing terms of endearment.

"Was it worth it?"

"To see the look on your face falling back into that chair? Yeah. Yeah, it was." I laugh just thinking about the surprised little grunt he made as I fled, and he's anything but amused by it.

He grabs my chin and holds my gaze; the next words sound more like a threat than anything else. "I'm glad you had fun."

I dart my tongue out over my lower lip, and I can feel the answering flutter of excitement in my stomach and then the warmth of it pooling lower. I've been dying for more of this side of him.

TWENTY-SIX

Ramsey

THE LOOK of anticipation on her face and the way her eyes sparkle with the taunt; I'm desperate to fuck her. I've fallen straight into her trap. Because this is exactly what she wanted, the thing she begged me for one night when she finally trusted me enough to tell me.

"Bend over. Elbows in the dirt," I demand. She slides into the position slowly, and I wrap my hand around the back of her neck to press her head down lower.

Her ass is up in the air, looking as perfect as it ever has, with the swell of her cheeks on full display beyond the lace edge of her little scrap of fabric, see-through panties. I wrap my hands around the sides of the elastic on her hips and wrench them down over her thighs. She's soaked for me already, glistening in the fading light of the setting sun.

"What are you doing?" she asks as I kneel down behind her.

"Kissing your ass, since you asked so nicely."

She laughs until my lips touch her skin, and then she exhales like I've stolen her breath. I kiss her left cheek and then move to her right, running my tongue over the curve, then biting her in soft, gentle nips and scrapes of my teeth until I reach her center again. She tastes like sugar melding with salt as my tongue runs the length of where she parts for me, her legs spreading wider as she whimpers. I fuck her with my tongue, and she rocks back against my face begging for more.

"Oh fuck..." she cries out softly when I use the pads of my fingers to massage her clit. I'm obsessed with the taste of her, lapping up every fucking drop she gives me. She gets louder as I take her closer to the edge, and she begs for me, saying my name over and over and cursing everything in its wake. She sounds so good like this, so perfect that I can't stop myself when the time comes to pull away.

I'd planned to deny her. To make her suffer for being so careless with her safety and making me chase her out into the night like this, but I'm too fucking in love with the sound of her moans and whimpers. The desperate way she rolls her hips, grinding back against my tongue as my fingers circle tighter around her clit, has me needing to hear her come for me.

"Oh god. Oh please. Ramsey... just a little more, and I think I can," she pleads, and I'm careful, working her clit with just the right amount of pressure while I let her ride my tongue. I can hear a whimper of frustration from her as she tries to chase it. I pull away for just a moment, squeezing her thigh in reassurance before I slip underneath her and pull her thighs down so she's straddling my face.

"All the way down, sugar. Ride my tongue as long as you need, and we'll get you there. I've got you," I promise her.

She does as I ask and grinds down on me while I slide my fingers inside of her, curling them to give her the extra bit of friction she needs as she fucks my face like I'm the last chance she's got at anything good. I can hear the change in her moans, getting closer with each pass she takes over my mouth. One of her hands is loose enough from the rope that she slips it through my hair and tightens, giving her the hold she needs to fuck my mouth harder. A moment later, she's coming loudly, telling me how good I am in between gasps. She soaks my chin and my beard as she does it, and I think I might have forgotten how good it feels to be used like this. To be nothing but her escape for a night.

She rolls over to my side, tangling her legs with my arms for a moment until we can pull the scrap of fabric meant to be between her thighs back into place. I pull the ropes from her wrists, and she rubs the marks left by them as she stretches her joints again. She takes a deep breath, staring up at the first glimpses of the star-scattered sky, and then her eyes fall to mine.

"I feel like I'm about to pay for that twice over now, aren't I?" There's amusement in her tone.

"You've got a few more minutes until the taste of you wears off my tongue. Then you're putting my shirt on, and I'll give you a thirty-second head start back to the house." I'm exhausted, and I need the thirty seconds as much as she does.

"And if you catch me?"

"*When* I catch you, then it's my turn."

TWENTY-SEVEN

Ramsey

I HAVE to steel myself when I walk inside Seven Sins because, even from across the room, I can tell Dakota is already in fine form. She's talking to a coworker and shaking her head, her eyes rolling and then darting to a man at the far side of the bar. Hazel's friend has never really liked me much and catching her on a bad day is going to make the ask I have that much more unlikely to get a positive reception. But she's the only one who can really help me with my problem.

It's at least quiet in here, early enough in the afternoon when most of the locals are still working and the tourists are out on day trips that keep them out of town. But the place is still dark, and the music is low with a heavy beat as she fixes a couple of other guys at the bar their drinks. She finishes them just as I step up, and she pushes a napkin in front of me without making eye contact at first.

"What can I get—*you*." Her eyes narrow and sweep over me for a moment before she gives me an impatient look.

"I was hoping to talk to you."

"If you need directions out of town, I'm happy to call you a car to take you to the airport. Hell, if you give me ten minutes, I'll drive you myself." She gives me a saccharine little smile for show.

"No. But I do need a favor."

Her eyebrow arches, and her lips curl in a half-formed smirk.

"Oh, I can't wait to hear this. I mean, the answer is going to be no. But I still want to hear it."

I just need to remember I'm doing all this for Haze. If it means I get points with her, it's all worth it.

"I need someone to teach me how to dance. Nothing fancy like you all usually do around here, just enough that I don't fuck it up." I force the words out before I can change my mind.

Dakota and her staff teach line dancing and country swing on Fridays and Saturdays in the after-dinner hours of the evening to try to get the crowd coming in earlier and keep some of the braver tourists entertained outside of Cowboy's. It's an open-floor opportunity for anyone who buys drinks, but I'd rather not embarrass myself in front of a crowd of people. Doing it in front of Dakota would be enough.

"Why? You planning on coming to Hazel and Curtis's wedding?" She grins.

"I'm asking Haze out on a date, and I know she likes to dance. I feel like I let her down the other day when we came with my friends, but I didn't want to look like a jackass."

"You always look like a jackass, so I wouldn't worry too much about that."

"Fucking hell..." I shake my head and push the napkin back to her. "I just want to do a nice thing for her. I could use some help. If you're not willing, maybe someone else is?" I glance down at one of the other bartenders.

"Yeah. Haze won't like that." Dakota shakes her head at the blonde down the way. I start to smile at the idea of Hazel being jealous but smother it immediately before Dakota sees. That Dakota thinks she would be? That's gonna fuel me for the next week at least.

"So?"

"Fine. It's quiet right now anyway. But I can't teach you everything in an hour, and that's all I've got."

"I'll take what I can get."

A few minutes later, we're out on the floor with her reluctantly giving me advice on how to two-step and telling me to keep my elbows in as we make our way along. It's not coming as easy as I hoped it might, but I'm still picking up the basics.

"FUCK ME SIDEWAYS. This is what you're doing now? Dancing at a bar in the middle of the day?" Grant's voice breaks my concentration, and I miss the next step nearly an hour later. I look up to see my older brother laughing as he leans back against one of the high tops.

"Better this than whatever you're doing. Don't you have mud to be wallowing in somewhere?" Dakota flashes a look of derision at Grant without missing a beat.

"Lovely to see you too, Hartfield." Grant's laugh fades, but his smile doesn't, and I don't miss the way his eyes wander their way up her legs.

"I thought I told you you were banned from this bar," Dakota calls out as we make another pass.

"It's hard to ban the person who owns the building," Grant

argues, and that's enough to get her to drop her hand from my shoulder and turn her full attention on him.

"The building, not what's inside it, Stockton." She motions for him to quit leaning on her table, and he complies, but in a manner so slow that they're locked in some sort of hate-filled, eye-fucking situation that I'm feeling increasingly out of place to be witnessing.

I clear my throat. "Dakota's just teaching me some steps so I can take Haze out one of these nights."

"I'd have thought she'd have ripped your balls off by now." My brother smirks, but there's a look of sympathy behind his eyes too.

"Still standing, balls intact—at the moment." The song comes to an end and turns over to something slower I don't recognize.

"All right, cowboy. This is your final test. See if you can turn me around the floor without stepping on my toes." Dakota reaches out for me, and I take her hand in one of mine, placing the other in a very loose position on the side of her lower ribcage. I'm not looking to lose one, and I'm looking even less to do anything that might piss Haze off.

I manage to keep up with her steps, whirling around the floor and turning her almost as well as I saw some of the other people here doing the other night. I let her lead as we spin one more time, and then I dip her gently before she comes back up. We're making our way back to the starting point when I see Grant take a couple of steps out onto the floor.

"All right. You gotta let me show my little brother how it's done. It's painful to watch." He holds out his hand, and Dakota eyes it warily. Her gaze shifts back up to mine, and I nod.

"Thank you," I say softly, honestly appreciative because she was able to pack more into the last hour than I've probably learned in a lifetime.

"Of course," she says easily, like she didn't chew me out the second I walked in here. "And don't listen to this asshole." She flashes a look that could kill at Grant even as she considers taking his hand. "You did just fine. Hazel will love it."

"You want those two back together? I thought you hated all Stocktons," Grant asks Dakota as he gives up waiting and takes her hand, pulling her close. They start to move around the floor together, faster than anything I'd attempted.

"I hate some more than others. Also... if this is you trying to show him up, you're already failing." Dakota stares down at his feet.

"Stop fighting me taking the lead, and maybe you'll change your mind," Grant counters as they drift away to the other side of the floor.

I head to the bar to grab a beer while I watch them finish out the song, settling onto one of the worn pleather bar stools as the other bartender pours for me. I feel like I need to keep watch over them to make sure no one loses an eye.

My brothers and I have barely spoken in the last five years, the three of us only communicating to wish each other well on major holidays and to check in about the occasional significant moment with their casino or my team. My older sister, Aspen, is the one who keeps us all united, so it's been an adjustment now that I'm home to just casually run into each other at the bar.

The song comes to an end, and the two of them exchange more unpleasantries before she returns to her station behind the bar, and he pulls up in the empty seat beside me. His two-thousand-dollar suit looks out of place against the worn wood and the eclectic decor, but it doesn't seem to rattle him any.

"If you're already bored of the ranch, I told you there's an office waiting for you. A whole casino to play in if you want." Grant looks me over inquisitively.

"I'm not bored of the ranch. I just needed Dakota's help, like I said." I tilt my head as I study the details of his suit. "What are you doing here anyway?"

"I saw the ranch truck outside. Figured I'd come in and see if it was you and get a drink if it wasn't." He shrugs, but I'm not entirely sure I believe him.

"Are you ordering something? This isn't rented out for a family reunion, and I don't have space for people who aren't paying customers." Dakota wipes down the counter and then looks at Grant impatiently.

His lips press together with amusement as he looks her over. "Yeah, give me a whiskey. Neat."

"Well or shelf?"

He smirks at her like it's a ridiculous question. My brother always loved the finer things our parents could afford, and he couldn't wait to get off the ranch and into a condo in the city when we graduated. I'm not sure he's ever had a well drink in his life.

"You have Oban or Ardbeg?"

"I got Jack or Jim, sweet cheeks. You want the fancy stuff? I suggest you go back to your golden tower."

"Jack is fine."

She slams a glass on the counter and pours it without spilling a drop, capping the bottle and sliding him his drink before she takes off to the other end of the bar where one of her bartenders is waving her over.

"She hates you," Grant notes as she walks away.

"Not as much as she hates you." I look back at him, my brow furrowing as I watch him watch her. "You got a masochist thing going on these days?"

"If I do, that makes two of us. You should come to work with me and quit wasting your time chasing after the Briggs girl. I know you loved her, but she's moved on. It's been the gossip in town for months about how well those two get on and how fast he fell for her. I've got half a dozen girls at the casino prettier and more amenable."

"She's my wife." I'm not even going to dignify the rest of what he said with a response.

"For now. You want to game this out, go for it. But don't leave town without coming to see me again."

We both jolt at the slam of metal against wood and turn to see the source. Dakota's pulled a bat out and is waving it at two of the patrons sitting in front of her. The other bartender is standing behind her, and both of them are yelling at the two men. I watch as one of the guys fingers the holster on his hip.

"Holy fuck." I go to stand, but Grant's heavy hand is on my shoulder shoving me back down in my seat.

"You're on fucking parole. Don't you dare fucking go anywhere near it. I got it." He slides past me and makes his way calmly to the scene.

"Gentlemen!" he says loudly, spreading his arms wide and stealing the attention away from Dakota. "Do we have a problem here?"

"...of this shit!" I can only hear part of what he says in return. She answers Grant in the wake of one of the assholes' complaints, and the men start to talk loudly over her, apparently pissed that she's speaking at all.

"Whoa. Whoa. Don't worry, gentlemen. If you're not getting the service you like here, I've got somewhere better you can go. Have you heard of The Avarice? It's a little casino up the way. Fucking fantastic drinks and service. Gorgeous women. Everything you could want on a day like this. Let me get my card out." He pats his breast pocket to indicate that he's reaching for it and not something else, and the guy eases up on his holster, his hands going back to his drink. "Here we go. You just give them this, and it's on the house, okay?"

The guys seem placated by the gesture. They gather themselves and move off the stools at that end of the bar in a relatively orderly fashion. They head for the back door, and I see Dakota muttering under her breath as Grant gives her a sharp look. Once they're gone, I make my way to them.

"What the fuck was that about?" I ask, looking to Dakota for answers.

"They were asking a lot of fucked-up questions about people in town. Who certain people were. Even asking about the ranch. I asked if they were cops. They didn't like that. Then they started pressing Ruby for answers, and I told them this isn't that kind of bar, and they could go to Morton's."

"One of them said they didn't like her mouth," Ruby pipes in.

Well. I could have told them that was a mistake.

"The other one said something similar but in a language I didn't understand. Irish accent, maybe? Do people in Ireland speak another language?" Ruby looks to Grant and me like we might have answers.

"They can." Grant looks to the door.

"Fucking tourists," Dakota mutters. "They all want to recreate some Wild West saloon. And you just keep bringing more of them in." She sneers at Grant.

"You need security," he answers her, a disapproving tone to it.

"I have it." She points the end of her bat at him before flipping it over and tucking it back under the bar.

"It's not a joke. You're going to get yourself or someone else killed, antagonizing them like that with no backup plan." He lectures her, and I can see the way she bristles at the implication.

"Grant—" I start, but she's already ready to tear into him.

"I'm going to get someone else killed? You're the one who

keeps advertising to these jackasses to come up here. If you'd stop dragging them all into town, we'd be just fine."

"Because business in here is fucking booming." Grant glances around at the nearly empty bar.

"It's four p.m." She gives him a dismissive look as she wipes down the counter.

"I guarantee I have a full house right now."

Dakota looks like she's about to jump the counter to rip his throat out—her hand gripping the rag tightly and her focus slowly lifting from the counter to the two-thousand-dollar suit in front of her. I can see her imagining shoving the rag down his throat and how much damage she can do to him with a metal bat and a broken bottle. She closes her eyes and turns to me, opening them slowly with a saccharine smile on her lips before she speaks.

"Ramsey, if you don't remove your brother from my bar, I'm going to say things I can't take back, and you'll have to decide which body you're helping to bury."

"Yep." I nod and turn to Grant. He starts to open his mouth to argue again, and I shake my head. "Let's go."

I manage to get him back out onto the street, blinking as my eyes try to adjust to the late-day sun. We walk slowly down Main toward the lot where we're both parked, passing another group of tourists headed in Seven Sins' direction, only pausing to take pictures of the old city hall building. I hope for their sake they pick Cowboy's instead.

"Do you ever think you might catch more flies with honey?" I mutter as I glance back at Seven Sins.

"Maybe I don't want to catch. Maybe I just want to badger to the brink of insanity." Grant's self-satisfied grin hasn't left his face, and I'm not in the mood to argue with him further. I just want to get home to Hazel.

TWENTY-EIGHT

Hazel

WHEN I GET HOME from the inn, I'm frazzled and more than a little tired. I'm half ready to melt into a tub when I notice something on the bed. I'm surprised when I find a new dress laid out on the quilt and a pair of my old black cowboy boots sitting on the floor just beneath it. I'm half worried he found something else to burn when I see a small handwritten note.

> GET DRESSED AND COME MEET ME DOWNSTAIRS.
> TAKING YOU OUT TONIGHT.
> —R

I lift the dress up to get a better look at it, and it's a black dress with a tea-length tule underskirt, a corset top with ribbing, and two thin straps. It's pretty and way sexier than anything I've worn lately. I'm gonna have to dig deep in my makeup drawer to see if I even have red lipstick that could live up to it. I shift on my feet, wiggling my ankle back and forth and biting my lip. I *am* tired, but it's been forever since I've gone out in something fancy, and the idea of being out on the arm of my famous football-playing, kidnap-plot-busting hero of a husband doesn't exactly sound terrible. We could at least set a few gossips on fire tonight. I grin to myself as I play with the lace edge of the corset and then hurry to get ready.

When I'm done, I stand in the mirror, doing one last check to make sure my curls are sufficiently undone and messy and my lipstick is staying firmly within the bounds of the liner I put on. I don't look half-bad when I clean up out of my admittedly dowdy innkeeper outfits and the torn jeans and tanks I usually wear taking care of the horses. I spritz my apple perfume on my wrists and rub a bit behind my ears before I hurry down the stairs to meet Ramsey.

But if I don't look half-bad, he looks positively heart-stopping. He's in all black, from his boots and pants to his button-down shirt and cowboy hat. His sleeves are rolled and all of it highlights the tattoos and the tan he's been developing since he got here. The muted tones of his outfit make his green-gold eyes that much more brilliant in comparison.

I might have to rethink how much I hate him.

"You look gorgeous." He flashes a panty-melting grin at me as I make my way down the final steps. I try to remind myself I've been married to this man for years, and I don't have to be nervous just because we're going out on a date.

"Thank you. You clean up well." I raise a brow and make a point of running my eyes over him. His grin widens in response, and my heart skips a beat.

"I'm glad you think so." He kisses the side of my neck and pauses. "And fuck do I love that perfume."

"I know." I can't help the bashful grin that comes, and I

catch myself nibbling my lower lip. He kisses his way down my neck and buries his nose against me as his arms go around my waist, a low growl rumbling from his chest.

"Fuck. Okay. We're getting out of this house first." He tears himself away and holds out his hand for mine.

"Do I get to know where we're going?" I ask as he leads me out back toward the truck.

"Dinner first. Then a surprise." He winks at me.

"Where's dinner?" I'm curious if it's somewhere in town or if we're traveling for this dinner.

"I was going to take you to Daniel's, but I found out they closed." It's the steakhouse we used to have in town. One we went to for fancy occasions only but I used to love going to growing up. It always meant a big accomplishment or celebration in my family, something that pulled us all together at a table dressed up for the occasion, and made my dad pull out his credit card. I can still feel the red pleather under my legs and smell the warm bread they used to serve at the table with apple butter.

"Yeah, your brothers' steakhouse ran them out of business a couple of years ago." I pout because I'd loved that bread and these perfect little twice-baked potatoes they had that I'd been obsessed with since I was a kid.

"So... we're going to The Avarice, to eat there." Ramsey introduces the idea reluctantly, knowing what my reaction will be. I might have the Stockton name, but I don't support their business practices.

I let out a little sound of protest at supporting the town's enemy.

"But..." Ramsey looks to me to see if I'll let him finish before I say no. I press my lips together and give him an expectant look. "Only because they promised me they could make the dinner you always used to love."

"With the potatoes?"

"With the potatoes and the bread pudding with the brandy sauce and ice cream for dessert." He gives me a worried look like he's half afraid I'm going to say no.

"I usually try to stay away from anything Stockton-run. But I'll make an exception this once." I grin at him. Inside I still feel a little guilty for being a traitor to the town's cause, but half of them have looked at me that way anyway just for having fallen in love with the youngest one—as if it was a thing I could ever control.

AN HOUR LATER, we're halfway through dinner, and he's just absently grinning into the distance like he's daydreaming about something amusing. It makes me smile in return, though I try to suppress it so he doesn't realize I'm watching him. I missed this version of him so much that it almost hurts the way my heart swells to see it.

"Something amusing?" I ask, twirling my fork through the last of my potatoes.

He focuses back on me, and the grin grows.

"Yeah. Just remembering that first time I took you to Daniel's. For that dance?"

"Prom. My junior prom. Your senior prom."

"Yes. Shit. That was prom, wasn't it? I'd forgotten that part."

"I didn't. I felt guilty because half the senior girls were hoping you were going to ask them."

"I had better plans." He gives me a mischievous look like he'd had designs on me all along.

"Oh please, you weren't dying to take out your best friend's sister. You just felt bad for me after Eric was such a dick."

"Eric's loss, my gain. I'd been waiting for him to fuck up."

"Secretly in love with me all along?" I tease, knowing full well he wasn't.

"I don't know what you'd call it. You were just under my skin. You always had some smart-ass comment. You weren't scared of me. Didn't give a shit about impressing me. I was so used to girls running around in low-cut tops and skirts that you in your cut-off, old jeans and dirty, tight white tees did it for me, I guess." He laughs.

"I didn't bother. You always treated me like I was just one of the guys. Another brother who just happened to have tits." I shake my head remembering that I considered it once or twice in front of a mirror and forgot it just as quickly.

"Jesus, Haze." He nearly sputters his wine onto the table but manages to swallow.

"What? It's true. It wasn't worth my time. Not to mention you weren't about to ruin your Bo bromance for me, and I wasn't going to suffer that kind of heartache." I set my fork down and take a sip of my wine instead.

"But you went to prom with me."

"I did. And then what happened after?" I ask, raising a brow and crossing my arms. "Nothing. That's what."

"You know what happened after. I got that scholarship, and I was going to be in college, on the road with games, and you were still going to be in high school."

"Mm-hmm." I shake my head, pretending to still be mad about the first time he left me for football. "Always for football."

"I was always thinking you could do better." There's a pained expression on his face as he folds his napkin over.

"Isn't that for me to decide?"

He doesn't get a chance to answer because the waiter comes to take our food away, disappearing and returning with the coveted cast iron skillet bread pudding a few moments later. I take a bite and let the flavors play over my tongue.

"And?" he asks.

"It's not quite the same, but it's not a bad imitation."

"They've got the cook from Daniel's back there these days," Ramsey adds, like it might sway my opinion.

"Then maybe the cast iron was seasoned better. They should have stolen those with everything else they've taken in this town," I grumble while I eat another bite. "I should see if Marlowe could make her own version."

Ramsey shakes his head. "I think you need another whiskey and Coke."

"Yes, please." I grin.

He calls the waiter back and orders me another drink.

"Are you trying to get me liquored up?" I tease him as I lean over to feed him a bite of the dessert, and he takes it. My thoughts flash back to the night of the cake tasting, and I think of how much more he deserves.

"Maybe. Is it working?" His lips pull to the side even as he chews his bite.

"Yes." I take some of the vanilla ice cream, letting it melt away the heat of the last mouthful. "You have a room for us upstairs already?" I hope he does because I'm ready for him to be out of the black Wranglers he has on and on his back so I can ride him.

"No. We've got another place to go to after this. I'm not a cheap date, Mrs. Stockton." He presses a palm to his chest, pretending to be wounded.

"Well, that's unfortunate." For both of us—but I am curious about the surprise.

HE SPENDS the rest of dessert flirting with me heavily, and on our way to the truck, someone stops him for an autograph for their kid. He takes his time talking to them and thanking them for the kind words they offer up in support of his career and his early parole.

"Well, that was hot," I say as we climb into the truck. "I think I regret missing that part of the experience."

"What?" He glances at me as he starts the engine.

"The part where you're all sexy and famous. Where people fawn all over you and how talented and brave you are. I think I might have just discovered a new turn-on."

"Whatever helps my cause, I'll take." His face turns thoughtful as he looks out at the road, but his smile doesn't fade. "You think you might be willing to do the jersey thing for me again?"

"I might." I smile back at him. "You think you might play again? I know Cooper was encouraging you when he was here."

The smile drops from his face, and I feel sorry I stumbled on the wrong discussion. I thought the idea of playing again might make him happy, and apparently, it's more of a minefield than I realized.

"I don't know. I miss it. A lot, if I'm honest with myself. Watching it on the TV isn't the same. But I don't know how great my chances would be, and I..." He glances over at me and then back at the road. "I have other priorities that are more important to me right now."

"Like what?" I play coy as I run my hand over his thigh.

"Like my wife looking gorgeous tonight," he answers, shifting in his seat as I lean against the center console. He glances down, and his eyes fall to my cleavage.

"So sweet of you to say, Mr. Stockton." I run my hand along the seam of his jeans, first teasing his balls and then following it up to where I feel him going hard under my hand.

"Fuck, I love it when you call me that," he rasps as my fingers run back down.

"I know you do," I say softly as his eyes snap in my direction when he sees me lean further, reaching for the buttons on his jeans. I make quick work of them, one after the other all the way down until I've only got the cotton of his boxer briefs keeping my palm off his cock.

"Haze..." he hisses when I run my hand over him again.

"I haven't had you in my mouth yet, and I need it." I coax the band of his underwear down gently with the tips of my fingers until the head of his cock is free. I see the tension in his forearms, and I follow the sight down to where his hands are white-knuckling the steering wheel.

"Not on the road. I can't handle it." He lets out a weighted breath.

"I tried to get you to go to a room." I tease the pads of my fingers on the underside of the head.

"I'm trying to get you where we're going in one piece." He grits his teeth when I wrap my hand around him.

"You could pull over," I offer, lifting my lashes to watch him contemplate the idea. I can tell he's fighting with himself, trying to be a gentleman and listening to his better angels, but I'm desperate to push him over the edge. A low rumble of want and frustration comes out of his chest, and he drums his fingers on the steering wheel.

"Haze, darlin'... have some mercy on me. I'm begging you," he pleads, glancing over to shoot me a pained look before his eyes return to the road. It's enough that it has me letting him go and sitting up straighter.

"You're serious about this?" I ask, more curious than upset. I want him, but that he's trying so hard to hold back has me invested in where we're headed.

"Just for the next hour or so. Then I promise I'll make up for it by doing unspeakable things to you the rest of the night."

"I'm going to hold you to that." I flash him a look, smiling at the way relief floods his shoulders. I readjust the fabric on his boxers and pull his shirt down. "Just don't forget to button back up before we go in."

"Noted." He smirks at me.

TWENTY-NINE

Ramsey

WHEN I WALK her inside Seven Sins, she looks at me skeptically, waiting as I pay the cover charge, then letting me have her hand as we walk toward the bar for a drink.

"I don't want to criticize your choices since dinner was amazing, but this is the reason we couldn't just go home?" She raises a brow and glances around the crowded bar.

"Just gotta trust me, sugar." She nearly had me in the car and destroyed any chance of me getting her here. But I managed to drum up just enough willpower. I wave down the bartender because I need a shot before I embarrass myself, and she might need another drink so she doesn't laugh. Mostly I'm just biding time, wishing I hadn't put myself up to this.

But as I look at her sipping her whiskey and Coke, talking to Dakota, and looking as happy as I've ever seen her, it feels worth it. They're laughing about something, and then it quiets, and Dakota looks up at me, amusement dancing in her eyes.

"You ready, cowboy?" she asks.

"As I'll ever be."

"All right. I got you." She winks and then takes off down the bar.

Haze whirls around, and her brows lower with confusion and a hint of accusation.

"You'll see... Finish your drink." I nod to what's left of the amber liquid in her class, and she complies.

She finishes just as the first notes of "Neon Moon" come over the speakers, and I hold out my hand. She stares at my palm for half a second, like she's not quite sure what I want, before she finally puts her hand in mine. Her lashes flutter, and then she looks at me again.

"Dance with me?" I ask, my heart hammering to a staccato rhythm that's already out of sync with the music. Her lips curl with a smile, though, and she nods as we head to the floor. It's not too crowded yet; there's enough room that we can move around together. There are only a few locals who know us well enough to be watching with bated breath to see if I make a mess of this. It's still enough to have my anxiety rising as I pull her close. Who knew dancing in a small-town bar could rival the nerves I feel before a playoff game?

I put one hand low on her waist, just above her hip, and she places hers on my shoulder. We slowly start two-stepping our way into the crowd, moving around the floor counterclockwise as the music floods over us. I keep repeating the advice Dakota gave me in my head: watch my toes so I don't step on her. Slow, slow. Fast, fast. Slow, slow. Fast, fast. Lead but don't drag. I'm focusing so hard on it that it takes me through half the song before I actually look up from my feet.

Haze has a smile on her lips, her eyes wide and glassy, and my heart constricts in my chest. She bites her lower lip, and her hand drifts down my chest as we make another turn. I can see her mind whirring with something as she watches the couple next to us spinning around, and then she looks back up at me again. Her eyes flood with something I can't quite read—something between nostalgia and love, if I had to guess, or at least, if I could hope.

"You remembered," she says, and it's quiet, so quiet I read the words on her lips more than I hear them over the music and the roar of the bar. I smile slowly, half afraid to do anything to mess this moment up.

"Sugar, when it comes to you, I remember every single thing. Like you were branded on my soul." I press my lips to her ear and say the words loud enough for her to hear before I kiss her cheekbone softly and pull her closer. I feel the answering press of her fingers into my chest, and I tighten my grip on her as we make another round on the floor. She rests her head against my chest, and I'm not ready for the song to end as the last chords start to drift over us. I wish I could keep her like this forever, content and safe in my arms.

But the spell breaks a moment later when "Copperhead Road" starts, and several of the couples around us break up and yell as they get ready for the line-dance portion of tonight's events.

"Shit. We better get out of here before we get run over." Haze looks around smiling and starts to tug on my hand as she pulls away.

"Or..." I tug her back to my side. "We can try to keep up."

"You didn't..." she calls out as she side-eyes me, amusement playing in her eyes as the opening chords fade and the first lines of the song play. The people around us start to move in unison, and I do my best to remember the steps Dakota taught me. Haze follows in kind, having done this a million times at weddings and parties over the years. She giggles as she sees me keeping up with the first few steps.

"Just remember when I fall on my face and make an ass of myself, it was for a good cause!" I answer as the stomping starts to drown out my words.

I falter after a few more steps, but I feel her hand on my forearm. She guides me through them again, and we migrate to the back of the line where I won't cause anyone else to trip. She manages to get me back in sync with the beat. A minute later, she's in tears she's laughing so hard at how well I'm able to keep up with her.

"Oh my god! Is this Dakota's work?" she asks, beaming so brightly I wish I could bottle it for the rough days. The ones I might have to live without her.

"She mighta helped," I answer, raising my voice again as the crowd starts to holler out.

"Who's idea was it?" Her brow furrows. Her confusion is understandable. Dakota isn't a matchmaker, and I'm not one to make an ass out of myself in the name of love.

"Mine. She agreed reluctantly."

"You still manage to surprise me, cowboy." Haze's lopsided grin feels like a reward all on its own.

"I try!" I grin back, and the din of the song and stomping reaches a fever pitch; we're both drawn back into it. We manage to finish the song, and then stumble off the dance floor and through the crowd as another starts up. Her fingers thread through mine, and she squeezes my hand as we make our way out of the crush of people wanting to join in the next dance.

"You want another drink? We can go sit and watch for a few before we get back out?" I offer.

She stops, pausing to look up at me, a question in her eyes like she's not quite sure if she should say what's on her mind. "Do you want to dance more?"

"Is this a trick question?" Because I can tell she's teasing me. "I want whatever you want."

"Will you come here with me again sometime? To dance?"

"Sure. Whenever you want," I answer, confused a little by the question.

"Then make good on your promise." Her soft smile turns wicked, and she pulls me toward the back door of the bar, waving at Dakota on the way out. I tip my chin to Dakota, and she nods back, laughing and shaking her head before she moves to the next person at the bar.

THIRTY

Hazel

"JUST GIVE ME ONE MOMENT!" I say as I slip into the master bathroom after we get home. I make a quick tour of all the essentials, slipping out of my dress and freshening up, but then I stand in front of my closet. I dab the perfume on my pulse for a moment while I pause to make sure I'm making the right decision by letting him in on this secret. I'm nervous, and that this man can make me nervous after everything probably says something on its own. I reach into the drawer, though, and pull it out, slipping it on and then taking a deep breath before I walk back out into the master, flicking the light off in my wake.

He's leaned back on the bed, boots and hat gone and his shirt half unbuttoned from where I mauled him on the way in. I'm busy staring at his tattoos, and I only look up to meet his eyes when there's a sharp intake of breath on his part.

"What's that?"

"A jersey with my name on it," I muse as I climb into his

lap, straddling him on the bed. He reaches out absently to support me, his hand brushing over my ass and then digging in as I wiggle down into a seated position.

"Why do you still have it?" He looks down at his college jersey as it pools on the tops of my thighs.

"I still wear it sometimes."

"When you burn effigies on a full moon?" He smirks, and then his smile darkens. "Cause it better not be when you're with him."

I roll my eyes. "When I go see the Chaos play the Rampage in Denver. This way, I don't have to pick sides, and I get all sorts of compliments from the sports bros on knowing who the home-state boy is."

"Do you tell them how you stole it?" His eyes grow heavy with lust as his fingers play with the hem.

"You mean tell them how you stole *me* out of your team-mate's room and made me cover up with it?"

"I maintain Reynolds had no business fucking touching you." He shakes his head like it still pisses him off.

"I maintain that it was none of *your* business."

"You didn't complain when I had my head between your thighs later that night."

"I was just making the best of a bad situation." I smirk at him, and he answers it for a moment before his eyes suddenly cloud with concern and his brow furrows.

"When did you go to a Chaos-Rampage game?"

"Last year." I lean forward and kiss the side of his neck. He lets out a soft sound of approval, tilting his head to the side and closing his eyes. "And the year before that." I dot another kiss. "And the playoffs before that."

I barely get the last word out before his hand wraps around the side of my neck, his thumb bracketing my chin as he pulls back from me. His eyes burn into me as they travel over my skin, like he's trying to make sense of what I've just said.

"What do you mean?" I can hear the suspicion in his tone.

"I mean... if you were in Colorado playing, I was in the seats watching. Like always." I promised myself I'd never let him find out. I'd sworn my friends to secrecy when they went with me. Made them commit to a social media blackout of our attendance on any platform he or anyone he knew might see. So I can't believe I'm admitting it so freely now.

"Why didn't you tell me?" He blinks rapidly, and his mouth twists like he's fending off pain.

"What would it have changed? You had your life, and I had mine."

"I would have gotten to see you. There were days I would have killed for a glimpse of you."

"I'm sorry..." I say softly. "I didn't think you'd want—"

"I always want you," he cuts off my explanation, his hand skimming down my jaw, and I lean into it, closing my eyes.

His thumb runs over my lips. "Why won't you let me kiss you?"

"Boundaries."

"For you or me?"

"For my icy little heart." I smile at him. This conversation has gotten so heavy, and I hate that I somehow ruined the night. I knew the jersey was a risk, but it was one I thought would make him happy or amused, maybe even tease me for being obsessed with him.

"I see. Is there any hope for me?" he asks as he absently rubs his thumb over the swell of my lower lip, back and forth, like he's considering the possibility. "Melting it, I mean?" His eyes lift to meet mine, and it feels like he's asking me something much more pointed than whether or not he can kiss me.

"If anyone can melt it, it's you. I never count you out,

Stockton." I press a kiss to his thumb. His eyes go soft and drift over my face for a moment, lost in thought, before he comes back to me.

"You should have told me about the games," he repeats, his brow furrowed.

"I'm sorry. Do you want me to make it up to you?" My hands go for his belt, undoing the buckle slowly while he watches me.

"Show me how sorry you are." His eyes glitter with the challenge.

THIRTY-ONE

Ramsey

SHE MAKES quick work of the belt and buttons, her fingers hooking into my boxer briefs and dragging them down my thighs along with my jeans. She's greedy as fuck to have her mouth on me again after I denied her all night.

Fuck. Let's be honest; I'm greedy for it too. I need it. To fill her pretty little mouth and take the edge off so I can take my time with her after.

I feel her breath on my cock as her fingers tease their way down the underside a few moments later. I thought I was ready for this, to finally let her have control over me, but when her mouth wraps around the head of my cock, I have to dig my fingers into the sheets.

"Fuck..." I moan as she teases me relentlessly, giving me soft touches but not the full depth of her. "Sugar... Your mouth... Fuck." I'm lost for the right words, but she doesn't care. She's just happy to be getting what she's wanted all evening, and I'm thanking every lucky star I have that I have a wife with a mouth like this. One she knows how to use so fucking well. One that she's this happy to use to bring me to my knees.

So warm and wet and so fucking perfect. Her tongue dances over the tip and then circles around it as she explores the vertical piercing. She sucks gently and takes me a little deeper before she pulls back, the sound of her mouth on me wet, sloppy, and so fucking sweet to my ears after all this time.

I groan at the loss of her as she replaces her mouth with her hand, slowly stroking me as she looks up at me thoughtfully, enjoying having me at her mercy.

"How long have you had it?" She runs her thumb over the end of the barbell.

"Got it after I signed the divorce papers," I admit and she pauses, something flashing over her face that I can't see well enough in the dim light to understand. I almost start to explain it, but it goes as quickly as it came, and she's already on to the next question.

"Did it hurt?"

"When I had it done, yeah. Saw fucking stars."

"Good. You deserved some pain back then." She says it like she means it, but when her eyes meet mine, they're soft, and her lips curve just the slightest bit in amusement.

I choke on the laugh I have in response to her sadistic side because she leans down, sweeping her hair off her shoulder and wrapping her fist around the base of my cock as she takes me deep. I see stars for real then, brilliant against the back of my lids as she starts to work me over. A low moan rumbles out of my chest, and it spurs her on.

"Christ. You suck cock like you were fucking made for it," I mutter, torn between trying to watch her and feeling so fucking good I can barely keep my eyes open. "The way you take me down your throat, Haze..." I curse again, loudly, and she eats it up like she does the rest of my praise.

She releases me after the next pass of her mouth, taking a break for air, and her hand runs up and down the length of me in a perfect rhythm. I risk opening my eyes, and it's like something out of one of my prison fantasies, her in my jersey, cheeks flushed and lips swollen, so focused on the task of making me come that she's barely noticing anything around her.

This time when she takes me, her hair slips forward, brushing the tops of my thighs with each bob of her mouth. I missed this. This little gesture, a memory of her I'd clung to long after I'd accepted that I'd never see her again. I'd imagined the feel of her hair over my skin a million times when she was gone, so much so that it's hard to believe it's real now. I reach out for her, my fingers threading into her long, soft strands, the feel of them grounding me. I tighten my grip as she starts to moan around my cock; the vibration is the extra push I need. The two of us play off each other like we always have, reading what the other needs before we even have to ask.

"Sugar..." I warn but she only works me over harder, eager to have me coming for her. "You're so fucking merciless. Let me come on your pretty lips. If you won't let me kiss them, at least let me paint them. Please."

A soft whimper of a moan from her is a promise as she starts to take me faster, letting me fuck her throat as my hips counter her desperate attempts to take me deeper. I tighten my grip on her hair, dying to have the real-life version I've been conjuring in my head for years.

"Fuck, sugar. Yes. Just like that. Suck me harder." She obeys every request, silent and spoken, and I start coming inside her mouth until she lets me slip out. I grab the base of my cock and stroke myself hard and fast as she helps. My come lashes over her pretty red lips and cheeks, staining her perfect makeup and slowly dribbling down her chin.

"You're so fucking gorgeous. All dressed up for me like this. My jersey. My come." I run my thumb over her lower lip as her tongue dips out to taste me, and I take some for myself, drawing it down her chin and over her throat to the top of the jersey. Some of it has already dripped down onto her necklace, and I go to wipe it away for her. I'm making so many mental notes, committing this "photograph" to memory for when I need it on the long nights.

She comes closer, climbing onto my lap and straddling me. Her lips are at my neck, kissing their way up as my breathing starts to return to normal.

"I love all the sounds you make for me when you're in my mouth," she whispers against my skin as she kisses my throat, smelling like sex and feeling like heaven as her body settles against mine. "I was looking forward to that for weeks. You so desperate and needy for me. Coming so hard on my tongue like a good boy. You've got me so wet now," she confesses. "I've loved everything about tonight... dinner, dancing, this—you've been so sweet."

"Anything to see you happy." My hand runs up her thigh, and her eyes track the slow drift. "I'm gonna get a washcloth for you." I kiss her forehead, plant her back on the pillows, and stand, pulling my pants back up before I head to the bathroom.

When I come back, she's lying back on the bed waiting for me, and I can barely handle how fucking beautiful she is. I have no idea how I ever left this woman or how I'll do it again if she asks me to. My eyes dart to the suit jacket I left on the floor. I couldn't bring myself to give her the gift I bought her earlier. I didn't want to envision the possibility that she might actually use it, not when she was laughing and dancing with me like we were still twenty years old.

Visions of her marrying him start to play in front of me, haunting me as I try to force a smile when she gives me a questioning look. I sit next to her on the bed, taking the warm washcloth to her chin and cheeks and slowly down her neck—gently washing her clean again as she leans into my touch.

"But I do have one favor to ask." I'm hoping it won't change her mood. I drop the washcloth to my side and look down over the jersey.

"What's that?" She smiles, and her fingers trace over the tattoo on the back of my hand.

"Now that I've seen you in this." I tug at the hem of my Highland State jersey. "Let me see you in the dress."

"The dress? The one I wore tonight?" She looks at me perplexed.

"The wedding dress." I need to see her in it. I want to know what she picked for him.

Her face falls immediately, and her eyes go to the window. I watch as her throat bobs hard on a swallow.

"I burned that dress."

"Ours?" I say it like it belonged to me too. She nods, and I'm not prepared for the way that guts me. My chest is tight, and my stomach's turning. I'd loved the way she looked in it, and now, I'll never see it again. I start to pull back, but she grabs my wrist.

"I couldn't bear to look at it anymore, Ramsey. Every time I saw it, it broke my heart. Bristol saw me crying one day when she was over, and we were having a girls' night. I went to look for something in the closet, the bag it was in fell down, and I lost it. She was furious I was still letting it get to me. We were all a little drunk already. So we had an impromptu burn-the-dress party."

"I see." I guess I can't blame her. I kept the cowboy hat, but the rest of the suit I'd worn had been lost to time when I'd bulked up in college. I hadn't been sentimental when we were still together, but I guess I thought that we would never end. That it would never hurt like it has the last five years.

"I wish I still had it. I would if I could." She looks at me thoughtfully.

"I want to see the one you're going to wear for him."

"Ramsey." She lets out my name on a discouraged sigh.

I cross the room and extract the box from the suit jacket pocket, handing it to her. I feel like I'm playing a constant game of brinksmanship with her, just hoping for a glimmer of a chance of winning.

"I just want to see how it looks with this." I hold it out for her, and she takes it reluctantly, her eyes locked on mine, searching for an answer there.

THIRTY-TWO

Hazel

I STARE at the box he holds out for me. It looks distinctly like it contains jewelry, and my hand shakes as I take it from him. I'm not sure what it means—if he's still mad, if he's accepted that I'm getting married to someone else, if it's just meant to be another taunt... the possibilities are endless with him, and right now, his face is a mask.

"I figured you've let me help with everything else—the honeymoon, the cake, the invitations. Gotta let me in on the last bit." There's a small reassuring smile.

I open it carefully and inhale sharply when I see what's inside.

It's a stunning pear-shaped sapphire necklace. I pull it out of its container and hold it up in the light, biting my lower lip as I stare at how beautiful it is. I look at him with a silent question, but he's lost in his own thoughts, staring at it with me before he realizes.

"I figured it could be your something blue." There's a sad smile on his face. "To match your hair."

"Ramsey..." I'm lost for words. I have to take a long deep breath to keep from crying. Whatever mood he's in tonight, I'm not prepared for any of it.

"Please?" He asks to see the dress again, and I can't bring myself to tell him no. Even though it's the last thing I want to do right now.

"Okay," I agree, setting the necklace back in its box on the bed next to him.

WHEN I RE-EMERGE in the dress, it's not zipped up in the back, so I have to clutch the front of it to my chest.

"Can you zip it? I need help with it." I turn my back to him, and the train drags with my movement, making me look like a statue standing in the midst of a giant pedestal of champagne-colored marble.

His fingers move deftly up the back of the dress, pulling the zipper and leading with one finger to make sure it doesn't catch my skin. The bodice is skintight and perfectly tailored. It makes my breasts look like they did when I was nineteen and my waist the hourglass figure that I can never quite achieve in my usual T-shirts and jeans. He doesn't say a word as his fingers slip under the necklace I wear every day.

"I know you usually wear this one. I figured you need something special for the wedding though." He undoes the fastener from my neck, pulling it away and then moves to rejoin it, his large fingers still managing to skillfully work the clasp. He sets it gently on the dresser, next to my ring holder and perfume. "Did he get this for you? You wear it all the time, but I don't remember it."

"No. I had it made."

"It's pretty. Looks like you."

"Well, you would know. You picked it out," I confess softly.

"What do you mean?" He frowns at me. It's another thing I shouldn't be admitting to him. Another thing like the jersey and the games that tells the truth about the last five years.

"It's my engagement ring. I just had the stones reset." The way he looks at me, I feel like my heart might stop in my chest. Apparently, I've finally caught him off guard tonight with that information. "It was just... so pretty. I wanted to be able to still wear it."

"Oh... well..." He's lost for words for a moment and then practically chokes them out when he does speak again. "I'd rather not be your something old that day. Blue it is." He puts the sapphire on me and takes a step back to admire his work.

"You look gorgeous," he compliments me, but his eyes are distant, studying the dress, and I can tell his mind is a million miles away.

"Ramsey, it's beautiful..." I hold the sapphire up to let it catch the light again.

"It's a lot of dress," he comments absently, studying the ornate detail on the bodice and following the line down to the long train. "Fancy as fuck compared to what you married me in." I can hear his mood shift with his tone.

"Well, the wedding is in March, not the summer like ours was..." I don't know why I'm explaining this. I should be getting out of the dress because I don't think trying it on was wise, given the effect it's having on him. "Could you unzip it now? I want to put the jersey back on." I offer him a small smile.

"It's gonna be hard to fuck you with all those skirts." He grabs the train and pulls it back around, lifting it and letting it catch the air to fall to the floor again.

"Ramsey..." I try to use my most placating tone, but it fails.

"I think we should try. Give it a test run to make sure it'll work on the big day. What do you think?" He paces in my direction, his knuckles brushing over the back of my cheek when he reaches me.

"I don't think that's a good idea." I try to bargain with him, and he's clearly disappointed, his eyes darkening as he looks over me.

"No? Why not? We already went through all the lingerie. The cake. The invitations. Seems likes we should do this one too. That's what I'm good at, right? Giving you a chance to try it all out first." His hand wraps around one side of my throat, and he kisses his way up the other. "You know I'll make sure you get it exactly the way you want."

The heavy breath that escapes when he nips my neck is the only confirmation he needs that I'm still on the verge of no return for him.

"That's my girl. One more thing we can check off your wedding planning list."

He walks me to the edge of the bed and gently presses up my spine until I'm bent over it, face down, ass in the air as he starts to pull up my skirts. There's a mound of them, and it's not light work, but he's dedicated to the task. His fingers slip between my thighs when he's finished, and he tests me through the cotton, groaning when he finds me still ready for him.

"Am I making you wet, sugar? You want me to fuck you in his dress?" His fingers gently massage me through the fabric, just enough to give his taunt a physical presence too. I grind down on the edge of the bed, desperate for more friction, and not even a little bit embarrassed, even though I should be. "This way, when you say your vows to him, I can be right there with you. My collar around your neck, the smell of me on your skin. That's how you like it, isn't it?"

I bury the sound I make when his fingers slip under my

panties, and it only serves to make him angrier. He tears them off, wrenching them down my hips and ripping the lace on one side in the process. He tosses what's left next to me on the bed.

"Look how soaked you are, just from letting me come all over that pretty little face. I doubt you get that wet from sucking his cock. Do you?" he demands.

"No," I answer quietly.

There's a grim chuckle from him, and then he's on his knees, his face buried in my pussy as he starts to lick and kiss and suck in earnest. He gives me just enough to tease and torment but not nearly enough to sate how much I need him. My fingers twist in the quilt as he lightly flicks his tongue over me for the hundredth time, and I let out a muted scream into the quilt I've bunched under my head.

"Ramsey, please," I beg. "Please."

"No, Haze, darlin'." He chuckles as he pulls away. "We're going to make sure you come hard tonight. As long as it takes. I want to make sure the memory sticks for you."

I can feel how wet I am from how the air cools my skin in his absence, and I shift on my feet, grinding against the spot where my dress is bunched up on the edge of the bed. I want to put myself out of my misery and keep him from being able to torture me more than he already has. But I can't seem to chase it, not like I need, and there's too much fabric for it to do any real good.

His shadow falls over me before I hear him, and his hand comes down hard on my ass, my exposed cheek stinging with the crack of his palm. I gasp and turn back to glare at him. He answers me with an intimidating glower.

"Don't take what's mine to give." He growls, and I feel the weight of several toys drop onto the bed at my hips.

"Then fuck me. Now." My patience is wearing thin.

"I will. In good time," he promises, and I hear the sheets

rustle underneath the toys as he chooses one. "But first, I want to see what it's gonna be like when he fucks you on your wedding day, listen to you make all those little mewling fake cries you make for him."

I feel the press of Curtis's toy as he slips it inside. I know which one it is by the feel of it, that sensation of being full but not full enough. The taunting awareness that I've had better, but without any of the man to make up for what's lacking in the toy. Not that either compared to the man in the room with me. The one who owns my body, whether he's there with me or not.

"Fuck, Ramsey. Don't... I'll lose it." I'll cry if he doesn't let me come tonight after all this.

"Don't worry. I won't let that happen. I've got other things to keep you sated, or at least on the edge." I don't like the soft devilish laugh that he has, and the dull buzz confirms my fear. It's one of my clit vibrators, turned down to the lowest setting. The same style Ramsey always liked to torment me with. "Raise your hips."

Stupidly, I comply because, for some reason, I crave this man tormenting me over everything else.

"Fuck," I curse as I lower back down, his fingers coasting over my hip and the curve of my ass as he watches me rock forward against it.

"It shouldn't be too high, but if it gets to be too much, tell me," he whispers, sweeping some hair out of my face as he does it. He grins at my suffering and kisses my temple. I want to scowl at him, but I'm easily distracted. He's peeled off the shirt he had on earlier, and I can barely stand to look at him. The man has an unfair advantage at almost every turn.

He uses Curtis's toy on me again, teasing me with the tip and then taking it deeper. He changes his rhythm and depth until he finally has the perfect combination—the response he wants from my body and the soft curses of me not getting enough of what I need.

"I know he leaves you feeling empty, sugar, but I want to hear you try to fake it. I want to hear those little pretend gasps of awe you make for him while you fuck yourself with his cock again."

"Ramsey..." I let out a frustrated sigh. "Fuck."

"I don't think he'll want to hear my name on your wedding night," he muses.

"Fuck off."

"I'm trying... would it help if you call me 'daddy' too?" He snickers, and I let out a shrill little scream that I don't bother to bury in the quilt, which only makes him laugh harder. I want to curse him. Tell him how much I hate him—that I'm never letting him touch me again, but those would all be lies. So I offer the truth instead.

"Please. I want *you*."

Those are the magic words because the toy disappears, and his cock replaces it in one deep thrust. A loud gasp slips free, and I swallow hard as I adjust to the difference, burying my face in the quilt as I feel his piercing again. I want to thank whoever or whatever gave him that idea.

"Fuck me," I curse, and there's an amused half-groan as he slides out of me and back in again.

"That better?" he asks. It's rhetorical. He knows it is, but I also know his ego likes to hear it.

"So much." I moan when he hits a pace that finally starts to spark and bloom little currents through my body. He keeps it for a minute, letting me chase the edge and counter him with the roll of my hips. But then he slows again, and I hear the sound of him opening a bottle.

I feel the cool drip of lube against my ass, and then the tip of something silicone follows, barely brushing against my skin.

"I know we're still working you back up to me, sugar, but you can take him. He's so much smaller. Just the tip first. You can do it." His voice is the perfect mix of raspy need and soothing comfort. I could drown in it—so distracted by it that I don't have it in me to argue.

I pant as he teases me with it, starting to press in and then pulling back again, slowly and carefully warming me up to the sensation. I grip the bed, curling my fingers around the edge of it, and try to breathe.

"Not with you inside me. It's too much."

"Nah, darlin', it's gonna be perfect. You're so close. This is gonna help take you over the edge." He teases it along the seam again, and I take a deep breath to try to steel my nerves. "Besides, we're practicing, right? Gotta get you ready for the big day... When he finally gets his turn to have you here, but you're still imagining it's me inside you instead."

"Ramsey!" I protest, so distracted by scolding him that I don't even notice him slipping the toy inside me at first. Not until the fullness of it starts to sink in, and I whimper his name a second time. "It's so much," I murmur. It's good and too much all at the same time.

"You can take it. You're a good little wife, Haze. So good for me. I'll reward you with my mouth later, suck on that sweet clit of yours for hours on my knees if you give me this."

He eases more of the toy inside me while he fucks me, and I roll my hips to try to get more of the vibration on my clit. I need it to help me stay focused while I adjust to how overwhelmingly full it feels. Especially when Ramsey's already taking up so much room that I feel like I can barely breathe.

"You good, sugar?" he asks once he has it in as far as he planned.

I take a breath and a quick inventory. I'm full, tormented, and dying to fucking get off, but I'm good.

"Yes," I say softly.

"That's my girl. I knew you could do it." He starts to ease in and out of me with slow thrusts of his cock while he holds the toy still, and the vibrator hums on a low setting. It's torture—pure and simple, but the kind that's so good I can only manage to moan and mutter out a curse against his name in reply. "Fuck... You're being so good for me. You feel so good, tightening around me like this. Fuck, Haze."

He groans when he takes me deeper before he does the unthinkable and uses the toy to counter his next thrust, sliding himself in as he slides the toy out. He continues until I'm just a moaning mess being fucked from all angles, all of them in his control and me at his mercy. Then he presses me further, closer and closer to the precipice, syncing them back up again until I can barely use words. Every inch of me is on edge, so near to the release I need I can almost feel the feather's edge of it.

"Fuck, listen to you. So sweet when you're all filled up like this. Trying to take both of us at the same time without falling apart. You're a mess, sugar. Such a beautiful fucking mess like this. I wish you could see how good you look with both of us inside you. Fuck Look at you." He rubs my hip with his free hand. I glance back over my shoulder. It's not a perfect view, not the one I really want, but it's enough. The sight of us—him all muscles and tattoos, and me spread out in front of him in a pile of satin and tulle while he takes what he wants.

I shift to get a better look, and it brings my clit flush against the vibrator. I gasp and murmur how close I am before I try to rock back to take more of him and bring myself over the edge.

"You gonna come for me?" he asks, slowing down his rhythm to force me to answer him when I try to fight for control.

"Yes." I gasp for my next breath. "Fuck. *Please*. Please make me come."

"Please make me come, who?" He stills inside of me, and I'm stuck on the edge, hanging by a thread and desperate for the fall.

"Please. Please, Mr. Stockton, make me come. Please!" The last please is more of a demand than a request, but it appeases him all the same.

"That's better." He gives my ass cheek a playful squeeze.

He fucks me with the toy slowly for a few more slow thrusts of his cock before he takes it away in favor of gripping both my hips, taking full control, and fucking me fast and deep. I feel it start to surface at last, my nerve endings blooming with the sensation, and his piercing hits every spot perfectly in the rhythm I need.

I start coming so hard I almost see all the colors of the aurora in the blackout. I cry out his name and curse him at intervals. It's one wave after another, and every nerve ending in my body feels like it's rushing to its own end.

I can feel him follow, coming hard inside me. I watch him in the mirror in the corner of the room as his arm wraps around my middle, and he bends over, fucking me through his own release. His jaw tightens, and he comes loudly, moaning so loud it vibrates through me.

I'm lost, staring at him in the mirror. He looks fucking gorgeous and unbroken and powerful. I wish I always got to watch him reflected like this—see him at his best—when he knows just how much he's desperately needed.

He groans as he pulls out, and the last of him spills onto the backs of my thighs, hot against my already warm skin. He looks down and surveys his work, kneeling and disappearing behind my skirts.

"Fuck, sugar. You're leaking." He kisses the inside of my thigh and uses his fingers to push his come back inside me as his tongue teases me softly. I raise my hips in response, trying to cant myself up and out of his reach—still too close to my orgasm to be able to take the torment he's giving. He licks me one last time and stands. "The only thing better than seeing you in this dress with him will be getting to watch you have to pick a new one because this one's too small." He flashes a roguish grin at me in the mirror and then helps me stand, turning me around to face him.

"Ramsey," I chide.

"You want it too. Don't lie. The number of times you begged me to fuck you bare in the last few weeks... I know, darlin'." His fingers trace their way down my jaw. "You aren't ready to admit it yet, but I know. You will."

I ignore his accusation. If it's true, he's right. I'm not about to divulge those kinds of secrets, so there's no use in discussing it. His self-satisfied smirk is endearing and irritating in equal measure, though, so I do what I do best.

"So I did a good job faking it that whole time?" I ask, and his eyes snap to mine, his brow darkening. I laugh when he realizes I'm teasing him.

"Turn around," he instructs, unzipping the dress for me. "Get in the shower, brat. I'll be right in after I clean up." He nods over his shoulder to the bathroom and then starts to pick up the toys.

"Yes, sir." I smirk, and he flashes a look at me that tells me to watch my mouth.

"Don't say that. I might like it so much I'll make you use it everywhere." He gives my ass a gentle push, and I hurry my way across the room. "What would Grace and Kit think?"

"I don't think they'd be nearly as scandalized as Albert." We both devolve into snickering, and I kiss his cheek on the way out.

I turn the knob on the shower and jump out of the way of the stream. I'm thankful it doesn't take long for the water to heat up. I want a hot shower and a fresh, fluffy towel, and then I want to sprawl out on the bed and sleep for a year. My body's exhausted from being so thoroughly worked over, and this dress has me so overly heated I'm ready to peel my way out of it.

He joins me a short while later, after he washes off the toys and puts the lube away. Grinning at me as he steps in through the shower door; a boyish one that wraps around my heart. I wish I could keep him like this, always have him this happy and free.

"Bed's ready to crawl in," he whispers against my forehead before he kisses me there.

Ramsey makes light work of the shower for me, sudsing and rinsing every inch of my skin and then slowly lathering my hair while he massages my scalp. His fingers run circles over my temples and down behind my ears, making soft strokes up and down my spine before he starts over again. He repeats the process until I'm melting in his hands, and then he rinses me off.

For a man as coarse as he is, he's always been good about this part—making sure I felt completely safe and cared for in the wake of whatever rough sex we had. It's more meaningful on this night, too, when we can't seem to decide which side of the fence we want to stay on with each other—love or hate, rough or gentle, facing the truth or more of us avoiding it. But I'll take as many more nights like this with him as I can get.

THIRTY-THREE

Ramsey

"WHAT'S THIS?" I ask as I walk out onto the back deck to see Bo jumping out of his truck. I can see my bike in the back, and she looks like she's gotten a bit of a detail job in addition to whatever work they did on her.

"What's it look like, jackass?" Bo calls back.

"I didn't realize it was ready yet. You didn't have to bring it over."

"Well, technically, I am still your brother. I figured for the time being you still get the family discount and the door-to-door service," he answers as he pulls the tailgate open.

I hurry down to meet him as he pulls the ramp he's got in the back of the truck out. Once he's got it fixed, I climb into the bed, help him undo the bike from its restraints, and walk it down.

"Thanks for this."

"Sure thing. Where do you want it?"

"Uh. We can probably put it in the pole barn."

He walks with me as we get the bike moved, but when he goes to open the pole barn door, he stops short. He looks back at me, brow furrowed, and motions for me to stay quiet and come to him. I put the kickstand down, abandoning the bike, and walk toward the pole barn, giving him a confused look as I make my way over.

When I get to the door, I hear the sound of something rustling around inside, furniture shifting and scrapes across the floor.

"It's probably just an animal," I say in a low whisper. The place wasn't exactly as airtight as it should be, and it wouldn't be unheard of. His frown gets heavier, and he shakes his head, pointing for me to listen. Then I hear it—the low sound of a man's voice talking to someone on the other side of the building.

I rack my brain for who it could be. Kell and Elliot are both in the bunkhouse; I already saw them duck in for the night after talking about going into town for a drink later. None of the guests from the inn would have wandered out this far, that I know of, and none of the boarders renting space would be here this late, even if they got confused about the barns.

My frown matches Bo's now as we listen to try to hear what they're saying.

"Look over there," I hear him say.

"Can't see shit without a light," another guy answers louder, and he's much closer to where we're standing.

"Shut the fuck up," the other hisses.

All the hairs stand up on the back of my neck, and I flex my fists as Bo and I exchange looks of understanding. He nods for me to take one side of the door, and he takes the other. We do a silent count, and then he moves in before me. We walk slowly around the edges of the room, and I make my way to the left, looking for the barn gun I saw in here the other day and praying it's still loaded if I need it.

I watch Bo disappear behind a large, old bookshelf, and I crouch when I hear the guys talk again. He wasn't kidding about not being able to see. Without the overhead lights on, it's damn near impossible. The only ambient light is coming from the far door, where the earliest rays of moonlight are barely creeping in to illuminate the space.

When I step forward to get a better look around the room, I hear the scurry of a mouse under my feet. The skittering attracts their attention, and I see one of their shadows freeze.

"The fuck was that?" Number Two whispers again.

"Probably a bird or a mouse. It's a barn," Number One growls low, still annoyed that his partner won't shut up.

There's the sound of footsteps again, moving in my direction, and I reach my hand up on the desk, feeling around for the gun. It rustles the heavy furniture cover that's draped over it, and I hold my breath, waiting to hear if they heard it, and letting out a sigh of relief when I hear them continue to talk.

I feel around one more time, and finally, my palm collides with the buttstock. I wrap my hand around it—and thankfully, just in time.

"Hey, asshole!" I hear Bo call out, and a second later, there's a loud smack and a groan followed by the sound of a body collapsing against the floor.

"What the fuck? Shane?" Number One calls out for Number Two, and there's only another muted groan in response. "Who's there?" he calls out, the anxiety reverberating through his words. They didn't anticipate being found.

Number One steps out of his corner, and he's illuminated by the door. I can see his silhouette aiming his gun wildly, trying to find the source of the noise.

"Put the gun down," I call. Grabbing the gun off the desk and aiming it in his direction.

"Fat fucking chance of that, you prick," Number One returns. "Go fuck yourself."

"You first." I hear another sound, like a blunt instrument against flesh, and this time, I hear the distinct sound of metal clattering across the concrete floor. I see Bo's silhouette next to the other man, and the gun is missing from his hand.

They both drop to the floor a moment later, scattering to find it in the darkness and tussling with one another in the process. I pull myself out of my hiding spot and run over, hitting the guy on the back of the head and forcing him back to his knees.

"Let it go, or you'll get one in your head." I'm desperately hoping I can make good on that promise.

"What are you doing here?" Bo asks the guy, grabbing him by his collar.

"I'm not telling you shit." He spits on the ground and shoves back at Bo. It elicits another smack on the back of his head from me, which he meets with disdain. Something about his voice hits me as familiar, and I'm racking my brain as I hit him again with the buttstock of the gun.

"You'll fucking do what he—" Before I can finish my sentence, I feel the searing heat of pain across my cheek and face. It's like being hit with a tackle with no helmet. So painful that I drop to my knees.

Bo turns to me, trying to make out what happened to me in the dark. The guy he's holding hostage takes advantage of his distraction and shoves him so hard he falls back against the bookshelf. I grip the gun tightly. It's the one thing I can't afford to let go of as I try to clear the pain and my mind to refocus my attention back on the situation.

"The door. Let's go!" the second guy yells to the first, grabbing his shoulder and shoving him forward as he looks between us, before he turns to run. They race for the door, but they're slowed by the maze of furniture and tripping hazards that are in here in the dark. One of them hits his knee and screams out in pain as he tries to run on it.

"Ramsey?" Bo calls to me to make sure I'm okay.

"I'm fine. I'm coming. Go!" I yell to him to get a head start, and he takes off after the intruders. I climb back to my feet, setting the gun down, and rub the side of my cheek; it feels tender where he hit me, but I don't feel any blood. I roll my shoulders as I step over the furniture, and then I take off after Bo as soon as my feet are under me again.

The light out in the field is only slightly better, illuminating the silhouettes of the guys as they race across it. Bo is on their heels, but he's not in the same shape he was when we were kids playing ball, and while he can more than pace them, it's not enough to catch them. I reach him, but the guys are over the far fence where they've left a car, and they tear off in it across the field.

We watch as they disappear over the horizon as we catch our breath.

"What the fuck was that?" Bo asks, leaning over with his hands on his knees.

I stretch my neck, running my fingers over my cheek once again to make sure I'm still not bleeding.

"Fuck if I know." I take a deep breath of the night air. Prison made me soft, I guess. Not enough time sprinting down a field, and I'm out of shape. I need a lot of time back with a trainer if I'm going to run for a living again.

"Do you think they're headed toward the casino?" Bo breaks through my existential crisis as we watch the car speeding in the direction of The Avarice. It's the only thing in that direction off the property, but it's also the easiest way to get back to civilization if you can't go out through our front drive.

"I don't know. It seems like that's how they came on to the ranch. There are a couple of gates out that way, I guess."

"No cameras on them?" He looks at me.

"There might be one. I'd have to ask Haze. I don't know what she kept of my parents'." Given the business my parents were in, we'd originally had a lot of cameras on the property, but Hazel preferred privacy over technology.

"Back to the house then, I guess." He stretches out his back, rubbing a palm across his chest as if it'll ease his lungs.

"I need a fucking beer after that. That's for sure."

ONCE WE GET BACK to the house, Bo and I stand out on the back porch, sipping our beers and enjoying the crisp night air. It's that time of year now when the temps drop low at night, even if they still manage to get reasonably warm in the daytime. Without a beer or a jacket to keep you warm, the chill runs down your spine and tunnels through your bones until its deep inside. The kind you can't shake, a bit like the worry I have tonight after what's unfolded. The blood's still drying on my knuckles, and I'm studying the pattern of it when Bo finally sits up straighter.

"I have a bad feeling," he says, staring at the pole barn in the distance that we'd found the intruders in.

"About them?"

"That's the same place I saw Curtis."

"That barn?" I guess I never did clarify. I'd just assumed it was the garage they park most of the cars in. "I thought you meant the garage that's attached."

"No. That one." His brows lift in question, wondering if

I'm as worried as he is. I let out a long breath and take another sip of my beer. Definitely a bad feeling or two.

The barn we found the guys in really only has my and my parents' things in it. They used it for extra storage when they were alive, and when they died, and Hazel and I took over the house, we moved most of their things out there. Then when I left, I'd followed suit. It's essentially the Stockton family heirloom and furniture graveyard, but no one outside the family knows that either.

"Fucking weird that they'd pick that one and not one of the others," I mutter.

"Right? If they were just off the street snooping around, you'd think they'd go for the stables where they'd know they might find some stuff of value."

"Right," I agree.

"This is what I mean... So much of this stuff happening has been weird as fuck. I can't put my finger on it, but I don't like it." He shakes his head and downs another sip of his beer.

"Yeah. The one guy's voice. It sounded almost familiar, but I have no idea where—" I stop dead in my tracks because it hits me. His voice sounded like one of the guys from the other night at Seven Sins. The ones my brother had sent to the casino.

"What?" Bo asks, clearly realizing I was coming to terms with something.

"One of the guys. I think he might have been in Seven Sins the other night."

"What makes you think that?"

"He got into it with Dakota. She said he was asking a lot of questions, and she didn't like his attitude. It nearly came to blows. Her other bartender said they'd asked about the ranch."

"That's not fucking good." Bo states the obvious; his face clouded with concern.

"No. It's not. What's weird is that my brother chased him

off and sent him to The Avarice. Then he headed back that way... might not be a coincidence."

"Sounds like you and your brothers need to have a chat."

"Yeah. I think that's what I'll be doing first thing tomorrow."

I'm not leaving this ranch until I get to the bottom of what's happening. No way am I letting Hazel stay here alone or, worse yet, with Curtis until I had answers. And my brothers are going to cooperate with my investigation, whether they like it or not.

THIRTY-FOUR

Hazel

"I'M SO sorry it's taken me this long to get some time in with you," I apologize as I sit down in the dining room with Amelia.

"No worries at all, sweetheart. I've been having a lovely time. Grace has kept me busy with all the different excursions to antique markets and visiting with the horses. It's been lovely just to sit and read in the library too." Amelia gives me a soft smile as she places her napkin on her lap.

"Well, I'm glad you've been having a good time. It's just been a wild few weeks around here, and I'm barely able to keep up."

"It does seem busy around here. Like you might need to start thinking about hiring some more help." Amelia gives me a pointed look before she sips her water.

"Oh, yes..." I feel a bit of shame at the fact we don't have as many people on staff as I'd like, but we need to cut any corners that we can afford to. "I'm hoping next season. It's so late in this one that it didn't make a lot of sense. It's pretty quiet here in the winter."

"Still focused more on the horses, then?" She nods out the window to where Kell is bringing a couple of riders and their horses into the stables.

"They're still a big focus, yes." Amelia, who'd run her own real estate business when she was younger, always likes to give me a little bit of unsolicited business advice when she visits.

"It doesn't seem like many people from the inn are riding though?" Her brows raise in curiosity.

"No, lately it's been mostly older folks who'd rather feed them some sugar cubes or carrots than ride. A few folks come up from the city for lessons though."

"That's too bad. Have you considered closing down the ranch?" Amelia's blunt with a side of sweetness. She has the ability to laser-focus in on the questions that cut to the heart of something that's been bothering me, and it's one of the reasons I've always liked her. There's no beating around the bush with her or time for gentle hand-holding and discussions about the weather. It's just raw and unfiltered thoughts and questions that make me feel like she could run an excellent interrogation ring.

"It's crossed my mind, but we have boarded horses and rescues here, so it'd involve a lot more than just me changing my mind on a whim. I have commitments. People and horses that I care about deeply."

"Well, if it's the right business decision, it's not a whim. If you closed down the ranch, I'd imagine you could sell off a lot of this property. Focus more on your inn."

"I've thought of it. My fiancé and I talked about it at one point." Curtis had a similar opinion. Sell the ranch, keep the money and use it on the inn, reduce the costs of the ranch staff and upkeep, and focus on excursions at local public parks and forest preserves rather than trying to be a one-stop shop for everything. It isn't a bad idea, but it means making choices about the Stockton family land and legacy that I'm not ready to make. Ones that I couldn't now on my own, even if I wanted to.

"Yes, I've been wondering where your fiancé is. I haven't seen him around. You said you were on a break? Something about your ex-husband?" Amelia looks at me thoughtfully, her brow slightly furrowed.

"Oh well... about that... we're on a bit of a hiatus, I guess you could say. Or, at least, I think it's just a hiatus. I'm really not sure at this point."

"Oh dear. What happened? You seemed so happy!" She reaches over to me, and her face clouds with concern.

One of the waiters sets down Kit's famous breadbasket in front of us and fills our water glasses, letting us know that they'll be out with the first course soon before I can answer.

"Well... like I mentioned a bit before, it turns out I'm still married. Fluke thing with the paperwork, and we've just figured it out. We have a waiting period before they'll let the divorce go through, and in the meantime, I'm stuck with my ex. He's going through some legal trouble, and he needs some stability. This is his family ranch, and most of his family and friends still live around here, so he came home while we wait for all of that to go through." Trying to explain this whole predicament makes me feel like I'm living a soap opera, and I cross my legs nervously under the table. I imagine to someone like Amelia, who oozes so much money and class, I look like a mess in her presence, that this whole thing seems like some backwoods drama.

"Curtis was just okay with all of that?" Amelia's frown deepens.

"No, but he's practical. He was called away for work

anyway, so being on hiatus kind of works for us really." It seems easier to just tell her what we've been telling everyone else.

"It doesn't sound like it's working for you. It must be killing you to be separated from someone you love so much." Amelia looks at me sympathetically.

"Yes, it's hard." I swallow because, if I'm honest with myself, I've been so caught up in Ramsey lately that I've barely thought about Curtis. We've barely kept up with texting each other, and I've only spoken to him twice on the phone since the incident with Ramsey. Things are as distant between us as they've ever been. He's grown increasingly cold whenever he talks to me, and I can tell he's not as content with the Ramsey situation as he claimed to be.

"Have you tried calling him to talk through it? Maybe see if he could rearrange his work plans and come back early? Or are you not hoping to make things work?" Leave it to Amelia to ask the questions I don't know how to answer.

"I..." I don't even have a good boilerplate response, let alone a real answer. Not when I really listen to my gut. I'm torn. "I'm not sure what I am right now, to be honest. Having my husband back has been a change... And while he's got a lot of flaws, there's a lot about him that I'd forgotten how much I've missed. You know?" I regret the words almost as soon as I say them when I look up and see the disappointment in her face. I'm sure I sound like someone who wants to have their cake and eat it too.

"I can't say I do. My ex, the one I was married to before my dear sweet Louis." She looks thoughtfully into the distance as she thinks about her second husband, who passed away a few years ago, and then blinks before she resumes. "That man was a nightmare. He was cruel and unthinking. He always put himself first. Never taking care of his family. Running off to do God knows what God knows where instead of having his priorities straight. He always brought his work home with him. I'm grateful for my children, but that's the only good that ever came out of that man."

I nod along my understanding as our first course is brought to the table, and she looks livid just thinking about her ex. I never felt quite that kind of blind animosity for Ramsey. There was mostly just a gaping hole of misery that turned into bitterness over time.

"I'm sorry you had to deal with that. I can't imagine."

"Can't you? From what you told me in the past, your ex didn't seem that much different." Her brow raises as she assesses me.

"I've been angry with him. Bitter about what happened. But I also know he had his reasons for acting the way he did, just like I had mine."

"You're going soft on him then. Thinking about taking him back?" She puts her fork down and looks at me with pointed curiosity.

"I think that I'd forgotten there were a lot of reasons why we were together in the first place." I feel like I'm in a therapy session, forced to say things out loud that I'd barely even let myself think.

"Huh." She presses her lips together and takes a bite of her salad.

"You don't approve?" I smile at the way she's trying to contain her opinion.

She tilts her head in thought and takes a sip of the lavender lemonade Kit made especially for her stay before she answers the question.

"I just think Curtis didn't cause you any of the problems your husband did. I've only seen you happy with him. I don't understand why you'd want to even consider going back to someone who hurt you when you have someone you've told me has always been good to you. I feel like you're too serious for games like the ones your ex plays." She pauses to take another sip, and continues, looking me over thoughtfully. "You're like the daughter I never had, and I worry. I just want what's best for you, sweetheart, you know?" Amelia gives me a soft smile, one that reminds me a little bit of the ones I used to get from my mother as a child.

"I know." I look out the window, staring at the stables and the wide stretch of land beyond it. "But sometimes, working through the hurt makes the love stronger in the long run, you know?"

"Sometimes you find yourself burned again for believing him a second time," Amelia counters, her eyes sweeping over me before she takes another bite.

"I suppose that's a risk," I acknowledge as I look out the window.

"That's the part I don't get. Why take a risk when you have a sure thing?"

It's a good question. One I've been asking myself since Ramsey's been back.

THIRTY-FIVE

Hazel

WHEN I GET BACK to the house from my dinner with Amelia, Ramsey's sitting on the couch in Chaos sweats and a tee with wet hair, watching football on TV. I tilt my head in curiosity as I notice an ice pack pressed to his face. As I round the corner and get closer, I can see his knuckles are scraped and scabbed, highlighted with purple bruising. I feel my stomach tumble with worry.

"What happened?" I move between him and the TV. He hits the mute button as one of the announcers loudly analyzes the previous play and takes in the sight of me in my sundress and cardigan with a smile. His lips twitch with amusement, but he doesn't comment.

"Some guys were in the pole barn, and Bo and I ran them out." His face sobers as he explains.

"What guys? Bo was here?" I feel my heart skip in my chest, and I have a million questions now.

"I don't know what guys. They were in the pole barn snooping around. Have you had any issues like that before?"

"No. Things are usually pretty boring around here. When was Bo here?" I didn't see my brother's truck today, and I'd just been over at the inn getting work done before my dinner with Amelia.

"He dropped off my bike from the garage. They finished up the work this week. He walked out with me to park it, and we heard voices. So we went in to check it out." He shrugs like it's no big deal, and I reach for his hand, turning it over so I can get a closer look at his knuckles. He lets me examine them for a moment and then pulls them back, giving me a dismissive grunt like I'm overreacting.

"You fought with them? Did you call the police?" I pull the ice pack away from his face gently next and cringe when I see the bruising and swelling on his cheek. His eyes narrow when I mention the police, and I realize what a stupid idea that is. "Sorry. I wasn't thinking about the parole and all. This looks terrible." I click my tongue at the sight of his cheek.

"Thanks," he grumbles. "One of them hit me. It's fine. Just bruised."

"Did you put something on the cuts?" I move toward the kitchen because we might still have something there.

"I took a shower. Cleaned up. Got the ice on my cheek. I'm good." He takes a deep breath, and I can tell I'm agitating him with my mothering. I try to remind myself he's spent the last five years on the field getting beat up like this on a daily basis—to him, it really is nothing.

"You're lucky they didn't have guns or something though. You should have called me. You and Bo going after them; that's not smart. You're both so hotheaded sometimes. Is Bo hurt?"

"Bo's fine. It was a split-second decision." Another grumble.

"Why the hell would anyone be in that pole barn?" I frown

pacing back to the window to look out at it, as if somehow seeing it will give me answers.

"That's my question. Does anyone know we're storing stuff in there? That there might be something of value?" He gives me a curious look.

"I mean... just family and, of course, Sam when he's doing groundskeeping. He goes in there sometimes for equipment and to spray for bugs and set traps and things." I walk back to Ramsey and sit down next to him on the couch, pulling the ice pack back again to look at it while he gives me a grumpy look.

"What about Curtis? Could he have told someone in passing?" Ramsey asks, looking past me to the TV like he's not particularly concerned with the answer or excited about discussing my fiancé in exile.

"Curtis? No, I don't think so. I keep it locked up. I know there are some valuables in there, and I don't want inn guests or ranch visitors wandering in on accident," I add, just so that Ramsey knows that I do my best to keep the things still entrusted to me safe.

"I don't know how someone would know to try to break in there then."

"Maybe they were just snooping around?" I offer.

"Maybe." He doesn't seem reassured by my answer. "Do you still have cameras on that building?"

"We should. But I haven't checked them in a while. I usually let Elliot or Sam handle the security stuff for the barns."

"You have kids handle security?" Ramsey doesn't like that answer.

"We don't usually have a need for it. It's just the stuff left over from your parents. Sam checks it every so often to make sure it still works, and sometimes Elliot checks the one to the stables to keep an eye on the horses, especially if one is sick. Otherwise, it's pretty quiet around here."

"You should be having Bo or someone handle that for you. You need to take it more seriously." His green eyes are bright with concern, and I sigh.

"It's not like it was when you and your parents lived here. It's just old ladies on vacation and people from the city who want to board their horse or get riding lessons. There's nothing to worry about."

"There's always something to worry about." Ramsey sits up straighter and drops the ice from his face. "You're out here exposed by yourself. Anyone could come out here—if those guys could..."

"Ramsey... I promise you. It's been quiet. And I'm not by myself. I have you."

His eyes soften at that and search over my face for a moment before they go back to the TV. The flash of it illuminates all the perfect angles of his cheek and jaw—the side not covered in an ice pack—and I'm distracted by how pretty he is.

"I just want to make sure you're safe. I can't be here all the time." I can see the stress in his shoulders, and I lean over, rubbing them gently. I know he's thinking about his parents and the fact that he wasn't here when they died. He still carries so much of that guilt with him, even though he was barely an adult himself when it happened.

"I'm safe. We'll check the cameras. We'll put more up if we need to. I'll talk to Anson and Bo about what options there are." Anson works in construction, but both of my older brothers run businesses that require a certain amount of security.

"I think you should see about Cade coming to live in the bunkhouse. He needs a place. You've got one. You need more family around here. People you can trust."

"I've got Kell and Elliot in the bunkhouse. Kit's out in the gardener's cottage. Usually, I have—" I stop short because I don't think he wants to hear about Curtis. I see the flinch in his face at the name I don't mention.

"I'd feel better if one of your brothers was here to keep an eye out on you. Someone I know can throw a punch," he explains.

"Well, Cade's been talking about bull riding lately anyway. He was asking about seeing if he could train on the ranch—if he could pull the resources together," I answer Ramsey absently, thinking about my younger brother's latest foray into danger. Cade always needs to be in one kind of thrill-seeking, life-altering adventure or another to feel alive it seems.

"I thought he was going to school? Had that athletic scholarship?" Ramsey's distracted glance turns on me, and he frowns as he considers Cade as a bull rider.

"He graduated in the spring, but he didn't get drafted, and he's a bit lost at the moment for what to do next. He's been helping Bo out at the garage and staying at Bo's house. I think Bo's getting tired of him moping around, though, wanting him to figure his shit out." I'm worried about my younger brother, too, but I go a little easier on him than Bo does.

"All that just so he can come back and get thrown around by a pissed-off bull?" Ramsey frowns.

My eyes follow his to the TV, and I raise my brows as the lines collide and bodies go flying across the turf.

"Is it really all that different from you bull-rushing into three-hundred-pound, seven-foot-tall linemen?"

"There's a difference," he grouches, slouching back into the couch.

"Oh yeah? Explain it to me," I sass back at him with a smile creeping onto my lips.

"I'd rather do other things with you." A boyish grin spreads on his face as he side-eyes me over his ice pack.

I kiss his temple and run my fingers over his bicep. "Let me get my shower really quick, and we can discuss your options."

"I'll be here waiting." His eyes slide over me in a slow perusal, and then he leans over to kiss the side of my neck. He hits a tender spot with his lips, and I close my eyes as I imagine them elsewhere. "So hurry up." He dips his hand beneath me and gives my butt a squeeze that has me up and out of my seat.

I'm trying to remember Amelia's sage advice as I trudge up the steps, but when I look back at my husband, all I can do is wonder if it's possible to fall in love with the same person twice.

THIRTY-SIX

Ramsey

THE NEXT DAY, I'm in my brother's office in the tower of The Avarice again—the receptionist thankfully remembers me this time. As I wait, I pace around the office looking for any signs my brothers might be involved in this, like somehow there'd be some sort of tell. It's ridiculous, I know, but I'd spent the night tossing and turning after Hazel fell asleep.

"What do you need?" Grant draws my attention as he comes into the room, ready to get to the point like I told his receptionist I would. Lev follows behind him, looking at me curiously and wondering what my summons is for.

"Curtis Reed. He works here?" I ask bluntly. No use beating around the bush.

"Yes. I believe so." Grant looks to Lev. "Lev handles most of the staffing."

"I recognize the name. He works here. He's a low-level floor manager, I believe," Lev adds.

"And?" I press because I'm suspicious about the coincidence of their employee dating my wife.

"And?" Lev shrugs, raising his brow.

"Don't pretend like you don't know why I'm asking." There's an edge to my tone.

"I'm not pretending. You're going to have to spell it out for me." Lev gives me the same tone in return.

"He's engaged to Hazel," Grant interjects, and we both look at him. "He thinks we're involved somehow now."

"So you are familiar." I eye him because he's playing coy, and that's never a good sign.

"I knew she was dating *a* Curtis. It doesn't take much to figure it out if you're asking about one." Grant gives a half-hearted rise of his shoulder, but the way his eyes dart to the side, I feel like there's more than what he's sharing.

"How did you know?" I press on.

"The town gossip makes its way up here. People talk while they're sitting at the tables or the bar, brother. It's not exactly a secret. I told you; it's been the talk for a while that she met someone she likes better than you."

"Because you planted him in her life?"

Grant smirks, gives a small click of his tongue, and then it spreads to a full smile. "Why would I do that?"

"You've always had your eyes on the ranch. Always been plotting expansion projects onto my land. Always trying to convince me to come work for you. That doesn't work, so you go after Haze. She's as stubborn as me, so you move on to options you have more control over." I'd come up with a million scenarios in the middle of the night last night.

"Well, as much as I wish I'd thought of that. He's not ours." Grant stands from his desk and walks around to the front of it.

"He came in through the normal channels. He's been here a little over a year," Lev speaks up again, and I look over to see him scrolling through information on his phone, presumably employee records.

"What's made you suspicious of him?" Grant studies my face, like somehow he can tell more from it than my answers.

"I have my reasons."

"He's on a leave of absence for a few months," Lev says and then sets his phone down on the shelf.

"A leave of absence?" My brow furrows. "He's not at a training in Vegas?"

"Training in Vegas?" Grant repeats like I'm speaking a foreign language.

"You didn't send some of your staff off for training in Vegas?" I clarify.

"No," Lev answers. "Why would we do that? We could just bring someone out here."

"I don't know fuck all about casinos or how you run them," I grumble at my brother, but my stomach is sinking at a rapid rate.

"I'm not after your goddamn ranch, Ramsey. I don't need that backwater anymore. We make ten times what the ranch brings in here and then some with the projects we have on the side. I have plans to expand, most of them I told you about, so you know I don't need your land." Grant's charm has lapsed, and he sounds more like our father now. "So you don't have anything to fear from me, but it looks like you might have other concerns. I suggest sharing them with people who can help you do something about them."

"We're brothers first, yeah?" Lev's face softens as he sees the panic in mine.

I might not always trust my brothers when it comes to money, but when it comes to my life, that's a different story.

"I don't think Curtis is who he says he is. I don't know more than that right now. I'm still trying to piece together what I've got. Some guys turned up at the ranch last night—I think they might be the same ones from the bar the other day. Did they end up coming here?"

Grant looks thoughtfully at his desk. "I'm not sure. I never followed up. I can check though. The card I gave them would have been run if they did."

"Check," I say, and he nods to Lev, who starts typing something into his phone again.

"While we wait... What did the guys want at the ranch?" Grant raises a brow.

"I don't know. They were in the pole barn. All that's in there is Mom and Dad's stuff and some of mine from when I moved out. Hazel usually keeps it locked, but I've been in and out since I got here. It was like they were looking for something."

Grant straightens from his lean against his desk, and there's something in his eyes I can't read. "Like what?"

"I don't fucking know, but I'm going to assume antique dealers don't raid private property with guns at night."

Grant and Lev exchange looks, and I don't like the way it makes me feel like I'm not read in on something.

"What?" I ask impatiently.

"Nothing," Grant answers. "I'm just trying to think of what they could be after. Or how anyone would even know what's there."

"Do you know something about Curtis? If you do, you better fucking tell me now. Because if I find out that you let him around my wife and then you lied to me about it, too, I'll fucking kill you."

"No. I don't know anything about Curtis. I'm as curious as you are."

"There were a couple of guys who stayed after they ran the

discount card you gave them. They checked out this morning," Lev offers.

"Run the names. Get any information you can on them," Grant instructs Lev.

"I'll need to get one of the security team on it." Lev pauses as he heads for the door to look back at us. His eyes meet mine. "If there's something going on, we'll get to the bottom of it."

"All I care about is Hazel and everyone at the ranch being safe."

"We've got it. We'll keep you posted on what we hear, and you let us know if anything else happens, okay?"

"As soon as you know." I narrow my eyes at Grant, and he nods.

"Of course," he assures me.

As I drive the long way around back to the ranch, using the time to try to get my head back on straight with this information, my stomach turns with anxiety. Now I have to figure out how to tell Hazel about all of this. Bo's warning rings in my head as I try to think of ways to tell her that don't end with her telling me I'm jealous or making shit up.

But there's no way Curtis is innocent in this—Bo saw him in that pole barn, saw him searching the property, saw him arguing with a person no one knows, and now, these guys show up when he disappears and lies about where he's going. It's too many coincidences, and where there's smoke there's usually fire.

A sentiment that becomes all too real when I notice smoke rising above the tree line on the road. It's coming from the direction of the ranch. I hit the gas and tear down the road as fast as I can back home.

THIRTY-SEVEN

Ramsey

WHEN I GET to the ranch, it's chaos. Smoke rises in a giant plume over the stables, and Kell, Elliot, and Sam are all running wild, trying to get the horses out. I throw the truck in park and jump out, racing to the doors. My heart feels like it might explode in my chest when I see Hazel at the door, her hand holding the reins to one of the rescues and a bandana wrapped around her mouth. She rips it off as soon as she's free of the barn doors, and she coughs, bending over to try to catch her breath, and then yelling and motioning for someone to go back in.

When she sees me, she beckons for me to run faster to her. I try to press my out-of-shape muscles to run like I'm still on the field, but my boots aren't cleats, and the gravel isn't turf. She starts yelling directions at me before I even reach her, using her raspy, smoke-stained voice to let me know who's left in the stables and who's in the most danger.

"Get Wolfsbane!" she repeats as I reach her. Her face is muddied with soot and sweat, her cheeks red with the exertion.

"Are you okay? You need air!" My heart hammers with worry as I see the smoke billowing out over her head.

"I'm fine. Wolfsbane." She coughs and then takes another deep breath, racing through her next words. "He won't budge for anyone else. He's panicked, and he needs you. There's not much time!" She urges me on, and I race through the stable doors, my boots pounding the pavement as I make my way through to the back.

He's on the far side of the stables from the doors, and as I race through it, I can feel the heat from the fire. It seems to be coming from the east side of the stables, furthest away from the horse stalls, and mostly full of equipment. It buys us time, but it's also fueling the fire and the smoke. The heat of its burn has me sweating by the time I reach his stall, and I can tell that we don't have much longer to get the last of these guys out of here, so I'm just praying he cooperates.

Wolfsbane stamps his feet and neighs at the sound of another stall slamming as Kell rushes Lady Luck out of her slot. The fear and tension is evident in how he paces the enclosed stall and rears up more and more frequently as he hears the cacophony of the evacuation. His eyes bulge with fear, even as I approach. No wonder Hazel wasn't able to him out of the stall, let alone the barn. In my hurry to get into the stall, I notice his halter is missing, and I scan the floor for it, spotting the cobalt blue lead rope attached to his halter in the shavings. I'm thankful Hazel always pushed for the horses to wear bright colors that didn't always live up to the tourists' aesthetics. I grab it and approach Wolfsbane slowly, my hands up and practicing the most soothing voice I can muster under the circumstances.

"Hey, buddy," I call to him. "It's me. I'm here now. I've got you. Just let me finish this, okay?" As soon as he hears my voice, his eyes dart down, and he falls back to his four legs from his rear. He turns his head to me and blows air through his nostrils, an intimidating sound for most, but I know him. That's his way of telling me it's about damn time I got here. "That's right, buddy. It's all right. Good boy." I soothe him as I come closer. "I'll get you out of here, bud," I reassure him in a soothing voice.

I maneuver his halter in my left hand while I keep patting my way up his neck and down his jaw, eventually managing a hold on him that allows me some sort of control while I halter him, still saying his name softly and telling him he's a good boy. I keep telling him it's going to be okay until the coughing fit I have takes my voice away. The smoke is drifting lower, and I glance up to see it filling the rafters of the stables. I rip my shirt off, thankful I'd only worn an old cotton tee, and tear it in two quickly, wrapping it around my face and tying it.

I slide his stall door open, and he stomps his feet again as another stall door shuts. Kell and Elliot yell to one another that the fire is spreading faster now, and I hear them say they've got four more horses to go.

"Okay, buddy. Let's get you out of here so I can go help them. You can be good for me, right?" I sweep my hand over his nose and forehead, trying to reassure him, but I can see the anxiety in his eyes. "I've got you. I promise I've got you."

He blows out another loud snort, but he starts to move with me. I breathe a sigh of relief as we get halfway out of the stables, mopping the sweat off my brow with my free hand as we move toward the doors. Hazel's coughing and guiding another horse out of a stall that I pass, but I see her eyes flood with relief, and she nods to me when she sees Wolfsbane. We exchange a look, and I nod to her, trying to let her know it's going to be okay.

"Three more!" Kell calls as he runs back into the stables

past me, startling Wolfsbane enough so that he misses stepping on my foot by a centimeter or two and forcing me to pause to calm him one last time before we cross the threshold.

I walk him out to the corral with the rest of the horses. He's not keen to go in or for me to walk away from him, but I call out one last reassurance, letting him know I'll come get him when I'm done, and lock the gate behind him. I run like hell back into the stables, taking the last horse as Kell and Elliot get the other two.

Hazel starts to come in to help, bent over and coughing before she even gets past the first stall.

"Haze! Go back outside. Check on the horses in the corral."

"I need to do a last check." She shakes her head no, and I run to her, kneeling down to look up at her.

"We've got them all. I'll be sure of it. You're gonna collapse in here, and then we'll have to save you instead of the horses. Please don't be stubborn here, darlin'. Please," I beg her, and her eyes open. They're red with irritation from the smoke and crying, but she nods and goes back to the barn doors.

I run one last time to the stall. It's Admiral that's left, and he's one of the best trail horses we've got. Calmer than the rest, and even now, when I can tell he's agitated and nervous, he lets me halter him and lead him out with ease. He follows me with very little struggle, and it gives me the chance I need to check the stalls visually one last time to make sure everyone's out.

I'm grateful for it because no sooner do I get Admiral through the barn doors, one of the beams on the east side of the stables tears away from the roof, the fire and the heat too much for it to take. It clatters to the ground, taking out a smaller crossbeam on the way down and smashing into a pile of equipment and feed. It ignites almost instantly, and the hay dust fuels its rapid spread across the floor.

"Jesus Christ." Kell's at my side as we both stare, and he

takes the lead rope from me to take Admiral to the rest of the horses. "We're so fucking lucky."

"Lucky..." I mutter in agreement. I rip the shirt off my face, the heat of the day and the fire and smoke all conspiring to steal the oxygen from my lungs. I bend over in another coughing fit, all the while searching for Haze and not seeing her.

I panic then, forgetting my own discomfort and spinning in a circle as I try to find some sign of her in the chaos of people and animals around me. I'm half worried she ignored my warning and went back in. But I finally spot her in the distance, sitting under a tree as Kit hands her a bottle of water. I head toward them, hoping that Haze didn't get hurt in the madness.

Kit sees me first, and she pulls another bottle of water out of a pocket in her apron and hands it to me. She looks like she was just dragged out of the kitchen at the inn in the middle of prepping dinner. Green and red smears across her apron and her neatly tied-up hair is fraying at the sides. Her eyes sweep over me, looking for damage, and she seems satisfied when she finds nothing life-threatening.

"Drink some water. You need it too. You both look like hell. The fire department's on the way," she reassures us.

"Thank you." I uncap the water and guzzle it down as I collapse under the tree next to Haze.

"You two should go to the hospital and be seen for smoke inhalation."

"I can't leave. The horses—we'll need a plan for the night, and the fire's not out yet," Haze protests the instruction, even as she coughs again and leans back against the tree to try to open her lungs for a deeper breath.

"You should go," I encourage her, my voice raspy from the smoke. Her eyes slide to me, and she shakes her head.

"There's something you should see." Sam comes over to us and nods back toward the stables.

"What?" I ask, but he doesn't answer and just nods for us to follow.

When we get to the side of the stables, we can see the words scrawled in spray paint on the side, even as the fire licks at them. I watch as Sam snaps a couple of pictures of the warning the arsonists have left for us. One that isn't very creative but has a clear message.

ALL STOCKTONS WILL DIE

Hazel starts bawling her eyes out at the sight of it. I turn to comfort her, but she just pushes past me, a sob racking her body as she pulls her hair up into a bun off her shoulders and ties it off.

"Haze, it's going to be okay." I approach her just like I did Wolfsbane, slow and steady so I don't get the brunt force of her anger.

"It's not, Ramsey. It's happening again. Everything was so quiet, and then you come back, and now all of this." She has to take a deep, stuttered breath between the crying and the irritation from the smoke. She can barely get her next words out. "It was so quiet before. So quiet, and then you come back, and now it's people breaking in and horses being set on fire."

"The horses are all okay. We got them all out." I feel guilt and my own tears claw their way up my throat.

"They're not okay. One of the rescues reinjured her bad leg rearing up into her trough in her panic. I saw Johnny Boy had a big gash on his face when Kell brought him out. We have to get the vet here." She shakes her head, tears streaming down her cheeks. "And it could have been so much worse. When Wolfsbane wouldn't come with me..." Her words fade into another sob, and I reach for her, wrapping my arms around her shoulders and pulling her close.

"I'm sorry. I know it was fucking terrifying. I was scared

too. But they're all out. We'll get the vet here tonight. I'll pick him up myself if I have to."

"Kell's already on it."

"Hazel?" a woman's voice calls, and I turn around with her to see the older woman approaching us. "Oh, my sweet girl. I am so sorry. This is terrifying!" She runs to Hazel and practically knocks me over trying to get to her, pulling her into a tight hug.

"They could have died, Amelia!" She sobs into the woman's shoulder, and she rocks her back and forth slightly like she's a colicky baby.

"It's okay. You're okay. I'm so sorry!" Amelia repeats, and I'm irrationally agitated that this woman is comforting my wife instead of me. It feels like she's edged in on a private moment, but I don't want to argue in front of everyone.

"It doesn't feel okay. I can't believe this is happening." Hazel raises her head for just long enough that she can peer over Amelia's shoulder and see the flame lick through the roof of the stables. The sound of another crash on the inside is enough to tell us that it's not going to end well.

"I know, and with all the worries you already have. Life's unfair, sweetheart. The bad luck that sometimes comes into our life; it just isn't fair," Amelia reassures her and looks up at me, her eyes traveling over my form and not finding much she likes. "You. Why don't you go get her some more water? She needs it." The older woman instructs me, and I can't really disagree.

I head into the house as the sirens blare in the distance, no doubt making their way down the state road from town to the ranch as I climb the stairs. I glance back over my shoulder as more of the stables collapses, and the smoke billows high into the air.

Whoever did this is going to pay. My brothers and I will make sure of that much.

THIRTY-EIGHT

Hazel

AMELIA COMFORTS me as I finish crying my way through the aftermath of the stables fire. Kit brings me another water from the inn and a small plate of dinner that she insists I eat while I sit at the picnic table outside. The embers are still smoldering as the fire department finishes their work, and I feel like I should be doing something—anything—to begin picking up this mess. The idea of just walking away and letting it all sit here like this is killing me inside.

"There's nothing you can do right now but take care of yourself." Kit's brows raise as she gives me a pointed look and motions to the plate.

Grace has come back out to the ranch and told me to take the night off, promising me it's no big deal for her to work the night shift. I feel guilty, though, since she's only just come off of one the night before, but she won't hear any arguments. I'm grateful I have staff that feel like family; people who have my back like this in a crisis. If I didn't, I'd probably be losing my mind more than I already am.

After I eat, Dakota and Marlowe show up to lend some support too. Dakota brings several cases of beer for me and the guys, including my brothers, who've all made their way over here. They're currently on the porch with Ramsey looking conspiratorial as they have some sort of hushed discussion and motion erratically to different spots on the ranch. It's another thing I should be worried about. The four of them are bound to be plotting something I'll want to know about, but I simply don't have the energy. My whole body feels heavy with the weight of the day, and I can only bring myself to stare at what's become of the place.

Marlowe brought leftover donuts and gives them to the first responders as they pack up their equipment. Distributing them like they're magic and will somehow cure everyone of their exhaustion. I smile at the way she insists on handing one to the grouchy fire chief, who only takes the sprinkled pink sugared dough when she makes him taste it. His bushy eyebrow popping up in surprise is one of the few highlights of the day. That and the fact all the horses survived with seemingly minor injuries.

The fire department is leaving, and the police department is wrapping up the last of their witness questioning. A short while later, they're giving Ramsey and me their information, and he's reluctantly stuffing their card into his pocket as they drive away. I see him shake his head, muttering something to Bo as they agree about something.

I hear Anson and Bo starting to say their goodbyes a few moments later, and soon everyone else is as well. I stand for the assembly line of hugs and reassurances. People say all the right things and promise me that it'll all be okay as they pile into their cars and drive away. Leaving me staring at what's left of the stables in the darkness, the moon illuminating the giant crater in the roof and the pile of rubble underneath it. One full side of it collapsed and the whole structure is dangerously canting over like it's bowing to a higher power. The latest victim in whatever feud the Stocktons have managed to land themselves in. The only solace is that, at least this time, no one lost their life.

"I hope the police don't come back tomorrow," Ramsey grumbles as he walks up behind me.

"I'm sure they will. They're going to want to investigate more. You need to tell them about the situation you and Bo encountered in the pole barn. Tell them what happened. That they attacked you." I give him a hard look, but he's too busy staring at the aftermath to see my reactions in the darkness.

"No. I don't want them involved."

"Why not?" I raise my voice slightly, frustrated with Ramsey's reaction to this. Usually, I side with him. I'd rather not have the police involved in things if they don't have to be, but the kind of people that would kill horses to make a point seem like the kind of people I don't want to deal with on my own. At some point, Ramsey will leave, and I've got to keep everyone here safe.

"Because I don't want my parole officer involved in this. I don't want to go back to prison on some fucking technicality. I'm supposed to stay out of trouble, even if it comes to me."

"You were defending your own property."

"You think the cops will care about that? They look at me and my record. They see a high-profile murder case. They see the tattoos and that video of me beating the life out of a man. They don't remember that it was the guy who tried to kill Coop. That hurt Bea. They don't see a man just trying to defend his family, Haze. They see a family with a history of crime. It's too risky to involve them. I don't want to bet my life and yours on the right one coming to help us."

"We need to know who did this. If it's starting all over again. Guests could have been trapped in the stables. Kell or Elliot could have gotten hurt helping us get the horses out. Wolfsbane would have died if you didn't come home when you did. You won't be here all the time, and we can't handle everything in-house."

"We can handle it a hell of a lot more than some small-town police department. They're cut out to handle domestic disputes and the occasional car accident, Haze. This is more than that. It's deeper than that."

My heart sinks. There's more to this than I know.

"What aren't you telling me? What are you and my brothers plotting?"

"I was going to tell you when I got home, but then the fire was happening..."

"So tell me now," I demand.

"There's no good way to do that. I don't have enough information yet, and I don't want to—"

"Fucking tell me, Ramsey. I'm not some delicate little flower that needs to be protected."

"I think the guys that did this are the ones who were in the pole barn the other night."

"No shit." I scoff at his ridiculous declaration—as if anyone couldn't easily put that together.

"I think it runs deeper than just disgruntled thieves though. I think it's related to what my parents were involved in somehow. Enemies of theirs."

"Enemies of the Stocktons, you mean, since they made that clear." I can still see the note scrawled on the side of the stables in my head, burned forever now.

"Yes."

"So one of their past rivalries is coming back to haunt you?" I press for more information because I hate being held in the dark.

"I'm not sure." He shakes his head, and when he sees the doubtful look on my face, he winces and looks out the window.

"What else?" I feel my stomach turn. Whatever he doesn't want to tell me, it's big.

He takes a deep breath before he speaks, studies my face for long minutes and looks like he'd rather die than tell me the next piece of information. So I brace myself when he finally says the words.

"I think Curtis could be involved."

Whatever I thought he was going to say, it wasn't that.

"Curtis? Are you fucking serious? He's not even here, Ramsey." I feel the anger bubble up in my gut. I can't believe he'd take a moment as serious as this one to try to rope Curtis into this mess in some wild attempt to get one over on him.

"It's curious that he disappeared right as everything started happening." Ramsey's voice is low and lethal.

"You appeared right as it all started happening. It's you who's getting into fights and chasing people off the property. It's you with the spray-painted threat against you on the side of the stables. It's your family who always seems to be at the bottom of whatever drama is happening in this town." I gesture to the wide range of places this ranch has seen violence.

"You should talk to your brothers too, then, if you don't want to listen to me," Ramsey suggests, a thing that makes me feel even angrier—like that meeting on the porch might have been about managing me and Curtis rather than the heart of the matter.

"I don't want to talk to anyone right now, Ramsey. I want to go take a long shower and get the dirt and smoke and misery off me and try to get some sleep before the vet comes back in the morning," I snap back at him.

"I can meet the vet," he offers, looking over me, and I'm sure finding me haggard and worn down from the day's events. He's probably already deciding how he can tuck me out of the way and take this whole thing over. Probably discussing with my brothers how they'd fix this and keep me busy in the inn. It's *not* happening.

"No. Absolutely no way," I answer firmly. "I need to be the one to do it. They're not your horses. This isn't your ranch anymore. It's mine, and it's my responsibility to take care of all this mess. This is exactly what I meant when I said you'd come back and turn everything upside down, and then I'd be left to clean it up. I just didn't realize the path of destruction would be quite so literal."

"I'm right here offering to help however I can." His tone is bordering on incredulous.

"You're not here. Not really. You're not dealing with the practical realities of the aftermath of this fire. You're making up accusations against Curtis and conspiring with your brothers and mine. Hell, you almost missed the fire entirely because you were over in that golden monstrosity doing God knows what with them. Dragging their problems at the casino all the way back here to the ranch. Wolfsbane could have died, Ramsey. Worse—Kell or Elliot could have been under that beam." The tears threaten again, but I hold them at bay. I'm not about to look like I can't handle this on my own or give him any reason to pity me.

"I'm well aware of what could have happened. It's why I want to make sure I'm getting to the root of it and snuffing it out."

"The root of it? I can tell you what's at the root of it— anyone and everyone with the Stockton name." I tear out of the room, not interested in discussing this further. I want my shower. I want to cry long and hard without witnesses, and I definitely don't want him trying to be the one to comfort me.

I don't want to lean on him any more than I already have—I can't. Because if this does turn out to have to do with him or his family, the chances that he'll run again are high. He can go back to the happy version of his life in Ohio, back with all his football friends, and all the laughter and money and fame. The better life—the better version of himself—the one not tangled up in all the misery this place represents.

And I'll be the one still here. Left alone to run the inn and the ranch the same way I've been doing for the last five years—with a broken heart and a mean spirit. One that just won't seem to let me quit.

THIRTY-NINE

Hazel

IN THE MORNING when I get up, I can tell Ramsey never came to bed last night. I peek into the guest room to see if he slept there instead, but the bed is already neatly made. If he did sleep there, he's long gone now. I hoped to at least apologize. I was emotional last night, lost in how scared I was for the horses and my friends. I hadn't been fair in how I treated him, even if I did think that his conspiracy theories about Curtis were wild allegations. The shower and the sleep has cleared a lot of the pain, and now I just want to clear the air too.

I make my coffee, pour it into a thermos, and stuff a donut from yesterday's breakfast into my mouth before I make my way out to where Kell and Elliot are already working. My brother, Cade, and one of his friends are helping to get the horses situated in the other barn.

The vet is here, too, working with the two horses that were injured when they were startled by all the commotion. It could have been much worse, and frankly, we were lucky that it was just that. Not that we really have funds for more vet bills on top of the ones we are already paying for the rescue horses we took in last month. But where there's a will, there's a way.

As I step out onto the back porch, though, I'm met with shock.

"Curtis!" I nearly drop my thermos.

"When I got your text last night about the fire, I just got on the next flight I could and drove out from Denver this morning."

I didn't want to believe what Ramsey said last night, but I couldn't write it off either. Standing here now in front of Curtis, my stomach turns.

"Oh. You didn't have to do that." I shake my head. "I've got things under control."

That's a lie, but I'm getting there. I'd at least managed to pull myself out of my anxiety death spiral and formulate a plan for how I'll get this all under control. I'm fairly certain Curtis showing up out of the blue is going to ruin it all when Ramsey finds him.

"I just want to be here to help. To support you. However you need." A sympathetic look crosses his face, and he takes a step forward and kisses my cheek. My heart swells with the fact that he raced up to the ranch from Vegas to be here for me. It's the kind of guy Curtis is—always thinking about how he can help, asking what he can do instead of just making decisions on my behalf. Not conspiring with my brothers to outmaneuver me.

Amelia's voice echoes in my head, and I'm starting to wonder if I've been letting myself get too caught up in Ramsey's web to see things for what they really are. If I really have my head on as straight as I think I do.

The hairs on the back of my neck go up a moment later,

though, as I feel the breeze whip at the damp spot on my cheek where Curtis kissed me. I glance around, hoping Ramsey wasn't nearby to see it. It feels like I'm cheating on my husband, and I'm fairly certain Ramsey will have even stronger opinions than that.

"Thank you for doing that. That means so much." My eyes drift over him, and I offer a small smile before I have to be practical. "But I'm not sure that's going to work with Ramsey being here," I say softly, looking down at the boards of the deck.

This isn't an easy topic, and I don't know that I have it in me to negotiate this kind of thing today. Not after the emotional and physical drain of yesterday, and especially not before I've had my coffee.

"Fuck Ramsey and his delusions. This is serious. The stables burned down. Horses are hurt. You've got threats against your life sprayed on the barn. I'm your fiancé. It's gotten too serious for us to still be playing this stupid game he wants."

"I appreciate your concern and that you showed up here for me. Truly. But... it's not a game to him, and I don't need the added stress. It's his ranch—legally speaking. He has a vested interest," I explain even though Curtis is smarter than this. He shouldn't need this explanation.

"I don't care. I'm here for you. He'll just have to get used to it."

"Don't you need to be in Vegas?" I question. It's a Sunday, but I assume he'll need to be back for training on Monday.

"I don't care about anything else but you, Hazel. If they want to fire me, they can." Curtis shrugs like it's nothing that he'll lose his job. Like we don't live in a small town, and he can just as easily pick up another one.

Although, if Ramsey's suspicions are right, he might push for Curtis to lose his job anyway. I swallow hard. There's really no might about it. If the Stocktons decide something, there's no stopping them. They mete out their own justice, and the whole town just has to brace for the impact of it.

"They will fire you, and possibly worse, if we don't hold up our end of the bargain, Curtis." I shake my head. I could just imagine them beating him to a bloody pulp and all the guilt I'd feel for it.

"If you're worried about them, then what if we leave for a bit? We could get you out of here and away from all of this?"

"Leave? I can't leave. The stables just burned down. I have a million things I have to take care of."

"You just said yourself it's Ramsey's ranch and not yours. Let him deal with the fallout."

"Legally, not literally. Even still. I have the inn to take care of."

"I'm sure Grace can handle it. She's been wanting more responsibility, right? Here's your chance to give it to her. You can get away and relax, escape all the stress from Ramsey and his drama. We can reconnect. Hell, maybe we can go to a beach, or you could come back to Vegas with me." Apparently, I'm wrong about Curtis too. He might have come back, but it seems he wants to manage me the same way everyone else does —to his benefit.

"No. I'm not abandoning my home when everyone needs me. There's too much that needs to be done. It's all hands on deck." I'm surprised he would even suggest it when he knows this is where my heart is.

"Fine. Then I'm staying. I'll be your extra set of hands."

"Stay where? Ramsey won't let you back in the house—not until the ninety days is over."

"The inn? Don't you have extra rooms?"

"He won't like that." I shake my head, and the anxiety in my stomach doubles when I hear boots through the house approaching the back door. The footfalls are heavy enough that they could only belong to one six-foot-five man I haven't seen yet this morning.

"I won't like what?" Ramsey asks as he opens the screen door, and I can practically feel the animosity radiate off him when he sees Curtis. "Oh yeah. I won't like that at all."

"It's not about you. It's about Hazel," Curtis counters.

"My wife, you mean. I've got everything under control, and you're the last person we need here. Aren't you supposed to be in Vegas?"

"Doesn't seem like you have anything under control by the looks of it. I came when she texted me about the fire."

I can see the slightest bristle in Ramsey's countenance when he hears that. He won't love that I texted Curtis about it, but it's not like I could keep it a secret from him.

"Well, you can go back to wherever you came from. No one needs you here."

"Ramsey, stop it," I warn him.

"I'm just telling him the truth, sugar."

"Should I just talk to Grace or Tabitha about getting a room?" Curtis ignores Ramsey and looks at me.

"You're not staying at the inn. You're not staying anywhere on this property." Ramsey takes a step closer to him, and I fear we're only a few minutes away from the two of them throwing punches.

"You don't get a say in where I stay. Only Hazel decides."

"I don't think it's a good idea." I look between them warily. "It's just going to add to the tension here. We need to be focused on the horses and getting things in place for them."

"Fine. Come and stay with me at a hotel downtown then. It'll give you a break from all of this at night. Let you escape a little," Curtis pleads with me.

"We made a deal." Ramsey looks at me. Something about the finality in his tone irritates me. Like he's not trying to convince me I should choose him, but that he's telling me I don't have a choice at all. Given that we haven't even resolved our argument from last night, it builds on every frustration I've already been feeling since then.

"I said you could stay here. I didn't say that I would," I argue.

I can see Curtis stand up a little straighter, a self-satisfied smile touching his lips. Ramsey doesn't miss it either, and I can see the moment his temper hits. It flashes over his face before he reins it back in, and his own smirk appears. I feel like a rabbit trapped between a snake and a wolf.

"Before you take off with him, why don't you ask Curtis where he's been all this time?"

"I've been training. She knows that."

"Training for what?" Ramsey asks calmly, staring Curtis down. "Because we both know it has nothing to do with the casino."

My heart drops as the two of them stare each other down.

"What are you talking about?" I look to Ramsey first and then to Curtis. "What is he talking about?"

"I have no idea." Curtis defends himself, but there's something in the way he does it—the small half-step back he takes, the way his face falters, the shift of his shoulders that tells me there's truth to what Ramsey's saying.

"Someone explain," I demand, my temper finally surfacing. All before I get my fucking coffee.

"Your boy toy here's been lying to you. There's no training in Vegas. Nothing to do with the casino. He took a leave of absence from his job."

"That's a lie!" Curtis shouts, taking a step toward Ramsey.

"You don't want to do that." Ramsey holds his hand out to stop Curtis in his tracks. He's right. Curtis would lose. Ramsey has six inches and probably sixty pounds on Curtis, most of them muscle. He'd just be asking for pain, and Ramsey doesn't need the trouble.

I stare at Curtis, trying to make sense of Ramsey's accusation. Ramsey wouldn't lie about something like this, so he must have known. His brother's must have told him. Which means he's known for a while and didn't tell me.

"How long did you know he wasn't in Vegas?" I turn on Ramsey.

"I was coming to tell you last night when I saw something was on fire, and then with everything, I didn't get a chance to tell you."

"You should have found a way!" I turn back to Curtis. "Where were you?"

"I can explain everything if I can just have some time alone with you. Come stay downtown with me. We can talk. You can relax." Curtis reaches out for me, and I recoil from it.

"She's not fucking going anywhere with you, you lying sack of shit!" Ramsey steps between us.

"Stop this! I don't want to talk to either of you. I have things to do around the ranch and no time for these bullshit games. Don't talk to me. Don't follow me. Just let me do my job in peace." I take off toward the corral in a hurry, forcing myself not to cry. I don't need to look unprofessional right now. Not in front of all of my staff while we're facing a huge crisis.

But the fact that Curtis lied to me and Ramsey has been investigating all of this without saying a word to me? I thought that, finally, Ramsey had matured. I thought Curtis was a good man. I thought that my ability to pick someone I could trust might have finally improved, and that maybe, just maybe, my instincts were finally reliable, but now I realize I'm as lost as I ever was.

FORTY

Ramsey

I WANT TO FOLLOW HAZEL, but I know her well enough that when she's in this mood, there's no point in trying. Some of the bullheaded fury has to wear off her before she'll listen to my apology or an explanation. And she's not wrong. She has a job to do, and I don't want to distract her with minor details—like this asshole fucking all the way off. So I return my attention back to the problem at hand.

"*Leave.* Don't ever fucking come back here. Don't talk to her. Don't even mention her name in passing ever again." I close the distance between us until I'm almost touching him as he holds his ground, looking up at me because I tower over him.

"Fat fucking chance. She's my fiancée, whether you like it or not."

"You keep saying that word like it means something. It doesn't mean shit. Not against everything she and I have."

"She loves me. Get that through your thick fucking skull. Or did you get too much brain damage on the field?"

My laugh is cut short by my fury.

"I don't know what you thought you were pulling with her. If you were just a plant the entire time or thought you'd take a nice buyout when the opportunity presented itself... But I know you're not who you've been saying you are, and I will find out who that is, and then I will crush you under my boot until nothing's left but a stain." I'd enjoy it too. I don't say that part. I don't want Hazel to know just how much I'd love the opportunity to make him cry like the little bitch he is. I want him to suffer for every single one of the lies he told her.

"Is that a threat? I imagine your parole officer would want to hear that." He thinks he's fucking clever, but nothing would stop me from keeping her safe.

"Maybe they would. It won't change a thing."

"It'll change when you're back in prison, and she has a chance to listen to me without you in her ear feeding her packs of lies."

"I've got my brothers and hers to fill my shoes if they put me back in prison, and they'll keep her protected all the same. Whatever game you *were* playing, it's over now."

"We'll see about whose game is over, Stockton." Curtis storms off the porch and back to his car, tearing out of the long driveway a few minutes later.

I'm going to have to figure out more security for the ranch and convince Hazel that Curtis can't be trusted once she's had time to herself. I've already been worried for her, but knowing he's in town means that Hazel isn't safe. Especially not when he seems so desperate to get her alone.

She's the only priority I have right now, but it means resolving what the source of all this is. My brothers and I, in-law and blood, have too much work and too little time to figure it out.

But one thing's for sure—he won't put a single finger on my wife again as long as I'm breathing.

FORTY-ONE

Hazel

THAT AFTERNOON, after all the immediate needs of the horses, the ranch, and the inn are met, once I thank Grace and Tabitha for all their hard work, give Amelia my apologies for missing another dinner, and make sure Kell and Elliot have the extra help they need from Cade and his friends—I pack a bag and head to Bo's house. My knuckles are rapping on the door as soon as I confirm that his truck is in the driveway.

His brow furrows when he answers it and sees the bag in my hand, but he steps aside and lets me in all the same.

"If you're moving in, we'll have to work on a room for you. Cade's been staying here, and he's got the other spare set up for his video games." Bo looks skeptically at the bag next to my feet in his entryway.

"I'm just staying the night. No need to panic."

"I assume Ramsey's done something to drive you away?"

"Him and Curtis."

"Curtis?" Bo asks, confusion coloring his tone.

"He's back in town." I look up just in time to see the flash of worry across Bo's face that tells me he's been read in on whatever's going on. "And that's what I thought!" I point a finger at his chest.

"What?" He holds up his hands palms out like he's innocent when we both know the truth already.

"You knew too. Was there anyone in this family besides me who didn't know?"

"You're going to have to give me a little more information."

I feel my temper climb as I stare at my brother, and my eyes narrow.

"If there are enough secrets floating around between all of you and Ramsey that I have to specify the details, we're going to be having a whole other conversation."

My brother's eyes roll to the side, and he closes them as he lowers his hands and shakes his head.

"Let's go sit out back..." He starts for the other side of the house, and I follow him into the screened-in deck he and the rest of my brothers built a few summers ago. It overlooks the lake his house sits on and has a gorgeous view of the mountains. Almost enough to distract me from my worries for a few moments. I melt into one of the chairs, so tired from the last two days—physically and emotionally—that I'm not sure I'll ever get up again.

"Did you at least tell him you came here? He'll lose his mind, and we'll have a whole other conversation *and* a set of problems on our hands while he tears up the town looking for you."

"I left him a note that I was coming here and to let me have the night away."

"I'm texting him too. I don't need him thinking I conspired with you." Bo gives me a worried glance.

As much shit as he's talked about Ramsey in the years since our divorce, it's funny that he worries so much about him now. I roll my eyes as he pulls his phone out.

"Do whatever you have to do. And then tell me about Curtis and Ramsey and whatever you've been conspiring about. Every. Single. Detail."

I wait patiently while he types out a message to Ramsey. I don't bother to pull out my phone. I sent a quick message to the girls group chat to let them know I'm doing okay today. I didn't have the energy to update them on the drama, and I didn't want to see any more desperate messages from Curtis either. He's been sending one every hour on the hour, it seems, and I just need time he isn't willing to give.

"Ramsey's right about Curtis. You should stay away from him," Bo says as he puts his phone away.

"That's hard to do when I'm engaged to him."

"Are you? I'm pretty sure you're married."

"Now you sound like Ramsey. If that's how this is going to go, I'll go to Dakota's." I sit forward in my chair like I might get up. Her place isn't much further down the road. I could muster one last round of energy. Bo holds his hand out and gives me a look to tell me I need to take a breather.

"I told him about Curtis. I warned him when he first got here that Anson Cade, and I had seen some shit we didn't like."

"Like what?"

"That pole barn that Ramsey's stuff is in? The one the arsonists were running around in? He was in there one day when I was over, and you were at the inn. Another time, he had a metal detector out in one of the fields claiming he was looking for a watch. Did you know about those things?"

It immediately makes my stomach swirl. I've never shown Curtis inside the pole barn. In fact, I didn't even think he knew where the key was. And I've never seen Curtis wear a watch in my life. But I also have no idea what he could have been doing with a metal detector. There must be plausible, simple answers to them, but I don't have them.

"That's what I thought." Bo's eyes travel over to me, a bit of pity and a bit of warning in them. "Then one night, Cade was on his way back from Springs, went down to one of Anson's team's games, and he stopped to get a late-night snack. While he was in the drive-thru off 50, he looked over at the motel parking lot when he saw a couple of people arguing—a man, who looked a little familiar from a distance, and a woman. It was real fucking heated, like they were having a couple's spat almost. He watched because he thought he might have to call the police, but then the guy got in his car and drove off. Which is when Cade realized—it was Curtis."

"And you didn't think to tell me any of this until now?"

"It was all random stuff. He could have had a fender bender with the woman. He could have bought a new watch. Maybe you asked him to go out into the pole barn. None of it was a glaring red flag; it was just enough little things that they were adding up to us having questions we were trying to get answers to."

"But you still didn't tell me?"

"You're supposedly in love with him. You don't have a history of listening to warnings when you're in love with someone."

"You should have told me. And supposedly? Really?"

"We were afraid you'd think it was ridiculous and that you might tell him. Then he'd know we were onto him, and any other clues we might have gotten would have been covered up. He just... has a bad vibe around him. I know you love him. I know he's been good to you, and I don't have anything concrete I can point to him the way you'd want it... I just, with some of these guys, when you know, you know."

"And yet you continue to hold steady to Ramsey's side. You two seem all chummy again. I thought you said it was family first around here?"

"Then I found out he *is* still family." Bo's lips quiver with half a smile, and I frown at him.

"Don't be a smartass."

"He's a fuckup, Haze. But he loves you. He'd do anything for you. The second he was back in that house with you, I just felt a whole fuckton of relief."

"Because I can't take care of myself?"

"Because you've been living with a fucking snake, Haze. I don't know what he's got up his sleeve, but you can't trust Curtis. And I hope to God you're not actually in love with him."

Of course he doesn't want me to be in love with him. Because he wants his brother-in-law back, firmly ensconced where he thinks he belongs—on his ranch at my side.

"But I can trust the man who ran off?" I give Bo a skeptical look.

"He ran off because he thought it would keep you safe. He believed that. I know he did. And you know he wanted you to go with him. You were just determined to stay here and run your inn, and he wasn't going to come between you and your dream either. I told you my opinion then, and nothing's changed—neither of you was in the wrong."

"So you told him about Curtis, and then what? He went to his brothers, I assume, since he knows about Vegas not being a real thing?"

"When those guys were in the pole barn the other night, I told him it was the same barn I saw Curtis in. It all just seemed too coincidental. Especially since when his parents were killed, it seemed like the murderers were looking for something on the property then too. So the next day, he went to see his brothers, hoping they'd have more on him with his employee file. He thought maybe they knew more than they were letting on because Grant had told him to give up on you too," Bo explains.

"Give up on me?"

"Don't be naïve. You know he doesn't want the divorce to go through."

"He's never said that to me."

"Maybe not plainly. But I promise he's said it loud and clear if you were listening. The whole town knows that's what he's here for, so if you're claiming you don't—it's because you don't want to hear it.

"Well, maybe he should man up and ask how I feel about that idea instead of whatever this is he's been doing... Or, you know, vaguely any attempt at directly asking me what I want." I cross my arms over my chest.

"Haze..." My brother sighs loudly and runs a hand over his face.

"What?" I'm exasperated and currently regretting running to the brother that might love my husband more than I do.

My brother steeples his hands and runs his index fingers up the sides of his nose as he blinks at the floor and then lifts his eyes to meet mine.

"You two are some of the most stubborn, bullheaded, independent people I know."

"Please, Anson's worse."

"I said some of."

"And? So what?"

"He's *here*. He could be anywhere he wants to be. He has the money and the means."

"His parole officer—"

"You don't think his fancy-ass fucking lawyers could get him out of that if he really wanted? People as rich as his family... they don't follow the same rules as the rest of us."

"Maybe he was bored of life out East."

"I'm sure he was real bored of fame, good money, and endless women."

I glare at my brother for even bringing up the other women. I knew there were others, and I was fine with it. I didn't expect him to stay celibate while we thought we were divorced. I certainly wasn't. But I didn't need to dwell on them.

"And that reaction right there tells me everything I need to know about how you feel about letting him walk." Bo sits back in his seat with a self-satisfied smirk.

The idea of Ramsey leaving after this makes my heart twist and my lungs clench, almost like I can't get a breath. The thought of him now, with someone else after the last few weeks we spent together—well, that makes me imagine setting things on fire. Namely his clothes and his bike and half the things I'd saved for him while he was gone. He's mine now, and if he could force me to be his for ninety days on a technicality, well... two could play that game.

"Is he thinking about leaving?" I ask, trying not to sound as worried as I feel. I haven't exactly been kind to him.

"I haven't discussed it with him. I don't want to be in the middle of you two any more now than I did before. But I can't imagine he is. All he talks about is keeping you safe. You know, after his parents..."

"I know," I respond sharply. I knew better than anyone how much his parents' deaths—especially his mother's death—rattled Ramsey to his core. He'd been sweeter and more care-free before it. Always with a joke, always a laugh about something. Finding his parents like that had extinguished almost all of the light he had in his soul. It had broken him in a way nothing seemed to be able to glue back together again—not therapy, not the ranch, not me... not even football—his first real love.

"Then you know as much as I do about the state of his mind. Probably more."

"Does anyone really know his mind?" I shake my head, staring out at the water as a fisherman in waders wanders deeper in on his next cast.

FORTY-TWO

Hazel

"I NEED you to listen to me, Hazel. This is serious." Curtis had been lying in wait for me when I got home from my brother's today and is refusing to take the word no for an answer.

"Oh, I'm very serious, Curtis. I want you out. You lied to me repeatedly. If you need to get your stuff, do it quickly. Or if you give me an address, I can send it to you."

"And what? You're just going to let him stay here?" Curtis scoffs at the very idea of Ramsey.

"Let him? It's *his* ranch. He's my husband." I can't believe we're still covering basic facts.

"What happened to all the stuff about you loving me, and us being it for each other? The future we were going to have? None of that matters now?" He looks at me like I'm the one betraying him, and it makes my blood boil hotter.

"What happened is you lied to me," I say through gritted teeth.

"What happened is he bribed you into sleeping with him, and now he's got you so twisted up you can't remember all the reasons he ruined your life. You're distracted by the money. We can make our own. We're good together."

I slam the pot down on the counter. I won't even dignify the implications, especially not given how enthusiastic he was about the arrangement himself.

"Where were you all this time? Not Vegas."

"I can explain all that, I was... I'm working on a secret project, and I couldn't share details with you. It's all under-cover. But if it'll change your mind, I'm willing to risk it. I'll tell you." He bargains with me as if he has any kind of leverage in this situation. The only thing he has right now is his life, and he'll lose that too if Ramsey comes home and finds him in this house again.

"A secret project? Undercover? What are you even talking about? You act like you're FBI or CIA or something."

"Not quite." He says it with an air of authority I'm positive he doesn't have. Curtis was—or at least *I thought* Curtis was a lot of things—patient, thoughtful, pragmatic. But not once did I ever peg him for having any of the required personality traits to pull off being an undercover agent of any kind. So I have to smother the scoffing laugh that wants to bubble out.

"What does that mean?"

"I'm... I'm..." he falters, looking around the room like he's desperate to tell me anything but the truth. "I'm trying to recover something that was lost. Something that's very impor-tant to people who are not the kind of people you want to cross, Hazel. You don't want to be on the wrong side of this. And I promise you that the Stocktons are."

"Is that why you were in the pole barn? And in the field with a metal detector? Who were you arguing with at a motel a few months ago?"

He blinks rapidly for a moment, shock coming and going from his face before he rights himself. He didn't expect me to know those things. Apparently, he thinks my brothers are dull just because they're from a small town.

"Yes."

"Why didn't you tell me?" I want answers. Now.

"I wanted to protect you. I didn't want you to have to be involved in all of this. I was just doing what I had to do."

It hits me like a ton of bricks then. We didn't meet by accident. He didn't really think it was love at first sight. I was a mark. This whole time I've been nothing but a mark to him—a way for him to get something else he wanted.

"You used me. I was just a pawn to you. You moved in here. You charmed me and told me you loved me. You asked me to marry you!" I yell because I can't control my temper anymore. If I was still wearing my ring, I'd throw it at him. I have no idea who Curtis really is or how he might retaliate if I do something he doesn't like. I might not be anything but a speed bump in his way at this point. The thought has me calculating where all the knives are in the kitchen and how quickly I can get to them if I need one.

"I admit that when we met, it was part of a plan. I was hoping to get you to like me. I did and said things I thought would help that along. I admit that. It was wrong. I was wrong. But something changed over time. I fell in love with you—for real. You're beautiful and smart and everything I've ever wanted."

"Don't even start with that bullshit. I don't want to hear it. I don't care what you want."

"I mean it. I wish you could see into my heart. I wish you could see the truth. How much I love you and want to marry you."

"Don't talk to me about truth. You're a liar, Curtis. From

the very beginning, you lied, and anything that comes out of a lie that big..." I shake my head, holding back tears that I was just a fool. "None of it is real. Not the moments we had together. Not the love. And most definitely not the engagement."

"I'm risking everything telling you this. I could be killed for just admitting any of this to you. If that's not love, what is?" He grabs my arm and squeezes when I try to wrench it away.

"Hubris? Greed? I don't know what you call it. But you're not in love with me. You wouldn't have treated me like this, lied to me over and over again if you did."

"I fucking love you. Don't tell me I don't." His tone is more ominous now, and I can tell we're wading into a side of his personality I haven't met yet.

This isn't the sweet guy I thought I knew. The one who helped me haul hay around the ranch, sat on the porch talking to me for hours while we drank lemonade, and volunteered at the local food bank with me on the holidays—he's gone. He never existed in the first place. Everything I ever knew about him is flashing by like a movie I dreamed up and, somehow, only managed to ever see the projection rather than the real man behind it all.

"Curtis, you need to let go of me." I try to say it calmly, but the way his fingers dig in hurts like hell.

"It's not safe for you here. You're leaving with me before she changes her mind. If I have to make you, I will. You'll see that I'm doing this for you." Curtis drags me forward by the arm, even as I try to fight him. He's not that much bigger than me, only a few inches and a couple of dozen pounds, but the shock of it has me off-kilter, and I stumble forward to my knees when I try to resist him.

"Get up! We don't have time for this!" Curtis yells, jerking my arm. The motion tears at my shoulder, sending searing pain through the joint, and I yelp from the pain.

I hear the slam of a screen door and then the sound of something smashing to the ground as I try to tear myself free from Curtis's grip. I look up, and it's Ramsey, the box of bakery goods and coffees from Marlowe's that he was holding are scattered across the floor. The coffee streams across the floorboards and soaks the old blue rag rug that belonged to his mother.

"Let go of my wife, or I will smear your fucking brains on the wall," Ramsey threatens. He barely raises his voice, and he's across the room in a few quick strides. Curtis releases me like I'm on fire and tries to step backward, tripping over the baseboard and stumbling backward as he tries to regain his balance.

"Are you fucking stupid, or do you have a death wish?" Ramsey roars, and I realize if I don't intervene, this is going to get ugly fast. I rub my arm, trying to soothe some of the pain in my wrist, and slowly rotate my shoulder as I stand up. I need to shake this off and try to get Ramsey to see that I'm okay.

"Your wife." Curtis's laugh sounds maniacal. "She's not your wife. She's my fiancée, and she's leaving here with me."

"I'm not leaving with you, Curtis. I told you. Whatever we had, it's over," I repeat myself, praying it'll get into his head before Ramsey has a chance to do worse to him. I reach for my husband, brushing my fingers over his forearm to try to soothe him. "Ramsey, it's fine. Look at me, please. I'm fine."

He glances down at me, but he's not satisfied, the red marks on my arm still too bright for his liking.

"No. He doesn't fucking touch you." Ramsey's eyes shift from the marks on my wrist to the man who caused them. He's on Curtis a moment later, with two handfuls of his shirt as he drives him back into the wall. He slams him so hard, Curtis has the wind knocked out of him, and he gasps for air. Ramsey seizes on the chance to grab his throat and squeezes.

"Fuck you," Curtis chokes out, trying to punch and kick but failing with each desperate try.

"Oh, I'm gonna fuck you up for sure." Ramsey's threatening smile flashes over his face as he studies the way Curtis's goes red.

I'm not above wanting revenge, wanting to see Curtis suffer for all the hurt and betrayal. I'm so furious that I'm imagining doing it myself, and I know my husband can mete it out on my behalf with twice the violence I could muster. But I love Ramsey far too much to want to see him back in prison, and nothing is worth losing him again. Not when I finally have him back.

"Ramsey, please," I plead softly, hoping I can lower the temperature of the room.

"Nah, sugar. This one's been a long time coming. He needs to know exactly where he stands. We need to put him in his place." Ramsey's face twists as he looks over Curtis. "You lying piece of shit. You thought you could just sneak into her life and take what you wanted. That you wouldn't pay for that? You picked the wrong one for those games."

"You're just mad..." Curtis sputters and tries for another breath, practically squeaking out the next words. "That she loved me more. That I fucked her better."

I'm starting to question whether Curtis's self-preservation instinct is missing.

"Loved you more...Fucked her..." Ramsey repeats his words, and they dissolve into diabolic laughter as he shakes his head, but then his grin fades, and his eyes narrow. "Let's see about that."

FORTY-THREE

Hazel

RAMSEY SLAMS his fist into Curtis's stomach, and he doubles over choking and gasping, mewling out agonized cries as Ramsey drags him along the wall into the kitchen.

"You fucking piece of shit. I'll kill you!" Curtis threatens, though it's dulled by the way he's hunched over and clutching his stomach. "I'll fucking kill you and your whole family and fuck her on top of the pit I bury you in."

My heart drops to my stomach, and I have to bite my lower lip to keep from crying. I can't believe I let this man into my home—into my heart. That I was such a fucking fool, and worse that Ramsey is a witness to all of it. The hurt and embarrassment pool in my gut, swarming like wasps ready to envenomate and bleed me dry from the inside out.

Ramsey drags him up straight, squeezing his jaw as he uses his knee to pin him against the wall.

"I'd like to see you try." He brings his face within an inch of

Curtis's. "I'd drag my cold body out of the grave before I let you touch her again. Cut you into a thousand tiny pieces and feed you to the pigs on the other side of town."

Ramsey's eyes flare with rage, and he grabs a rag off the counter, pushing it into Curtis's mouth and practically shoving it down his throat to silence him.

"I don't want to hear one more fucking word out of your mouth." Ramsey squeezes his cheeks tighter.

"Get me duct tape?" Ramsey nods to the kitchen drawer, and I follow his orders, too dazed by the sudden violence to disagree. He rips a piece off the roll as I hold it and slaps it over Curtis's mouth a moment later. I can hear the soft whistle of Curtis's sinuses as he tries to breathe heavily through his nose and see the desperation in his eyes as he looks at me. I feel a flash of guilt, the smallest glimmer of it, before I remember that he's been using me and my affection for him to try to steal from the Stocktons.

A moment later, Ramsey's grabbed a chair from the table, and he shoves it violently underneath Curtis's knees, forcing him to sit down. He wrenches his arms back behind him, eliciting another now-muted groan from Curtis. Ramsey holds out his hand for the duct tape again, and I hand it to him reluctantly. He takes it and starts to wrap it around Curtis's wrists, weaving tighter on each round and then taping his bound hands to the back of the chair, wrapping it around one of the spindles. He moves to each leg, doing the same in quick order.

I stare quietly, watching him work and feeling my heart rate rise with each pass of the tape. Curtis moans again when Ramsey yanks one of his ankles into place and he squeezes Curtis's jaw.

"Shut the fuck up. You had no problem twisting her around like a fucking rag doll. I'm barely touching you."

Curtis tries to mumble out another threat, his eyes piercingly cold as he stares at Ramsey, but his words disappear into the cotton gag. Ramsey kicks the chair back into the wall, and Curtis is rendered immobile by the binds he's put him in.

"Fuck me..." Ramsey crosses his arms over his chest, shaking his head as he evaluates Curtis. "You're more of a little bitch than I took you for." Ramsey's head twists to look back at me. "Sugar, this is why you don't lie to protect a man's ego. They get all fucking caught up in themselves, thinking they're untouchable. Making rash decisions and stupid mistakes." His eyes shift back to Curtis, and he kicks his booted foot up on the chair seat between Curtis's legs, barely missing his balls with the steel toe of the boots he has on. Ramsey makes a clicking noise in the back of his throat, shaking his head and then tilting it as Curtis stares back at him, daring him, even though he's wrapped up so tightly I'm worried for his blood flow.

Ramsey leans back against the kitchen counter, looking over his shoulder and holding his hand out for me. I take it and slowly walk toward him. He studies the blooming bruises on my arm, and I watch as his rage levels up with each mark he catalogs. He checks it, though, and pulls me close, looking into my eyes.

"I'm sorry I wasn't here," he apologizes, and I can tell that it's eating him up inside. "I thought you were still with Bo for a while yet, or I never would have left."

"It's okay. I'm okay. Just a few little bruises." I stand on my tiptoes and kiss his cheek as he wraps his arms around me. They tighten like steel around my waist, and I know that whatever happens next, this man won't let anything else hurt me.

"You're gonna pay for these." Ramsey's eyes go from the bruises to Curtis. "You don't know how fucking lucky you are that you ever got to touch her at all."

Curtis narrows his eyes in response, and they shift to me,

something like another plea in them. Like he thinks he might still be able to convince me, even now.

"Don't bother." I shake my head slowly. "And for the record, I didn't love you more. I'm not sure I loved you at all."

I can see Ramsey's smirk out of the corner of my eye.

"You should at least admit you told a couple of white lies yourself." Ramsey's eyes flash with something like a taunt in Curtis's direction, and I frown for a moment before I realize what he means. "Or we could just give him a demonstration. I think he might deserve that for what he said."

My cheeks flush as Ramsey turns me back, and his hands go to the button on my jeans.

"Please, sugar. I want him to see it for himself. Want to see the realization when it hits him." Ramsey kisses the side of my neck, and his fingers dance under the edge of my waistband, brushing over my skin and teasing goosebumps out of me.

This is the thing about Ramsey—the reason I could never love anyone more than I love him; he can always bring out my better angels, but he's only too happy to help me set my demons loose when I need it.

"Yes... Let him see," I agree. Curtis's eyes go wide, and I see him pull on the duct tape restraints, trying and struggling against them but failing to do anything except make himself look pathetic.

Ramsey doesn't waste time, quickly unbuttoning my jean shorts and turning me to face Curtis, my back to Ramsey's front as his palm slides slowly over my stomach and abdomen. More goosebumps break out over my skin in its wake as his hand goes lower and lower. His fingers dipping under the band of my underwear, parting and slipping around either side of my clit as his mouth goes to my neck again. He teases me gently, giving me more pressure and less before his lips ghost over the shell of my ear.

"Fuck, you're so pretty like this. So fucking good for me. Tell him the truth, and I'll show him how wet you get for me." Ramsey's voice is at my ear, coaxing me on.

My mouth is dry from how quickly this turned, and I have to press my lips together to wet my tongue, darting it out to lick my lips before I can speak. A soft moan coming from the way he circles tighter with his fingers before I can get the words out.

"I lied... I lied when I said Ramsey couldn't make me come. I was just worried it would intimidate you since he was already so many things you weren't. I wanted to protect your ego." The words are quiet, but I know he can still hear them clearly from the way his body goes taut in my peripheral vision.

"That's my girl," Ramsey whispers against my skin.

I lift my lashes to look at Curtis, and if it was possible for him to kill me with one look alone, I'd be dead. His eyes drift over me with disgust but lock on the way Ramsey pulls my shorts and panties down. Ramsey turns me slightly, keeping me partially obscured from Curtis as he drags them over my ass and thighs, all the way down to the floor, where I step out of them. Ramsey's hands coast their way back up my legs, and my nerve endings all wake in their trail.

"Oh, he misses this," Ramsey whispers in my ear when he's standing straight again. "He can't stop watching." He dips his fingers inside me, and I close my eyes again, focusing on how good he feels. He starts to pump them in and out, and I can hear the sound of myself getting wetter as he works me over. It feels loud in this room with just the three of us, like it's echoing off the tiles.

"Fuck," Ramsey curses. "She feels so good. If I were you, I don't know if I'd want to live in a world where I didn't get to have her again. There were days I wished I would die out on that field if it meant I didn't have to miss her anymore. That much I pity you for."

My fingers drift over his traps as I try to steady myself when his fingers work me deeper, and his thumb starts to tease a circle around my clit. I inhale sharply when he hits me just right, and I can feel both sets of their eyes on me.

"The trick with her, by the way, is you have to listen carefully and take your time. Every breath, every moan—she tells you what she needs. If you're good enough for her, the way she comes is the most beautiful fucking sound on earth.

"I guess you wouldn't know, since she was always faking it for you, trying not to crush your ego. Then again, I guess you did hear the real thing once. I bet she didn't get a chance to tell you that yet, though... That when you were making her call you daddy on the phone, it was my tongue between her thighs making her moan like that. It was my come she was soaked in while you were trying to get that pathetic fucking dick of yours working. Me, who she's always begging for more of." Ramsey taunts Curtis, and I feel filthy in the best way. I'm dying for more from him—more of his hands, more of his words, more of Ramsey taking what he wants from me and giving me what I need. There's one thing I want more than anything though.

"Ramsey, please."

"You need more, sugar?"

"Yes. Your tongue."

He gives a wicked grin, and then he slides everything off to the side of the kitchen counter before he hoists me up on top of it, angling me so that Curtis can still watch us without seeing all of me.

"Spread for me, sugar; let him remember one last time." Ramsey's fingers make their way up and down the insides of my thighs. He looks over at Curtis and grins. "You're gonna like this show. Gonna be real sorry you didn't get one last chance to do this for her."

The second Ramsey's tongue hits me, I already know it

won't take long. I have a sick fucking kink I didn't know about, apparently, because I feel like every part of my body is on fire, swollen, tender, and ready to burst the second he touches me just right. I'm loving every second of making Curtis watch this —knowing it's probably ripping him apart the same way it did me to find out he'd been using me, lying to me. Knowing he's going to find out that my husband is better than him at everything.

Ramsey takes his time with me, though, like he wants to make a show of how much he loves tasting me. This was a thing he excelled at. He'd spend hours between my legs, kissing and sucking and teasing in intervals, edging me to the brink and back again while we'd watch a movie, until he'd get me well and truly begging for him.

My fingers thread through his hair as he starts to coax the first soft edges of my orgasm from me. I tighten my grip on his shoulder, digging my nails in and using it as an anchor to fuck his tongue. His fingers take on a faster rhythm, and I'm practically panting by the time I feel the blinding white bloom of my release.

"Oh fuck..." I cry out. "Please. Ramsey! Fuck!" I can feel the gentle scrape of his teeth and the tension as he starts to suck hard on my clit.

My nails slip down his shoulder, and I lose my grip. I'm sure I've torn into his skin with how sharp this set is, but he doesn't say a word. His focus is all on me. I let myself slide back on the counter and give him full control to finish me off. His tongue takes on a punishing pace, and his fingers work me into a second wave.

I glance over at Curtis, and his eyes are wide, watching every move we make. But I barely get to look before I'm cursing again, begging Ramsey to put me out of my misery just before he finally slows down, languidly licking over every last bit of me like he doesn't want to miss a single drop. It gives me one last wave of pleasure that licks through every nerve ending in my body. I collapse back against the cold stone counter, letting it cool my heated skin. I'm trying to let my heart rate slow when I see Ramsey stand and walk toward Curtis.

FORTY-FOUR

Ramsey

HAZE IS STILL COMING down from the high of being thoroughly fucked while her ex watches. Curtis can't seem to take his eyes off her, and I half wonder if I'm giving him more enjoyment than he deserves just by letting him see her fall apart for me. But I wanted him to know—needed him to know—that any thought he's ever had about her coming harder for him, wanting him more, or loving him more than me is dead fucking wrong. Haze and I could be separated by thousands of miles, and our hearts would still beat in sync like we were made for each other. I can only imagine how much it fucking hurts to be the one who wants her but knows he could only ever come in second best.

I stand over him; his brow is sweaty, and his eyes dart between me and Hazel. He struggles against the tape that's been keeping his hands secure again, trying to lurch forward in the chair like it might threaten me somehow. I rip the duct tape off and pull back the rag, grabbing his jaw in my hand and squeezing so hard I'm half worried I might break it. Then I spit straight into his mouth.

His eyes go wide with surprise, but when he starts to speak, I backhand him across the cheek. It's so hard that I hear the crack of my bones against his, and I feel the sting of it.

"That's the last taste of her you'll ever get. So fucking savor it."

He's still dazed and blinking when I shove the rag back into his mouth and put the tape back in place. It's struggling to adhere to his sweaty cheek now, so I double it, and then triple it. The last thing I want is to hear him say one more word about her. I look back at Hazel, who's easing off the counter and grabbing her clothes. She slips back into them quietly, and then she looks at me. There's a question on her face. It's a simple one, but one I don't have an answer to yet. I need time to think, and I haven't had that. It's only been act since the moment I saw his hands on her—wanting to kill him and then having to talk myself down, reminding myself that if I kill him, I'll lose her in the process. It's not worth it, however much I might want it. We need to find out who he works for. What he's looking for that he's willing to go to these kinds of extremes.

"Go pull the truck up to the back deck," I say soft enough that only she can hear me. "And call Bo while you're out there. Tell him I've got a one-point safety."

She nods her understanding, trusting that I've got a plan—and I do, it just might be a little half-cocked. But we'll figure it out, especially once I have Bo and my brothers' help. That's who I need more than anyone right now because I can't shake the feeling that they know more about this than they've been letting on.

I send Haze on her way, and then I take Curtis—chair, duct tape, and all—and drag him over the den rug. I shove the furniture out of the way as he watches, and I can see his wheels turn-ing. He thinks he's going to die, and the panic is setting in as he struggles against his restraints.

"I told you not to fucking come back here again. But you couldn't stay away." I shake my head, keeping an eye on him always as I move the last of the furniture off the rug.

He makes a groaning sound against the rag in his mouth, clearly trying to bargain with me, but I ignore him.

"Nah. You should have thought about all that before you got anywhere near Haze." I close the distance between us. "You thought you'd get to steal from my family and have some fun with my wife and you'd just walk away?" I slap his cheek play-fully, grinning at the way the panic sets into his eyes as they go wide, and his pupils dilate. He tries to talk again, and it's muted by the dirty rag half stuffed down his throat. I take both sides of his face in my hands, pinching a little before I do my worst.

"This is where you're going to learn not to fuck with my family." I slam his head down as I draw my knee up hard, the cracking of the cartilage and bone in his nose, a muted grunt, and the slump of his body in the chair is the only answer to the violence.

I make quick work of what I do next, grabbing the knife out of my pocket to cut the tape on the chair and rebind his wrists. I let his limp body slide to the floor, and I stretch him out. I roll him with the carpet, turning him into a little Swiss roll of stupid fuck filling. He could come to any time, and I need him immobilized and silent when I take him out to the pole barn.

I grab the rope off the decorative saddle stand, using the knife to cut it, and I tie either end of the rug. I'm just in time to hear Haze pulling the truck up to the back deck and idling it. I throw the rug and its contents over my shoulder and haul them out, meeting her at the back door while she swings the storm door open.

"No one's out right now. I checked." She nods to the truck where she already has the tailgate down, and I toss him inside and climb in alongside him.

"Take us through the garage door at the pole barn," I direct her, and her eyes briefly flash over the carpet and me before she's back in the driver's seat, taking us through the gravel lot between the house and the pole barn in rapid order. I just need to get him somewhere no one will see him. Somewhere we can keep him quiet until we decide how we're going to get the information we need out of him. I shoot off a quick text to Grant, hoping he's not indisposed at the moment.

She pulls the truck inside a few moments later, and the garage door comes down automatically behind us as she shuts off the engine and hops out.

"Tell me he's not dead, Ramsey." She looks at the rolled carpet, and her eyes meet mine with worry.

"He's not dead. I just knocked him out to make the transport easier. We can get him strapped to something in here while we wait. What did Bo say?"

"He said okay." Her eyes search mine again for answers.

"Good. Help me pull this carpet out?" I pull the tailgate out and she takes one end from me. I bear the weight while she helps guide the carpet as we walk through the pole barn to a place we can dump it on the floor. I'm not being particularly careful with the contents. If he breaks a bone or gets a little bruised up, it's no different than what he did to her as far as I'm concerned, and in his case—he deserves it.

She helps me move him along, getting him into the center of the room where it's mostly storage. We might as well start here so he can tell us what he and his friends were looking for. Because while I'm not worried about Curtis, his friends have me nervous. I have a feeling he's just their scout, trying to find an easy way to get what they want before they come with their full forces. We have no idea where they are or where they went or even if they'll be back. Never mind knowing who they are. Which means anything we do here needs to be quick and tireless until we can move him on—whatever that's going to look like—once Bo and my brothers get here.

"Where are we putting him?" Haze asks as she whirls around, looking for somewhere convenient.

"Can you go get one of the chairs over there? They're mixed in with some of that office furniture." I nod toward where I'd been hiding a few short days ago. I knew there were at least a couple there that might work.

"Sure." She skirts past me.

I pull the ropes on the carpet in the meantime, unrolling it and letting Curtis's body loose. He's still limp, and my heart skips a beat that I might have done more permanent damage than I thought when I knocked him out. I can't afford another dead body on my rap sheet right now. I doubt they'll overlook the second one the same way they did the first.

I kick his side, but he still doesn't move. Another flurry of anxiety floats through my stomach, and I turn to look around. I can't remember if the sink is still in here or if Haze removed it since she expanded the storage out here. I need cold water. That's the quickest way to bring him to again if the circumstances aren't worse than I planned.

I don't get to find it, though, because, a moment later, my legs are taken out from me with one swift kick. Apparently, I don't have to worry about Curtis being dead. Now I have to worry about me. Somehow, he's managed to cut through the duct tape, and he's got a small knife to my throat.

"I always knew you were stupid. But too stupid to check my pockets—I expected more of a challenge," he rasps, his throat still sore, and his mouth still dry from the gag. He has me pinned down with his body weight as he hovers over me, one knee in my gut. The knife brushes against my neck, and I swallow hard as I try to put distance between my skin and the blade.

"Curtis, don't!" Haze calls from across the room.

He laughs in return, a cackle that's cut short by the rawness of his throat.

"She's much more compliant when you threaten something she cares about. I learned that one from you." He presses the knife harder against my skin, and I close my eyes, cursing him and myself in the process. After what we just did, I worry about how he'll punish her if I'm not there to stop him.

"Curtis, please. I'll do whatever you want. If you want me to go with you, I will. Just don't hurt him," she pleads.

I open my eyes again. I have to fight him. I have to find a way to get him off me without him slicing my throat open because her fate will be worse. The damage he did already was when he thought he was playing nice.

"Oh, don't worry. You're going to do everything I want, sweetheart. Just as soon as I take care of him, you can blow me while you kneel over his body. Let him bleed out while you suck me dry." Curtis chuckles to himself, and I start to move, but he digs the blade in, not enough to rupture an artery but enough to make me bleed. I grunt out a protest, and he laughs louder. "You're fucked now, Stockton."

"Fuck you," I curse under my breath, my mind racing trying to think of how I can at least take him out with me.

"Curtis! Please!" Haze's plea is desperate, and my heart hurts for her. I can't leave her like this. Not with him.

"Shut the fuck up!" Curtis yells back at Haze.

"Don't fucking talk to her like that." I growl the words, and he laughs again, we tussle for a moment, but he maintains the upper hand by keeping the knife to my throat, nudging it against my jugular.

"Stop moving, or I'll kill her too when I'm done with you." Curtis grits his teeth, and the muscle at his jaw ticks, his face going red from leaning down over me. I hear Haze's soft footsteps reverberate across the concrete under my head, but he doesn't seem to register them. Too lost in his own rage to pay attention. "Now you better fucking listen to every word I say."

"Get your hands off my husband." I can see her just on the edge of my vision as I stare up at the ceiling. She's hovering behind him, a menacing look on her face if I've ever seen one. He's startled by her proximity, but he still grins like he's amused.

"That eager to suck daddy's cock?" He winks at me. "You can—" He stops short, and then I see why. She has the barn rifle I'd left sitting on the desk aimed at his head.

"Blow you?" I can hear the taunt in her voice.

"Hazel... you need to calm down." Curtis's tone changes immediately, and he turns back to look at her. I use the opportunity to shove him hard, trying to get him off me, but when he slips, his knee hits my balls, and he digs in. His attention snaps back to me, and I feel the knife start to press into my flesh a moment before I see red. Thankfully not mine own.

There's a flash from the muzzle of the gun and the spray of a million tiny droplets of blood. I blink as Curtis's body slumps on top of me, blood streaming out from the wound in his skull onto my chest. I look up at Hazel in shock, but she's already in motion. She tosses the gun aside and pulls at Curtis's arm as I push, and we manage to get him off me. I move to sit up, trying to get myself right and make sense of what just happened. But she's already in my lap, straddling me as her hands go to my chin. She lifts it and tilts her head to look at my neck.

"Are you okay? Oh my god! Let me see!" There's panic in her voice that starts to fade as she looks me over. "Okay. It doesn't look like anything more than a small nick." She lets go of me and sits back, looking into my eyes. "I was scared he got you before I could stop him."

"No. But Hazel..." My eyes drift to Curtis's lifeless body.

"He was going to kill you. I had to." Her brow furrows as she looks at him, her face shifting as she takes it in.

"Are you okay?" I ask, wrapping my arms around her, because my wife is strong as fuck, but she's never had to kill someone before. I'm not even sure she's seen someone die or shot at anything living. She never went on any of her brother's hunting trips, that I know of. But at least they taught her how to shoot. Thank fuck.

"I'm fine. As long as you're fine, I'm fine." She leans forward and her hands cup my face as she checks me again for good measure.

"I'm fine." I reassure her.

"Fuck me with a rattlesnake..." Bo's voice is low, barely above a whisper, as he takes in the scene. He's doing the math in his head that this has just gone from kidnapping to murder. Hazel knows it too as they exchange a look.

"It was self-defense. He was going to kill Ramsey." She pulls herself up from my lap, stepping one foot over my legs and then holding out her hand for me so I can try to stand again.

Bo's eyes meet mine as I stand, a seriousness there I've only seen a few times. We're both imagining the same fate. One where Hazel ends up suffering for her good deed. I look back at her, and she's staring at Curtis's body too, still trying to make sense of the situation.

"We can just explain to the police that it was a domestic dispute, and I had to do it," she says softly, in a tone that tells me even she doesn't believe that will work.

"Haze, come here." I reach for her, and she takes my hand. I pull her close to my chest, kissing the top of her head, and she squeezes me tight. "We can't call the police, sugar. But we're going to make sure you're okay." I look over her head, and Bo nods to me, already plotting how we're going to get ourselves out of this mess.

She'll be okay. We'll make sure of it. I'm not letting her life go up in flames because of me. Whatever it takes.

FORTY-FIVE

Hazel

I'M STANDING under a hot stream of water, scrubbing my skin clean with soap, still processing how this morning took such a sharp turn. It'd started out so well—having breakfast with my brother and planning to come back home and finally sort things out with Ramsey. The two of us were gonna tell Curtis to fuck off for good, and then we were gonna get started on a plan for rebuilding the ranch—and us.

Instead... it turned into a nightmare. Curtis's cruelty running so much deeper than I thought possible. The flash of the gun and the spray of his blood plays like a loop in my head when I close my eyes. I don't regret killing him. I should... I should feel guilt or sorrow or something that makes me feel like I should be on my knees begging for forgiveness. But I don't. Not if the alternative was that Ramsey died right in front of me. I'd pick the same option every single time.

But my heart still hurts for it, and I'm terrified about what it means for all of us—that I pulled the trigger and that I've made my husband and my brother an accomplice. Ramsey's brothers too, since they showed up just as Bo and Ramsey sent me to get cleaned up. They insisted I needed to get changed, try to make myself look normal in case anyone at the inn needed me.

Grant and Levi had just nodded at me like it was nothing, but then I imagine this isn't their first rodeo. The people in the inn on the other hand... I'd have to come up with a story. That Bo was running off a coyote that he thought had rabies or something that could explain away the gun shot. I can't imagine Grace or Kit would ever look at me the same if they knew the truth. Albert might have a heart attack if he found out. And that's just my employees... Amelia? She'd probably never speak to me again if she found out that I killed the man she was rooting for me to marry in order to save the one who had left me.

But she didn't know Curtis—hell, I didn't know Curtis. I couldn't have dreamed he'd turn out this twisted and sick. But then I don't suppose he guessed I would be the one to take him out of this world either. I imagine he would have left like I asked this morning if he had a second chance.

I run my fingers over the bruises he left on my arm. I'll have to hide them with a cardigan even though it's still a little too warm on these early fall days to justify it. We'll have to figure out what to do with his car. With all his stuff that's in my house. How we're going to explain his disappearance.

I hadn't even met his family yet. They were always on one trip or another—and now I wonder if I was ever going to meet them. If the people who were helping pay for our wedding were even his family at all, or more likely, whatever criminal element he was involved in. I blink and shake my head. Our wedding. That was probably never happening either. Not if he was only using me. Just coming to terms with all this makes me feel ridiculous. How gullible. How much of a fool he made me out to be. He must have been laughing every single night.

He certainly was convincing when he was using me. I believed he really loved me right up until this week. I thought I meant something to him. There were date nights and flowers and a ring, big shows of affection, but there were also quiet nights alone together, and tender kisses and inside jokes. We'd started planning the wedding, reserving all the chairs and tents and tables we'd need. I'd picked out a dress, and he'd picked out a suit—more things I'll have to burn right alongside my clothes that are covered in his blood now.

But it was all a lie. All a lie so he could find something that the Stocktons supposedly stole. The last forty-eight hours replay in my head like a movie reel, and then my heart stops.

He said it wasn't safe for me here. That she could change her mind. Who is she? Who could have that much control over him that he'd be scared of her? Another woman? His boss? Did they have eyes on the ranch? My heart skips in my chest as I hurry to finish my shower. I need to tell the brothers the rest of what I know.

As I towel off, I keep racking my brain for anything else Curtis said or did that didn't make sense, anything that set off my senses when I'd seen him in the last couple days.

It hits me hard now. The thing he said that I hadn't thought much of at the time. He'd said the horses were hurt. Except, I never told him that. I never said a word about the horses being hurt—just that the barn had burned down, and we were worried that arsonists had done it. I didn't want to elaborate, and when he said it, I figured at the time that he just assumed that the horses had gotten hurt, but now I wonder if he *knew* it.

If he was repeating something someone else had told him. Someone who was already here.

There's only one person on this property who's a bigger Curtis fan than I was. I throw my clothes on and take off running.

FORTY-SIX

Ramsey

WHEN WE OPEN the door to her room, Amelia's already furiously packing up her things. It'd only taken us a few minutes to look through Curtis's phone, after Hazel explained her suspicions, to figure out that she must have been his accomplice. She was keeping her eyes on the ranch and on Hazel whenever he was gone.

Amelia must have put together that something happened to Curtis when he didn't answer her calls and she didn't see Hazel. Whether she thought they ran off together or believed he was hurt, I don't know. But everything is starting to make sense.

"Don't panic. We just need you to come talk to us," Lev says as he walks slowly into her room, trying not to startle her. But she's worse than the horses.

Her eyes flash to us, panic searing across her face, and she reaches for her gun. Thank fuck, Levi's quicker than she is, though, and he tackles her to the ground before she can get a shot off. He pins her arm down, and Grant takes the gun, dispensing with the ammunition and putting the empty weapon in the back of his pants. His foot stomps on her fingers, squishing them as Lev squeezes her throat until she passes out from the lack of oxygen and collapses, going limp on the carpet, her cheeks ruddy from the exertion, and her perfectly coifed hair in tangles.

We have to move quickly. Hazel gave us a path to get back down the servants' stairs without being seen. Luckily, no one else is staying on this floor in this wing, and no one is in the room below. Amelia had always requested a quiet room with no neighbors, Hazel said, claiming she was a light sleeper. But that lie will give us what we need to get her out of here.

We move her the same way we did Curtis, navigating the back stairs and getting her into the truck with a blanket tossed over her as Lev holds his hands around her throat—ready to take her out again if she comes to before we're ready.

This time, though, we move her to a barn on the far side of the property. One where no one can hear her if she screams. One where the neighbors are miles away. I'm just hoping she cooperates and gives us what we want, that somehow, we can come to an agreement that stops the bloodshed today.

"TELL us who you are and who you work for," Levi demands of her.

"Like you don't know." She rolls her eyes, a manufactured smirk appearing and disappearing from her lips.

"Maybe I just want to hear you say it." He shrugs, sitting

back in the chair across from her. Amelia gives a false little smile as her eyes drift over Levi.

"I won't say a word until I know Curtis is safe."

"Who is Curtis to you?"

"Why don't you ask the dark-haired bitch." Amelia looks at Hazel who insisted on being present, despite me begging her to stay at the ranch house. My heart can't take her having to be part of any more hard decisions today.

"The dark-haired bitch? After everything, that's what you call me?" There are tears in Hazel's eyes, and somehow, this seems to be hitting her worse than the Curtis news. "You were like a mother to me."

"I would have been. But you had to choose him. You're such a disappointment. Years I invested in you. All for what? So you could spread your legs for this piece of shit again? I'm embarrassed for you. You could have had everything."

"What do you mean would have been? Are you his mother?"

"So there are brains in there after all. Impressive." Amelia's eyes glide over Hazel and find her wanting.

"You knew he was lying to me, and yet you talked him up. Over and over again, you encouraged me and the relationship. All that talk about women making better decisions for themselves, and you were just luring me into a trap."

"Of course I did, sweetheart. That was the whole point. He needed to marry you to get this ranch, get back some semblance of the money that was stolen from us. We both had to help you make the right choice."

"It's disgusting. Completely disgusting that you would manipulate someone in that way. I thought you were my friend."

"Oh please. I don't know how anyone could tolerate you. I don't know how my son tolerated you all this time. So crass and opinionated all the time. Always thinking you know better than everyone else. At least he's free of you now."

Hazel shakes her head, tears forming in her eyes, and I reach out for her, but she swats me away, charging toward Amelia.

"You're right. At least he's free of me." Hazel's grin turns cruel, and Amelia's eyes grow wider; she blinks, and then looks around at the rest of us.

"If you don't bring my son in here this instant, I will scream. And then I will bring down hell on this ranch. You'll wish you were all dead by the time we're done with you," she threatens, and Grant just grins and shakes his head, staring down at his phone like her lack of compliance is a temporary inconvenience to his evening.

"That won't be happening," Levi says as he nods for me to take Hazel.

I close the distance between us, taking her hand and pulling her close. She buries her face in my chest, and I wrap my arms around her.

"It's okay," I whisper into the raven-colored hair at her crown. Pressing a kiss to the silky strands while I work to comfort her. "It's okay, darlin. Don't listen to a word she says."

"Yes. Don't listen to me. Keep making the same stupid mistakes you've been making. It keeps turning out so well for you," Amelia taunts her.

"You sure you don't want to go back in?" I ask Haze when she looks up at me with tear-stained cheeks.

"I'm sure. I want to get to the bottom of this," she says quietly.

I can't hear what Lev says to Amelia next; he whispers it softly into her ear, smiling as he pulls back and takes her horrified look in. Amelia screams a moment later—a crystal rattling, blistering scream that echoes off the walls.

"Give me my fucking son!" She rattles against the binds that hold her in place, tugging on them like she's possessed and screams again, her voice too hoarse for it to be as effective this time.

"No one can hear you out here." I shake my head.

"Not a single soul. It's just us, and we don't give a fuck about you or your son." Grant leans back against one of the large wooden beams that holds up the center of the barn.

"She does though. She cares about my son. The way she fawned and obsessed over him. The way she planned every detail of the wedding. She said she loved him more than she ever loved anyone." Amelia attempts to get in Haze's head and mine, and I feel her hug me tighter.

"Leave her out of this." Grant steps in front of us, like he's worried one of us might snap on her. "And tell me what you're here for."

"You know what I'm here for. You're the smart one, right? He's your muscle. The other one ran away to play games with grown men every weekend. You must be the brains." Amelia looks between Levi and me and then back at Grant. "I'm sure if you think really hard, you'll know what we want. I just thought all these years you'd have kept it in the casino. Shame it wasn't there, and we had to come bother the poor defenseless ex-wife."

I feel a swirl of anxiety in my chest as it tightens. Grant doesn't flinch when she makes the accusation. He just continues to stare. No surprise or confusion on his face when she insists that we have something of hers.

"Huh. Looks like the big sporty one doesn't know what I'm talking about. You keep secrets from each other too? That's a dangerous business when it's your family on the line." Amelia's saccharine smile returns, and my heart drops with it. But I can't let it show on my face. The three of us can discuss this later.

Hazel picks up on my anxiety, and her hand runs gently down my spine.

"It's odd that you'd say that since Curtis kept secrets from you." Hazel whirls around. "He was insisting on getting me out of here before you changed your mind. Confessing to everything just for a chance to get me to leave with him."

Amelia's fake lashes flutter for a second, her rosy-red cheeks blushing just a little more at that information, giving away that she doesn't like it one bit. Then her eyes narrow, and she looks around the room before focusing back in on Hazel.

"So where is he? Seems like he took off without you." Amelia's tone turns dark.

"And without you." Hazel mimics the smile Amelia gave her. "But I'm sure you'll see him soon enough." Hazel squeezes my hand tightly, and Amelia doesn't miss the motion.

"Did you kill him? You jealous little prick!" Amelia rages at me, and Levi's hands press down on her shoulders.

"Calm down."

"I won't be calm until I see my son."

"Tell us what we need to know, and you can see him," Grant says calmly, looking like he's barely bothered by the scene unfolding. I worry for my brothers and what they've done in the last five years that this seems like a boring night to them.

"Bring him to me. Then we can talk."

"Listen to me." Levi comes around to the front of her chair, standing next to me as he takes her chin in his hand. "We have his cell phone. It's how we confirmed it was you that was stalking Hazel around, keeping an eye on her when Curtis was gone. It won't take us long to get the rest of what we need. If you tell us, though, and make all of our lives easier... we can go easier on you."

"If you have his cell phone, then I know everything I need

to know. I won't tell you shit." Amelia spits in Levi's face, and he blows out a breath as he wipes it off his cheek.

"Have it your way." Levi stands and moves back to her side where he keeps an eye on the ropes that secure her in place. She's given up fighting them now, though, leaning into her fate. I can tell in the way she looks off into the distance that somehow the knowledge of his cell phone confirms his death to her; a thing I'm fairly certain she already knew when we brought her here but was unwilling to admit to herself.

Amelia's eyes glitter in the dull light of the barn, almost like she might cry, but she swallows hard and chokes it back. However much she might disgust me, I have to give her credit for having that kind of strength. She blinks what's left of the tears away and then looks up at me, a smile at first that melts into a sneer as she looks me over.

"I regret feeling sorry for your bitch of a mother." Amelia spits at my feet. "She begged for your lives. As a mother, I felt for her. Let her pathetic little sobs worm their way into my heart and spread their poison. I spared you and your brothers, pretended like I didn't know where your sister was, instead of making sure they destroyed the whole family tree. It was the biggest mistake of my life. If I could go back, I would have put a bullet in every single one of your heads myself, starting with your sister and taking my time with you." Amelia's eyes land hard on me.

My world stops, and the color fades at the edges of my vision. All I can see is her in front of me and flashes of my mother and father soaked in their own blood.

"You were there that night?" My throat is raw, and I can barely get the words out.

"There? Who do you think shot that cunt in the face?" Amelia smiles like she enjoyed every moment of my mother's death. Like she doesn't have a single regret in her body. "She deserved it for—"

The gunshot rings out in the night, and the spray of blood against the barn wall is brilliant red. Splattering against the wood and the bull's head that's mounted on the beam above her. Dripping slowly down the bony face until it threatens to return to its owner again.

"Holy fuck!" Bo shouts, finally making himself known again from the corner of the barn as Amelia's body slumps forward in her chair.

The rope binds are the only thing keeping her from sliding to the floor at my feet where she belongs as Lev stares down from her side. I want to see her skull as mutilated as my mother's was when I found her, pieces of it everywhere on the porch and embedded in the furniture. Nearly unrecognizable if it hadn't been that she was wearing the same apron she always did when she made us dinner, and her tortoise shell hair clip still neatly holding her hair back from her caved-in face.

I raise the gun to shoot again. To make sure she suffers the same fate. I want her wandering hell faceless, her jaw hanging from her skull while she tries to explain how she could have been so coldblooded and cruel.

"Ramsey..." Hazel says softly, her hand on my forearm as she looks up at me. "She's dead."

"I want her more than dead. I want her in fucking pieces." The gun is shaking in my hand, and I realize I'm crying, sobs racking my body. I feel sick. Like I might throw up. I can imagine my mom seeing someone like Amelia at the door, smiling at her. Inviting her in to get her out of the heat of the day. Offering her a cold drink and a comfortable chair. Letting her sit at the dining room table and serving her a piece of pie. And she killed her. She fucking murdered her in cold blood.

Over what? Money? Greed? An endless cycle of hate between these families that never ends.

"Let me have the gun, please." Hazel's pleading with me, and I look down and see there are tears in her eyes. I take in a sharp breath, trying to assess why she's crying, and then I see the blood that's splattered across her shirt and arms.

"Oh fuck..." I mutter, turning to her. My hands searching over her body and trying to wipe the smears off her skin. She takes the gun from me gently and hands it off to Bo. His eyes drift over both of us and, for the second time today, I can tell he's worried. The reality of it sets in. That I've made my poor innocent wife who loved horses and taking old ladies bird-watching an accessory to two murders in one day. Fucked up her whole life so fucking quickly she barely had time to process it before I was making it worse. "Oh fuck. Fuck. Fuck. Darlin', I'm so sorry. I didn't think. I didn't think... I'm sorry." I hit my knees and press my face to her stomach. We'd spent so much time trying to make sure we'd cleaned her up and kept her safe after Curtis, only for me to fuck it up again. All I can seem to do is fuck up her life. She takes pity on me despite it, and her fingers run through my hair, and she wraps her other around my neck.

"It's okay. Shh. It's okay, baby. It's okay." She presses closer and rubs small circles over my back. "I've got you."

I lean into Hazel's warmth. Her touch is the only thing keeping me grounded right now when the whole world feels like it might slip out from under me. I turn my head and stare across the barn, watching as several more drips of blood tumble off the bull skull to the ground at Amelia's feet.

"Tell Anson it's a two-point safety now," I hear Grant mutter to Bo; the three of them exchange looks, watching me like I need the vigilance.

I can't make sense of much in this moment, but I do know

one thing—my mother and father's killer is finally dead. I've made sure of it. Too long and too late for it to serve any real good. It couldn't bring her back to me. My kids will never know her through anything but stories and old photographs. My dad will never get to see me play pro. But at least I've managed to do the thing law enforcement never cared enough to bother with—I've gotten them both the justice they deserve.

FORTY-SEVEN

Hazel

OUR BROTHERS ARE busy taking care of the mess we made today. I feel a flurry of guilt as I drive Ramsey and me back to the house, feeling like we should have stayed to help somehow. But Ramsey needs time to process; he's still unusually quiet, and he's apologized a half dozen times to me for what happened. No matter how many times I promise I'm okay, he doesn't seem sure enough, and I want his mind off everything that happened. I can't stand to watch him spiral into despair the same way I have before, and if I have to be strong for both of us until I can bring him out of this, I will. Our brothers can hold the fort down in the meantime. Plus, if you can't rely on your family to take care of the dead bodies—what kind of family are they really?

"Are you doing okay?" I ask. The night is late, and the moon is starting to fade over the horizon.

"I'm fine," he answers, his voice muted as he stares out the window.

"We need to get ourselves cleaned up. Burn the clothes. Take a shower."

"Yes." He nods. "I don't want any traces of this on you." He looks over at me, worry coloring his face. "I wish you hadn't been out there with us. It would have been better. You didn't need to see that. Losing both of them that way in one day."

"They weren't who they said they were." I try to shrug it off. I don't want him worried about me right now, but he's not wrong. It had sliced straight through my heart to find out two people I'd trusted and cared for so much had turned out to be manipulating me. It's something I'm not sure I'll ever fully recover from, but it's something I can keep marching through. After all, this is life—one hard thing after another. We just have to keep finding our way through to the other side. As long as I have the people I love with me, I can find a way to make it through.

"You're too good to people, Haze. They don't deserve you. They abuse it, and I wish I could fucking kill them again for it." He shakes his head, wincing at the thought, as he runs his fingers over the back of his knuckles.

"You don't have to worry about it anymore. They're gone, and I'm wiser for it. It's a shock, but I'll be okay. It was a surprise for all of us... what you found out about Amelia..." I risk a glance at him as we pull down the small dirt road, getting closer to the house again.

"I'm glad it was me. That I could end it. That's fucked up, I know. But it felt... good. Both times I've had to do it... It felt *good* to put an end to the misery those people brought on the world. I don't know what that says about me." It's a vulnerable admission on his part, one I'm sure he wouldn't make to my brothers or his. The kind of truth he'd only trust to me, and one I have to be careful with.

"I think it means you loved the people you were protecting," I say, turning to him as I put the truck in park.

"I'm sorry you had to make that choice with Curtis. He deserved it, that and worse, really, but I'm sorry it had to be you."

"I'm not. I'd do it again," I say softly, staring up at the stars through the windshield. I didn't feel the deep satisfaction from it the way Ramsey does, but I certainly don't feel any remorse. Good isn't a terrible word to describe it either.

I'm sure I should feel worse than I do. That someday this might hit me like a ton of bricks in a therapy session three years from now while I bawl my eyes out into a mound of tissues on the coffee table next to the therapy couch. But right now, I'm the therapist... "I know what you mean when you say it felt good," I add. His eyes meet mine, deep pools of empathy reflected in them, and he holds out his hand for mine, squeezing me tight when I return the gesture.

"Let's get cleaned up." I tilt my head toward the house, and he nods his agreement before we climb out of the truck.

THE STEAM ROLLING off the water fills the shower room in our master bathroom. I'm on my second round of soap and shampoo, trying to make sure every bit of Amelia and Curtis is washed off me. Ramsey has barely moved, leaning against the shower tile and letting the water run down his back. There's a sharp red line on his skin the rivulets of water follow as they make their way to the drain. I slip some conditioner into the ends of my hair and make my way over to him.

The gentlest touch startles him, and he looks back over his

shoulder. His eyes are rimmed with red, and his face is still tight with worry. This shower isn't doing nearly as much for him as it is for me.

"Come here," I whisper, motioning for him to turn around.

"I'm fine." He stands up straighter, apparently worried I might judge him for not being numb in the wake of the day's events.

"I know you are," I reassure him, and he turns reluctantly, letting me wrap my arms around his middle. I press a kiss to the center of his chest, and he leans down to kiss the top of my head. We stand like that, just holding each other for a few minutes before I step back, grabbing the teak chair that's pressed up against the wall. "Sit." I pat the seat, and he looks up at me, perplexed and frowning. "Just trust me."

He complies, slowly sitting down and dwarfing the small bench, adjusting once or twice like he's afraid he might break it before he finally settles down. I grab my shampoo bottle and pour a small amount into my palm, lathering it up between my hands before I start to run it through his hair. He freezes up at first like I'm taking too many liberties with him. But as my fingers massage his scalp and I drag my nails gently down the nape of his neck, he relaxes into my touch. His eyes close, and he leans back as I work the strands up into a bubbly lather.

"Keep them closed," I say softly as I reach for the handheld, turning it on to a gentle setting. I slowly rinse the suds from his scalp, cupping my hand around his ears and eyes as I go. I watch as some of the tension in his shoulders goes lax, and they fall an inch and then two by the time I'm done.

I move to the bodywash next. I don't think when I grab it off the small ledge, putting my harvest apple scent into my hands and then onto the washcloth instead of his woodsier version. I swear softly and go to wash it off, but he grabs my wrist and looks up at me.

"Leave it," he whispers and nods to the cloth.

I work just as carefully as I did with the shampoo, sudsing his neck and shoulders and moving down his back. I pause at intervals to make sure I've tackled all the spots that are extra dirty, stained with blood or grime from the aftermath of the day.

He holds still for my ministrations, allowing me to move and position his limbs as I need, and standing as I start to move over his lower back and his butt and thighs. I move to his front, working down his legs and knees, all the way down to his ankles and feet, making sure I cover every single inch of him.

When I finish, I toss the washcloth to the side and pull him close, placing my hand over his heart as I feel his body shudder. I look up, and there are tears in his eyes again, only this time they fall.

"I'm sorry." He mouths the words, and I press my lips together, my eyebrows softening as I study him.

"Don't ever apologize to me for loving your family and wanting to keep them safe. You don't owe anyone an apology for that. Least of all me. If anything, Ramsey, I love you more for it."

"Do you love me? After everything?" He can barely bring himself to ask the question. "I'm so fucking scared of losing you, sugar. So terrified of dragging you into this miserable life of mine, one you didn't ask for. One that keeps asking more and more of you, even when it's taken everything from us already."

"You'll never lose me. Not in this life or the next." I lift my eyes to meet his because I want him to hear the next bit, really hear it. "And it could take everything else from me, as long as the two of us are still standing at the end of the day, that's all that matters." I rise onto my tiptoes and press a soft kiss to his lips, one that takes him off guard. His eyes open wide, and he blinks for a moment.

"Let me melt the ice away, sugar. Please. I need you

tonight." His hands bracket my jaw, and his eyes search mine for any sign of hope.

"I need you every night." I kiss him again, so whisper soft that I barely feel his lower lip as mine brushes over it. Not until he answers it with a kiss so feverish that he nearly knocks me off-balance. It's wild and desperate, like a lifeline between us, as his lips move over mine in rough, pleading strokes. He's making up for lost time, finally taking what's always been his.

"I want you forever, Haze. Please let me keep you this time." The words are a mess, scattered in between one kiss after another as his fingers tangle in my wet hair. "Please."

"I'm never letting go again," I warn him.

"Never again," he promises.

I shut the water off as he backs me up against the wall, pinning me and kissing me, his body pressed against mine. We stay like that for long minutes until my teeth chatter against his next kiss. His eyes dart to mine, worry in them as he pulls me from the shower, wraps me in a large bath towel, and carries me to bed.

He only unwraps me once he's sure the fire's on in the fireplace, and I've promised him I'm warm as I slip under the covers. He makes his way slowly to my side, studying me like he's committing me to memory before he climbs in bed. He reaches for me, and his thick arms wrap around my body, dragging me to his side. I wrap my leg around his hip and my hand around his neck as he kisses me one last time before nuzzling his nose against my neck.

"Mine." His voice breaks through the night with a quiet declaration one last time before we both fall asleep so closely wrapped around each other that I'm not sure where I end and he begins.

FORTY-EIGHT

Ramsey

IT TAKES me two days locked away with Hazel and a visit from Bo, but I'm feeling myself again. Enough that I'm ready to confront my brothers. The conversation with Amelia has played again and again in my head, and it's obvious there's more to the story than they've told me about our parents. Fuck, there's more to this story with Curtis and Amelia than I think they know, especially after Haze finally has a chance to fill me in on everything that was discussed between her and Curtis the day he died. It doesn't seem to be a surprise to them either when they see me come in the door to Grant's office looking for answers.

"I was wondering when we'd see you." Levi looks at me thoughtfully.

"I was wondering when you were gonna stop gaslighting me," I reply tersely.

Grant's eyes slowly roll to the side as he lets out a small

sigh. "You had more important things to do, if you remember. Off on your little pro-football adventure instead of staying here when I asked you to."

"You know why I left."

"You don't think the rest of us couldn't stop thinking about Mom? Lev? Me? Aspen?"

"You aren't the one who found her like that. You didn't lean down to touch her one last time and find her body still warm. I was minutes away from being able to do something about it."

"You wouldn't have done anything about it. You would have ended up dead," Grant answers me flatly, stopping his pace in front of his windows to look at me like I'm insane for thinking it would have gone down any other way.

"At least I would have died trying." I grit my teeth.

"This isn't worth discussing. It's in the past," Levi interjects, looking between us like he doesn't have the energy for one of our brotherly spats today.

"Then tell me about the present. I want to know exactly why a madwoman and her fucked up son were on my ranch torturing and manipulating my wife. It's obvious you knew more than you let on."

"More but not enough. If you'd held your temper, we might have gotten more out of her." Grant flashes a derisive look in my direction.

"She killed our mother."

"All the more reason we should have gotten more out of her." Grant presses his point.

"Fucking hell. The two of you need to stop fighting each other. We don't have time for it. We killed two of theirs, and they still don't have what they're looking for. They'll be at our door soon enough, and we all need to be on the same page of a plan when that happens." Levi looks at us both like we're misbehaving toddlers.

"Fine. What are they looking for? Let's start there." I study my brothers.

My brothers exchange glances before one of them speaks, and apparently Levi wins the silent argument.

"A reliquary," Grant says flatly.

"A reliquary?" Of all the things I'd imagined, that was low on the list.

"Two weeks before Mom and Dad died, we were sent to help carry out a heist. It was part of a debt Dad owed to someone else—a favor he'd promised in exchange for an advance. One he needed to cover a bad bet. He sent us to ensure that it went smoothly, to have eyes on it since he couldn't be there. Something went wrong. We still don't know exactly what, but there was another team there at the same time as ours. The alarms were tripped, and in the process of trying to get out, we were attacked and robbed. Nearly killed. Managed to wound them in the process, but we never figured out who it was," Levi explains.

"You were robbed *during* a robbery?" I ask skeptically.

"We were double-crossed. They used us to get in and it gave them someone to pin the blame on. Then after we did all the hard work, they took what we'd stolen. We were scape-goats." Grant explains his side of the story while Levi crosses his arms.

"That's a theory." Levi looks at Grant. "We don't know for sure."

"There's no other realistic explanation," Grant answers, and it's clear they've been arguing about this for the last five years.

"So you don't have any of it, but someone thinks you do?"

Grant turns his back and looks out the window as Levi tilts his head and looks at the floor. I'm getting tired of their quiet little play they're putting on, one that's delaying the answers I need.

"Tell him," Grant mutters.

"We still have one piece of it. It was the rarest piece in the collection, so we took extra precautions with it. Stowed it somewhere safe before we ever went for the rest. When they held us at gunpoint, they took what we had—not realizing that they didn't have the most important piece," Levi explains.

"There isn't exactly time to double-check the order's right when you're fucking someone over, and the police are on their way." Grant turns around, his hands in his suit pockets as he shakes his head and leans back against the desk.

"Did Mom and Dad know? Why did they kill them instead of you?" I ask, perplexed by what the reasoning could have been. It was Grant and Levi who fucked up.

"We don't know. That's what we needed Amelia to tell us." Grant levels me with a look that tells me he's disappointed that my temper got the best of me.

"She wasn't going to tell you. Not once she realized Curtis was dead." I shake my head.

"And whose fault is that?" Grant looks at me.

"Whose fault? That's what you want to figure out right now? Because it certainly fucking seems like there's plenty to go around in this family. Starting with you two not being honest," I snap back at him.

"He's right." Levi looks at Grant, his brow furrowed, and Grant shakes his head, letting out a frustrated sigh.

"So they think Mom and Dad hid the reliquary somewhere on the ranch?" It feels like pulling teeth to get my brothers to give me any details.

"Yes. But whether it's the people who asked Dad to find it for them in the first place as payment, or the people who stole everything from us assuming it would be there... We don't know." Levi leans back in his chair. "We've always assumed it was the people he didn't pay back, pissed off enough that they wanted to make a point to everyone else in the community."

"How much of a community is it when you're all killing each other all the time?" I run a hand over my face, trying to scrub the frustration and confusion away and failing. "You were involved in the business, and you didn't know any of this?"

"Dad and Uncle Jay were only just letting us in on things. We were a stopgap measure when they didn't have another choice. Dad didn't like to provide details." Levi explains.

Uncle Jay was the youngest of my dad's two brothers. We'd only seen him a handful of times growing up, and after Uncle Creighton died leaving the casino to dad, the visits had grown even more scarce as bitterness permeated the dispersal of family assets.

"So ask Uncle Jay now." I demand, hoping they're still able to get in touch with him. It's the only way we get answers.

"He won't discuss it." Grant shakes his head.

"What do you mean he won't discuss it?" I press.

"Exactly what I said."

"So how do you know he wasn't involved?" I look between the two of them.

"We don't," Levi answers, his eyes drifting down to the floor again, like he's as disappointed to tell me as I am to hear it.

"Holy fuck..." I pace back and forth. "You never thought to tell me any of this?"

"What good would that have done?" Levi gives me a perplexed expression.

"I begged you to stay here and help us redress Mom and Dad's deaths. And you ran off to play ball. It would've only made you a liability if you weren't going to help. Possibly a target." Grant's eyes darken, and I grind my teeth to keep from lashing out at him.

"I might have stayed if you weren't keeping secrets from me. If I'd known Haze was still going to be in danger because they thought we still had something. Fuck! I thought I was keeping her safe by leaving, not painting a fucking target on her back."

"Nothing happened for years. We thought it was safe. It was only when you drew our attention to Curtis, and we started looking at his badge logs and some of his behavior that we realized something was off about him," Levi explains.

"That's a big fucking miss," I mutter.

"Yes, well... it seems to be a family trait." Grant's eyes sweep over me and then meet mine.

"We should focus on what's next." Levi tries to corral the argument.

"What's next? I hope you're pursuing this. Did you find out who the intruders were? The arsonists? One in the same?" I look between them.

"They used fake IDs, and they charged to the card I provided them for a free stay. It was a dead end." Levi shakes his head, and I can tell he's as frustrated as I am.

"So they could still be around." I click my tongue and shake my head. I only felt safe coming here because Bo and Anson were taking turns staying on the ranch alongside Cade and his friend. Knowing she's under constant watch is the only thing keeping me sane right now.

"We have to be cautious until we make the next steps." Grant's not sweating anything, probably because he lives in this tower surrounded by security.

"Cautious? That's easy for you when you live in a fortress."

"I told you to move in here." Grant shoots me a derisive look.

"And abandon everyone at the ranch to some unknown fate?"

Grant opens his mouth to say something but thinks better of it and turns his back to me again. He paces toward the window and then finally speaks.

"Close temporarily. She wanted to do renovations, right?"

"I'm not even going to approach that subject with her. It's a nonstarter. So tell me what the plan is. I think I deserve to be part of this family-bonding activity, considering I've already been helping clean up the mess."

"We have someone coming to pick up the reliquary. She's going to put it up for auction, and we're hoping it's going to draw out the people looking for it," Lev explains.

"If it's stolen, how's that possible?" I frown at the implications.

"The black market. Not Sotheby's." Grant presses his lips together.

"Isn't that risky? Can you trust her?"

"She comes well vetted and recommended, and she charges a hefty commission for the privilege of her services." Grant shuffles a few pieces of paper on his desk, and then gives me a pointed look. "This whole world is a series of calculated bets. You just have to plan to be the house and not the gambler."

FORTY-NINE

Ramsey

A WEEK LATER, at my insistence, we're standing in front of the vault at The Avarice, waiting for Levi to bring the courier down for the reliquary. Grant has it sitting out behind the heavily barred gate, and I roll my shoulders. Performance anxiety is rolling through me in waves. I've been able to adapt to the idea of being a killer, but the idea of exchanging goods in a clandestine tête-à-tête in the basement of The Avarice is, apparently, a bridge too far. The fitted suit I'm in isn't helping. I thought I might have been done with them when my pro career ended with my prison sentence, but instead, I'm in one Grant's tailor fitted to within an inch of my life.

"You're the one who insisted on being here." Grant flashes a look at me, warning me not to embarrass him.

"You wanted me back in the family business." I hold my ground. "This is what it looks like."

"Well, I retract my statement. Stay on your ranch with your mud and your horses."

A moment later, we hear footsteps coming down the hall, and I don't get to respond. Levi appears with a tall brunette woman. Her hair falls around her shoulders in thick waves, and her pale green eyes are hauntingly stark against her pale skin and dark lashes. She's dressed in a fitted, white blouse and wide-leg trousers that hide her heels. Another tall woman, even taller than the first, trails behind her, with dark-auburn hair bluntly chopped at her shoulders and ocean-blue eyes. She's wearing black leather pants and a black sweater with spiked heels that make her look deadly.

"You must be the courier..." Grant takes a step forward, holding out his hand to the brunette. Her eyes flash over him, but I can't read if it's interest or pure assessment that's dancing behind them.

"I am." She smiles, flashing a bright smile.

"Grant."

"Charlotte," she answers him and then turns to me, a small smile appearing on her lips like she's registering how uncomfortable I am.

"Should we be exchanging names?" I ask.

"No," the auburn-haired one says bluntly, looking between the three of us brothers like we're the worst excuse for men she's ever seen.

"Ramsey, right? I've seen you around." Charlotte smiles at me politely, and the face Levi makes behind her makes me regret I ever had such a public career.

"Around?" I ask, but she ignores my question and turns to Grant again.

"Do you have the item?"

"Yes."

"As we discussed, my policy is to leave a deposit with you

worth one half what the item will reasonably fetch on the market. Are we still agreed?" She looks at Grant as though he might say no.

"We're agreed."

"Good." She smiles. "The money." She nods to her assistant who presents a bag.

The exchange happens so quickly that I barely know why I came at all. I suppose this way, I've at least seen the reliquary, and I'd be able to identify the party who stole it if she never returns with it—a risk we have to take to dig deeper into this pit of vipers my brothers have stirred up.

"Now what?" I ask Grant when Levi disappears with the women up the elevator again.

"We wait. Hopefully she draws them out."

"And if there is a buyer?"

"We pay extra to find out who they are," Grant answers bluntly.

THAT NIGHT, when I get home from The Avarice and pull into the drive, my phone dings with a text. It's Cooper asking me to call him. I glance at the clock and see I have a bit before Haze is off her shift at the inn, so I hit the button to return Cooper's call.

"Hey, cowboy. How's it going?" Cooper greets me warmly. It feels strange, like he and that world are a lifetime away, and I'm somehow able to time travel with a phone call.

"Good," I lie. I can't drag Cooper into any of this.

"Well, I'm glad you're good because I've got even better news. Well, actually, that's fucked up... I shouldn't say that, but it's good for you. We've got a DE position open. One of the guys just found out he's out for the season, and the rookie was dismissed for misconduct. They're looking for someone, and they're willing to call you back to the practice squad if you think you can get into shape. It'll give you a chance to compete for a starting spot again. Coach Undergrove is planning to call you."

My heart skips a few beats at that news. The idea of being away from the death and destruction around here. Not having to be part of whatever game Grant and Levi are playing. Running down a field on a Sunday autumn afternoon. I don't hate the idea, but it feels too good to be true.

"I thought they weren't sure if I'd be a liability."

"I've been talking you up. So has Quentin, and you know he's got a lot of sway here. Plus, the PR team isn't worried. You're a hero around here, and they'd just be grateful to have someone healthy and formidable out on the field, you know?"

"Wow. I just... didn't think it was a real possibility. I thought you were just trying to give me some hope to get through things. I'm not sure what to say."

"Do you want to come back?"

"I do, but I don't want to leave Haze. I can't go through that again. Neither can she."

"I can understand that." I can hear the disappointment in Cooper's tone, but his love for Bea has made him see the world differently too. "Well... talk it over with her and let me know? I'll let Coach know you're thinking about it. Just... think quickly? They'll want to move in the next day or two.

"Of course," I say, looking out the truck window to see Haze making her way to the front door of the house from the inn.

"All right. Talk with you soon then. Later."

"Later, man."

We hang up, and I take a deep breath. I have no idea how to break this idea to Haze—if I even should. I don't want to put everything we've been building the last few months into jeopardy by making her think I'd leave her again. But with everything that's happened here, I have to wonder if she'd reconsider it. If we could let someone else run the place for a few months a year while I played and come back here in the offseason. Maybe it could be the best of both worlds for us.

BY THE TIME I walk inside, I've worked myself up to the idea of telling her. I'll caveat it by telling her nothing would make me leave her, and she has the final say in the decision we make. It's our future, not just mine anymore, and I can't imagine her not at my side, even if it means I get to play again. I know if I explain it that way, she'll understand. She knows I love football the same way she loves the inn.

When I find her in the dining room, though, she's reading a piece of paper from the mail and startles when she sees me. I hope it's not another bill. They've been piling up lately, and there'll only be more in the future as we work to rebuild the stables and hire more staff. That might have to be part of my pitch for playing again.

"Hey, sugar. How was your day?"

"Not terrible. Yours? Your brothers pull you in deeper?" She's agreed I need to sort things out with them and stay close to what's going on. But she's not thrilled it means I'm getting dragged deeper into the criminal underbelly of their business.

"Not terrible. I managed to mostly observe. I thought one of their couriers recognized me."

"I see." She frowns as she looks at me, and I'm worried she can tell how anxious I am about Cooper's news.

"I need to tell you something," I admit.

"Me too."

"Can I go first?"

"Um... I think I need to." Her lower lip wavers, and her eyes look down at the paper. "But you may not want to speak to me after I show you this."

"Sugar, there's nothing you could do that would make me not want to speak to you."

She turns the piece of paper around silently, and I skim the words. My heart stops, and my world bottoms out.

It's a final decree of divorce, signed and sealed by a judge.

FIFTY

Hazel

THE LOOK on his face makes me feel like I can't breathe. It's agony and fury all intertwined, and I see the way his hand shakes as he sets the paper down.

"I can explain." I try not to cry. I don't need to cry. We could fix this, easily.

"I don't know if you need to. It's pretty self-explanatory." His tone is so cold it makes my heart ache from the frost.

"I know I said I was going to put the paperwork in a safety deposit box, but I filed it. I figured the state requires the ninety-day cooling-off period anyway. This way, when it was over, we could go our separate ways without having to wait even longer for the paperwork to go through. We could get back to normal faster."

"So you weren't even going to give me a chance?"

"Ramsey, at the time... Please, remember, at the time I didn't know. I didn't want to admit to myself how much I still loved you or that Curtis was twisting everything and manipulating me. I didn't know you still loved me. I thought you just wanted the ranch back and wanted to punish me for moving on while I still lived here. I thought this would all be a disaster between us and that I needed to plan a wedding to marry Curtis. I thought you'd go back to Cincinnati to play again, and I could go back to my life the way it was." I rush through my words, hoping if I can say them fast enough, it'll stop the spread of the poison—like cutting off a limb to keep the rest whole.

A sad smile comes and goes from his lips, and I frown as I wait for him to say something—say anything at all—to let me know he's not quitting on us just because I fucked up.

"Well... that's my news. The team wants me back."

"What? When?" It feels like someone's just stabbed me in the gut with the way his words make my heart drop and take all of my hope with them.

"Immediately."

I can hear my heartbeat echoing in my eardrums.

"But you're not going, right? I thought that was over. I thought you were committed to the ranch and helping your brothers. That we were going to rebuild all this together." I try not to sound as desperate as I feel.

"I thought that too." He looks down at the decree. "But now we're not even married, and this is all yours." He lets out a huff of air and shakes his head. "It's funny how the world fuckin' works, huh?"

"You don't mean that."

"No, but you did. You got what you wanted. The divorce. The ranch. The inn. All of it. You don't need me."

"Ramsey! You're being fucking ridiculous. None of that matters. You can't do this to me again."

"What matters is you lied." He palms the piece of paper on

the table. "We don't lie to each other. That's the difference between us and everyone else in this fucked up world, Haze."

"You promised. You break that and you're a liar too. You promised me that you were going to be here for me. You said you loved me." The tears are coming hot and heavy now. I can't stop them and I don't care to. Not with the way he's looking at me now—like he can see straight through me to the other side, where there's a life waiting without me.

"And you ripped my fucking heart out!" He pulls the paper from the table and crumples it, tossing it to the floor. He turns his back to me and starts to walk away.

"Don't you dare fucking walk away from me!" I yell after him, furious that after everything he's just going to walk up the stairs.

He looks back over his shoulder, his face faltering for a moment before he regains his ire.

"Or what?" He dares me to say what I'm thinking.

"You can walk out of here for good!"

"Was already planning on it, sugar. Kinda the point of a divorce." He turns to the stairs and makes his way up, pausing halfway to look back at me. "I'm gonna pack tonight and get a flight out of Denver in the morning. Grant and Levi will look after you and the ranch if you need them. You've got your brothers here to keep you safe."

AN HOUR later I'm sitting at Seven Sins as Dakota pours me another shot.

"I thought we were gonna get to have a second burn-the-dress party. The first one was so much fun. This thing where you're crying and pouting, not so much." Dakota gives me a pitiful look.

Marlowe and Bristol push their empty shot glasses toward Dakota. I called an emergency meeting at the bar and had just finished telling them my sad sob story.

"You really filed it?" Marlowe scrunches her nose.

"I know I fucked up, but I thought..."

"You thought you were going to marry Curtis. Then he turned out to be a giant piece of shit." Bristol nods her head like it's a perfectly sensible thing.

I haven't told them the whole story. I'd kept it to the important parts. Curtis was manipulating me the whole time to try to get the ranch. I found out. He was gone. Drove out of town, never to return. I didn't want them to have to keep my dirty little secret, but I'm worried keeping it from them might eat me alive. Especially when the secrets are starting to mount up.

"But I lied to Ramsey. I told him I'd put the papers in the safety deposit box," I say as Dakota slides another drink my way. I take a sip. "This tastes like it's watered down," I complain.

"It is because you've already had three shots. I get wanting to drown your sorrows, but let's not drown you, too, okay?" She raises her brow.

"I don't want to remember any of this." I stare down at my whiskey and Coke. "I just want to go back in time and fix it. I can't lose him twice. I can't." The tears threaten, and Marlowe rubs my back, and I throw back the rest of my drink. It doesn't even burn like it should and for some reason, that brings the tears. Now I'm that girl, crying in the bar over her man while her friends huddle around her drunk ass trying to convince her she'll be okay.

"You know I love you, and I hate to say this, but..." Dakota shakes her head. "I think you're gonna have to go throw yourself at his mercy."

"How?"

"Beg?" Dakota winces as she makes the suggestion.

"Get naked?" Bristol adds.

"Oh, better yet—put on some of the lingerie you got for your honeymoon."

"Yes... let's remind him of how I tortured him when he first got here."

"I'm fairly certain that man likes being tortured." Dakota pours me another drink, this one very obviously ninety-nine percent Coke and one percent whiskey, and I frown at it and then her.

"Maybe just remind him of how much you love him?" Marlowe gives me an encouraging smile. "But the getting naked and begging thing might not hurt." Her smile turns slightly pained as I glare at her. "Sorry, but I don't think they're wrong."

"Men are easy creatures to manage once you figure out their weaknesses, and you already know Ramsey's. So use them," Bristol encourages. "And then once you've got him where you want him, tell him how you really feel now."

"Am I crazy for wanting to make it work with him?" I stare at the bubbles rising and breaking on the surface of my drink.

"No. Somehow... someway... it'll work out. You're like magnets, always finding your way back to each other no matter the obstacle in between. You're meant for each other." Marlowe's got all the right words even though she doesn't know exactly how right they are.

"He's going to try to run again. I know it. I'll probably go home, and he'll already be gone."

"Then you go to Cincinnati after him." Dakota shrugs.

"To Cincinnati?" I ask, giving her a shocked look.

"If you love him, and he loves football... maybe let the man have one last season." Bristol looks at me thoughtfully.

"But the ranch needs me. We have to rebuild the stables, and I had plans for remodeling the inn."

"Does it need you?" Dakota's brows raise. "Or could it manage without you for a few months as long as you make trips out here? Grace, Kit, Elliot, Kell... hell, even Cade is doing a good job of keeping things running while you've been dealing with the aftermath the last few weeks. Bo and Anson, I'm sure, would be willing to check in on things too."

I take a long chug of Coke, wishing it was more whiskey. She had a point. A point I didn't love because... I like feeling needed around the inn and the ranch. I like being the one to make sure everything's functioning. I like putting in the long hours it takes and going to bed exhausted.

But I also really love being married to Ramsey Stockton. I love watching the way he lights up on the field, and I've never gotten to see him play in his home stadium in the pros. I didn't hate the idea of listening to tens of thousands of people chant his name when he sacks the opposing quarterback for the third time like he did in college.

"She's thinking about it," Bristol notes.

"Maybe she needs another drink?" Marlowe points to my half-empty glass.

"Yes. One more shot for good luck. I'm going to need it for the begging I'm about to do." I push my glass forward, and Dakota tops me off before she looks at Marlowe.

"Can you take her home?" Dakota asks.

"Yep. I don't mind," Marlowe agrees.

FIFTY-ONE

Hazel

"WAIT... ONE PIT STOP," I mumble as Marlowe tries to keep me on track to the door.

"What's that?" Marlowe looks at me perplexed when I wander toward the truck Ramsey's been driving since he got here.

"I have to take care of something..." I rifle through my purse, extracting the switchblade I keep there in case of emergencies and pull it out.

"Um!" Marlowe lets out a little yelp of worry. "What are you doing?"

I slam the blade of the knife into one of Ramsey's tires.

"Making sure he can't get away. Obviously." I walk to the back side of the truck and stab another one.

"Hey!" There's a loud shout from the other side of the barn, and I hear footsteps across the gravel as I go for the third tire. I look up, and it's my six-foot-four brother's frame hovering over me and keeping me from the next tire. "What the fuck do you think you're doing, Hazel?"

"Cade! Get out of my way. I'm busy!"

"Doing what? Making us pay for another set of tires?" His brow sinks into a frown.

"Haze. Please... inside! You have a mission to carry out inside, remember?" Marlowe sneaks her arm around mine and starts to tug me in that direction. Cade goes for the knife in my hand, and I jerk it back. His eyes go wide.

"Hey!" I hold the blade up in the air. "Don't start with me. My house. My rules. If I want to stab truck tires, you just mind your own business."

"How many has she had?" Cade looks past me to Marlowe.

"Three, but Dakota was watering them down. She's more emotional than drunk right now," Marlowe answers like I'm not even here.

"She watered them all down? That hussy!" I complain, not that anyone cares how I've been wronged in this.

"What's wrong?" Cade looks at me for a moment but then back to Marlowe, and I frown at the way the two of them are communicating past me.

"There was a little mishap with some paperwork, and Ramsey might be leaving," Marlowe answers.

"Oh fuck..." Cade groans.

"I'm fixing it!" I argue. "Hence taking away his getaway vehicle."

Cade takes my other arm, and between the two of them, I'm corralled away from the car, stripped of my weapon of choice, and hustled in the door.

"Go fix it." Marlowe motions for me to hurry off, and I glare at her but thank her anyway for getting me home. "Of course. Now go get your man."

"I was gonna go in and get some food," Cade mumbles.

"I wouldn't recommend it. I think the two of them are about to tear the house apart one way or another," Marlowe muses as I pull off my shoes.

"I can still hear you," I mutter through the screen door, but they ignore me.

"Would you mind running me up to the Snack Stop for a slice of pizza? My friend's got my car tonight on a date, and since Haze has decided to take out the one car that I have keys to..."

"Sure. I've got some leftover sandwiches at the bakery, though, if you want?" Marlowe's voice grows softer as they walk away.

I shake my head. Marlowe's always talking someone into more food. Might as well be the bottomless pit that is my younger brother.

I get to the bottom of the stairs and stare up at the top floor. I can do this. Somehow, in fourteen steps, I was going to figure out the right words to get the love of my life to stay, even though I'd stupidly forced us into a divorce. I trudge up them, taking my time, and when I reach our door, I stare at it for a moment before I turn the knob.

I can do this. I'd beg if I have to. But when I open it... he's gone. There's no sign of him, and all of his things have been cleared off the dresser. I hurry into the bathroom and whirl around, checking the counter and then the shower. His razor and his body wash... all of it is gone. He's left. During the short while I was gone at Dakota's bar to try to figure out how to fix this, he already ran.

He was probably doing the same thing Curtis always did— driving up early to stay in the city so he didn't have the long commute to the airport in the morning. One of his brother's probably took him—and I'd fucked up the truck, so there was no chasing after him. Unless I could get Bo to take me. Except...

Bo would probably take his side. Tell me to let the poor man go and live his life. Find a woman that doesn't take him for granted.

I collapse in a heap on the rug in front of the tub, and the tears start to pour out. My lungs are racked with sobs as I try to pull in more air, and I can barely catch my breath. I can't do this again. The last time, it felt like I was dying, but somewhere... some part of me thought there might still be hope. That maybe somehow, someday—maybe not until we were old and gray and twice divorced with grown kids of our own, we'd find each other again. That somehow, I'd get more time with him.

Then I had him—with plenty of time left, and I squandered it.

"Haze?" I hear the quick padding of feet across the carpet, and suddenly, he's there. Standing in the doorway to our bathroom, shirtless in a set of Chaos sweats that leave nothing to the imagination. Like I conjured him to torture myself, except the disgruntled tone he has when he speaks wouldn't be my first choice. "Fuck. I thought you'd gotten hurt or something. Are you okay?"

I stand and march over to him, closing the distance so rapidly he takes a step back and tilts his head like he's bracing for impact.

"No, I'm not okay! I thought you left without saying goodbye. Everything was gone, and you were nowhere to be found." I shove at his chest but he holds his ground.

"I just got my stuff packed so I can leave early. I'm sleeping in the guest room. I figured with everything... it's best we keep our distance." His brow raises as he takes my emotional state in. The fact that he's not even shedding a single tear right now pisses me off.

"Distance." I shake my head, wiping the tears from my

cheeks. "Well... good luck getting to the airport. I slashed all the tires. Most of them, anyway. Until Cade stopped me."

His face screws up with confusion, followed by a strange combination of irritation and amusement.

"Well, that was silly. Bo's taking me."

"That fucking traitor!" I screech. "I knew it." I make a mental note to punch my older brother in the stomach the next time I see him. He'll know why.

"Is he though?" Ramsey looks at me like I've lost my mind.

"I'm his blood."

"And I'm his brother." Ramsey counters.

"Were his brother."

Ramsey's face hardens at that correction, and I feel my heart skip when he starts to turn away. I reach for his arm, wrapping my fingers around the crook of his elbow, and he halts in his steps.

"But we could fix it," I add quickly. "If you want him as a brother again, I mean."

Ramsey's eyes slide to the side and drift over me.

"I think it's a little late for fixing things now, Haze. We only manage to hurt each other." I can hear the skepticism in his voice and it hurts.

"Just hear me out," I plead.

He lets out a beleaguered sigh, but he doesn't move to leave again.

"You could still go to Cincinnati. Play for the Chaos and finish out the season. It's just a few more weeks, right?"

"Not if there are playoffs. Which there could be," he counters, but I can tell by the way his brow softens that he's interested in where I'm going.

"I could follow you. I might have to come back a few times here and there to make decisions about the ranch, but... Bo and Cade and the staff, they could handle things. I'd have to figure out how to hire an extra person or two... but maybe, if you're playing again, you might be willing to give a loan to your ex-wife?"

"The check for the million is already on the nightstand." He nods toward it, and I frown, but he jerks his chin like he wants me to know that he made good on his promise in black and white. I walk over, and sure enough the check is sitting there just like he promised it would be months ago. His flourished signature on the dotted line.

"You were serious..." I stare at it. "I don't know whether to be flattered or insulted."

"Flattered. I would have given you two million if it meant I could have you in my arms again, Haze. That's all I wanted. I thought if you remembered how good we could be when we aren't fighting... maybe you'd give us another chance. I didn't realize how dead set against it you were. I would have never pushed you like that if I didn't think somewhere deep down you might still want us."

"I would have been back in your arms again for free. It was the *letting you back into my heart* part that felt like it should have a high price tag. You broke me, Ramsey. When you left... I know I said I was okay. I wanted you to believe that because I wanted you to chase your dreams the way you encouraged me to chase mine. I wanted to see you out on that field, free from all the pain that this ranch represented for you. But... I laid on this floor, night after night, wondering how I could go on without you. Imagining you happy and free of me and all the other bad memories here... When all I wanted to be was yours. All I wanted was some way that I could be the one you ran to." A sob breaks free even though I thought I was done crying for the night. How I have any tears left yet to spill is a mystery.

"Haze..." His lower lip quivers the slightest bit as his eyes travel over me, and I watch the ensuing tears that stream down his cheeks. "I wanted you to run with me. I wanted you. But it's like I said... I didn't want you in a place where I thought my being there could hurt you or hold you back. I wanted to play... yes. I thought it would give me the ability to give us a better future, one where we didn't need Stockton money or Stockton land to make things work. Where it could just be the two of us, deciding our own fate."

"I still want that."

"You won't be happy away from this ranch or the inn." He shakes his head, his cheeks stained red from the pain of knowing it.

"I won't. Not long-term. But for a year or two. However long the Chaos will give you. We could move back and forth. There during the season. Back here during the offseason. I can go back and forth between." His eyes light up as I suggest it, and I'm hoping that's a good sign for me.

"And then we come back here?" he asks, the tears slowing as he considers my proposal.

"Yes. Then we come back here unless we decide we want to be somewhere else. I'd consider it if that's what you really want. But I think... I think we need to stay and fight. We can't let whoever killed your parents drive us away from our family and friends. As much as your brothers piss me off... they're family. And they're right about not letting awful people have the upper hand. They can't have this ranch or this town—it's already ours."

"Fuck..." he curses under his breath, and he scrubs a hand over his face. "I love this ranch, sugar. There are memories that hurt, yes, but this ranch is as much you as anything else it's ever been. Better for having been loved by you. Same as me. It's the only place I wanted to come when I was finally free again. So I'm not about to let anyone take it from this family."

My heart constricts in my chest as hope creeps in. The tears welling at the corners of my eyes.

"Is that a yes?" I whisper, too scared to ask it too loudly.

"When have I ever been able to say no to you?" His hand cups my cheek.

"About as often as I can say no to you." I risk a small smile, and he returns it. The corner of his mouth turning up just a little bit, enough that I think I might be on the road to forgiveness. My heart flutters with the excitement of a future with him, and he studies me, his eyes narrowing.

"You're not completely off the hook. I'm still pissed about the divorce. You know how much extra paperwork that's going to be to set everything straight again? I thought I was free of that shit with this parole over."

"But it means all that wedding planning stuff I made you do wasn't for nothing..." I point out.

"Oh, all of that's still getting burned, and you're gonna start over again. I guess we're getting married at the casino because I'm not marrying you where you were gonna marry him. Grant will love that idea." Half a smile comes and goes from his face as he considers his brother's reaction to hosting a wedding.

"We better get the family discount," I mutter, thinking back to how they dismissed me so thoroughly when I inquired months ago.

"We should. I'll package it up with one hell of a bachelor party."

"Excuse you. You are not a bachelor." My brow drops, and I scrunch up my nose.

"I'm pretty sure the paper on the floor downstairs says otherwise..." I can tell by the way his green eyes play over my face that he's just teasing me, waiting and hoping to get a rise out of me.

"I'm pretty sure you're going to be too preoccupied to think about being a bachelor."

"Oh yeah?" His brow raises in question.

I hold up the check and look between the two.

"A million dollars says you're in my bed every night until we get the paperwork fixed."

He scoffs and turns his head to look out the window. The devious grin that plays at his lips makes my heart take off like a racehorse in my chest. I put the check back down on the nightstand, closing the distance between us, and rest my palms on his chest.

"Deal?"

"I'm not that cheap, sugar."

"You have a counteroffer then?" My hands drift down his chest and over his abs.

"A million dollars plus half this ranch starts sounding sweeter..." he trails off as he watches my fingers play along the top of his sweats.

"Deal," I answer.

"I want it signed the second our lawyers draw up the new paperwork."

"Fair enough." I tilt my head.

"And..." His fingers tilt my chin up, forcing my eyes to meet his. "The first thing I want is you on your knees giving me a full-throated apology for that piece of paper downstairs."

"I can do that, Mr. Stockton." I hook my fingers around the waistband of his sweatpants and look up expectantly.

"Good, Ms. Briggs." The use of my maiden name stings a little, like it should. His eyes drift over the Bull Rush Ranch branded T-shirt I have on and the dirty jeans, smiling at my messy state of dress. "You're gonna have to put in a lot of work if you want to earn the Stockton name back."

"It's lucky for you that I like a challenge."

FIFTY-TWO

Ramsey

HER KNEES HIT the rug at my feet, and she frees me from my sweats. I'm already hard from the anticipation of having her again, knowing it's going to be twice as good as the last because she's so impatient to apologize, and I'm even more eager to let her. Her hand runs down the length of me, so soft and gentle, as her tongue teases the head of my cock.

"I was hoping you were gonna come find me. Hate fuck me half to death for one final goodbye." I run my knuckles down her cheek.

"You'll have to settle for me begging for forgiveness instead." She wraps her mouth around me and takes me down, testing her limits and getting me wet as her hand works in tandem.

"We'll have to find new reasons to hate each other. I like you mean, darlin'. It's hot as fuck when you tear into me." My fingers thread back into her hair as I brush it out of her face.

"Fuck..." I try to say more, but it fades into a series of soft curses. Her mouth, so perfect and warm, and her tongue, too fucking clever as it circles the head. I swear this woman could get me to do anything she wanted just by offering to let me have her mouth one more time.

She pulls away to answer me. "I like you mean too. Honestly, I could take you a few shades nastier." A devilish smile plays at her lips, and she drags her tongue down the underside.

"Don't tempt me. I went easy on you," I warn her.

"I know, and you shouldn't. Especially while I'm trying to make it up to you," she taunts.

"Don't worry. You will." I groan as she takes another pass over me, letting me bump the back of her throat. "Fuck... Your mouth is perfect, sugar." I risk a glance down at her, and it makes my heart hammer in my chest to watch her mouth bob over my cock again. "Look at me."

Her eyes lift to meet mine, but her lashes stay low, and I'm not prepared for what it does to me. It seems like a fucking joke that I ever thought I was going to walk out the door tomorrow, but I'm still getting over the fact she drove us to that point again.

"Take your jeans off. Panties too. I want to watch those thighs get slick from how much you like sucking my cock." She releases me, and I continue the slow stroke she'd started while I watch her strip down for me. "Your top, too, while you're at it. We can watch those nipples perk up while you think about me coming on them."

Her cheeks heat at that, and fuck, do I like making her blush. Her top is over her head and on the floor, and her bra joins it in the small pile—until she's completely bare for me besides the necklace that has my stones set in it.

"Touch yourself," I demand.

She's obedient as ever, her fingers massaging her clit then traveling lower as her eyes drift up to mine for approval. "Get them nice and wet for me. Soak them." She slips her fingers inside her sweet little cunt and closes her eyes, nibbling on her lower lip as she works them in and out for my benefit. "Now..." I almost hate to interrupt the scene I've created, but I need what's next. "Use them on me."

She raises up on her knees and wraps her hand around me, her fingers glistening as she coats me in her come. She strokes me slowly, her eyes searching mine as she waits for her next instruction.

"Now lick it up. Every drop. Nice and slow." Her tongue flattens, and she takes a long lick up the entire length, her hand going to my balls and gently gripping. Massaging me gently as her tongue licks me clean. "That's my good girl, cleaning up this mess and all the others you've made. We're gonna fix it all together, sugar."

She takes me down again once she's had her tongue over every square inch of my cock twice over, and she moans quietly when I slip my hand over the back of her head and fuck her throat deeper.

"It feels good to know you've got my cock down your throat, doesn't it? That it's the only one you're getting from now on." She answers me with another soft moan, her eyes lifting to meet mine in reverence. "You look so pretty like this."

I grip her hair and guide her up and down my cock as her tongue takes over, swirling and licking before she sucks and teases me with the edge of her teeth until I can't take much more.

"Take my pants off," I demand, and she drags them the rest of the way down my thighs, letting her nails scrape over my skin on purpose as I step out of them. "You want your reward for being so obedient?" She blinks, and her yes is another muffled moan.

I run my hand under her jaw, stroking her cheek until she lets me go with a quiet pop. Her lips are so puffy and swollen; I want them again. But I lean down to scoop her up off the floor, carrying her to the bed and pulling her into my lap, letting her straddle me. My cock brushes over, and a whimper escapes. She can't control herself once she gets a taste, her brow furrowing and her lip rolled between her teeth until she gives in. She rubs her clit against the head of my cock as she moves to get comfortable, her eyes closing as she's lost in it. I wrap my fist around her hair and gently pull until her eyes open.

"Look at me," I ask, and her pupils meet mine, wide and doe-eyed. She's so desperate to be fucked that it's a palpable thing hanging in the air between us. "You're gonna ride me, and I want you coming hard and fast on my cock." She nods. "Do you want a toy?" I ask because, once she starts, I don't think I'll be able to stop, and I want her taken care of.

"No. I'm already so close. Your piercing always hits so perfectly. Like a built-in toy." She smirks, and I can't help the small smile that forms in return. I stifle it, though, trying to keep the mean streak she likes so much.

"Get on," I demand, and she climbs up, guiding me inside her as her lush hips settle down against mine until she's fully seated. "Just like I remembered." I dig my fingers into her hip and lean forward to kiss her, biting her lower lip softly as she writhes over my cock, desperate for me to give her permission. "Ride me," I grit out, my voice raspy and strained as I struggle for my own control.

She doesn't waste time, fucking me hard and pressing her nails into my shoulders for purchase. They dig in so deep, I'm sure they're drawing blood, but I don't care. The look of determination on her face and the soft moans every time she takes me deep are all I can focus on.

"Fuck. I'm already so close..." she murmurs quietly, the sound of her wet little cunt sliding over me is almost loud enough to drown her out.

"Gorgeous. So fucking gorgeous. Faster..." I urge her on, my hand cupping her breast and my thumb toying with the sensitive tip of her nipple as she cries out. It spurs her on, and she's gasping and moaning a minute later.

"I'm coming. Fuck. I'm already coming..." she curses. The look of surprise on her face has me biting my tongue to keep from grinning too hard.

But the way she's fucking me relentlessly, shuddering her release around my cock makes it impossible for me to hold out any longer. I tighten my grip around her hair, tipping her head back and groaning my release into her neck, nipping at her and then sucking a small mark of possession into her skin as she starts to slow her rhythm. Her breathing smooths out, and mine follows until we can almost hear ourselves think again.

"Oh fuck, Ramsey. That piercing. I know I should be jealous, but I honestly want to thank whoever gave you that idea," she mutters as she collapses forward into my arms. I kiss my way down her neck and then lie back as she climbs off me. She curls up at my side as I wrap my arm around her shoulders, looking up at me, sated and happy.

"Look in the mirror then." I smirk at her.

Her brow furrows, and I reach forward and slip my forefinger under her necklace, running the pad of my finger back and forth underneath it.

"I didn't want to take my wedding band off either. I had to find a way to wear it out of sight." Her jaw drops, and I brush the back of my hand gently underneath her chin. "I figured that if I ever got you back, it'd be another toy for you to play with."

FIFTY-THREE

Hazel

A FEW WEEKS LATER, I find myself sitting next to Bea in the wives' box at the Queen City Chaos game. Ramsey teased me this morning about the fact I didn't technically qualify to be in here, and I reminded him that I was more than happy to elope at any time. He's the one insisting on the lavish wedding and honeymoon in the offseason. Not that I'm complaining. This time I'm going to be able to do it exactly the way I want without any of the family pressures and worries I had when we were just kids in college.

"All right. Cheese coneys and drinks as promised." Madison, the quarterback's wife and Bea's best friend, returns from the small catered food and drink bar at the back of the box and lays out the spread in front of us.

"I feel like I'm being spoiled." I look around, feeling a little out of place at all the luxury in this box. Not that we didn't have money, but I spend so much of my life in cut-off jeans and

T-shirts, mucking stalls and helping run orders out from the inn's café, that the idea of dressing up in designer clothes and sitting in a comfy climate-controlled lounge with catered food to watch football feels foreign to me.

"Get used to it." Bea grins. "You're stuck with us now."

I smile back at her, wrapping my arm around hers and leaning against her shoulder for a moment in a half-hug. She is my anchor here, keeping me grounded and helping me navigate this new life I have with Ramsey in the city.

They offered Ramsey a generous sum of money to play the rest of the season, and his agent is already in talks for a multi-year extension. Old me would have been incredibly nervous about what that meant. But new me? Well, all it took was a few practices watching Ramsey on the field, and a few friends and family dinners at the Rawlings household, to realize he belongs here—and we could easily make this our second home. My only worry is all the extra staff we need to hire to keep things running more efficiently.

I'd covered more shifts in the inn and stables than I was willing to admit to myself, and I'm not going to make any of the rest of the staff work those kinds of hours in my absence. Those, along with all the bills for the stable repairs and the inn renovations—it's all starting to add up. But I need to not think about that today. Today is Ramsey's first day back on the field, and I'm only too happy to celebrate it.

"Everything okay?" Madison asks as she takes a bite of her coney, using her napkin to delicately wipe at her lipstick after.

"Just thinking about the inn. I shouldn't be. Today's his big day." I stare down at the field as they're finishing pregame warm-ups and setting up for game intros.

"Well... I actually wanted to talk to you about that." Bea and Madison exchange looks.

"About the inn?" My brow furrows.

"Yes." Bea nods.

"She won't shut up about how amazing it is and how much she loved it. She keeps showing me all the pictures and telling me about the town." Madison grins at her.

"Well, I'm glad you enjoyed it. If you ever want to come back, we can always make space at the ranch house if the inn's booked up."

"Have you ever thought about expanding the inn? Maybe putting some small cabins down by the river or even out on the prairie? Those views would be breathtaking to wake up to," Bea asks.

"Can you imagine the morning yoga sessions?" Madison looks at Bea and then back to me. "Have you thought about offering spa services?"

"Well, I'd love to do all of that, but... we're still just figuring out how to recuperate from the fire and get back on our feet again with the horses. We have a temporary setup, but the sooner we can get them back to normal..." I explain, looking between the two of them, but the way they're watching me, I can't help but feel like I'm missing something.

"So... we might be able to help with that." Madison looks at me thoughtfully.

"We've been hoping to invest somewhere for a long time. We even had a place in Colorado for a while until it fell through. Water access issues among other things... But your place is infinitely better than anything we've found. We're actually building a place here in the hills, but we're doing so well and expanding so fast... we'd love to have a destination as well." Bea gives an animated explanation, and I can't help but feel the excitement of their energy.

"What kind of place?" I knew they owned a rapidly growing PR firm that mostly catered to athletes, but I wasn't sure what that had to do with me or my inn.

"A retreat of sorts. Somewhere our clients can go for some peace and quiet. To get away from everything. Time with the horses. Spa days. Hiking. All of that would be perfect for what we have in mind," Madison adds.

"We were hoping, maybe, if you'd want to talk through some of the ideas we have... we might be able to invest in Bull Rush Ranch and your inn. Help your horses and our clients. It's a win-win for all of us, I think." Bea looks at me hopefully.

"I mean... I'd love that, but are you sure? I'm not... we're not very swanky. I don't know if we could cater to some of your clients' tastes." I scrunch my nose in worry.

"First, the place is absolutely gorgeous and gives all of those quaint inn-in-the-country vibes that we want. And second, that's what we're here for. But only if it fits your vision. We don't want to interfere."

"No—I'm so excited about the idea of it. I definitely want to talk more." I grin at both of them.

"Perfect. We'll set something up this week before you fly back." Bea grins.

There's a loud roar from the crowd.

"Oops. That's our cue." Madison sets her food down and walks to the front of the box, and Bea and I follow. The tunnel is set up and the cheerleaders line up on either side with the smoke machines going at full force, billowing into the wind on this late fall day.

As they start to announce the defense coming out onto the field a few minutes later, they get to the last name, and I feel my heart swell as they introduce him.

"And last but certainly not least, our hometown hero. You know him. You love him. Ramsey Stockton!" the announcer bellows out, and the crowd loses their minds, screaming at the top of their lungs, and everyone in the box claps as he runs out onto the field. He holds his helmet up in the air, and a round of fireworks go off on one side of the field. I see him turn and point up to where we're sitting and pat his chest over his heart, and I press my palm to my own and blow a kiss down even though I know he can't see me.

I haven't seen him look this happy since we were kids, and nothing in the world could match how proud of him I am.

FIFTY-FOUR

Ramsey

WHEN THE GAME'S OVER, we head to West Field. The sports bar's owned by one of the guys on the team, and there's a private room where we're all able to celebrate our win. And I can finally bask in the fact that I got the second chance I'd barely even hoped for.

Hazel takes my hand as we walk into the room, her eyes darting around as she takes in the raucous scene. We needed this win tonight against our divisional rival to help clear a path to the playoffs, and everyone and their mom—quite literally in some cases—is here tonight to celebrate.

I squeeze her hand in mine and give her a reassuring smile as we make our way to the far corner where Cooper and Bea are waving us over.

"We saved you guys a couple of seats at our table." Bea grins and pats the seat at her side for Hazel to sit in. I'm real fucking thankful the two of them get along as well as they do because I'm fairly certain Bea's half the reason Hazel doesn't go home more often. She promises me regularly that she loves being here with me, but I know she's homesick for her friends in Purgatory Falls.

"The man of the hour!" Cooper hollers when he sees me, throwing his hands up.

"Can we give it up for this fucking badass right here?" Quentin yells out from the other end of the table. I'd sacked the opposing quarterback on fourth down with three seconds to go, killing their chances at a comeback. The crowd had lost their minds, and I felt like myself again for the first time in a year.

I take a dramatic bow as my teammates' cheering hits a fever pitch, and then I pull Hazel's seat out for her so she can sit down. The flash of awe in her face that fades to a proud smile has something twisting in my chest, but I just grin. I look to Cooper, and he nods.

"Hey, Westfield!" Cooper calls to our tight end and the owner of the bar. Westfield nods to both of us and then jumps on his chair.

"All right, everyone. Can I get some quiet in here? Please?" Some of the roar dies down, but there's still a group in the far corner being loud. "Breaker! Knox! Shut the fuck up, will you?"

"Language!" Westfield's wife calls as she puts her hands over their daughter's ears.

"Sorry!" Westfield looks down at his daughter. "Sorry, baby girl. Daddy didn't mean it."

The crowd dies down to a few murmurs and a few cooing sounds as the wives remark on the baby's dress. But I have the quiet I need.

"I just wanted to say a huge thank you to all of you. I know many of you lobbied on my behalf to the media and supported me through my extended vacation. Your letters and words of encouragement got me through one of the darkest parts of my life. I never thought I'd get to play ball again, and stepping out on that field tonight felt like a dream come true. It was like my first pro game all over again. So I want to thank all of you—and especially Cooper and Bea here for everything you've done to support me." I look at them, and there's a small round of applause. I try to hold back the tears of anticipation I'm feeling as I turn to Hazel. "And last, but definitely not least, I want to thank the love of my life. I wouldn't be here today if it wasn't for her. She's my true north and the center of my universe, and the second chance she's given me is the only thing that's better than being out on that field again."

Hazel presses her hand to her heart, tears slowly rolling down her cheeks as she looks up at me.

"So while we're here tonight celebrating second chances, I figured we might be able to put one more on the list. That is if she says yes." I reach into my pocket and pull out the new engagement ring I purchased for her. It's a bigger, better version of the one I'd gotten her when we were in college, and I kneel down in front of her.

"Ramsey!" Her jaw drops, and she shakes her head. I've managed to actually surprise her. "Yes. Of course, yes." She holds out her hand, and I slip the ring on gently as she presses her free hand to her mouth. She's shaking by the time I hug her, racked with happy little sobs, and I squeeze her tight.

"I love you to the ends of the earth, sugar," I whisper against her ear so she can hear me over the cheers.

"I love you too." She hugs me tighter and turns her face up to kiss me.

Somehow I'm lucky enough to get everything back together again in my life, not exactly the way it was, but the kind of well-worn patchwork that I might love even more after the work of having to put it all back together again.

EPILOGUE

Ramsey

WHEN I GET out to my car from practice, my phone rings, and I see Grant's number. He rarely calls to chat, so I'm hoping we might finally have an answer to some of our questions. It's been weeks since the courier had started shopping the item, and I'd hoped we'd have a bite on it by now.

"Hey," I answer.

"You have a minute?" Grant's immediately on to business.

"Yes. I just got out of practice."

"So you're alone?"

"Yes," I reply, wary of what's coming next.

"Good. I need you to do me a favor tomorrow night and meet with the owner of the Cincinnati Queen's Guard."

"What?" I ask, exasperation coming through my tone. If I'd run through a list of a hundred things Grant might ask me, meeting with the owner of the local hockey team wouldn't even make the list.

"You heard me. Tomorrow night at Kelly's Steakhouse." Kelly's is a swanky, upscale steakhouse on Vine Street. We sometimes took rookies there and made them buy dinner for everyone as part of the welcome to the team. It's popular with athletes and the rest of the upper crust in the city.

"Why do you want me to meet with him?"

"You're there, and it'll save me the trip of flying all the way out. I assume you can handle it?"

"I'm a little wary of his reputation. I'm off parole, but I'm still trying to make sure my image stays squeaky clean for the PR team. If I'm seen with him—"

"Do *not* be seen with him," Grant cuts me off. "When you get there just ask for a private dining room. Bring Hazel with you and celebrate your anniversary."

"The anniversary of what?"

"The first time you kissed. The first time she sucked your dick. I'm sure you'll think of something." His tone develops an edge.

"That's all you're going to tell me?"

"That's all you need to know right now."

"What time?"

"Seven. There's a dress code." My brother's always worried that I'll dress down for the occasion. Never mind the man's always overdressed, Kiton when it could be Armani.

"I'm aware."

"One never knows."

"Is that all?"

"The party planner Hazel hired is up my ass about every detail of this wedding. You do realize I have more pressing matters than your nuptials? I'm getting ready to open the new bar on New Year's Eve, and my focus needs to be there."

"I'll talk to her." I clear my throat. "But you do know that Dakota's planning a rival New Year's party, right?"

"I can handle Dakota," he answers sharply. I'm not sure he can, especially not going into it with that kind of overconfident attitude, but I won't argue. "Now if there's nothing else, I need to get back to work."

"You called me." I huff out a sigh of frustration. I'd mostly been communicating with Levi the last few weeks, and I honestly preferred it.

"Have a good night." Grant disconnects the phone before I can answer.

––––––––––––

THE NEXT NIGHT, Hazel and I are walking into Kelly's Steakhouse. She's wearing a gorgeous dress that Bea had helped her pick out a few weeks ago for a fundraiser she attended with the rest of the wives, and I'm wearing the suit I just had tailor-made. I bulked up when I started playing again, and unfortunately, it meant outside sweats and tees, I needed a new wardrobe.

I follow Grant's instructions, and the maître d' smiles as they check their notes.

"Yes, our private room is still being readied, and your other guest is finishing a meeting. If you'd both like to have a seat at the bar for a few minutes, I'll come get you to take you upstairs."

"Thank you." I nod, politely, hoping I'm doing a good job of blending into this role Grant has me playing.

Haze and I make our way to the bar. It's drenched in gold, and the bar is lit up with a brilliant purple. Chevrons and streamlines compliment sweeping curve patterns that are littered throughout the place, and I feel like I've stepped back into the 1930s.

"This is... wow." Haze looks up where several large chandeliers drip candelabra-lit crystals from the ceiling.

"Well... he doesn't exactly have a shortage of money." The owner of the Queen's Guard also owns this steakhouse and several other places throughout the city.

"It's beautiful. I looked him up... Did you know that he's one of the youngest billionaires in the country? He's only our age. He inherited the money when his grandparents died suddenly in a house fire a few years ago."

"Yes, well, he's a lot more than that." He has a reputation in Cincinnati, and I've never bothered to look into whether or not it was well-earned.

"You know him?" Hazel tears her gaze away from the decor to look at me again.

"I know of him. Enough to be nervous."

"You? Nervous?" Hazel's lips quirk in a smile. "I can't imagine a man who could intimidate Ramsey Stockton."

The bartender comes over and looks at us both expectantly.

"Oh, I'm sorry. We haven't looked at the menu yet," I apologize.

"Do you have a recommendation?"

"Our signature cocktail—the Queen of Hearts."

"What's in that?" Hazel's brow furrows with curiosity.

"It's a blackberry gin fizz with muddled raspberries added in."

"That sounds delicious. I'll have one of those." Hazel beams.

"Just a whiskey, neat. Something peated?" I ask when he looks at me.

"We have a nice Laphroaig we just got in?"

"That works." I don't normally drink during the season, but a sip or two won't kill me, and I could use it for my nerves.

"Neat?" He pauses and looks back. I nod my agreement, and then he takes off to make our drinks.

"They really like naming things after queens around here... Speaking of, he owns the Queen's Guard, right? Bea was just telling me we need to go to a game together." Hazel nods to the inlaid gilded tiles that form a vintage-looking hockey player on the wall behind the bar.

"Bea did seem to be a fan." I smile, thinking of a memory I have of her and Cooper. Hazel's eyebrow raises.

"You sure you never had a thing for her?" Her tone is playful when she asks.

"I'm sure. They just reminded me of us is all. If we were nicer people, anyway." We both are busy laughing when the maître d' appears and gives us a warm smile.

"I can take you upstairs now." She motions to the stairs at the back of the restaurant.

"Oh. We just ordered drinks." Hazel looks worriedly at the bartender who's still muddling the berries for us.

"Not a problem. I'll have them sent up for you. Follow me."

We follow her up the stairs and into an illuminated, amber-colored room which has a long narrow table down the center with more than a half dozen black velvet upholstered chairs down each side. Four place settings are neatly set on the end closest to us, and I glance at Haze to see her taking it all in.

The maître d' pulls our chairs out for us, and I stare at the array of forks and knives spread out around the place setting as I sit down. I sincerely wish that Grant had made the trip. I'd fail this test in a matter of minutes. The door on the other side of the room opens, and the green-eyed woman from the basement of The Avarice appears in a black cocktail dress, smiling warmly as she sees both of us.

"How is everything so far?" She looks between us.

I stand as she approaches the table, and Hazel follows suit.

"Very good," Hazel answers.

"Charlotte, right?" I hold out my hand, and she takes it, giving it a delicate shake.

"Yes. Ramsey, and this must be your wife?" Charlotte looks at Hazel, and they exchange their own greetings.

"Something like that. We're in the midst of, um... renewing our vows." Haze struggles for a good explanation, but I suppose it's as good as any.

"Ah. Complicated. I'm familiar with how that can be." She braces her hands on the back of the chair, and before I can say another word or sit down again, the door she came through opens once again, and the owner walks through.

I've never seen him up close in person. Only on TV or when I went to a Queen's Guard game and the camera had panned to his box. But the sharp inhale of breath that comes from Hazel's direction when he walks in the door would make me jealous if I didn't already know how in love with me she is.

He looks like every bit the descendant of old money. Perfectly styled blond hair and crystal-blue eyes. A jawline that could cut glass and a tailored suit that rivals anything I've ever seen Grant wear. I may not like them, but I'd spent enough years in the pros to spot them.

"Mr. Stockton!" He flashes a bright white smile at me as he holds his hand out.

"Mr. Kelly," I say in answer.

"Please. Just call me Hudson." He turns to Hazel. "Mrs. Stockton, I presume?"

Hazel just nods and shakes his hand, quietly smiling like she's meeting a celebrity. I'm going to give her a hell of a lot of shit for this later. Hudson pulls Charlotte's chair out for her, and she sits as he invites us to sit across from him.

Just as we do, the bartender reappears with our drinks, setting them down on the table. He turns to Hudson and Charlotte, taking their orders before he disappears out the door again.

"That's my favorite." Charlotte nods to the drink in front of Hazel.

"It sounded amazing."

"It is." Charlotte nods, and then she looks to Hudson, who smiles at her, a silent exchange in the look they give each other before he leans back in his seat and returns his attention to me. The suit I'm wearing immediately feels three sizes too tight as I consider how out of my depth I am.

"I'm afraid Grant didn't give me many details about tonight," I apologize for my ignorance.

"Ah well... It's quite simple, really. Charlotte here..." He looks at her again in a way that betrays something much deeper than a business relationship and stretches his arm over the back of her chair. "Informed me that our families have a mutual problem that needs to be snuffed out."

WHAT TO READ NEXT

SEATTLE PHANTOM FOOTBALL SERIES

Defensive End - Prequel Short Story

Pick Six - Alexander & Harper

Overtime - Colton & Joss

Wild Card - Tobias & Scarlett

QUEEN CITY CHAOS SERIES

Before the Chaos - Prequel Novella

Rival Hearts - Madison and Quentin

Mine to Gain - Beatrix & Cooper

OTHER BOOKS:

Thick as Thieves - Charlotte & Co.

ACKNOWLEDGMENTS

To you, the reader, thank you so much for taking a chance on this book and on me! Your support means the world.

To Kat, SJ, and Vanessa, thanks isn't enough for all the hard work you put in on this book. Not a single one would happen without you but this one especially. You always go above and beyond, and I'm so grateful to have such an amazing editing team.

To Autumn, for all of your tireless work supporting me and my books through all of the ups and downs. So grateful for you!

To Thorunn, thank you for your constant words of wisdom and support, and especially for holding my hand through this one. This book wouldn't have happened without you and all of your equestrian expertise. Thank you for answering all of my research questions and cheering on the M.A.D. era.

To Eva and Kelly, thank you for holding me up during the doubts and celebrating with me when I found my writing muse again. I'm so incredibly grateful to have your wit and wisdom in my life and to be able to call you friends.

To Matty, thank you for being one of the best friends a person could ask for and for patiently answering all of my tedious research questions.

To my beta readers: Emma, Shannon, Ashley, Jaime, Tiffany, Mackenzie, & Brittany, for your feedback—your thoughts on these characters and this new world encouraged me to chase new dreams and I'm so thankful for you!

To my Creator Team, thank you so much for all the support you give my characters, my books, and me. I wouldn't be able to do this without you, and I'm so incredibly grateful.

ABOUT THE AUTHOR

Maggie Rawdon is a romance author living in the Midwest. She writes men with the kind of filthy mouths who will make you blush and swoon and the smart independent women who make them fall first. She has a weakness for writing frenemies whose fighting feels more like flirting and found families.

She loves real sports as much as the fictional kind and spends football season writing in front of the TV with her pups at her side. When she's not on editorial deadline you can find her bingeing epic historical dramas or fantasy series in between weekend hikes.

Join her readers' group on FB here:
https://www.facebook.com/groups/rawdonsromantics

facebook.com/maggierawdon

instagram.com/maggierawdonbooks

tiktok.com/maggierawdon

Made in United States
Orlando, FL
02 April 2025